The Other You

ALSO BY J. S. MONROE
FROM CLIPPER LARGE PRINT

Find Me
Forget My Name

The Other You

J. S. Monroe

W F HOWES LTD

This large print edition published in 2020 by
W F Howes Ltd
Unit 5, St George's House, Rearsby Business Park,
Gaddesby Lane, Rearsby, Leicester LE7 4YH

1 3 5 7 9 10 8 6 4 2

First published in the United Kingdom in 2020
by Head of Zeus Ltd

A CIP catalogue record for this book is available
from the British Library

ISBN 978 1 00401 662 4

Typeset by Palimpsest Book Production Limited,
Falkirk, Stirlingshire

Printed and bound by
T J Books in the UK

For Andrea

Double, double, toil and trouble . . .

Macbeth, William Shakespeare

ONE WEEK EARLIER

CHAPTER 1

KATE

She used to be good at faces. So good they paid her. If you were living a lie, she would see it in your eyes. She could spot an impostor at a hundred yards. And she only had to pass you once in the street to remember your face forever.

'Kate?' Rob calls up the stairs. 'You coming?'

Kate glances at herself in the bedroom mirror. Rob is taking her to a new place today, a secret beach somewhere on the south coast. It's a change from their normal Saturday. Usually they begin with a swim in the bay, followed by coffee at their favourite café overlooking the harbour. Double espresso for him, flat white for her. Rob likes his routine.

'Just a sec,' she says.

He's by the front door, ready to go, but she knows it will take him a few more seconds to switch on all the alarms. The house is like Fort Knox. She leans in closer to the mirror in their bedroom, searching for a clue in her face, a tell-tale sign that the thirty-three-year-old woman smiling back at her is not quite as blissed up as she seems. Nothing. Her eyes are dancing, happiness radiating from every pore of her sun-kissed skin.

'Kate?' Rob calls out again, above a cacophony of beeping alarms.

'Coming,' she says, skipping down the stairs to join him in the vast hall. Stretch, the smooth-haired dachshund puppy he's bought her, trots in from the kitchen.

'See you later, little legs,' she says, scooping Stretch up to kiss him goodbye. He normally comes everywhere with her, but in another break with routine, Rob has asked that this morning he stay behind. 'Sure he won't set off the alarms? He's not very good at staying on his bed.'

'The system's smarter than that,' Rob says. 'Knows a naughty dog when it sees one.'

An hour later, they are walking arm in arm across a small beach that can only be reached by descending a treacherous cliff path. Behind it, granite rocks rise up like a giant stage curtain. The tide is turning, leaving a pool of deep turquoise water trapped by a bar of rippled sand that bisects the mouth of the cove. On either flank, the steep rocks flatten out as they extend into the sea. They've got the beach to themselves and no one passed them on the coast path.

'Why haven't you brought me here before?' she asks, stunned by the beautiful location.

'I didn't think you were strong enough – to climb down,' he says, walking on ahead.

They've been together five months now and it's true that she hasn't been in a good place, recovering from a car accident that nearly killed her. But she's feeling better by the day, physically and mentally.

Rob stops to pick up something from the tideline. It's a small piece of glass, heart-shaped and smoothed by the ocean.

'I think this may be yours,' he says, watching as she takes it in her hands. His faint Southern Irish lilt is more inflected when he talks quietly, almost musical.

Hearts don't usually do it for Kate, but for some reason this piece of sea glass, with its rough-hewn beauty, melts hers. Maybe it's because Rob's not a natural romantic, still learning.

'It's gorgeous,' she says, turning to kiss him. She closes her eyes, feeling the sun on her eyelids. They both know what's coming next. They can never help themselves. Or she can't, at least. Without saying anything, they strip off all their clothes and race down the beach, Kate slightly ahead of Rob.

'I won,' she says, running as far as she can into the water until it's too deep and she has to dive beneath the glistening surface. She knows he let her win. He always does. But this time she feels strong as she swims out into the deep translucent pool. Sometimes she gets a twinge of cramp in her legs, a legacy of the accident, but not today.

'I've been having some swimming lessons, up in

5

London,' Rob says a few moments later, treading water beside her.

Is he changing the subject, still embarrassed by her skinny-dipping habits? He can be a bit uptight like that.

'Trying to improve my front crawl,' he continues. 'You know, the breathing. Will you tell me how I'm doing?'

He doesn't wait for an answer and dives under, his white body shimmering below her.

'Ready?' he calls out, surfacing ten yards to her right like a seal.

Kate nods, trying to be enthusiastic. Rob has lessons for everything. Swimming, tennis, chess and recently beginner's French – he needs to speak it for his work. All she wants to learn is how to paint people again. The accident put an end to that. Destroyed her ability to recognise faces too.

Rob starts to windmill through the water, all long arms and legs. She can't say it's an improvement on his previous style, but his firm bum is impressive. As he passes, she leans forward and tries to grab him where he likes to be grabbed when he's not swimming. The result is spectacular, as if he's swum headlong into a brick wall. He comes up for air, gasping and choking.

'Was that you?' he says, shock giving way to a smile.

'I hope so,' she says.

'I thought I'd been bitten by a fish.'

'Next time I will bite you.'

'Is that a promise?' he asks, coming over to kiss her.

She takes him in her hand again, gently this time, and pulls him towards her.

'Do you dare me?' she says, nodding at a rock at the back of the beach as they tread water. It's overhanging the deep pool and just begging to be jumped.

Before he has time to answer, she swims off towards the shore.

'It's too high,' Rob calls out, but she's already out of the water and climbing up. 'Kate, be careful.'

He's always urging her to be careful, to lock the house, look out for strangers. It's become a bit of a mantra. And she always ignores him.

'Dive or jump?' she says from the top of the rock, peering down at the dark water below.

'Kate, please!' Rob says, looking up at her.

'You're such a pussy,' she says, raising her arms above her naked body. She feels good today. Better.

'Kate!' he calls out again, but it's too late. She's already diving through the air like a swallow and coming up from the cold depths beside him.

'Your turn,' she says.

'No way.' He kisses her with relief, glancing at her head as if checking for damage. 'You alright?'

'I'm fine.' She's never been afraid of heights, not since her mum encouraged her to leap off the harbour wall in Mousehole, a village further down the Cornish coast. They were on holiday, just the two of them, and she can't have been older than six. The local boys were impressed – she'd pencil-jumped from the highest point. No wetsuit either. She was terrified, but she's loved it ever since. The thrill of the jump.

Back on the beach, they warm themselves in the strengthening sun, drink coffee from a new 'smart' flask that Rob is testing – he works in tech, loves his gadgets – and talk. Their clothes are back on as a man with binoculars has appeared on the skyline behind them. Apparently, the beach will be busy with nudists later, and Rob doesn't think this man is a birdwatcher.

'You really are getting well, aren't you?' Rob says, pushing a comma of wet hair off his fore-head. 'I mean properly well.'

'We'll see,' she says. 'After all this excitement, I might need a lie down.'

'But you're feeling stronger?' he continues.

'Sure.' She smiles. 'Thanks to you.'

'I'm not here enough to take any credit.'

Rob only comes down from London at week-ends, and not every weekend, but he's the best thing that could have happened to Kate. In five short months, he has turned her life around. He's let her stay in his extraordinary house in Cornwall, spoilt her beyond her wildest dreams, and nurtured her damaged body and soul back to health.

'I just wish I was able to paint again.' She sighs.

'It'll come back,' he says. 'I promise.'

In recent days, she's been trying to capture Stretch on canvas, but painting portraits of people, her first love, is still beyond her.

'The thought of never asking anyone to sit for me again . . .' she says, her words tailing off. 'It scares the pants off me.'

He glances up, perhaps wondering if that's a cue for another race down to the sea, but she hasn't got the energy. Maybe she's not as well as she thinks.

'Does anything else scare you?' he asks.

'Hospitals,' she says, shuddering at the memory. She has tried so hard to forget the tubes, the breathing apparatus, the sense of helplessness after the accident, when she was lying in intensive care.

'Hey, it's where we met.' He smiles.

'That was different. I was on a ward by then.' And he was on a tour of the hospital, encouraging patients to visit an exhibition he'd organised in the main reception area.

'And you? Are you scared by anything?' she asks, doubting that he's troubled by much in life. It's her he worries about not himself. She used to think he was nervous when she first met him, but it's just his energy. Rob's protean brain never stops; it whirrs like a supercomputer. He's an Irish geek. His phrase, not hers.

It's a while before he answers.

9

'When I was a teenager,' he begins, 'I was terrified of meeting my doppelgänger.'

She glances up at him, surprised. 'It's supposed to be a bad omen if you see one,' he continues, looking out to sea. Rob's never struck her as a superstitious person. Far from it. His life is ruled by modern technology, not by fanciful myths. She doodles a pattern in the soft sand, hoping that he will continue. They don't often talk in this way, not about him, his fears. It's always about her.

'Are you still frightened?' she prompts.

'And now everyone's into posting selfies on social media,' he says, ignoring her question, 'it's well within the bounds of probability for all of us to be found by someone with an exact physical likeness.'

She feels a pang of disappointment. He's reverted to work speak just when she thought he was opening up. Returned to safer ground.

'There are several billion faces online, waiting to be matched. Believe me, I've done the maths, crunched the numbers.'

Of course he has. But she's taken aback by what he says next.

'We've all got a double out there somewhere, watching, waiting. Shadowless.' He looks around the cove, up at the clifftop behind them. The man with the binoculars has gone. 'And I've already met mine, a long time ago.'

'When?' she asks. He doesn't answer.

10

'They say it's bad enough to see your double once, but it's meant to be much worse if you meet them a second time.' He pauses. 'The day I see him again will be my last. He'll take over my life, me, you, the house, my company, all that I've achieved, everything that's precious to me.'

He pauses, eyes welling as the Cornish sun disappears behind a solitary cloud, casting the beach into sudden shade. 'He'll steal my soul.'

FRIDAY

CHAPTER 2

KATE

'What to do with ourselves, eh?' Kate says to Stretch, drumming her fingers on the Tesla's steering wheel. She's driven over to Newquay to meet Rob's Friday evening flight from London Heathrow and she's now waiting in the car park. It's like being on a first date. She's tried listening to the radio, but she can't concentrate. She's filed her nails, checked her lipstick in the rearview mirror, scrolled through her Instagram feed. Stretch is beside himself with excitement too, unable to settle on the plush leather passenger seat.

A Tesla's not her natural choice of car – a bit of a boy's toy – but she likes the fact that it's electric. Rapid too. Rob bought it for her personal use down in Cornwall. She still can't quite believe the new life she has. Her old Morris Minor Traveller used to spend more time at the garage being repaired than on the road.

She watches as a steady stream of people leaves the terminal: a few commuters but mostly holidaymakers. Despite herself, she starts to clock each face, noticing individual features – sallow cheeks,

Roman nose, spaniel eyes. Before the accident, she was employed by the police as a civilian 'super recogniser'. Two per cent of the population can't remember a face, a condition known as prosopagnosia, or facial blindness; at the other end of the spectrum, 1 per cent – dubbed the super recognisers – can never forget one. That was her. It wasn't her first choice of career – she always saw herself as a portrait painter – but she discovered that she was good at it. Very good. She once identified a suspect from just his eyes. The rest of his face was covered.

She sits up. Rob has appeared, across the car park to their left. Her heart stops. Cotton hoodie, white T-shirt and jeans, courier bag slung over one shoulder. He lowers his head to run a restless hand through his hair and looks up, taking in the evening sun with a sideways squint at the sky. She waves across at him, scrambling out of the car as he walks over. They kiss and hold each other tightly.

'What's with Stretch?' he says as he slides behind the Tesla's steering wheel.

She hadn't noticed, but Stretch is now curled up on the seat, head down. He was so happy a few minutes ago.

'Just tired,' she says, scooping him up as she sits in the passenger seat. His tiny legs are trembling on her lap. 'Walked too far today, didn't we, little one? We're both tired.'

Rob glances across at her and smiles. The

diffident smile that had so intrigued her as she lay in hospital, wondering if her life would ever be the same again. She knows what he's thinking. Has she just let him know that she's too tired for their usual Friday night routine? They'll have to see. She hasn't felt so well this week.

'Nice hair, by the way,' he says.

'Thanks.' She's pleased that he's noticed. She went for an undercut earlier today, in a bid to cheer herself up, make herself feel younger.

'I got you a present,' he says, legs bouncing like a schoolboy beneath the steering wheel.

'You shouldn't have,' she says, watching him use the sleeve of his hoodie to wipe away a smudge of dirt on the car's large touchscreen between them. She'd meant to clean the car before he arrived. He likes things to be spotless. 'I already have everything I need down here. Thanks to you.'

He reaches behind the seat, pulls out a small jewellery box from his bag and passes it to her. Inside, wrapped in tissue paper, is the piece of frosted beach glass that they found last week. It's now on a filigree silver chain. He knows she loves necklaces.

'It's gorgeous,' she says, suddenly overcome with emotion. 'Thank you.'

'I wasn't totally sure about the sizing.' He stares at her neck, a look of intense concentration on his face. 'Whether it would be too loose. I wanted it to be snug – you know, like a choker.'

She lets him fasten it, her neck tingling at his touch, but then the clasp catches a pinch of her skin at the back and she flinches. 'Ouch,' she says, playfully. It might be her imagination but he seems to hesitate a moment too long before apologising.

'Sorry,' he says. 'It's a little tight.'

Kate glances across at Rob's smooth, sleeping body and slips quietly out of bed, wrapping a cotton dressing gown around her as she steps out onto the terrace. It's a warm August evening and no one can see her here. The isolated house, all glass and oak and concrete, is cut deep into the Cornish hillside and faces out to sea, which is empty tonight, apart from the winking lights of tankers moored in the distance off Falmouth.

'You OK?' Rob calls out.

She swings around. It's too dark in the bedroom to see him properly.

'I couldn't sleep,' she says, turning back towards the bay, where a ribbon of moonlight has been laid across the water.

A moment later, his arms are wrapped around her from behind. 'Come back to bed,' he whispers in her ear.

She can feel him against her, a familiar swelling. She rests her hand on his smooth forearm and thinks again about the necklace he gave her earlier, his insensitive response to her squeal of pain. It still niggles.

'Thank you for the present,' she says. He must have just been tired. Hardly surprising after a long week at work and then the flight down.

'Not too tight?' he asks.

'It's perfect.'

Back inside the bedroom, they snuggle up in the darkness. In all other respects, he's played it well this evening. He ran her a bath with Moroccan rose oil and brought in two glasses of chilled champagne. Her exhaustion of earlier slipped away. Afterwards, he was the one who fell asleep almost instantly, like a laptop closing.

'Talk to me,' she says now, quietly. 'Tell me about your week.'

She still doesn't understand exactly what Rob does in London. One of the articles she read about his meteoric career described him as a serial 'tech-preneur', the youngest ever founder of a British 'unicorn' company and a pioneering champion of something called 'direct neural interface' tech-nology – the interaction between brain and machine. She likes the sound of unicorns. The 'disruptive' tag is less appealing. He also runs a charity on the side that puts on art shows in hospi-tals, which is how they met.

'That's so interesting,' she offers, filling the silence. 'You've developed an app, you say, that makes women wake up in the middle of the night begging to give their man a blowjob? That's incredible. What a smart, selfless piece of coding.'

He nudges her playfully. And then all she can

19

hear is the faint in and out of his breathing, and the sound of the waves below.

Sleep soon starts to lap at her own consciousness, but something's preventing her from dropping off. What Rob said about doubles last weekend has been on her mind all week. She hasn't been able to forget it, his words chasing her through her days of painting and nights of restless dreams. *And I've already met mine, a long time ago.* What must it be like to actually meet your double? And when did Rob encounter his? Where? *We've all got a double out there somewhere, watching, waiting. Shadowless.* It's revealed an unexpected side of him. A new insight.

She turns over, her interest piqued all over again. She remembers being fascinated by identical twins in primary school. The teacher used to tell her off for staring at them in class. Maybe it was an early challenge to her powers of recognition. Spot the difference. And there was the French-exchange girl at secondary school who apparently looked just like her. That had freaked her out.

She lies there, sleepless, her thoughts running loose and wild. What if the French girl were to suddenly come back into her life, discover her on Instagram, decide she'd like a piece of Rob . . .What was it he said? *It's well within the bounds of probability for all of us to be found by someone with an exact physical likeness.* Would Rob be attracted to her? The woman would have a fight on her hands if she tried it on with him. Kate

20

smiles at the ceiling. It's a preposterous thought. But then she recalls Rob's tone of voice, how serious he'd been, and her stomach tightens. *He'll take over my life, me, you, the house, my company, all that I've achieved, everything's that's precious to me.* Imagine living with that sort of fear. And what if it became reality? She shoves the idea to the back of mind.

Secretly, she's thrilled that Rob has been so honest with her, admitted to such fragility. It's a sign that he trusts her, no longer feels obliged to be the strong one all the time. She will ask him about it again when he's unwound from London. Diplomatically, of course. Tomorrow they'll walk the coast path and swim, have coffee at their favourite café overlooking the harbour. She starts to drift off to sleep, warmed by the prospect.

And then she's awake again. Her eyes spring open in the darkness, the sound of blood pulsing in her ears. Rob always insists that he sleep on the right side of the bed. He's a creature of habit, of quotidian routine. Tonight he's lying on the left. Should she prod him? Check he's not been replaced by his double? *Relax.* She's being silly. It's just another sign that Rob's loosening up, going with the flow a bit more. She rolls over, searching for sleep again. He might be helping her to recover, but she's doing him some good too.

SATURDAY

CHAPTER 3

KATE

Kate's up early the next morning, trying to paint Stretch on his bed. It's not easy as he follows her every time she walks over to the sideboard to make a tea. She loves this room, a vast atrium of a kitchen, one end of which she uses as a studio. The room doesn't face north, but there's so much glass that it feels like she's painting *en plein air.*

The sea below the house is as still as a millpond this morning, like a painting, streaked with cyans and ceruleans and framed by a high cirrus sky. In the distance, Gull Rock stands sentinel off Nare Head, the headland where she walks with Stretch, who loves to dart along the hidden paths between the yellow-flowering gorse.

Rob will be back soon, answering emails, making calls. No boundaries, never stops. She's a fine one to talk, trying to paint on a Saturday morning.

'It's just not happening, weenie toes,' she says to Stretch, who lifts his head from his bed at the sound of her voice. She puts her brush down and clutches her mug of tea, studying the canvas, trying not to panic. It will come back. Rob is certain.

She picks up the canvas to show to Stretch. 'What do you reckon? Can you see yourself?' She moves the picture around like a hairdresser with a mirror. 'No? More like a guinea pig, you think? A piglet?'

She looks at the canvas again and places it back on the easel. 'I see what you mean,' she says, throwing a snort in his direction.

She used to paint a lot of dogs before she became a super recogniser. Not by choice. When the portrait commissions dried up, she had no option. Labradors mainly. The occasional retriever. A few racehorses too. The price she paid for living in Wiltshire. Now, it seems, she can't even do dogs.

'Hockney painted forty-five pictures of his dachshunds,' a soft Irish voice says behind her.

She spins around to see Rob leaning against the bedroom doorway to her left, a tennis racquet in one hand.

'Took him a long while to get it right. Easels all over the house, apparently,' he adds.

Rob practises with a machine when he's down here, out on the court at the rear of the house. Two hundred balls on his backhand before breakfast. He peels off an electronic bandana, no doubt another piece of wearable technology he's testing. Kate takes in his sweaty smile, his windblown, tousled hair. Something's wrong. He folds his arms approvingly, glancing out to sea and then back at her, before looking at his trainers. He usually does that when he's trying to get her into bed. One moment pleading, the next all bashful. But then he fixes her in the eye.

'I know it's taken time,' he says, 'but you're looking so much better, Kate. And that necklace – it really suits you.'

The necklace. She raises a hand to touch it, remembering the pinch of pain, and time seems to slow down. She stares at him, his familiar face, his blinking puppy eyes, but she no longer recognises him. Her brain tingles, like déjà vu, but this is different, the opposite feeling. It's as if she's never seen this man before.

'Kate?' he says. His voice is far away, distorted. 'You OK?'

She can feel the mug slipping through her fingers, but she can't do anything about it. It falls and shatters on the concrete floor, splashing tea over her bare toes. Stretch trots off to another room.

'Are you hurt?' he asks, rushing forward, his hands on her shoulders as he kicks away a jagged shard of mug from her feet.

She shakes her head slowly, still staring at him, reality fracturing around her. Rob holds her close but it only makes things worse. Who is this person? She feels disorientated, nauseous, disconnected – from Rob, the house, her life, as if she's suddenly watching herself from a distance.

'You've been overdoing it, that's all,' Rob says, glancing at the canvas. 'When did you get up?'

'Just after you went out,' she manages to say. What's wrong with her?

'You mustn't push it,' he says, leading her through to the bedroom, where he closes the curtains and switches off the light. She's suffering from a migraine, he thinks, and needs to rest in darkness. She had a lot of headaches in the immediate aftermath of the accident, but none recently.

Once she's settled in bed and he's brought her a mug of herbal tea, he sits by her feet, one hand resting on her legs as he goes through emails and messages on his phone. Normality starts to return. Is this how it's going to be from now on? Irrational, late-night thoughts about doppel-gängers? Weirdness creeping up on her when she least expects it, reminding her that she'll never be fully herself again?

'I'm sorry,' she says. 'The painting – it's just taking so long to come back.'

But she can't help worrying that it's something else. The feeling when she saw him in the kitchen and thought he was a different person – it was so strange, sickening. The world seemed to split in two. Rob looked the same, but something – her instincts? her old self? her imagination? – was telling her that it wasn't him.

'Patience,' he says, leaning over to kiss her.

Rob loves her work and is determined that she'll

be a fulltime artist again. He knows that she never wants to return to her police job. She doesn't want to let him down. Maybe she has been pushing it recently.

'Art's the best healer,' he'd said that day they first met on the ward, lingering to chat at her bedside. 'Art and technology.'

When she was strong enough to walk down to the exhibition he'd organised in the hospital foyer, she was amazed to discover three of her own portraits on the walls. And she can't deny that her euphoria at seeing them on display worked more wonders than any medicine. Two years earlier, she'd been let go by her own gallery, forced to take up a proper job with the police and ditch her career as an artist. It had been a while since she'd had any work shown in public.

'I don't think it's a migraine,' she says.

'You just need to sleep.'

She knows he's right. But she's not sure she can face more dreams about Rob being replaced by a stranger.

CHAPTER 4

KATE

When Kate wakes from a light sleep, Rob is still at the end of the bed in his tennis gear, checking his phone, getting up to walk around in circles, settling again. A bit like Stretch. Sometimes she thinks he has enough energy and ideas to solve all the world's problems.

'Rob . . .' she says, but before he can reply, his phone rings.

'You OK?' he mouths to her, one hand over his phone. She nods and he walks out of the bedroom onto the terrace.

Kate closes her eyes again and lies back, listening to his animated tones as he talks about an upcoming 'IPO' in language that she barely understands. The mindless 'spray and pray' of some tech venture capitalists. The need for algorithms and the human brain to work in partnership, his hopes for a new project in Brittany.

Her name is mentioned, but his voice drops and she can't make out exactly what he's saying. And then she hears him again, cold and dispassionate, like she's never heard him before, ordering someone to 'boil the ocean' for new customers. She guesses he has to be tough at work, not like how he is with her, but his tone is surprising. Two minutes later, he ducks back into the room and pulls out a familiar headset from a cupboard. Rob recently launched a disruptive medical start-up that makes portable headsets for assessing traumatic brain injuries. He gets her to wear one occasionally to help monitor her recovery.

'There's a problem in London,' he says. 'An unhappy investor.'

'Do you need to go back?' she asks.

The thought of being on her own again is suddenly very appealing. She feels guilty, but she needs to work out what's happening in her head, why she dropped the mug when she looked at Rob. It was a step back, to when she was first recovering down here and dizzy spells and migraines were part of her life.

'I told them it would have to wait until Monday,' he says.

'Because of me?'

'I can't leave you like this,' he says, adjusting the headset in the dim light. He explained once how it works. Apparently, it uses algorithms to compare a patient's brain activity against normal data and then highlights any deviations.

'I'm fine. Really.' Kate ties back her hair. 'You should go.'

'Let's just check,' he says. 'Peace of mind.'

She sits up in bed, keeping her eyes firmly closed as he slides the device over her head. It looks a bit like a swimming cap, except for the matrix of colour-coded electrodes all over it. When he's being tender like this, tucking her hair behind an ear as he adjusts the headset, she feels so loved, cared for, cherished. No pinched skin.

She sits there in silence, like a good patient. The device is cool on her scalp.

'All seems fine,' he says after a couple of minutes. He's reading from his smartphone, which is linked to the headset via the app his team of 'brogrammers' in London has designed. 'When's your next check-up with Dr Varma?'

'Monday.'

'That's good,' Rob says. 'He might be down here already.'

'How do you mean?'

'He sometimes likes to make a weekend of his visits. Bring the family to the seaside.'

Kate smiles at the thought. Dr Ajay Varma, a neuropsychiatrist, often talks about his family, how well his two young daughters are doing at school, his parents back in south India. He's been overseeing her recovery since she left hospital, looking out for any lasting post-traumatic effects of the accident – mood swings, anxiety, depression. It all seems a bit unnecessary, but Rob insists, arranging and paying for his visits. She doesn't mind as he also happens to be a really nice guy.

'I'll give him a call,' Rob says, 'see if he can come over this afternoon.'

'Are you sure?' Dr Varma's never mentioned to her that he stays down here. But then she's never asked.

'It's important. You're doing so well. We don't want any setbacks.'

'If you say so.'

'I do. And I love you.'

'Rob?' she says, eyes closed. She so wants to build on his new-found openness, get him to confide in her again, talk some more about his fear of doubles. Make things more equal between them.

'Yes?'

She takes a deep breath. It suddenly all seems too much. Her funny turn feels like a step back and he's in carer mode again, seeing her questions as intrusive and deflecting them.

It'll wait. She gives him a defeated smile. 'I love you too.'

CHAPTER 5

KATE

'It still doesn't feel right,' Rob says.

This time it's him who's drumming his fingers on the Tesla's steering wheel. They are back in a car park, at Truro railway station. The evening flight from Newquay to London was full.

'Honestly, I'm feeling so much better,' Kate says, stroking Stretch on her lap.

After the results from the headset came through on his phone, she talked Rob into returning to London and said that she would drive him to the station. He was reluctant, suggesting he took a taxi, but he eventually came around to the idea, particularly as it turns out that Dr Varma is down for the weekend and has agreed to visit her this afternoon.

'Are you sure you'll be alright on your own?' he asks.

Despite his genuine concern, Kate can already sense Rob's restlessness, his desire to be back on the train to London. 'I'll be fine. Dr Varma can look after me.'

'Just remember to keep the house locked,' he says.

She sighs, turning to gaze out the window. Sometimes she thinks he forgets they're in Cornwall not London.

'I was going to give Bex a call,' she says. 'See if she fancies coming down for a few days.'

Bex is her best friend, a bridge between her previous life and this one.

'Good idea. We like Bex.' He pauses, looking at her. 'It's all coming back, isn't it?'

'What?' she asks, searching his face.

'That brilliant brain of yours.'

'Not if my painting's anything to go by.'

'What are you saying? You really captured Stretch today.' He opens the car door. 'Coming in?'

'Mind if I stay here?' she says, turning away. Something's not right. Again.

'Sure.' He grabs his bag from the back seat and leans over to kiss her goodbye. She closes her eyes.

'I'll call you,' he says. 'Hope it goes well with Dr Varma.'

Kate fingers the beach glass around her neck as Rob walks across to the station building. Just before he enters, a woman she doesn't recognise comes up to him and they hug, smiling, laughing. Long face, like a horse. Rob isn't a natural social animal – his first instinct is always to swerve away – but Kate can see he's making an effort, eyes blinking. Maybe this woman is another investor.

She watches the two of them chat and thinks

35

how little she really knows about Rob's London existence. It doesn't bother her. He'd probably say the same about her life down here. The weeks are long without him and she's made some good friends in the village. Who does he see in London? Or in Brittany, where he's been going a lot in recent weeks? She's not a jealous person, but she knows Bex thinks it's odd that she's never been to Rob's flat in Shoreditch or his offices in Old Street.

'Rob needs to know how much we love him,' she says to Stretch, determined to shake off the unnerving thoughts that are starting to inveigle themselves in her head.

She grabs the dog under one arm, climbs out the car and strides over to where Rob is still chatting. He hasn't seen her approach. And then he turns.

'Kate! Everything OK?' he asks.

She stands there, frozen to the spot, to the right of him. It's that same tingling sensation again, a lurching nausea, only stronger this time – the disconcerting feeling that the man in front of her is both Rob and not Rob. Familiar but unfamiliar. Recognisable but a stranger. Not so much déjà vu as jamais vu.

She inhales deeply, tries to focus on the red bricks of the station wall, something solid, definite, steadying. Her vision starts to blur. Is she about to have another migraine? This feels different. Rob is definitely acting strangely, like someone she doesn't know.

He'll take over my life, me, you, the house, all that I've achieved, everything that's precious to me.

Kate swallows. She should have had the conversation with Rob, got him to talk more about his fear of doppelgängers, open up about his vulnerabilities. She turns towards horse face, whose strong nose suddenly strikes her as beautiful. Is that why Rob is behaving like this?

'I just . . .' She hesitates, sneaks a look at the woman's slender figure.

'Give me a second,' Rob says to the woman.

'Sure.' She glances nervously at Kate. 'See you on the train.'

'I just wanted to say goodbye properly,' Kate manages to say. 'We both do,' she adds, nodding at Stretch in her arms.

'You need to rest,' Rob says, hugging Kate and Stretch. She mustn't cry. 'And talk to Dr Varma. I've got to go.'

She watches him walk into the station, wondering what's happening to her.

CHAPTER 6

KATE

'Bex, I wouldn't be asking you to do this if it wasn't important.'

Kate's still in the Tesla at the train station car park, on the phone to her best friend.

'You think he's having an affair or what?' Bex asks.

'Maybe,' she says, turning to stroke Stretch, who is asleep on the passenger seat beside her.

'So what exactly am I meant to be looking out for?' Bex asks.

Bex is a schoolteacher. Lancashire born and bred, she is also Kate's best friend, which is kind of her, as she doesn't suffer fools gladly. They used to live in the same Wiltshire village and watch *Fleabag* while eating butter pie at her place. And now Kate's asking a massive favour.

'I want you to see if Rob's with anyone when he gets off the train . . . and tell me how he seems to you,' she says, realising how absurd she must sound. 'How he looks.'

'What? Mark him out of ten? He's well fit, Kate. We already know that. Tens all round, even from Craig.'

38

Why's Bex in such an annoying mood? Probably because Kate's asking her to intercept Rob at Paddington, see if he's different in any way.

'I was behaving really strangely just now,' Kate says. 'When I waved him goodbye.'

Bex laughs. 'That's not like you.'

'Seriously, Bex. Rob bumped into this woman at the station and suddenly he seemed like a different person . . . I can't explain what I felt. I just know it was one of the weirdest moments of my life.' Up there with the time she saw Jake, her ex, with another woman.

'You was acting strangely? Or he was?'

Bex's accent might have been softened by years of living down south, but she's lost none of her northern bluntness.

'If I told you what I was thinking, you'd laugh at me,' Kate says.

'Do I ever? Even that time you tried doing the paso doble in the pub, I never once giggled.'

She's lying. They'd both laughed like drains that night. Her relationship with Jake was on the rocks and she'd needed cheering up.

'I thought Rob . . .' Kate's words tail off. She's crying. Stretch raises his head.

'You alright?' Bex asks, more gently now. 'Is it that woman at the station?'

Kate bites her lip, wondering where to start, how to explain. 'There's something else,' she says, wiping away a tear, trying to keep it together. 'Rob and I, we had a talk last weekend, about our worst

39

fears. I was worried I might not be able to paint again, after the accident. And Rob, he said he's scared of meeting his double. You know, his doppelgänger.'

'His evil twin?' Bex says. Kate can hear the amusement in her voice.

'It's meant to be a bad omen,' Kate continues. 'He met his once, a long time ago, but he's worried about seeing him again. That he'll take over his life. When I saw Rob off just now, I thought it was his double. Seriously. I know it sounds crazy, but it was fucking terrifying, Bex.'

'OK,' Bex says quietly, clearly surprised by Kate's sudden outburst. She doesn't often swear. 'Maybe seeing Rob with this woman triggered something,' she says. 'Hardly surprising, all things considered.'

Bex has helped Kate through some tough times in recent years. She never thought much of Jake, or the leaky narrowboat he and Kate lived on together in Wiltshire, and she's been a big supporter of Kate's new life with Rob. Thinks it's time Kate got a break. And a twenty-nine-year-old tech toyboy fits the bill perfectly. *Go for the money, girl.*

'Why don't you call Rob now, make yourself feel better,' Bex suggests.

'I don't want to worry him about it,' Kate says. 'And, you know . . .' She pauses. 'It might not be him I'm talking to.'

Oh God, she's sounding like a mad person. She pictures Bex pulling a face.

40

'I just want you to tell me what you think, when you see him,' she adds. 'Reassure me that Rob hasn't been replaced by someone else. That I haven't just spent the night with a complete stranger.'

'What time does his train get into Paddington?' Bex asks.

Kate closes her eyes with relief.

'Four hours from now.'

She loves Bex for being prepared to do this for her. She knew she'd be heading up to town today. She always goes to London on a Saturday to do the galleries. They used to travel together. But it's still a big ask.

'I could take a later train up to Paddington,' Bex says. 'To coincide with his. But you need to stop all this doppelgänger talk. I'm doing this to put your mind at rest. And if Rob's having an affair, I'll rip his balls off. Obviously. For you.'

Kate has to smile. Bex can be salty like that. 'Thanks, Bex. Really. Just make sure it looks like a coincidence, though. You being there.'

'I'll see what I can do. As it's you. And because I know you'll pay me back big time. Maybe a trip on his fancy yacht or something.'

'Thanks.' Kate pauses. 'Rob hasn't got a yacht, you know that. But I'll buy you fish and chips. I told him I was going to call you, see if you'd like to come down here for a few days.'

'Is that what you'd like? For me to come down?'

'He'll pay for your ticket.' Rob always offers.

41

'I'll buy my own, thanks.' And Bex always refuses.

'Seriously, it would be nice if you could come,' Kate says.

Bex is currently single, a rare state of affairs. She's not a stunner, but she does a lot with what she's got. Kate's seen how men notice her, the way she moves. She's also thirty-three, like Kate, with no sign of children. Something else they have in common.

'Actually, I could do with getting out the village,' Bex says. 'Might find myself a tasty Poldark, you never know. I'll see what the trains are doing.'

'Call me as soon as you see him?' Kate says, much happier now.

'How will I know what I'm looking for,' Bex says, 'if he, well, seems the same?'

'You'll know. Trust me.'

CHAPTER 7

KATE

It feels good to be back in the village after dropping Rob off at Truro. She was held up for ages driving through the narrow Cornish lanes – Saturday is changeover day for many of the local holiday lets – and to cheer herself up she pulled in at her favourite bakery and bought a cinnamon bun, an object of swirling, sugar-dusted beauty. She licks the last of it from her lips as she turns into the drive. To her horror, Dr Varma is already there, waiting by the front door. She should have come straight home.

'I'm so sorry, Ajay,' Kate says, showing him through the front door. She's called him Ajay since their first session, at his request. Rob still uses his formal title. 'I didn't realise the time.'

'It's quite alright.' Ajay smiles at her as he walks through to the kitchen and sits down at the table. 'I was early anyway.'

Kate knows he's lying. She never used to be late for anything, hated it when Jake was not on time.

'Thanks so much for coming,' she says. 'Rob tells me you were down for the weekend.'

43

Ajay smiles benignly. She's talking too much, not used to seeing him in anything other than a suit. This afternoon he's wearing chinos, a polo shirt and deck shoes. The only clue he's here for work is his familiar black attaché case.

'Can I get you anything?' she asks, hovering by the sink. 'Tea? Something stronger?'

'All good.'

She can tell Ajay wants to get down to business. She sits opposite him and tries to relax.

'Rob says you've been feeling a bit unwell,' he continues. 'Maybe a migraine.'

She shifts on her seat and thinks back through the strange episodes of the last week. Ajay will be sympathetic. Scientific.

'It was nothing,' she says. She feels bad for wasting Ajay's time, but she'd rather just confide in Bex for the moment.

Ajay senses her discomfort and gives her one of his chubby, reassuring smiles. She's forgotten what a good bedside manner he has. He won't rush her. He will bide his time until she's ready to tell him.

'He also said you're making fantastic progress,' he continues, beaming. 'Thought you'd really turned a corner when he arrived last night.'

'I've been feeling a lot better,' she says, watching as Ajay removes a laptop from his attaché case and opens it on the table. He pulls out a headset similar to the one that Rob put on her earlier, also covered with electrodes.

44

'He's asked me to run some more recognition tests — try to establish whether the part of your brain that was damaged in the accident has fully recovered.'

'Recognition tests? Sounds suspiciously like police work,' Kate says. When she did her interview for the super-recogniser job with Wiltshire Police, she was shown inverted faces and altered images. There was also a 'before they were famous' test, in which she had to identify celebrities from poor-quality images taken when they were young.

Ajay smiles. He knows Kate never wants to work for the force again, but he agrees with Rob that her powers of recognition, almost non-existent after the accident, remain the best indicator of her brain's overall recovery. The surgeon who operated on her talked of damage to her right temporal lobe, including the fusiform gyrus, the part of the brain that processes faces. He warned that facial blindness was a possibility. Kate was more worried about her ability to paint, particularly portraits of people.

'We're going to use the EEG headset to monitor a brainwave called a P3,' Ajay says, checking his laptop.

'What's a P3?'

'Electrical activity that occurs in the brain a fraction of a second after you recognise a face. The response spike is markedly stronger in super recognisers.'

'Should I be flattered?' Kate asks.

'What's interesting is that the reaction is involuntary – you can't stop a P3 brainwave,' he says. 'It's why they use it for lie detection.'

Ajay turns the laptop towards her and explains that she's going to be shown two faces for five seconds each. She'll then be shown hundreds of random facial images in quick succession, about ten per second, using a process called rapid serial visual presentation, or RSVP. Buried among them will be the two faces she was shown at the beginning. If her recognition skills are working, the deeper cognitive responses of her brain will trigger a P3 spike.

'Are you ready?' he asks.

She nods, adjusting her sitting position as he switches his laptop to full screen. A moment later, she studies each face for five seconds. First Brucie and then Jeff. Silly, she knows, but they used to use nicknames in the force when they were mentally storing images of faces, based on instant associations. Big chin? Bruce Forsyth. Prominent ears? Jeff Goldblum. It helps to make their faces stick.

Brucie and Jeff disappear and a series of images starts to flash in full screen before her eyes. She doesn't have enough time to clock each one in detail, but she's aware that they're what they used to call 'dirty' shots, when the faces are partially obscured.

After thirty seconds, she feels tired. Despite the speed of the images, her brain is desperately trying

46

to analyse each one, process it, match it against memories. The curse of the super recogniser. It's like playing pairs on speed. Or Pelmanism, as her granny used to call it. Kate always used to win against her as a child, but it was put down to her younger brain rather than any special gift. She only discovered her ability to recognise faces a few years ago, although she should have seen the signs earlier. Whenever she watched TV, she'd recognise walk-on extras in the background that she'd seen in other films. She just thought everyone did.

She doesn't know how long the test lasts – two minutes, maybe longer – but she's relieved when it's over.

'That was hard,' she says, blowing out her cheeks. It feels like she's just sat an exam.

'You have to relax,' Ajay says, studying his phone. 'Allow the images to wash over you, let your subconscious brain do the work.'

'I don't think I spotted anyone,' she says.

'You did.' He turns his laptop for her to see. There's a graph on the screen and a noticeable spike. 'Image number 213.'

Jeff. 'What about the other person?'

'The spike was less pronounced.' He scrolls through the rest of the graph and shows her more of a gentle hill than a mountain peak. 'But it's still an impressive response.'

She's not convinced. Brucie got away.

Ajay pauses, shaking his head. 'It's still remark-able. Your powers of recognition are undoubtedly back, which is encouraging, given the damage that your brain suffered.'

She doesn't need reminding. Six months ago, returning home after a particularly difficult day at work, she drove into a tree just outside the village. Not that she can remember any of it. They think she fell asleep at the wheel. She was lucky to survive, given her traumatic brain injuries. No airbags in a 1969 woodie. After an extensive investigation, the police concluded that it was a tragic accident.

'Does that mean my ability to paint will return, too?' She glances over at the canvas of Stretch on the easel.

'It should do. In time. Rob's so pleased,' Ajay says, putting away the headset.

A part of her was hoping she could blame her funny turns on a still damaged fusiform gyrus. But if her brain is healing, it might not be playing tricks on her. And Rob might have been replaced by his double.

CHAPTER 8

JAKE

Jake snaps shut his laptop and looks around the cramped narrowboat. It's not happening today. If he's honest, it's not happening every day. He thought he might write more after Kate left him, but his productivity has gone down, if that's possible.

He locks up and steps onto the bank, glancing back at the boat. One end of the roof is piled up with logs seasoning for the winter, the other is covered with solar panels. All part of living off grid. He needs to water the flowerboxes down by the bow. They were planted with petunias by Kate and are dying.

The canal has a rare beauty this morning, layers of gossamer mist hanging above the surface of the water. A plump of moorhens retreats into the deep reedbeds on the far bank as he walks on down the towpath. Up ahead, Jake's favourite bridge, a perfectly poised redbrick arch, reflects in the water to form a shimmering circle of sorts. It's the one thing that keeps him going: this idyllic haven where he lives like a floating nomad.

The post office in the village has texted to say

there's a package for him. He enters with a spring in his step – maybe it's a forgotten translation of one of his books? – and tries not to look at the croissants. He can't even afford the gas to bake his own bread any more.

'The usual?' the woman behind the bakery counter asks, sliding one into a paper bag for him.

'Not today, thanks,' Jake says, sweeping back his long hair. His empty stomach rumbles in protest. 'I think you've got a package for me.'

'Here we go.' She passes him a padded envelope. Jake knows at once that it's not a book. Too small. At least it's not a bill. Or a court summons. He's had too many of those recently. On his way out, he stops to look at the small ads: teenagers offering to babysit, mow lawns. He could do that. Easier than writing. His novels are only published in Finland now.

He crosses the street to walk in the sunshine and heads back to his boat via the station. As he passes, he spots Bex, Kate's best friend, on the crowded platform, all big hair and chunky shoes. He likes to chat with her even if the feeling is far from mutual. She's his last remaining connection with Kate. He didn't cherish Kate enough, according to Bex. It's not easy when you're broke. He hasn't seen Kate since she left hospital. Since she shacked up with her tech millionaire.

'Alright?' Bex says as Jake approaches.

'Off on holiday?' he asks, glancing at her wheelie case.

He suddenly feels like a hick in his canal clothes that smell of diesel and woodsmoke. There was a time when he was on this platform every morning in a suit, commuting up to London to work as a crime reporter. Kate used to complain that he'd turned feral, become more interested in spotting otters than writing bestsellers.

Bex nods awkwardly.

Is she going to see Kate? 'Somewhere nice?' he prompts.

Their conversation is even more stilted than normal. He's only two years older than Bex, but he feels disconnected, out of touch.

'London,' she says, without conviction. 'Friend of a friend.' With that, she raises her eyebrows and turns to the train that's just pulling in.

Back at the narrowboat, Jake steps on board, ducks down below and opens the small package at the galley table. There's no note, just a memory stick. He checks the printed address label again and looks at the postmark: East London.

Why was Bex being so weird?

He slips the stick into the USB port of his old laptop and clicks on the new icon. A video file appears. He leans in closer, watching the grainy CCTV footage that's already begun to play.

It takes a few moments to realise that the woman sitting at the bar is Kate. She's on her own, looking at her phone. Jake glances at the date in the bottom right corner of the screen: '10.05 p.m., 14 February'. He shudders at the memory. In the other corner it says: 'Bluebell 2'. The only Bluebell pub he knows of is on the way to Swindon. A barman comes over and starts up a conversation with Kate. Jake stares, transfixed, as the barman turns his back, fixes a bright orange drink and passes it to her. An Aperol spritz, her favourite.

The image judders and the CCTV feed is now looking down on Kate. Jake watches the scene play out again from the new angle. 'Bluebell 3'. It's like trying to spot a magician's sleight of hand. And then he sees it. There. A definite pass across the top of the glass, just before the barman slips in the ice.

Jake sits back, his mouth drying, and picks up the package again, checking inside in case he's missed anything. Empty. Whoever sent it has spotted something that they want Jake to see too. Why now, six months later?

He gets up from his desk and glances at his watch. It's too early for a beer, even on a Saturday. Not that he's got any. All there is to drink is his kombucha, fermenting in the corner. He puts on the kettle, trying to order his thoughts.

Valentine's Day is a date he'll never forget. Kate was working late, a relief as he hadn't planned anything romantic. When his phone rang, he thought she might be calling to suggest they meet for last orders. Instead, she accused him of cheating on her. As part of her job, she'd been trawling through hours of recent CCTV footage and by chance had spotted Jake with another woman in a shopping mall. It was a cruel twist of fate and Jake never got the chance to explain.

An hour later, Kate crashed her Morris Minor Traveller on her way home. He's always thought it was an accident.

He doesn't now.

CHAPTER 9

KATE

After Ajay has gone, Kate settles down at the easel, determined to finish the painting of Stretch – less pig, more dog. The results of the recognition tests were encouraging, giving her hope that her painting skills will return too. Stretch, though, has other ideas and won't lie still. He's almost six months old and already likes a thirty-minute walk every day.

'You win,' she says as he trots off out of the kitchen towards the back of the house. She watches him for a second and wonders where he's going. He doesn't usually disappear out of her sight. She gets up, paintbrush still in hand, and is about to follow him when she pauses at the fridge. She bought some Cornish Yarg yesterday, thick and creamy. She pulls on the fridge handle, but it doesn't open. She tries again without success.

'Rob, the fridge won't open,' she says a moment later, talking to him on the phone. She's a lot calmer now than she was a few hours ago. He's still on the train to London.

'Sorry, it must still be in diet mode. Stops you snacking between meals.'

54

'But I'm not on a diet.' Sometimes she despairs of this house, Rob's love of so-called smart technology.

'I am,' he says. 'And it thought I was down for the whole weekend. Try now.'

'Thanks.' She shakes her head in disbelief. The fridge door opens. Rob controls everything in his life from an app. Everything except her.

'You OK?' he asks. 'No more migraines?'

'Hungry.'

'How was it with Dr Varma?'

'He did some tests, thinks my brain is recovering.'

She suspects that Ajay has already sent over the results to Rob and that Rob is just humouring her.

'That's great news,' he says. 'I said you were improving.'

'I guess so,' she replies, looking forlornly at her half-finished painting of Stretch.

After a quick chat – Rob interrupted a work call to take hers – she lets him go. Stretch has not returned. She walks down the long corridor, eating a piece of Yarg. At the far end, it's right to the big spare bedroom, where Bex always stays, or left to a storeroom. Where's Stretch gone?

She stops in her tracks. The door to the storeroom is open. That's a first. It's been locked ever since she's been here. Rob's got an obsession with laptops and computers and once told her he keeps quite a few of them in the storeroom for security. The whole house is very safe – security lights and cameras everywhere, triple locks on the outside

55

doors. Kate told him it wasn't necessary, but he installed them soon after she moved in, thought she was being naive about her previous life, the nature of her police work.

Stretch appears in the doorway.

'What are you doing in there?' she says, as if it's his idea to be nosy.

She follows him through the door. It's more of an office than a storeroom, dominated by a large black desk and a picture on the wall behind. In the corner there's a stack of old laptops, at least ten of them. There are no windows, which is out of keeping with the rest of the light-flooded house. The back wall is cut into the hillside and the front wall adjoins the guest room.

'Bigger than we thought, isn't it?' she says to Stretch, switching on the main light. 'Much bigger.'

She walks around the workstation, running her finger across the smooth black marble. There's a computer screen on the desk, flanked by sound-stick speakers, but it's the black-and-white picture propped up against the wall that catches her attention, even though it's partially hidden by some card and wrapping.

She lifts it up, blows off the dust and studies it more closely, her head spinning. It looks pre-Raphaelite and has been done in pen and ink and brush. The inscription in the corner says 'DGR' – Dante Gabriel Rossetti. A couple dressed in medieval clothes are walking through woodland. They appear to have stumbled across their doubles, identical in every respect: same physical features, medieval clothing, matching feathers in their caps. The woman has fainted and her terrified man has drawn a sword to confront his double, staring into the whites of his eyes. The only thing that distinguishes them is that the couple on the left has been framed with an ethereal glowing light, to denote that they're the doppelgängers.

If only it were that easy.

She perches on the edge of the office chair and stares intently at the picture, her heart racing as she looks for clues: how to tell when your boyfriend's been replaced by a double.

She stays like that for a long time, holding the picture in front of her as she tries to recall some of the tricks and techniques from her old police job. Gait, facial features, tells – she knew about them all once. Her boss even sent her on a behavioural analysis course. She reminds herself that she was pretty good at recognising people, one of the best. She was never wrong.

So what is it with Rob that's different?

She replays the details of her recent funny turns as dispassionately as she can. Something about him has definitely changed. It's hard to describe, but it's almost as if he's impersonating himself, over-emphasising the little tics, the blinking eyes, the hand through his hair. Physically he looks identical, but there's something about him – is it his blue eyes, what they're hiding? – that doesn't sit right with her.

She props the picture back against the wall, walks over to a row of bookshelves and glances at some of the titles. Most are to do with business investment. Some are about coding, others are about health, neurotechnology and bio-engineering. There are several books about consciousness, exploring the twilight zone between life and death, another about locked-in syndrome. And on the bottom shelf a row of paperbacks. She bends down and pulls one out. It's an old, well-thumbed book by Fyodor Dostoevsky: *The Double*. She reads the blurb on the back, returns it to the shelf and pulls out another faded paperback: *The Private Memoirs and Confessions of a Justified Sinner* by James Hogg. Written in 1824, it's about a Gothic double.

She doesn't know what to think about all this doppelgänger stuff. Rob is clearly more obsessed with it than she realised. So obsessed that he keeps it under lock and key.

That doesn't mean he's been replaced by one. Of course he hasn't. Bex was right to call her out on that. A double would have to look identical, imitate Rob's mannerisms, perfect the way he talks. He would have to learn everything about Rob's history, about her . . .

She pushes the thought away. She's just being silly again. She also feels – unreasonably, perhaps

58

– a little misled about the storeroom that isn't. It's a full-blown office, full of Rob's things. Maybe he does work in here, when she's asleep, which is often.

She calls Stretch and closes the door after him. Rob must have forgotten to lock it in their rush to get to the train station earlier. And then she goes back in to take the copy of *The Private Memoirs and Confessions of a Justified Sinner*. She'll have plenty of time to read and return it. But before she's reached the desk, her phone rings. It's Bex.

CHAPTER 10

KATE

'I feel like an undercover cop on a stakeout,' Bex says, whispering. 'Is this what you used to do in your old job?'

'Where are you?' Kate asks, trying to put a lead on Stretch, who is desperate for his walk.

'Pret a Manger, Paddington station. Rob's train is about to arrive on platform one.'

'Are you actually going to meet him?' Kate asks, closing the front door behind her. She can't be bothered to follow Rob's instructions and triple-lock it. And she hasn't set the alarm in weeks. This is rural Cornwall, not Shoreditch. She heads on down to the lush green field below the house, Stretch pulling on his lead, and cuts across to the coast path that runs along the bottom of their land, marked by a herringbone slate wall.

'I'll say hello if . . . if something doesn't seem right . . .' Bex's words tail off. 'I'm tucked away in a corner,' she continues. 'Got a clear view of people walking past. I'll chat to him if he sees me.'

Kate tries to picture her in the window of Pret. 'Thanks, Bex.'

Bex explains that she'll do some galleries after

intercepting Rob and then come on down to Truro this evening.

She's really going the distance – and for what? Kate holds onto the memory of that unfamiliar look in Rob's eye, the overwhelming sense of disconnect that she felt.

'I had nothing planned this weekend anyway,' Bex adds. 'Just the usual gang in the Slaughtered Lamb tonight. It's not been the same since you left.'

Kate used to go to their local a lot with Jake, found herself drinking more and more. She tells herself she doesn't miss him, the claustrophobic life they shared, particularly on days like today. The salt-fresh air, blue sky, the sea laid out like sheet glass below her. She'd been going out with Jake for years, since they met at university. Perhaps it was the combination of their jobs – a portrait artist and an author – that did for them in the end, living and working in each other's pockets on a tiny narrowboat. Or the fact that they couldn't seem to have children. Their careers never quite took off either, which didn't help. It was why she took the police job in the end. One of them had to earn some money.

'Hold up, here comes his train now,' Bex says.

'He'll be at the front,' she says. 'First class.'

'Of course he bloody will.'

They both stay silent for a few seconds. Kate can picture the crowds of people flooding onto the platform, some back from their holidays, others

61

in town to shop. She used to spend a lot of time watching crowds, guessing what they did as she looked for the match. Too much time.

'Can you see him?' she asks. Why is she so nervous?

'Not yet.'

'You remember what he looks like?'

'Relax, Kate. I'm on it.'

'Sorry, I'm just—'

'I know you are.' Bex pauses. 'No sign of him yet.'

Maybe Rob's tricky investor isn't in London and he got off the train at Reading. Bex's silence seems to last forever. The coast path's high hedgerows are humming with bees. Above her, seagulls soar in the rising air currents. And then she hears another noise, one that she's heard a few times in recent weeks. She scans the clear sky and spots a drone out in the bay, heading towards her.

'There he is,' Bex suddenly says. 'Even more of a looker than I remember.'

'Is he with anyone?' Kate asks, watching as the drone approaches. The sight and sound of it make her uneasy, cutting through the coastal calm. Rob has recently invested in a start-up drone courier company. He tests a lot of his gadgets down here. Is that one of his? It can't be. He's in London.

'On his own,' Bex says.

'That's good.'

'I can't see anything strange about him, Kate.

That's all I can say. Right lanky sod, isn't he? And so young! How old is he again?'

'Twenty-nine.' The drone is above her now, hovering high above the coast path.

'Cheeky. Dead cool bag over one shoulder. Sound familiar?'

'All good. What about the way he's walking?' You can tell a lot by the way someone walks.

'Preoccupied,' Bex says. 'He's just pulled out his phone.'

Kate's own phone flashes up a message that he's on the other line. 'He's trying to call me,' she says, not sure whether to be reassured or scared.

'Are you going to answer it?'

'No.' She lets the call go to voicemail. The drone starts to move away, back out to sea.

'He's stopped on the platform. He's glancing around,' Bex says. 'Nice smile. Looks like he's leaving you a long, loving message.' She pauses. 'Hang on.'

'What?' Has Bex noticed something about him?

'Shitters, he's heading in here.'

'What are you going to say?'

'Better go.'

'Just tell him the truth, that you're coming down to see me, waiting for your train,' Kate says, but the line's already dead.

CHAPTER 11

KATE

Kate stops on the coast path and leans against the drystone wall. London feels so far away. At least Bex has got an excuse for why she's up in town. Rob knows Kate was going to ask her down. And Bex is a good bluffer. She tries to guess what they'll talk about. Rob will confide that he's a bit worried about her but won't go into details. He's too decent to be indiscreet. And Bex will flirt with him, pick some fluff off his shoulder, which will make him blush and blink.

'Shall we carry on?' she asks Stretch, who is pulling at the lead again. 'Keep ourselves busy?'

She turns to breathe in the pure sea air. No sign of the drone now. Two people are walking towards them on the coast path. Below, a sailing dinghy heads out into the bay, a tiny blade of brilliant white slicing across the haze of blue. And there, on the far side of the bay, is the field where she and Jake used to camp in the summer. Ironic that she's ended up living within sight of it but not with Jake. It always rained for the week they were down. They argued a lot too – he liked to go

64

sailing, she didn't – but she still feels a pang of nostalgia. It's the laughter she misses. His reassuring presence too. Was he a father figure to her, as Bex always used to say? She was brought up by her mother, a West End actress. Her father died before she was born.

She smiles weakly at the couple as she passes them, allowing their dog, a black Labrador, to sniff at Stretch. Ten minutes later, she's about to enter the village when her phone rings.

She almost drops it as she whips the phone out of her back pocket.

'He's worried about you, pleased that I'm coming down,' Bex says. 'Told me to make sure the house is triple-locked and alarmed at night.'

Sounds like Rob. 'Did anything strike you as odd about him?' she asks breathlessly. 'Different?'

'There really wasn't anything, Kate. Short of grabbing his balls and asking him to cough, I couldn't have examined him any closer. He must have thought I was right weird, the way I was standing in his face.'

'Did he offer to pay your fare?' she asks.

'Of course. And I declined. Let him buy me a coffee, though.'

Out of nowhere, a treacherous thought snakes into her head. 'What did you have?' she asks.

'Cappuccino, why?'

'How about him?'

'What is this, twenty questions?'

'Please, it's important.'

Her brain is already getting ahead of itself.

'Flat white, I think,' Bex says.

'He asked for a flat white?' she repeats, feeling dizzy, trying to buy herself time.

'Like a latte only with less foam. Can't see the point of them myself.'

'I know what it is,' she snaps. There's no need to be short with Bex. She has gone out of her way to help her. It's just that a flat white is what Kate usually has.

'Rob only ever drinks espresso,' she says. 'A double. He's a man of ridiculous habit.'

She's always teasing him about his routines, telling him he needs to let his hair down more often. In truth, she envies his discipline. She can't seem to focus so well since the accident.

'Maybe he fancied a change, I don't know,' Bex says. 'It's just a bloody cup of coffee, Kate.'

But Kate can tell that she's not convinced, that Rob's choice has disconcerted Bex. Kate too.

CHAPTER 12

SILAS

'This better be worth it,' Detective Inspector Silas Hart says as Jake sits down opposite him in the café. Silas tries to avoid work at weekends, but his current in-tray at Swindon CID is making that difficult.

'Sorry I'm late,' Jake says. 'Bus from Marlborough was delayed.'

'What sort of bestselling author travels by bus?' Silas asks.

It's a cheap shot, below the belt. Silas was happy to help Jake with his books when he approached him a few years ago, assumed he'd soon become the Morse of Swindon. But it turns out his thrillers aren't so bestselling after all. They're not even published in English.

Jake takes out a small padded envelope as a waitress comes up to ask if he'd like anything to eat. Silas is halfway through a bacon sandwich.

'No, thanks,' Jake says to the waitress.

The guy really is broke. They haven't met up for a while and, these days, when they do, they spend more time discussing rare birds than police procedure.

67

'Get him a tea and a bacon sandwich,' Silas says, turning to Jake. 'On me.'

'Thanks,' Jake says sheepishly, and retrieves a small memory stick from the package. Jake is a big man, and his long hair and flecked beard make him look a bit wild. It's a mystery how he manages to live on a narrowboat.

'What's on it?' Silas asks.

Jake swings his bag around, rummages through a mess of books and old newspapers and pulls out a battered laptop. Silas catches a whiff of diesel.

'Is it suitable for public viewing?' he asks, glancing around the café, one of his favourite greasy spoons. It's in the town centre, near the courts, where he's been most of this week for a human-trafficking trial. Until recently, Swindon's nail bars weren't really his sort of place. Now he's got to know them well. Extensions, overlays, the lot.

'There's no sound,' Jake says, but he still turns the cracked screen away from the middle of the café. All he'd said on his text was that he had been sent a video and it had something to do with his ex's car accident. An RTA wouldn't normally be the concern of Swindon CID, but Jake's ex, Kate, is not a normal person. For a year before her road traffic accident, she worked for Silas as a super recogniser, identifying more criminals than the courts could cope with.

'It's the Bluebell, in Rockbourne.'

Silas looks up at Jake at the mention of the

Bluebell. The pub was recently flagged in an ongoing county lines heroin network. He peers more closely at the screen, wondering how Jake has managed to get hold of the pub's CCTV feed. And what the hell Kate was doing there.

'Look carefully,' Jake says, as the barman fixes the drink. 'See what he did, just before the ice went in?'

Silas tears another bite off his bacon sandwich.

'Watch it again now – it's clearer from this angle.' Jake adjusts the screen.

Silas leans forward, mopping ketchup from his mouth with a paper napkin.

'There.'

Silas sees it. Something appears to go into the drink before the ice. But the footage is not conclusive.

'She was exhausted,' he says. 'We've been through this.' He scrutinised the RTA report carefully, made his own inquiries, tried not to dwell on how tired she was that night, how hard he'd been working her. How hard he'd worked everyone in the super-recogniser unit. 'And she'd had a drink – she was right on the limit.'

'Shame they weren't looking for something else,' Jake says. 'A sedative of some kind. Her drink must have been spiked. Must have been. It would explain her falling asleep at the wheel.'

Silas isn't convinced. Not yet. He's more interested in where the memory stick came from. 'Who sent you this?' he asks.

'No idea.' Jake turns the package over. 'Just arrived this morning.'

'And your mucky prints are all over it.' Silas takes the package by one corner, as if he's holding a fish by its tail. Whoever sent it to Jake knew to address it c/o the village post office.

'I didn't know what it was,' Jake says.

'We'll take a look at it – if you're happy to hand it in.'

'Sure. I've made a copy.'

Silas watches Jake take the stick out of his computer and drop it into the envelope that he's holding out for him. 'Do you hear from Kate much?' he asks.

'Nothing.' Jake looks down at his mug of tea. 'I don't even know where she's living.'

Silas took a personal interest in Kate's recovery, visited her most days at the Great Western Hospital in Swindon, on his way to or from Gablecross police station. He also tried to stay in touch when she was discharged, but she wanted to cut all ties with him, her job, the force. With Jake too, it seems. The last he heard, she was living in seaside splendour somewhere on the south coast of Cornwall with a wealthy entrepreneur who does something clever in tech.

'Everyone at the station misses her,' he says. He knows it's of little consolation.

'Me too.'

'She was an extraordinary woman. Gifted.'

They both fall quiet. Silas is saying all the

70

wrong things today. Kate is the only reason why he's prepared to forgive Jake for his poor book sales. It was Jake who introduced Kate to him in the first place. Brought her remarkable talent to the force's attention.

'I'll check out the video,' he says, watching enviously as the waitress puts Jake's bacon sandwich in front of him. He still marvels at his own short-lived vegan phase last year. 'Let you know what we find.'

'If it wasn't an accident, if someone was trying to harm Kate . . .' Jake pauses, eyes welling at the thought. '. . . was it because of the work she did for you? It was in the news again yesterday.'

Silas hesitates. He's asked himself the same question many times, particularly this last week while he was sitting in court watching a modern slavery gang being sent down for a total of thirty-three years. The original arrests were made by his team, almost entirely as a result of Kate's exceptional work for the police. It was one reason why he went to such lengths at the time to reassure himself about the circumstances of her accident.

'Let's not get ahead of ourselves,' he says, but the discovery that Kate visited the Bluebell on the night of her accident worries him. At the time, Silas and his unit were investigating possible links between modern-slavery and county-lines gangs in Swindon. The Bluebell was under suspicion, but there was no hard evidence of a connection.

He looks up at Jake, who's wolfing down his bacon sandwich. The thought of someone targeting Kate, a decent, ordinary human being who happened to have an almost superhuman gift, sends a shiver through him.

CHAPTER 13

KATE

The flat white at Kate's favourite café in the village doesn't taste the same as usual. It's not the coffee, or the artistic way it's been prepared, and she can hardly complain about the al fresco venue, looking out across the beach and harbour. It's the thought of Rob ordering one. She knows it's just a bloody cup of coffee, as Bex says, but he's never had a flat white in all the time they've been together. Why start now?

She pulls out her phone and listens to his voice-mail message:

'Just ringing to check you're OK. I'm at Paddington, about to head over to the office. Wish I was still with you in Cornwall. I'm so glad it went well with Dr Varma. Don't worry, your pictures will be hanging in the National Portrait Gallery soon – I just know it. Be careful and, you know, sorry I had to bail. I'll make it up to you, I promise.'

It sounds like Rob, always telling her to be careful, ever optimistic about her art. She smiles to herself, glancing along the line of other customers. There's only one outside table, a long, wooden bar from where you can look down onto the busy beach below. She needs to stop worrying. She's got so much to be grateful for. At the far end of the table, a pair of binoculars has been provided by the café for admiring the view – or the tanned bodies on the beach. 'Perv-oculars', as Rob calls them. Everyone's perched on chrome bar stools and Stretch is at her feet, his lead tangled around one of the legs. She realises how hungry she is. Bex is always moaning that she eats like a horse and never seems to put on weight. Must be her metabolism. Glancing at the man next to her, she abandons Stretch and her half-drunk coffee and goes to buy some flapjack from the café.

When she comes back, Stretch is whining and the man has gone. She slips Stretch a piece of flapjack, finishes her coffee and leaves, chatting with some people at the café counter on her way out.

'I won't be long,' she says to her friend Mark, who runs the gallery around the corner. He's got a dog too and she leaves Stretch and her phone with him whenever she goes for a swim. She's wearing her costume underneath her jeans and heads down to the beach, where she strips off and plunges into the crowded waves. She likes to swim out to the floating platform, about fifty yards offshore. At Rob's suggestion, she's been swimming most days. Another healer, like art.

She makes her way through playing families

and into deeper, calmer waters, wishing Rob was with her. They had fun last weekend, swimming at the secret cove. Happy days – before she started to have these doubts. She's just being silly about the coffee, over-analysing everything. It's good to be out here. The sea is crystal clear, shoals of silver fish passing below her, glistening as they twist and turn through shards of slanting sunshine. Below them, translucent jellyfish pulse hypnotically.

And then her calves begin to tighten up. Shit. Cramp.

She swims on towards the platform, only twenty yards away now, trying not to kick too hard. It's happened before. Nothing to worry about if she just relaxes and stretches. But it's not going away. Treading water, she stops to bend down and massage the cramping muscles. A spasm shoots up her left leg and she cries out involuntarily, swallowing seawater. She coughs and gulps for air, panic rising. And then the other leg goes, a bolt of excruciating pain that doubles her up. She's in trouble here. This is the worst cramp she's ever had.

She tries to call out to a group of bronzed teenagers who are now pushing each other off the platform, but she's coughing too much, desperate for air. The teenagers don't seem to hear her. She shouts again, thrashing about in the water as she tries to get their attention. She can't breathe. Each time her head goes under, she sinks further down into the deep before somehow coming back to the surface. This time though she's too far under, losing consciousness. She knows she won't make it back up. She's dropping, further and further.

And all she can think of is Jake brewing tea in their tent in the rain.

CHAPTER 14

JAKE

Jake asks the bus driver to stop at Ogbourne St George on his way back from seeing DI Hart in Swindon. Five minutes later, he's walking the Ridgeway, a kestrel hovering in the warm currents up ahead of him. His destination is the Bluebell at Rockbourne, a village two miles to the east, where he thinks Kate stopped off that night to have a drink. A photo of the bar on the pub's website matches the interior on the CCTV footage.

It's good to be back on the ancient route, which covers some of the most remote parts of the North Wessex Downs. Soon after they met, he and Kate completed all eighty-seven miles of it with old friends of hers, walking a different section each weekend. Vast open skies, rolling chalk downlands, Iron Age forts and lively conversation. It's the chats he misses most. Kate was a great listener.

Jake sets off at a decent pace, the wind in his long hair, knowing that there's a drink at the other end. He's got just enough cash for a pint. He should leave the pub to DI Hart, but he wants to talk to the barman himself, see the place Kate visited on her way home. He's been over that last night so many times, blaming himself for the accident, for initially arranging the police job. If he earned more as a writer, she could have stayed a portrait painter. And then there was his tryst, caught on camera.

He considers again the footage he was sent. Is it really proof that someone wanted to harm Kate? The police insisted her crash was an accident. She should have kept her head down when she got the job as a super recogniser, not done any media interviews, but hers was a remarkable story: 'The Woman Who Can't Forget a Face'. And when she started identifying criminals, lots of them, the force couldn't resist the good publicity. This week, they've been at it again. At least Kate's name hasn't been mentioned in the newspaper court reports.

Half an hour later, Jake is at the Bluebell in Rockbourne, propping up the empty bar with a pint in his hands. It's a traditional no-frills country pub: low-beamed ceilings, beer barrels behind the bar. All floorboards and blackboards and a no-nonsense landlady. And he's definitely been here before, when he was walking the Ridgeway with Kate and their friends all those years ago. It's not how he remembers it and, annoyingly, the barman on duty is not the person in the CCTV footage.

'Don't suppose you remember seeing a friend of

mine in here a while back?' Jake asks him, pulling out a photo of Kate.

'No, mate,' the barman says, shaking his head.

The landlady comes over to look at the photo.

'Never seen her before,' she says dismissively.

Jake's sure the pub wasn't this unfriendly when they stopped by on their walk.

'Who's asking?' the barman says, watching the landlady disappear out the back.

Jake clocks a further hardening of tone. 'She's an old friend, that's all,' he says.

'Left you swinging in the wind?' The barman grins. His teeth aren't great.

'You could say that.'

Jake is overwhelmed with a sudden urge to confront this man, challenge him about Kate's spiked drink, the terrible consequences. He knows something, even if he's not the barman in the video.

Picking up his pint, Jake moves over to a corner table in case he does something stupid. Kate must have stopped off here to decompress after work, make the switch before joining him on the boat. She was drinking a lot by the end of their relationship. So was he. Maybe she came here more than once.

He glances around the pub, at the camera above the door, the one next to the optics behind the bar. A lot of security for a quiet country pub. And a strange place for Kate to visit on her own.

He's about to leave when the barman comes over

to clean the adjacent table. He's then at Jake's table, unnecessarily wiping down its spotless surface.

'If you're a journalist, you need to fuck off,' the man says under his breath, still wiping.

'I'm not a journalist,' Jake says, sipping from his pint. 'And I'm not fucking off anywhere.'

He feels a sudden surge of adrenaline. When he was a cub crime reporter, his boss told him to always push back at the first opportunity.

'Who are you, then?' the barman asks.

'I write books. Crime thrillers.'

'Should I have heard of you?'

Jake hesitates before telling him his name. 'Big in Finland,' he adds, trying to lighten the mood.

Was it a mistake to reveal his name? He's carrying a little extra around the middle these days, but he's more than capable of looking after himself.

The barman wipes the table one final time and looks him in the eye.

'Then I suggest you fuck off to Finland, Jake.'

CHAPTER 15

KATE

When Kate regains consciousness, she's staring up at the sun, her whole body swaying. Faces peer down at her, kind teenage faces full of fear and worry. Her head hurts. It takes her a few moments to realise that she's lying on her back on the floating platform in the middle of the harbour.

'She's awake,' one of them announces, as if the kettle's just boiled. She loves kids, their matter-of-factness.

'Here's the lifeboat,' another says.

The lifeboat? For her? Kate closes her eyes again. Everyone will be watching from the shore, from the café. She likes to observe others, not be the centre of attention herself.

'I'm alright,' she says, trying to get up. But her head starts to throb and her legs buckle beneath her so she lies back down again.

'It's OK,' one of the teenage girls says. 'We've called for help.'

'What happened?' Kate whispers. All she can remember is swimming out to the platform. Why has she got such a splitting headache?

'I think you had a cramp attack, almost drowned,' the girl says, glancing admiringly at a boy standing next to her. 'Ned dived in, brought you onto the platform. He's done a life-saving course.'

Good old Ned. Kate will thank him later, when she's feeling stronger. Rob will kill her when he hears about this. And Bex. She'll be here in a few hours, telling Kate she's become a liability. She never used to be accident prone, but the stats aren't looking good. Two in six months now. At least this was only cramp.

She turns her head towards the harbour, watching as the inshore lifeboat comes alongside the platform. She can't help feeling she's wasting good people's time. She was too tired. Shouldn't have gone for a swim. Stretch will be beside himself, wondering where she is.

As she feared, there are crowds of rubberneckers on the beach, observing the scene unfold. And a man on his own, up by the café, looking in her direction through a pair of binoculars.

CHAPTER 16

SILAS

'This new facial-recognition software is officially shit, sir,' says DC Strover, sitting back at her desk. 'I assume it's not going live anytime soon.'

'That's not like you,' Silas says, glancing at his young colleague.

They are in the CID corner of the open-plan Parade Room at Gablecross. Strover is an expert when it comes to computers and a champion of all things digital, constantly berating Silas for not embracing social media.

'And stop calling me "sir", will you? "Guv" or "boss" but not "sir". Makes me feel like a schoolteacher. And I hated school.'

Silas recruited Strover to work with him eighteen months ago. Apart from still calling him 'sir', she's a quick learner, proving invaluable last year when they nailed a serial killer. He likes her sense of humour too, now that she's grown confident enough in his company to speak her mind.

'I'm a big fan of deep learning, don't get me wrong – boss,' Strover says, emphasising the last word in her strong Bristol accent. 'I just don't think computers will ever properly understand human faces.'

'You're in danger of sounding like me,' Silas says. He's never heard her badmouth technology before.

'Airport scanners are one thing – nice, clean, head-on face shots, a constrained environment – but big unruly crowds . . .?' she says. He nods, encouraging her surprising bout of heresy. 'Forget it. Poor lighting, funny angles, grainy resolution, scarves, beards, you name it. The messy real world that the software has to work with is just too variable compared with the neat and tidy images it was trained on. I mean, take a look at this.'

She passes Silas a printout of a mugshot. 'That's meant to be a match for our barman in the Bluebell.' She pauses, letting Silas study the image. 'My cat's arse looks more like him.'

Silas puts the mugshot down and sits back, smiling. She's right about facial-recognition software, confirming his own worst Luddite fears. The system has tried and failed miserably to match the CCTV image of the barman with one of 21 million images of faces and distinguishing marks currently stored on the UK's custody image database. And that's after Strover narrowed the search first with the relevant metadata. He doesn't know why they even bothered. When South Wales Police tested new facial-recognition software on crowds in Cardiff a couple of years back, 92 per cent of the matches were false. No wonder the Met, his old force, have abandoned using it at the Notting Hill Carnival.

'I've been asking the boss for weeks if he'll consider giving the super-recogniser unit another go,' he says.

'And?'

'Not unless Kate comes back. And we know the answer to that.'

Twelve months earlier, Silas set up a small intelligence unit to help identity criminals from Swindon's vast database of CCTV footage. The town has more than six hundred local-authority-run cameras, making it one of the most surveilled places in Britain outside London. But the unit wasn't about new software. It was about people, half a dozen 'super recognisers' – a mix of local police officers and one civilian, Kate – all of whom had been selected for their preternatural powers of facial recognition.

Kate's results during the screening process were 'off the scale', according to the professor of psychology who had overseen her assessment. He'd never come across anyone like her. And much to Silas's delight, Kate proceeded to identify dozens of criminals in her first six months, working off grainy images and mugshots as she watched hundreds of hours of CCTV. She also operated out in the field, identifying troublemakers in large football crowds, pickpockets in shopping centres. In retrospect, Silas should have seen that she was exhausted, but everyone was blinded by her results.

'Why don't we go to Kate, instead of trying to get her to come to us?' Strover says. 'She might be more interested in helping, given that this involves her.'

The same thought has crossed Silas's mind. Kate would spot a match if there was one. Unlike this new software, Centaur, the lucrative contract for which was signed off a month after his unit was closed down. To be fair, it's a long way off going live.

'Our problem is the boss,' he says. 'Much as I'd like to go to Cornwall, the nail bars of Swindon are calling.'

'Kate was in hospital for six weeks,' Strover says quietly, glancing at her own nails. Silas notices a touch of sparkle. 'If it was deliberate . . .'

Silas considers again whether Kate could have been targeted. It's been troubling him ever since his meeting with Jake at the café. After the accident, he gave Jake and Kate reassurances that no one could be arrested and charged on the basis of one super-recogniser's word alone. But there's no denying that a particularly violent organised crime gang are now behind bars as a result of Kate's initial idents. And he now knows that on the night of the accident she visited a county lines pub that might have links to the same gang.

He studies the still from the CCTV footage again. 'I'll go over to the Bluebell this afternoon,

86

talk to the barman,' he says, glancing at Strover's screen. 'What have you come up with?'

'Looks like Kate's living outside a village on the Roseland peninsula,' she says. 'South of Truro.'

Silas knows she's living in Cornwall, but he has never tried to find out where.

'According to Companies House, all her new partner's businesses are registered at the same address down there,' Strover continues. 'Nothing's listed in London.'

Strover tilts her laptop so that Silas can see the various websites. She's also called up a photo of the new man. At least she's found love. Young love. And money, by the sounds of it.

'We could go down there tomorrow morning,' Strover suggests.

He glances across at her. Long queues on the A303, Cornish pasty for lunch. Not much of a weekend, but he's got nothing else on and no commitments at home. An ex-wife who doesn't want to see him and a twenty-one-year-old son, Conor, currently AWOL. He would like nothing better than to get Kate back on board, the super-recogniser unit up and running again. This time he would manage her properly. He also wants to ask her about the Bluebell, find out what she was doing there. But he knows his boss is never going to sanction a trip during office hours.

'Two hundred and twenty miles, three and a half hours,' Strover adds. 'Maybe a bit less with blues and twos?'

CHAPTER 17

KATE

'Tell me exactly what happened,' Rob says, his voice calm but concerned. 'It was a lot of fuss about nothing,' Kate says.

She's back at the house, lying on her bed and talking to Rob on the phone. Not on FaceTime like they usually do, just an old-fashioned call. He didn't seem to mind that they couldn't see each other when she rang him, didn't ask any questions, and she didn't offer an explanation.

She doesn't want to see his face, not right now, but it feels good to hear his voice, reassuring. He sounds like the Rob she knows and loves. She's still fragile after what happened in the harbour and she's looking forward to Bex's arrival. She was meant to pick Bex up from Truro station, but she's only just been given the all-clear by the paramedic who checked her over on the harbour slipway beside the café.

'I was having a swim, like we always do,' she continues telling Rob. 'Out to the platform.'

'And then?'

'I got cramp in my legs, that's all.' She's trying

to downplay it as much for her benefit as his. She doesn't want to dwell on how close she might have come to dying.

'And nearly drowned. Doesn't that worry you?' he asks.

It terrifies her. But if she admits as much to Rob, he will rush down to see her and she can't cope with that right now.

'I must still be in shock,' she offers. Her calf muscles are almost too tight to walk.

'What were you doing before the swim?' he asks.

'Having a coffee. Like we always do.'

'And what did you have?'

This is too weird. Rob interrogating her about her coffee choices. Now would seem the obvious time to quiz him about his own choices, but she can't bring herself to ask. It suddenly seems so petty.

'A flat white.' She pauses. And then she can't resist. 'Ever tried one?'

'Sometimes. When I'm missing you.' His turn to pause now. 'It's like I'm tasting you in my mouth.'

She blushes. And feels so foolish. He had that flat white at Paddington because he was missing her.

'I had some flapjack too,' she adds, overcome by a sudden welling-up of love for him. 'I was famished, hadn't had lunch.'

'Were you sitting with anyone?'

89

'Just the local village stud. We're inseparable when you're away.'

'I'm serious.'

'What's this about, Rob?' She's irritated now. Must be another symptom of shock. 'All these questions.'

He hesitates before speaking. 'Have you seen the papers today?'

'Not yet.' His weekend *Financial Times*, delivered this morning, is still lying unread on the chair in the hallway, folded like crisp pink linen.

'There's been a big trial in Swindon. Modern slavery, people trafficking. The organised crime gang was sentenced yesterday.'

'And?' But she knows already what he's going to say.

'The judge said the original arrests were made on the basis of identifications by Wiltshire Police's super-recogniser unit. Singled it out for special praise.'

'Mention any names?'

'No.'

That's something, at least. Working on that case was addictive – and particularly draining. She knew that the trial would be coming up soon, but she'd put it out of her mind. Blanked it from her memory. That whole world is behind her now, part of another life.

She props herself up on one elbow and thinks about the man in the café, whose face was turned

90

away from her. She feels a pang of unease. It was just cramp, nothing more.

'There was a man sitting near me,' she says slowly. 'I didn't see clearly who it was. I just thought he was someone on holiday.'

'What did he look like?'

An image of the side of his face comes into focus. 'Big forehead, dark, slanting eyebrows, receding hairline. Late forties, maybe early fifties.'

'Familiar?'

'I'm not sure.'

She always used to be so certain.

'It doesn't add up, Kate, that's all I'm saying,' Rob says.

'How do you mean?'

'You're a strong swimmer. You'd had something to eat. And then all of a sudden you get cramp so badly you nearly drown.'

'I've had cramp attacks before,' she says. But they both know she's never had one like that. She's still in denial.

It's a few seconds before he speaks again. 'Did you leave your coffee unattended?'

Jesus. She starts to panic. Was she poisoned? Stretch senses her anxiety and tries to hop onto the bed. She scoops him up and holds him close to her chest. He was in a state when Mark from the gallery dropped him round a few minutes ago. And now it's catching up with her.

'When I went to get the flapjack,' she says, frightened by where he's going with this, 'I left my unfinished coffee, yes. For a minute, no longer than that.'

Silence. Rob is annoyed, she can feel it. Eyes closed, he's trying to control his frustration. She thinks of the café again, scared by the thought of someone spiking her coffee here in idyllic Cornwall.

'You've got to be more careful,' he says, gently now. 'I'm coming back down. Tonight.'

'It's fine, really,' she says, trying to disguise another wave of panic. She's not ready to see him in person. She just wants to be with Bex, on her own, give herself the chance to process everything that's been going on. She'll tell Bex about the cramp attack, see what she thinks, whether Rob's being paranoid.

'I could drive,' he offers.

'Honestly, I'm OK.'

She tries to tell herself that Rob is worried about her because he's a naturally cautious person, safety conscious. It's one of the things she dislikes about wealth. It seems to make people more fearful, oblige them to live behind high walls and locked doors.

But she knows his worries run deeper. Rob thinks she's in danger from the people she recognised when she worked for the police. She hasn't told him all the details of her old job. She's not allowed to. But he is aware that her memory for faces was instrumental in convicting some deeply unpleasant people.

92

'You really think someone spiked my coffee?' she asks, determined to downplay the possibility.

'Maybe.'

'Why would anyone do that?' She laughs nervously, but before he has a chance to answer, she hears a car pulling up outside.

'Bex is here,' she says, grateful for the interruption.

'Keep the doors locked,' he says.

'I always do,' she lies.

'And remember to set the alarm.'

'I promise,' she says, but this time she means it.

CHAPTER 18

JAKE

Jake closes his laptop and looks down the narrowboat to the bedroom at the far end. There's not much in there these days. He had a big clear-out after Kate left. A purging of sorts. The lighting is low and for a moment he thinks he sees her engrossed in a book, lying on the bed. She liked it down there, away from the noise of the engine. In the early days, she used to be his first reader, annotating embarrassing sex scenes with perceptive comments about emotional intelligence.

A male tawny owl hoots in the woods behind the towpath. Jake gets up from his desk and walks out into the cockpit. The sky is scattered with stars, partly hidden by clouds. Is Kate looking at the same sky tonight? They used to lie on their backs in the summer, on top of the boat, making plans and dreams as they spotted the Space Station circling the earth. Two children, a country cottage with her artist's studio in the garden, the boat kept as his writer's retreat. It never quite worked out like that.

A sound further down the canal. Metallic.

Unusual. It's hard to see anything in the dying light. A figure crosses the bridge by the lock gates. Someone returning from the pub, perhaps. A late dog walker. He thinks of the barman he saw today, the way he threatened him. Either he was lying and knew about Kate, or there's something else going on at the pub that they don't want journalists to discover. It had a strange vibe. All those CCTV cameras.

Back inside the boat, Jake reopens his laptop. The beginning of a chapter stares back at him. He doesn't know why he bothers to turn a good sentence these days, or agonise over an alliteration. It all gets lost in translation. Learning Finnish might be easier. Save everyone a lot of time.

He hears another noise, closer now. Muscles tensing, he steps back out to the cockpit, stands on the seat and peers into the darkness. He's just imagining things. It's happened a lot recently. The boat feels so empty without Kate. Sometimes he talks to her when he's writing, as if she were in the galley. Snippets of dialogue, passages of descriptive writing. His account of what she saw that night on the CCTV. She's never given him a chance to explain.

Below deck again, he calls up a photo of Rob, Kate's new partner, trying to ignore a tightness in his chest. There are always noises on the canal at night. He holds his fingers out above the keyboard. They're shaking. He dislikes Rob with a passion and hates himself for it. A better person than him would get on well with his successor. A man who has brought happiness to the woman he still loves, happiness that he was singularly unable to provide. He should be pleased for her. There are enough sickening reasons to like the guy – the tech fortune and his love of art, the unique blend of geekiness and entrepreneurism, his random acts of bloody philanthropy. Jake knows he ought to accept them all with equanimity, but he's consumed with a jealousy so intense that it frightens him.

More noise outside. This time he forces himself to sit still and listen, straining his ears. Silence, only broken by a return hoot from a female tawny owl, further away. His own breathing has become shallower.

There's one thing about Rob that troubles Jake more than anything else. The first occasion he met him – the first time Kate met him – was at her hospital bedside, when the two of them were deep in conversation about art. Kate had already told Jake on an earlier visit that it was over between them and his arrival was clearly an unwelcome interruption. It wasn't that, though. It was the ineluctable feeling that Jake had seen Rob somewhere else, a few weeks earlier. *Before* the accident.

He's thought about it a lot since, wishes he had Kate's powers of recognition, but he can't remember where he could have seen him. Maybe in the Slaughtered Lamb, the village pub? He's done a lot digging online, dusting down his old journalism skills to search through Rob's various companies and high-profile life, but with no results. Perhaps it doesn't matter if he's seen him before. It just makes the apparently chance nature of Rob's first encounter with Kate seem less serendipitous.

Another sound outside, this time followed by a telltale seesaw rocking motion. No imagining this time. Someone has either just stepped on or off the boat. Jake rushes out into the cockpit and sees a shadow disappearing down the towpath. He shouts after it, a deep, guttural roar. No response. And then a strong smell of petrol. The strike of a match.

Out of the darkness, a line of flames licks into life, racing along the towpath towards him like a burning snake, slithering up the mooring rope and onto the bow, where it rises into a fireball that lights up the night sky.

Jake is thrown backwards by the sudden heat, holding up his arms to shield his face. Instinctively, he grabs the rusty fire extinguisher from the locker under the seat, praying that it's not too old, and tries to approach the fire on the foredeck. He knows already his efforts are futile. The fire is quickly taking hold of his old wooden boat, wrapping it in its flaming embrace. He curses himself for stacking so many logs on the roof to season.

And then he is aware of people on the towpath, rushing towards him from other boats moored along the canal. Some are calling out his name, others beckoning him to come ashore. He's not abandoning his old boat yet. He's had her for too long to let her go down without a fight.

'Buckets!' Jake shouts as his extinguisher runs out. 'Get some buckets!'

He ducks back inside the cabin, now swirling with thick black smoke. Struggling to breathe, he grabs a rusty bucket from under the sink and goes back outside. The heat is intensifying, the bow of the boat starting to drift away from the shore, no longer held by the burnt-out rope. He leans over the stern, scoops up the canal water and hurls it onto the flames, desperate to save his beloved boat.

To his relief, other people on the shore have started to fill buckets too and are throwing water at the fire. A human chain of sorts has formed and with it a kernel of hope.

'More buckets!' Jake shouts, encouraged, ignoring the heat. The fire can be beaten, his boat saved, but then a man's thick arm is stretching out into the cockpit. Jake grabs hold of it and is pulled onto the towpath.

'Is there anyone else on board?' the man asks close to his ear, an arm round his shoulders. It's a fireman. 'People? Any pets?'

Jake shakes his head, watching as the whole boat starts to list and drift into the middle of the canal, shrouded in smoke and flames like some ancient fireship. He needs to talk to Kate.

CHAPTER 19

KATE

'Don't answer it,' Bex says as Kate's phone vibrates. It's Jake.

Bex and Kate are sitting in wicker chairs on the terrace, watching the moon rise above the horizon like a polished sixpence. Her phone is on the glass table between them.

'Ignore it,' Bex urges as the phone starts to vibrate again. Her voice reminds Kate of when she was training Stretch. 'I've switched mine off for the weekend and I suggest you do the same. How often does he ring you?'

'He hasn't for a month or two,' Kate says.

They've had the occasional terse text exchange about practical matters – could he return an overdue book to the library, can he remember to forward her mail once a week – but no conversation in months. She's still too angry.

'So why's he suddenly calling you now?' Bex asks. 'At eleven o'clock at night?'

'I've no idea. That's why I want to answer it.'

'Well don't. He's a two-timing little—'

'Please, Bex.'

Kate knows Jake must be calling her for a good

reason. He rang her once, a week or so after she'd left hospital and was living with her mother. It was late at night and he was drunk, on his way back to the boat after a session in the pub. He was asking her to come back, let him explain, give him another chance. She told him never to ring her again.

'Does Rob know Jake still calls you?' Bex asks.

'I told you, he hasn't rung me in ages.'

The phone starts vibrating for a third time. She reaches across to pick it up, but Bex snatches it away and turns it off. Kate knows Bex is right. Jake is her past and she must keep moving forward.

'Tell me about today,' Bex says. 'What happened.'

Kate takes her through her swim out to the platform, playing down the cramp attack, the possibility that she might have been poisoned, but her mind is still on Jake, trying to work out why he's calling her so late and so persistently. Something's wrong. He wouldn't keep phoning. She knows him too well. Perhaps his elderly mother has died. They were close and Kate misses seeing her. Jake would want her to know.

'You really frighten me sometimes,' Bex says. 'The things you choose to care about in life. You seem more troubled by Rob's choice of coffee than the fact that you nearly drowned today.'

'He told me tonight that he has a flat white when we're apart because the taste reminds him

100

of me.' She thinks again of the relief she felt on the phone.

'That's alright then. I'll try not to think that I wasted my bloody time at Paddington.'

'You didn't. And I'm very grateful.'

'Maybe you should see someone, Kate. You know, your dishy Dr Varma.'

'I saw him earlier today.'

'You never said. I would have caught an earlier train.'

'He's married, Bex.'

Bex has met Ajay once and flirted so much with him it was embarrassing. Ajay was having none of it.

'Did you tell him about Rob? About believing that he's . . .' Bex hesitates. 'That he's been replaced by a double? I was thinking about that on the train. That's not a normal thought, Kate. Not normal at all.'

'I will. I'm seeing him again at the end of next week.'

'So you didn't tell him.'

Jake is still trying to ring her. She can feel it.

'Are you OK?' Bex asks as Kate gets up from her seat.

She knows she should tell Bex about the court case, that Rob thinks her coffee might have been spiked, but she needs to speak to Jake first.

'Just going to the loo. Back in a sec.'

She walks into the kitchen, sweeping up the cordless telephone from the sideboard with the

101

deftness of a thief. Once inside the bathroom, she locks the door and dials Jake's number, pressing the keys as quietly as she can. It's engaged. She tries again. Still engaged.

'You alright in there?' Bex is outside the door.

'Fine. Won't be a sec.'

She loves Bex, her concern for her, but sometimes she wishes she'd cut her some slack.

'Don't want you cramping up again,' she says.

'I'm OK. Honestly.'

Kate waits a few seconds, confident that Bex is back out on the balcony, and redials Jake's number. This time the phone rings.

'Kate,' Jake says.

She knows at once that something is badly wrong. 'What is it?' she whispers.

'The boat. It's burnt out.'

For a moment she thinks he's drunk, complaining about the boat's engine. He was always mending it, head down in the sumps, asking her to pass him a spanner. And she was always saying they needed to replace the boat with one that didn't break down all the time, didn't leak and didn't constantly smell of diesel fumes. She knew he never would. He loved it too much, arguably more than he loved her.

'What do you mean?' she asks.

'Someone set fire to it tonight. It's gone, completely destroyed.'

'Are you OK?' she asks, trying to take in what he's saying.

'I was on board when they torched it, but I got off just in time. Everything's gone. Some of your stuff too.'

She only left a few things with him, old clothes and books that she was going to collect one day, but she's still sad. Not for their value but because a tiny part of her left them there deliberately.

'I'm so sorry, Jake,' she says, wiping a tear away. 'You're safe, though.'

'I'm fine. Why are you whispering?'

'I've got to go. I'll call you tomorrow. Have you got anywhere to stay?' she adds.

'One of the other boats, they're going to let me sleep the night with them. Remember Bruce and Sue?'

Of course she does. How could she forget? They lived on the water together for twelve years, got to make some great friends. People take care of each other on the canal.

'Look after yourself,' she whispers.

'Is Rob there?'

She pauses before answering. 'He's had to go back to London.'

'Business?'

'Yeah.' She doesn't know why she's telling him this. 'He's usually down for the whole weekend.'

'It's nice to hear your voice,' he says.

She hangs up.

Back outside on the balcony, she sits down next to Bex, trying not to cry. They both look ahead, staring out into the inky darkness of the sea.

There's a warm wind and the lights of a few fishing boats dot the water beneath Nare Head.

'You called him, didn't you?' Bex says. 'On the landline.'

'Yes,' Kate says, sniffing.

'I'm sorry. I shouldn't have tried to stop you. I'm not your bloody mother. I was just worried you—'

'It's OK,' Kate says, swallowing hard. 'It's nothing like that.'

She can't hold back the tears any longer.

'What is it, Katie?' Bex comes over to kneel down beside her, a hand on her shoulder.

Kate leans forward and lets her hug her, staying like that for a minute or two until the sobs subside.

'I knew something was wrong,' she says. 'He hasn't rung me for months, I promise. That's why I wanted to pick up.'

'What was it?' Bex asks. 'What's happened?'

'His boat, the one we lived on, it's been gutted by a fire. Tonight. Totally destroyed. He thinks deliberately.'

'Oh my God. Is he OK?'

'He's safe. Sounded pretty shaken up. Who would do that, Bex? Burn a beautiful old boat deliberately? And knowing someone was on board?'

'I don't know.' Bex looks for her phone and turns it on. 'I'm so sorry,' she says as her phone comes to life and starts to ping with messages.

'Loads of people in the village have been texting me about it. I shouldn't have switched my phone off.'

'What are they saying?' Kate asks, trying to picture the scene on the canal. It was a good community, tight-knit.

'Same as you. Everyone thinks it was arson.' Bex scrolls through a few more messages. 'They found a metal jerrycan up at the lock,' she says, reading. 'The fire brigade took fifteen minutes to get down there, by which time the boat was too far gone. I'm so sorry.'

'No one hurt, though?' Kate asks.

'No.' Bex pauses. 'Shit. And I was so off with him today.'

'Who?'

'Jake. I saw him at the station. When I was going up to London to spy on your Rob. Poor bloke.'

'You never said.'

Bex raises her eyebrows at Kate. 'I didn't think I needed to.'

'Where's he going to live?' Kate asks.

'The pub maybe. They'll put him up for a few days. They're good like that. And he's given them enough business over the years. If not, he can always stay at mine.'

'Yours?'

Bex nods.

Kate's shocked by the offer. Bex has never shown any inclination to be kind to Jake, even before they split up.

'Why not? It's just sitting empty.'

'Thanks, Bex.'

They sit in awkward silence.

'What is it, Katie my love?' she asks quietly. Bex knows her too well, senses that she's holding something back.

'Rob thinks that my coffee might have been spiked today, before I went for a swim.'

'Spiked? Bloody hell, Kate. Who by?'

She tells Bex about the court case, her role in it, the assurances she was given at the time that she wouldn't be in any personal danger. Jake was convinced at the beginning that her car crash hadn't been an accident, but Kate was just surprised it hadn't happened before. She'd started to drink and drive, something that she'd never done before. She was a total wreck, wrung out from the work she was doing, her empty life with Jake.

'I mean, I know it was exciting and all, but that job was so not you,' Bex says. 'You're free of it now.'

Kate's not sure she'll ever be free of it.

CHAPTER 20

SILAS

Silas can see the stationary fire engines up ahead, their blue lights sweeping across the water meadow and reflecting off the dark canal. He's parked as close as he can get and wonders how the units managed to get so much nearer.

'You didn't have to come out,' he says to Strover, as they walk along the towpath. He's impressed that she's there.

'Not so easy to ignore a text from your boss,' she says.

'You'll learn.'

There's no need for a torch. It's a clear night. At least it was, until a column of black smoke from Jake's boat rose up and stained the firmament. There are no casualties, but Silas wonders how the author will cope. Bets are off that he didn't have any insurance.

'You think it's arson?' Strover asks.

'Let's see. If he hadn't brought in that CCTV footage today, I wouldn't be here now. It's the timing that worries me.'

They walk on in silence, approaching the

107

burnt-out shell, smouldering and partly submerged like a stricken submarine. An area of the bank and towpath has been cordoned off with police tape. There's still a crowd, but people are starting to disperse. One of the fire units is also about to leave. It feels strange to be back on the canal. Last time Silas was there, a year ago, he'd taken charge of an Armed Response incident. He would rather be tucked up in bed right now, but when he heard over the radio about a fire on a narrowboat belonging to a local author, he told a surprised Control Room that he'd take a look.

'Thanks for coming,' Jake says, walking over to Silas and Strover.

'Have you given a statement?' Silas asks, nodding in the direction of the two uniforms on site.

'Not yet.'

'Strover will take one.'

She pulls out her notepad and pen on cue.

'It was deliberate,' Jake says, turning from Silas to Strover. 'I saw someone running away moments before.'

'You can tell Strover everything you saw in a minute. First I want to know what you did after we met for lunch today.'

'Me?' Jake says, blanching like a guilty schoolboy.

Silas knows at once that he's right. He's had a hunch ever since this afternoon, when he paid the Bluebell pub a visit. The barman in the CCTV footage wasn't there. According to the unhelpful landlady, he left six months ago, around the time when Kate's drink was spiked. She also revealed, after a little persuasion, that someone had been in earlier asking questions.

'Did you talk to anyone at the pub?' Silas says.

'Do you think the fire's connected?' Jake asks, ignoring his question.

'Did you talk to anyone?' Silas repeats. He's sorry about Jake's boat, but he's also annoyed with him.

'I spoke to the landlady and the barman – not the man in the video,' Jake says.

'And were they pleased to see you?'

'I've had warmer welcomes.' Jake stares at his feet.

Silas shakes his head, glancing across at the narrowboat behind him. It seems to have sunk lower into the water, tilting drunkenly. 'It might not be such a cosy country pub,' he says. 'More into drugs than draught beer.' He doesn't want to say too much.

'County lines?' Jake asks.

Silas nods, remembering that Jake used to be a crime reporter before he became a writer. County lines is a force-wide priority for policing in Wiltshire now, as it is for the whole country. Drug networks in London and Manchester, keen to develop new heroin markets, are extending their reach to towns like Swindon, targeting surrounding villages through secondary local lines.

'You shouldn't have gone,' he says. 'Should have

left it to us. Looks like you poked the wrong bear.' He glances again at Jake's boat.

'So what was Kate doing there?' Jake asks.

'That's what I was hoping to find out.'

Silas has a horrible feeling that she wasn't at the Bluebell by chance. Kate had taken to her police work, became intoxicated by her ability to identify criminals. He had too. It was like investigating on steroids. But the unit had to be focused and the priority at the time was modern slavery. When Silas started to suspect that the gang they were investigating might also have links to a new heroin network operating out of Swindon, he was told by his boss to stick to his brief and leave county lines to the force's dedicated Proactive Team. It was a frustrating time for Silas and the super-recogniser unit, particularly Kate, who was not used to being told what to do.

'What about the trial this week?' Jake asks. He sounds tired. Desperate. 'Is that why I was sent the footage?'

'We don't know yet,' Silas says. He wishes he did.

Jake cuts a tragic figure as he turns to the boat and then looks back at Silas. 'You think this is related to my visit to the pub today, don't you?' he says. 'You wouldn't have come out here at midnight otherwise.'

Silas feels a pang of shame. Is he really that transparent? 'You shouldn't have visited the Bluebell,' he says. And nor should Kate.

'The jerrycan was found over there,' Jake replies, changing the subject. He points down the towpath and pauses, struggling to keep it together. 'If I hadn't been awake . . . The fire started above where we sleep. Where I sleep.'

'Talk to DC Strover,' Silas says. 'You got somewhere to stay tonight?'

Jake nods, blinking hard. It looks like it's all suddenly caught up with him.

'Have you told Kate about the fire?' Silas asks.

Jake nods again.

'How did she take it?' It's very unlikely she's involved, but they'll still have to eliminate her from their inquiries.

'Pleased that I'm safe.'

'Is she still with her new man?' Silas shouldn't be asking. It's none of his business.

'He's had to go back to London. Usually comes down for the weekend.'

Jake's still in love with Kate, poor sod. At least it was mutual when Silas and Mel, his ex, split up. No arguments, just a heavy-hearted acceptance that they no longer had anything in common.

'Leave it to us from now on, eh?' Silas says, putting a hand on Jake's shoulder. 'And try to get some sleep.'

CHAPTER 21

KATE

Kate can't sleep, not after talking to Jake on the phone. She wants to call him back, let him unload a bit more about what's happened, but she knows he's no longer her problem. He's safe and there her concern should end. She's just not sure that Bruce and Sue, the kind couple who are putting him up for the night, will want to listen until dawn. Jake never keeps things in: he likes to discuss a problem until it has been examined from every angle. It's why she's not given him the chance to give his side of what she saw on the CCTV that night. She doesn't want them to talk about it until they reach the point where his infidelity somehow becomes forgivable or acceptable.

Bex went to bed after they chatted some more on the terrace and Kate is now in the open-plan sitting room, tucked up on the sofa, about to surf through late-night TV channels on the vast home-cinema screen. When she asked Rob if such a big TV was necessary, he said he needed it for his work. He hasn't watched anything on it yet, apart from the tennis.

112

She turns on the TV and gawps. A naked couple are having sex on a benchpress in a gym, the woman lying on her back, head hanging awkwardly off the end of the bench as she sucks off the man, who is standing. Instinctively she switches channels, shocked by the explicitness of what she's just seen, and then switches back to watch again, turning her head ninety degrees to see the poor woman's face. There's nothing remotely arousing about the couple, who seem more focused on holding their positions than giving each other pleasure. What concerns her is why the TV has been left tuned to a porn channel. Did Rob come in here last night while she was asleep? Wasn't he satisfied after they'd had sex?

She works her way through some dodgy films, darts and a shopping channel, trying not to feel disappointed, hurt. Does he need porn as well as her? She knows Jake was an occasional user, but that was after they'd stopped having sex. And then she acknowledges the thought that she's been struggling to keep out of her head. It doesn't feel like the sort of thing Rob would do: slipping out of bed in the middle of the night to watch other couples having sex. Coding, perhaps, answering emails, maybe practising his backhand, but not porn. He doesn't have enough hours in his day as it is.

She pushes the thought away and alights on France 24, the French news channel, half watching a report about another gilets jaunes riot. It's followed by an item on the rise of the tech sector in France and the growth of Station F, the world's largest start-up campus, in Paris's 13th arrondissement. She's about to change channels again when news footage of Rob flashes up on the screen. He's in Brest, talking about the 'rich digital ecosystems' of western Brittany. Talking in fluent French.

She holds her hand to her mouth and stares at the screen in disbelief. Rob is hopeless at French. It's why he's recently started to have lessons. She's always been good at languages, speaking decent French and Spanish, and has been teaching him too, marvelling at how little he can recall from his schooldays. She steps closer, listening to the words coming out of this man's mouth. It looks like Rob – same blinking eyes, shy smile, lanky gait – but it's not him. She's sure of it. It can't be. 'Jesus,' she says quietly. The presenter is speaking, but she's not listening.

She rushes down to Bex's bedroom, opposite Rob's office, and opens the door. 'Bex? Are you awake? Bex?' She can't disguise the urgency in her voice.

She's forgotten what a deep sleeper Bex is.

'Bex?' she asks again, rocking her shoulder.

'What time is it?' Bex asks, bleary eyed.

'I'm sorry,' Kate says. 'I need to show you something.'

'It's one thirty in the bloody morning, Kate,' Bex says, glancing at her mobile phone on the

114

bedside table and sinking back on her pillow with a groan.

'I know. I'm really sorry, but it's important.'

It's the second time today she's shared her worries with her. She's not sure she could cope without Bex.

'It always is,' Bex says.

Five minutes later, they're in the sitting room on the sofa, a confused Stretch at their feet. Bex is watching France 24 while Kate tries to find the footage of Rob on her laptop.

'It was on a few minutes ago,' she says, wondering if she's imagined the whole thing. 'A feature about the tech sector in France. Rob was being interviewed in Brest, but I swear it wasn't him. He was speaking in fluent French but he's crap at languages.'

'When was he there?' Bex asks.

'I'm not sure. I didn't know he'd gone.'

Bex has every reason not to believe her without seeing the footage for herself. Where is it? And then Kate finds the story and she's shocked all over again by the words.

'Here,' she says, turning the laptop so that Bex can see it. 'Take a look at this.'

They both watch the item on the France 24 website, Kate offering a rough running translation.

'He is saying how his company was drawn to that part of France . . . one of thirteen regions recently awarded "Capital French Tech" status or something . . . because it has a history of military

115

digital expertise and investment in health tech.' She stops, unable to go on. They both listen as Rob talks about Brest providing the perfect culture for developing neural networks and machine learning. It's complicated, technical French. '*Brest est la culture parfaite pour nous alors que nous cherchons à déveloper des réseaux de neurones profonds et un apprentissage automatique.*'

'See what I mean?' Kate says, glancing at Bex.

Bex looks at her and then back at the laptop. 'It looks like him, Kate,' she says quietly, still staring at the screen. 'That's definitely Rob. The man I met at Paddington yesterday. Who I've met several times before. Your fit new boyfriend, you lucky bugger.'

'Who's suddenly fluent in fucking French.'

'Maybe he's got a good teacher – you said he's having lessons.'

'He's rubbish, Bex,' she says. 'And I mean truly rubbish. I was trying to help him just the other day.'

They stand in silence, watching as the video finishes. Bex appears troubled by it too, at least momentarily.

'Just the other day?' she asks.

'A couple of weeks ago.'

Bex leans down to stroke Stretch, who seems to have picked up on the tension that's suddenly flared between them. 'You've got to stop this,' she says.

'I know,' Kate says. 'I'm sorry. It's late. I saw the

news, I'm tired, my brain began to get ahead of itself.'

'It's OK,' Bex says, putting an arm around her. 'Rob's a bright boy. Must be a quick learner.'

Maybe she's right. Rob can turn his hand to anything when he tries. Even French, it seems. Kate's still not convinced, though.

'What are we going to do with you?' Bex asks.

'I just thought, you know, maybe someone has taken Rob's place . . .' She stops, her lower lip beginning to tremble as the feelings return.

'We need to get you some help for this, Katie,' Bex says, her arm still around her. 'When did you say that nice Dr Varma is coming down to see you next?'

'End of next week.' Kate takes a deep breath, regains some composure. 'What's happening to me, Bex? Who's doing this? I'm losing my mind.'

'No one's doing anything to you,' Bex says. 'And you're not losing your mind. You just need to rest.'

'I don't know if I can cope,' Kate says. 'I see Rob speaking in French on the news and I don't think he's been lying to me, or keeping a secret. My first thought is that he's been replaced by a French-speaking double.'

'Except that it wasn't his double, was it, Kate?' Bex repeats. 'It was Rob.'

'But it does happen,' Kate says. 'Unrelated people can look identical.'

'Sure it can happen. My sister looks weirdly like

Lily Allen. Amber Heard is the spitting image of Scarlett Johansson. But that was Rob on TV, who we now know speaks good French. Not someone who looks like him.'

Bex walks over to the door, staring at Kate. 'Come on, you,' she says, without much conviction. 'Bedtime.'

'It's the only thing Rob's frightened of,' Kate adds, still on the sofa. 'His doppelgänger.'

The day I see him again will be my last.

SUNDAY

CHAPTER 22

JAKE

Jake leans over the edge of the lock gate with a long branch and scoops out the last floating item of clothing. It's one of Kate's old dresses, grossly misshapen by a bubble of air trapped under the orange material. Until this morning, Jake has never had to divide his worldly possessions into those that float and those that sink. And as he drops the sodden orange dress onto the grass next to the other items he's retrieved, he hopes he'll never have to again.

It's been a long, difficult night. Bruce and Sue did all they could to console him after Strover had taken a statement, but he couldn't sleep.

'What are you going to do with them all?' asks one of the locals, gesturing at the large pile of wet clothing and ruined books. Kate was always complaining the boat was like a waterborne library.

'Chuck them,' Jake says, quietly. Everything except Kate's orange dress. He'll keep that. She used to wear it to Womad, their nearest festival. Before they could no longer afford to go.

He picks up the dress, wringing it out as he walks

back around to the towpath and his boat. It finally sank in the night and is now resting on the canal's muddy bottom with just the remains of the roof showing. His few possessions are still trapped inside. He's been in a daze all morning, retrieving clothes and logs and kettles and plastic mugs from the water with the help of kind villagers and narrowboat owners. He even found his passport, sealed in a plastic folder. The generosity of others has been overwhelming. Even Kate was sympathetic, but it was unfair of him to call her. The last thing he wants is for people to feel sorry for him.

His plan is to finish clearing up and then move out of the village as soon as he can. He doesn't feel safe hanging around. The fire was clearly deliberate – DI Hart suggested as much last night. Besides, there's not much left for him here. No boat, latest book destroyed. And no partner. It's safe to say his life has now officially hit rock bottom, just like his narrowboat. And, in all honesty, he feels strangely liberated by the unambiguity of his circumstances. If he can't make a fresh start in life now, he never will.

He bundles the dress into a plastic bag, turns to take one last look at the sunken boat and sets off down the towpath, away from the village, passport safely in his pocket. It's a longer route, but he'll avoid having to walk past the line of moored narrowboats and the obligation to make more polite conversation. Christ, he could do with a pint right now. By the time of Kate's accident, he was drinking heavily, but he's cut down a lot since then and is determined not to lapse again. Even if he could afford it.

All part of trying to sort his life out, triggered by a small, misguided belief that if he can regain some of the mojo he had when he first met Kate, he might be able to win her back. There was a time when he was going places: published author, sharing his bohemian life on a watertight narrowboat with a beautiful portrait painter. Where did it all go wrong? On which rocks did their idealism run aground?

He keeps walking, towards the fields and railway line beyond, his brain struggling to process all that's happened. What worries him is that if the fire was a result of his visit to the pub, Kate's drink must have been spiked that night by dangerous people. Might they target her again? If, as Hart hinted last night, it's connected to the modern-slavery trial, there could be organised crime gang members still at large who want revenge for the hefty sentences imposed on their colleagues – people who were put away on the strength of Kate's identifications.

As Jake approaches the next set of lock gates, an attractive woman he doesn't recognise appears out of nowhere with a black plastic bag.

'Brought you some spare clothes,' she says. 'Used to belong to my husband. He left them when he moved out. I heard what happened, thought they might help. You're about his size.'

'Out of shape, you mean,' Jake says, grinning. 'Thanks. That's kind.'

'I've seen you around but never said hello,' she says, smiling at him.

Jake smiles back at her, flattered by the attention. Maybe there's an upside to everything that's happened. He remembers the nurse who circled his father, a GP, when his mother passed away, turning up announced at the house before she'd even been buried. Her haste was unseemly, but it had given his father hope, a glimpse of a life beyond. No one's died but maybe that what's going on here.

'I read one of your books,' the woman continues, squinting in the sunshine.

'Really?' It's the first piece of good news Jake has heard in a while.

'Yeah, bought it in a charity shop for 10p.' Ouch. 'You got somewhere to stay tonight?'

'I'm fine, thanks,' he lies, all interest in the woman wilting. He doesn't know what he was thinking. *Ten p in a bloody charity shop?*

One half-formed plan is to hitch down to Cornwall and camp where he and Kate used to stay. It's busy this time of year, but the owner always used to squeeze them in. His tent was his only possession not on board the boat – he'd lent it to a friend in the village. It just depends if the police or the Canal and River Trust want to speak to him again today about salvage.

'See you around then,' she says, smiling at him again before walking on down the towpath.

He's about to call after the woman, ask her name, maybe see if she wants to meet for a drink, when his phone buzzes. It's a text from Bex. No doubt more grief for the shabby, hopeless life he leads. But it's not.

Just heard about the fire. Glad you're OK. Please stay in my place. There's a spare bedroom downstairs. Key's under flower-pot by back door. Bex x

CHAPTER 23

KATE

'Where's Bex?' Rob asks on speaker-phone as Kate makes herself a fruit smoothie in the kitchen. He taught her the recipe: blueberries, avocado and chia seeds. Superfood for the brain. He tried to facetime her first, but she kept cutting him off, hoping that he'd think the signal wasn't strong enough. It often isn't, down here, much to his frustration and her relief. She's feeling better this morning, but she still can't cope with seeing his face.

'Sleeping,' she says. 'We had a late night.'

'Heavy one?'

Rob knows she hardly ever drinks these days, not since the accident. Neither does he. It's Bex he's worried about. She can fill her boots.

'Wild,' Kate says, not very committed. 'You know me.'

She's trying to pluck up courage to ask him about the news item she saw in the night on France 24, his sudden ability to talk in French.

'But is she with you now?' he says. 'In the house?'

'She's here, don't worry.'

'I should be there with you too. It's just all these meetings . . .'

'It's fine, honestly.'

'I'll be back down soon, I promise.'

Rob is at his flat in Shoreditch. At least she assumes he is. He might be at the office. It's the one drawback of not being able to see him. And he's feeling so guilty today, it's almost funny. A woman rang first thing to ask if Kate would be in all day. Said she had a flower delivery for her. Kate knows they're from Rob. He's done it before. When she first moved down here on her own, he sent her flowers two or three times a week. Since then it's been more random, whenever guilt strikes. Last time no one rang in advance, though. A huge bunch of white lilies just appeared one morning, piled up against the front door like an overnight drift of snow.

'How is it down there?' he asks.

She looks through the vast windows at the beautiful scene outside. Fields rolling down towards a calm, cobalt sea; solitary Monterey pine trees punctuating the vivid skyline. Her Cornish idyll, though, has been tarnished by the sight and sound of Rob speaking fluent French on TV.

'I saw you on the news last night,' she says, not as casually as she'd hoped. 'France 24. I didn't know you'd been back to Brittany.'

She can't bring herself to ask about his French. Not yet.

'Flying visit last week,' he says breezily. 'Looks

127

like we're going ahead with the new office in Brest. I didn't have to be there – should have sent someone in my place.'

Rob's often singing Brittany's praises, says it has so many similarities with Cornwall, its big beaches, rugged cliffs and coves. Their languages, Breton and Cornish, are closely related – *mor* means sea in both, for example. There's even a region of Brittany called Cornouaille, popular with artists because of its unique peninsular light. It sounds so similar. He's promised to take her one day, when she's fully recovered. She can paint *en plein air* and feast on crêpes rather than pasties.

'I could have come with you,' she says, coyly, hoping to disguise her line of questioning as petty jealousy. 'Kept an eye on you.'

'You wouldn't have enjoyed it,' he says. 'There and back in a day, wall-to-wall meetings. No time for play. We'll go when there's more time, I promise. Right now, things are kicking off in the London office with the IPO. Sometimes it feels like I'm in two places at once. What were you doing watching French TV anyway?'

'I couldn't sleep.'

Sometimes it feels like I'm in two places at once.

Is he mocking her? Mocking her paranoia?

'You should have called,' he says, sounding distracted. She can tell when he's started to do something else on the phone. Reading emails, checking his products' rankings in the App Store.

'It was late,' she says, thinking back to the

explicit sex she stumbled across. Should she ask him about that as well? It was shocking, so unlike Rob. God, she's suddenly behaving like the jealous wife, questioning her husband's business trips, porn habits.

She stays silent, listening as Rob tells her that she can always call him, day or night. He's worried she's tired, pushing herself too hard. She closes her eyes, soothed by Rob's voice. When she can't see his face, life is so simple. Why can't she just relax and appreciate that she's a right lucky bugger, as Bex would say? She's with a kind and caring man, her life has started anew.

And then she thinks of the news again. She needs to ask him, challenge him. Find some daylight between the Rob she knows and loves – the man who is talking to her now – and the impostor who might have replaced him.

'Rob?'

'Yes?'

She closes her eyes. 'You were speaking in French on the TV. Good French.'

'You heard that?' he asks, casually. 'Not bad, eh? They got me to do it in English and French. Had to practise for ages. You know what I'm like. Maybe you could be my translator next time, when you come with me to Brittany.'

Kate doesn't know what to think. She should be relieved but she isn't.

'That would be nice,' she manages to say.

'You OK?' he asks.

She's not OK. Not OK at all. It's a while before she speaks. 'There's something I need to ask you.' She pauses again, struggling to get the words out. 'Remember when you told me . . .'

She can't do this, can't bring herself to ask him about his double. She hangs up.

CHAPTER 24

JAKE

Jake walks on, crossing the field beside the railway line, the woman's black bag of clothing slung over one shoulder like he's Dick Whittington. He glances at Bex's text again, hearing her Lancashire accent in the words. In the past, she's always given him a hard time, thinks he spends all day 'liggin' about in bed. Now she's offering him a place to stay. She must be with Kate. He's sure of it. That's where she was going yesterday when he met her on the station platform.

He puts his phone away, looks up and sees a man ahead of him, up by the pedestrian railway crossing on the far side of the field. Except that he's not crossing the tracks, he's just standing there, listless, glancing one way and then the other.

A knot tightens in Jake's stomach. It looks like the man's a rough sleeper: matted hair, torn trousers, a ripped jumper. Could be him in a few days if he doesn't get a grip. Something's not right, though. The sheep in the field beyond seem to glance up as one. The morning air is too still.

131

Jake increases his pace, walking more quickly now, adjusting the bag on his shoulder as he looks around him. The atmosphere today seems purer, the greens of the trees more saturated. His mind is clearer too, senses heightened. Life feels more real after last night. Precious.

A moment later, he drops the bag and breaks into a run. Because to his right, about half a mile away, an intercity train has appeared, curving around the bend to bear down on the crossing. And this time he's not going to do nothing.

'Stop!' Jake calls out to the man. 'Stop!'

The man either can't hear Jake or has chosen to ignore him. He's moved through the metal kissing gate and is standing now on the stone ballast beside the tracks. Jake is ten yards away, running hard, lungs starved of air. The train is almost at the crossing. And then he's at the gate and spinning through it and lunging at the man as he steps forward.

The man swivels, his bloodshot eyes staring back at Jake, full of anger and fear. And maybe gratitude too.

'Please,' Jake says, breathless, gripping his arm.

Ten years ago, at Southall station in London, Jake saw a woman in trouble at the end of a platform and did nothing. A minute later she stepped out in front of a passing train, a sight – a sound – that has haunted him ever since. Now Jake braces himself for the man to tug himself free, but he doesn't resist. Instead they both flinch as the intercity train hurtles past, carriage after carriage, the scream of its horn fading in the turbulent air.

CHAPTER 25

KATE

Kate paces around the kitchen, watched by Stretch from his basket as she waits for the call to reconnect to Rob. She wishes Bex would wake up. She needs to talk to her, check that she's doing the right thing by challenging Rob, but she can't disturb Bex's beauty sleep again.

'What's going on, tiny feet?' she asks Stretch. 'Promise me there'll always be just the one of you.'

She looks at him again, just to make sure, cocking her head to one side. And then there's an electric click behind her. She spins around to see all four gas rings fired up on the hob, blue flames blazing brightly. For a second she stares in disbelief, before rushing over to turn off each of the knobs. Jesus. What if she'd left something on it? A tea towel? It's the second time this has happened. The house, Rob's pride and joy, runs on smart technology, but one day it's going to burn itself down.

Her phone rings: it's Rob. She presses connect before she realises he's facetiming her. Too late.

'What happened?' he says.

The voice is loud and clear, but the picture is blurred. Thank God. A message on the screen says: 'Poor connection'.

'We got cut off,' she lies.

'Can you see me?' he asks.

'No. I can hear you, though,' she says, trying to conceal her relief as she glances at the hob. Once again, a weak signal suits her just fine.

'I've got to get our comms sorted down there,' he says. 'It's embarrassing. Can you imagine if *The Cornishman* ever found out? "MD of Tech Empire Can't Get Broadband In His Own Home".'

He sounds cheerful, still the Rob she knows.

'You need to sort the gas hob too,' she says, staring at her phone's screen. His outline remains a frozen shadow. He could be anyone. 'Lit itself again just now.'

'Are you serious?' he asks, a sudden concern in his voice.

'It's OK,' she says. She can't complain. It's a dream kitchen, fitted with everything she could ever want. 'It just scares me sometimes. Like it has a mind of its own.' Last week the boiling-water tap came on while she was washing up and burnt her hand.

All the domestic appliances can be controlled from Rob's London flat. And she's got used to them going wrong. Welcome to the Internet of Broken Things.

135

'You need to tell me if it does it again,' he says, still anxious.

'Is there a problem?'

'It shouldn't be happening, that's all,' he says. 'I'll check the firewall.'

'You think someone's hacked the house?'

It sounds so ridiculous, but he's mentioned the possibility once before.

'You were going to ask me something,' he says, ignoring her question. 'Before we got cut off.'

She wants to ask him more about the house, but now's not the time. It's important they talk about what she saw on the TV. 'There was a reason I couldn't sleep last night,' she begins.

'Because you were missing me?'

She knows he's teasing her, but he doesn't realise how right he is. She's been missing the real Rob.

'You remember you once told me about your doppelgänger?' she continues.

'We've been through this,' he says casually. He's doing something else again, sounds distracted.

'I know, but it's been really troubling me. Has done ever since you mentioned it.'

'Listen, it was just an old phobia, nothing more. Read too many gothic novels when I was a teenager.'

'But does it still frighten you?' she asks, more firmly now. 'Meeting your doppelgänger again. Being found. Having your life taken over by a double.'

136

'It seems to worry you more than me,' he says, making light of her question. 'I would never have mentioned it if I'd known that it would upset you like this. I was on my own when I had all those fears – a lonely geek, coding in my bedroom and playing too much Mortal Kombat. I'm not on my own now, Kate. Still a geek perhaps, but definitely not lonely – thanks to you.'

'I'm just worried for you, that's all,' she says, trying not to become emotional.

'You worry way too much, you know that,' he says, pausing. 'And I love you for it.'

'I lost Stretch today,' she says, thrown by his sudden expression of affection. 'Found him in your office.'

'My office?'

'The door was open.'

'I left in a rush yesterday,' he says, 'and I can't seem to lock it remotely. More teething problems. There's a lot of valuable stuff in there, computers mainly.'

'That picture must be worth a bit too,' she says. 'The one behind your desk – Rossetti's doppelgängers.'

A brief pause. '*How They Met Themselves*?'

'You never mentioned it before. Is it an original?' She knows he collects art privately as well as holding his charity exhibitions in hospitals.

'I bought it at auction years ago. Long before we met. As an investment. Rossetti did four versions. The other three are in public galleries.'

137

It must have cost a fortune. 'I want us to be honest, that's all,' she says, once again conscious of how little time they've actually known each other. Theirs was a whirlwind romance. If she hadn't been strapped up in a hospital bed, she would have been swept off her feet. It had been a long time since she'd felt such a sudden, urgent attraction for someone. When he subsequently invited her to move to Cornwall, she didn't hesitate. It seemed the right thing to do – for her and for him, his career. He talked of opening a regional office in the Truro tech cluster, becoming a part of Cornwall's burgeoning digital landscape – 'Kernowfornia'. It never quite happened. Instead, he became more interested in Brittany, Cornwall's Celtic twin, apparently drawn by Brest's own tech hub.

'I'd just like you to tell me if . . . you know . . . you ever get worried that he might come back into your life again,' she continues. 'We're meant to share these things.'

She's being disingenuous. Ever since he mentioned his fear of doppelgängers, she's been worrying herself sick about it, and yet she's never discussed her anxieties with him. 'You said you met him once, a long time ago.' She shivers, bracing herself. 'What exactly happened?'

'You're right,' he says. 'No secrets. It was in Thailand. On a beach. I was twenty-one. Different time, different place.' He pauses. 'But thank you. For caring.' She wants to ask him more but there's a finality to his tone, as if he's said all he's prepared to say. 'Have you told Bex about what happened yesterday?' he asks, changing the subject. 'When you were out swimming?'

'She's heard the whole embarrassing story.' Kate flinches again at the memory of being rescued so publicly. And by the lifeboat.

'She's a good friend,' he says.

Her best friend; Bex's northern nous a perfect counterweight to Kate's southern skittishness.

'Did she mention we bumped into each other at Paddington?' he asks.

'She did.'

She starts to well up. Should she tell him about Jake and the boat? She leans in towards the phone, staring at the blurred profile on the screen, wishing she were with him now. Rob is back to how she knows him: kind, interested, open. A man who sends her snowdrifts of white flowers. She can cope like this.

'There's something else,' she says.

He'll be upset when she tells him about Jake's boat, offer to help. There's never been any hostility between them, at least not on Rob's side. It's a mark of his kindness, his confidence in their relationship, what they've built together in five short months. And she likes to think Jake has been good about it too, in public at least, an acknowledgement that what they had was no longer enough.

'What is it?' he asks.

And then the signal improves and she's looking at a clear picture on her phone. Rob's staring directly at the camera, smiling in a way that she hasn't seen before, top lip curling a fraction into what looks like a taunt. Almost a snarl. Is she imagining it? The tingling feeling returns, her scalp prickling as the room begins to spin.

'Rob?' she asks. His smile seems to adjust, flatten out, as if he's suddenly remembered he's on camera. It's the Rob she knows again, but the damage is done. She grabs the phone and smacks it face down on the kitchen table, like she's trapping a wasp in a jar. She leaves it there for a few seconds, breathing fast and hard.

CHAPTER 26

JAKE

'Thanks,' the man says. 'Back there—'

'No problem,' Jake says, interrupting him. He is still buzzing, in a shaken-up sort of way. It's not every day he saves someone's life. And within twelve hours of almost losing his own. After leading the man away from the railway track, Jake suggested they go for a walk together and he didn't protest.

They are now seated on a bench in the woods on the far side of the railway, looking down through a line in the trees at Hotspur House, a country pile on the distant horizon. It's an old vista, a legacy of when this whole area of woods and parkland was landscaped by Capability Brown. All around them are stacks of timber, ready to be taken away and logged.

'Were you really going to go through with it?' Jake asks. Although the immediate danger has passed, he still wants to keep the man engaged.

'Of course,' the man says, almost indignantly. They sit in silence. 'Maybe,' he adds quietly.

'So what's the problem?' Jake asks.

He is happy to wait for an answer. He can never

141

bring back the woman who died on Southall station, but it feels like he's finally made amends of sorts. Kate would be proud of him. And the woods look so beautiful today. They used to come up here together in the spring, have picnics amongst the bluebells.

'I never asked you your name,' he says, a seed of an idea beginning to form in his mind. The man doesn't answer.

'Do you drink?' he continues. No reply. 'I'm Jake, by the way.'

He resists offering his hand. Too formal for a pair of washed-up bums on a bench. It was Jake's idea to come up here, far from the railway line, from his boat. He smelt alcohol on the man when they walked through the trees, where the ground was recently a carpet of blue.

Bluebells.

'I drink too much,' he continues, filling the silence. 'Can't resist a pint in a nice country pub. Never been into drugs, though. I mean, we used to have the odd spliff on the boat, in the early days, but it always gave me such a headache. Food's my drug. Love to cook. When I can find the right ingredients. I like to forage. You can get some great chanterelles up here. Wild garlic too.'

Maybe he's got this wrong. The man remains taciturn, not rising to Jake's elaborately laid bait.

'You into drugs?' He glances at the man's sallow skin, his sunken eyes. The village has its alcoholics, a few people who sit outside the pub each day, waiting for it to open, but nobody who looks like this. Hollowed out, as if rotting from the inside.

The man leans forward, head lowered, hands clasped so tightly together that Jake can see the white of his knuckles. He senses he's getting warmer, but there's still no response. So he decides to come straight out with it, ask him if he's got caught up in a county lines operation. It might explain his sudden presence in the village.

'Gone cunch?' Jake says quietly.

The man looks up at him, surprised by the question, maybe the language too, and lowers his head again. Jake remains silent, watching him, willing on the faintest of responses. *You can tell me, pal. I've just saved your bloody life.* After what seems an age, the man nods.

Jake takes a sharp in-breath. Already he can feel his sympathy for this man melting away like deer in the forest, but he needs to sideline his own feelings. Stay focused. He might prove useful, know something about the man who spiked Kate's drink in the pub. Drug networks operate in a small world – at least they did when he used to report on them.

'No choice,' the man eventually says, staring at the ground.

Bollocks. In Jake's experience, there's always a choice. The man's too old to be a mule, but Jake knows the way county lines operate, how they use people of his age – early twenties, at a guess – to recruit teenage dealers.

'Swindon?' he asks.

The man nods, staring at his feet.

'Ever worked out the Bluebell?'

He looks up at Jake, sadness replaced by a hardening of his features. The name of the pub seems to have changed the mood. 'Wouldn't know, mate,' he says, standing up.

'Rockbourne, outside Swindon,' Jake says, watching as the man starts to walk away. Their conversation is clearly at an end. He knows something about the pub, Jake is sure of it. And maybe about the barman who served Kate that night.

'Couldn't you go to the police?' he calls after him.

The man spits to one side. And then he stops, about twenty yards away, his back still to Jake, and looks around him, as if taking in the forest for the first time, the still summer air. A shiver runs through Jake. Has he pushed him too far? The man pulls out a cigarette, lights it with a rasping strike of a match, and walks on.

It's a sound that Jake has heard before.

CHAPTER 27

KATE

Kate stares at the phone screen, watching it power down to darkness. She can't go on like this. Her paranoia is killing her. She's fine when she's just talking to Rob. It's when she sees his face that this feeling kicks in, a sickening, gut-wrenching sense that it's not him but someone who looks identical.

A moment later, Rob starts to call her on FaceTime on her laptop. She snaps it shut, looking around the kitchen. *Shit.* The landline in the hall. She rushes out and pulls the handset cable from the wall socket. There's no other way for him to communicate with her now. The house is isolated. She feels better already.

Bex is still asleep. Kate walks down the corridor towards the guest room and stands outside the door. She can't wake her again. Not after last night's drama. Bex would never forgive her. Instead, she opens Rob's office door, pleased that he's still been unable to lock it remotely, and steps inside, followed by Stretch, who's come to see what she's doing.

She's not sure herself. She just wants to get a better sense of the Rob she doesn't know so well, the man he was before she met him. She walks over to his desk, picks up the Rossetti and stares at it again, the frightened faces. *How They Met Themselves*, as she now knows it's called.

'What's this place?'

Kate spins round to see Bex in her pyjamas, standing bleary eyed in the doorway.

'Rob's office,' she says.

'His Cornish man-cave?'

'Did you sleep well?' Kate asks, ignoring the comment out of some strange sense of loyalty. She said something similar once to Rob and he didn't find it funny.

'Good, thanks. Apart from being woken up in the middle of the night by this crazy best friend of mine who doesn't realise how bloody lucky she is.' She bends down to pet Stretch, who is at her feet, tail wagging like a demented windscreen wiper.

Kate smiles at her. Where would she be without Bex? 'Sorry about that.' She pauses, her smile fading. 'I've just spoken to Rob. Asked about him talking in fluent French on the TV.'

'And?' Bex asks, looking up at her.

'He says they got him to practise it for the cameras.'

'There we go,' Bex says. Kate turns away, recalling Rob's explanation. 'There's always a rational explanation for these things,' Bex adds.

'I guess so.' Kate's still not convinced.

'What you doing in here anyway?' Bex asks.

146

'Looking at this.' She gestures at the picture behind her.

'Bloody hell, don't tell me that's an original Rossetti,' Bex says, coming over to study it more closely.

'There are four versions, apparently,' Kate says. 'It's called *How They Met Themselves*. Those two people on the right are the doppelgängers.'

'Complete with a Ready Brek glow around them.'

They both stare at the picture in silence.

'You want some breakfast?' Kate asks, leading her out of the office.

'Wouldn't mind a bit more of a nosey around first,' Bex says, lingering at the door. 'Any more hidden masterpieces?'

Bex loves her art. It's one reason they're such good friends.

'He doesn't really like people to come in here,' Kate says, about to close the door behind them. And then a book catches her eye. She takes it off the shelf by the door and looks at the cover: *Le Bouc émissaire*. She reads the back, conscious that her hands are trembling.

'What is it?' Bex asks.

'A French translation of *The Scapegoat* by Daphne du Maurier,' Kate says, flicking through the well-thumbed pages. 'About doubles.'

Kate replaces it on the shelf, trying not to dwell on the book, what its presence in Rob's office might mean.

'Tea?' she asks, as they walk back down the corridor to the kitchen.

'Could murder a coffee,' Bex says, watching as Kate opens one of the cupboards. 'It's just a book, Kate. Might not even be his.'

'It's in French, Bex,' Kate says, spooning some coffee powder into the espresso machine. 'Why read Daphne du Maurier in bloody French?'

'We've been through this,' Bex says. 'He's trying to learn the language.'

Kate can't hold it together any longer and turns away, her eyes stinging.

'Oh, Katie,' Bex says, coming over to comfort her.

'I hung up on him,' she says, steadying herself against the sideboard. She's feeling dizzy. 'When we were talking earlier.'

'Why d'you do that?'

'We were on the phone and then the signal improved and I saw his face and . . .'

Kate starts to cry, big hot tears, the last few days finally catching up with her.

'It's OK,' Bex says quietly, still holding her.

After a few moments, Kate unpeels herself from Bex's arms and fetches a glass jar of granola, placing it on the table. She feels better when she's doing things. She takes out a pot of yoghurt from the fridge, which is now behaving itself.

'His smile,' Kate says. 'It was as if he was mocking me.'

'Don't be daft. Rob would never do that.'

'I know.' Kate pauses. 'That's what's worrying me.'

They catch each other's eye. 'Will he be angry with you?' Bex asks, turning away. 'For hanging up on him?'

'He doesn't do anger,' Kate says, laying out some cutlery on the table.

'Count yourself lucky. Nothing wrong with a bit of anger, mind. Shows passion.' Bex raises her eyebrows suggestively as she sits down at the table, idly stacking away some magazines. She grabs the top one, a copy of *Wired*, and flicks through it.

'Actually, he was angry with me once,' Kate says, sitting down opposite Bex. 'Early on, when he came to see me at Mum's.'

'Staying with in-laws can be very stressful.'

'It wasn't that.'

Kate tries hard to think back to the visit, soon after she'd left hospital. She was spending a few weeks with her mum before the move down to Cornwall. Rob used to visit at weekends. Did he ask her about her memory? She was still heavily medicated for her injuries and those early days remain a blur.

'What was it, then?' Bex asks.

'I failed a recognition test of some kind. He showed me some images of faces.'

The details start to come back, but it's like she's seeing everything through a thick fog. Her mum had gone shopping and they were at the kitchen

149

table in her house, photos laid out in front of her, as if they were playing pairs.

'Do you recognise this man?' Rob had asked, pointing at someone – a doctor, she thinks it was. White coat anyway. She'd shaken her head and his fist had slammed down onto the table. So hard her herbal tea had spilt. She remembers that. He suddenly became very kind to her, mopping up, apologising, saying he'd had a stressful time at work. And then he'd asked her to put on the headset. It was the first time and she was scared, although her fear was numbed by the medication.

'You OK?' Bex asks.

'Fine,' she says, putting that day out of her mind.

'He's just trying to help you,' Bex continues, resting a hand on hers. 'And he's done a pretty good job, I'd say.'

'You're right.'

She tucks into the yoghurt, deciding not to tell Bex what she can remember. She's not sure if she's imagining it all anyway.

'I texted Jake this morning,' Bex says, changing the subject. 'Told him he can stay at mine.'

'That's kind of you.' And surprising. Maybe they'd make a good couple. Bex would be better at knocking him into shape than Kate ever was.

'Poor sod.' Bex pauses. 'You'd better ring Rob back.'

She's right. She turns on her phone and a

voicemail message pops up. Before she can play it, though, the phone starts to ring.

'I'll leave you to it,' Bex says, getting up from the table with her coffee. 'I'm going to take a shower.'

'It's showing "Number unavailable",' Kate says.

'Answer it, Kate. It's probably him.'

She takes the call. It's not Rob.

CHAPTER 28

SILAS

Silas waits for what seems like half the car-owning population of Cornwall to drive out of the village before he steers down the single-track road to the quayside. Miraculously, he finds somewhere to park. The sandy beach is spread out below them and beyond it the wide expanse of the sea.

He and Strover sit still for a few moments, admiring the view across to Nare Head. His father, who was also a detective, used to tell him stories about stakeouts when he was with the Regional Crime Squad in the 1980s. Everyone preferred the Mark 2 Vauxhall Cavalier in those days because you could put the seats back and sleep. Which was fine until a joint undercover operation, when half the force would turn up in the same car.

'Mountains or seaside?' he asks Strover, still looking ahead. It's been a quick drive, three hours from Swindon, including the judicious use of a blue light on their unmarked car on a congested section of the M5.

'Sorry, boss?'

152

'Are you a mountain or a seaside person? People tend to be one or the other. Like Africa and India – you prefer one continent or the other. Edinburgh or Glasgow. London or New York. Mountains or seaside.'

'Neither really,' she says, clearly confused.

'Where do you go on your holidays, then?' he asks. Silas loves to travel.

'City breaks.'

He nods his head in approval. He likes a good city break himself – Krakow last time – but he's a seaside man at heart. Always has been. Not the big beaches but rugged coasts and hidden coves. Western Isles of Scotland, the Pelion peninsula in Greece.

'Should you call her again?' he asks. 'Check that she's still in?'

Strover rang Kate earlier, before they set off from Gablecross, exaggerating her Bristol accent to explain that she had a special Sunday flower delivery and asking if Kate would be in today. Silas was taken aback by how naturally Strover slipped into character, wondered if she'd ever considered undercover work. The deceit didn't sit comfortably with either of them, but they needed to talk to Kate. And Jake had revealed that Kate's new man had had to return to London. Flowers might work. If they gave her warning of their arrival, there was a good chance she'd choose not to cooperate.

'I'll call her again now,' Strover says, as Silas

gets out of the car. 'Are we walking?' she adds, surprised.

'What flavour?'

'Sorry?'

'I'm buying us ice creams. You must have ice cream at the seaside.'

'Honeycomb if they've got it,' she says hesitantly as she puts the phone to her ear.

Funny, he had her down as a mint choc chip. You can tell a lot about someone from their choice of ice cream.

'And you'd better buy some flowers – decent ones,' Strover calls after him, before slipping into Bristol florist mode to talk on her phone.

Silas walks off, Strover's words carrying in the summer breeze. 'Is that Kate?' she asks. 'This is the florist's, I called earlier . . . Just checking you're in for a delivery today? About ten minutes?' He smiles to himself. Strover's coming on nicely.

Ten minutes later, they pull up in front of the house where Kate's living, Silas licking the last of his rum and raisin ice cream from his lips. It is the weekend, after all. In truth, he's nervous. He hasn't seen Kate for nearly five months, not since she left hospital and disappeared off their radar.

'*Grand Designs*,' he says, getting out the car and looking up at the house. 'Got to be.'

The entire front of the single-storey house is glass, most of the interior hidden behind blinds.

To the left of them, a shiny Tesla is hooked up to a charging point in front of a standalone double garage. He's sure they've got the right place. The address matches the one Strover found for Kate's partner's businesses. And she established from the DVLA database that the only car in Rob's name, a Tesla, is also registered at this address.

'Different,' Strover says, joining her boss at the front door.

He's holding a large bunch of carnations, the best he could find in the village shop. If there were another way of doing this, he'd do it. The last thing he wants is to frighten Kate. She's been through enough already.

'Not my bag,' he says, standing back to take in the property's glass and steel frontage. 'Good for growing tomatoes in though.'

'I like it,' Strover says, glancing across at the drive. 'And the Tesla Model S Performance. Nought to sixty in 2.4 seconds. Three-hundred-and-sixty-five-mile range. Top speed 155 miles per hour.'

Silas shakes his head in bewilderment. 'You are the source of the most unlikely information.'

'Girls not meant to know about cars?'

'Did I say that?'

Not convinced, Strover leans forward to press the doorbell. 'Driving one of those things is like sitting in the future,' she says, looking across at the Tesla again.

'Wait,' Silas says, gesturing at the security camera. He moves forward and holds the carnations up close to the tiny lens, blocking the view with flowers.

CHAPTER 29

KATE

The phone call was from the florist again. This time the woman was ringing to say that the delivery would be in ten minutes. Kate knows it will be lilies. More white ones. She guesses Rob's still feeling bad about returning early to London yesterday. Jake used to give her flowers too but never bought ones. He used to cut them when he was out walking in the forest. Honeysuckle, dog-rose and cow parsley, tied up with meadow grass. Rob isn't a great one for getting his hands dirty in the woods and he wouldn't have survived one night on their leaky old narrowboat. Everything has to be clean and in the right place, like the house. It's a measure of the man that he's allowed her to come into his home and make such a mess.

Bex is still having a shower as Kate half-heartedly tidies up their breakfast things. She's filled with a sudden desire to drive up to London, try to recapture some of the loved-up feelings from before. Rediscover the Rob who walked onto her hospital ward that first day, his eyes full of kindness and curiosity. Maybe it's only seeing him at weekends that's messing with her head, making everything feel so disconnected. She needs to be with him in London, stay at his flat, meet him for lunch at the office. Be an ordinary couple.

She wanders over to the easel where her painting of Stretch sits half finished. Behind it, on the mirror, she's stuck up a collection of photos of her and Rob from their first few weeks down in Cornwall together, when he was working from here. She leans forward and looks at him, the man she loves: emerging from the waves with a surfboard, teasing her by a rock pool with a crab in his hands, standing on the harbour wall at sunset drinking Provence rosé.

These photos all look like Rob, a reminder of those first few weeks here. She was still in considerable discomfort then, but the pain was lessened by the ease of her new life. She and Jake used to say that they didn't want a lot of money, just enough to make things run a bit more smoothly. That's how it feels with Rob. He hasn't let his ridiculous wealth change him. They go to the village pub for dinner – coconut vegetable curry for her, cod and chips for him. There just isn't that flinch any more when the bill arrives. And she doesn't worry that the car will break down.

A recent photo of Rob sitting at the harbour café catches her eye. She remembers when she took it. He was grinning at someone using the 'pervoculars' to scan the suntanned bodies on the beach below. She looks more closely at the picture,

158

grateful to be able to study Rob's handsome face without feeling strange. And then she notices someone in the background, standing in the coffee queue. It's the same man who sat next to her yesterday, before her swim. And he's staring at the camera. At her.

The front doorbell rings.

CHAPTER 30

SILAS

'Hello, stranger,' Silas says, holding out the bunch of carnations. It's good to see Kate again.

'You bastard,' Kate manages to say, visibly shocked as she takes the flowers.

Silas should have warned her. He tenses his foot, ready to insert it into the doorway in case she slams the door in their faces. She looks well though: healthy, barely recognisable from the woman he last saw in hospital, bandaged and full of tubes. Her long brown hair's up, shaved at the nape. Edgy, stylish. She must have struggled to conform when she was working for the police.

'It's OK, we're not here to ask you back,' he says, palms held up in front of him. 'We just want to show you one picture, that's all.'

'A long way to come for one picture,' Kate says, still holding her ground on the doorstep.

'One picture's often all it takes – as you know.'

'Has this got anything to do with the court case?' Kate asks.

'Can we come in?' Silas peers past Kate into the

airy hall, which looks bigger than his entire flat in Old Swindon. 'Please?'

'Don't give up the day job,' Kate says to Strover. She looks dismissively at the carnations and turns to walk into the house, leaving the door barely open behind her.

Strover raises her eyebrows at Silas as they follow Kate in. They've had warmer welcomes.

'Sorry about the phone calls,' Strover says, but Kate ignores her.

'You look well,' Silas says, keen to change the subject. 'Really well.'

They walk through the hall, past large modern artworks on the walls, and into the kitchen, where Silas sits down in the sunshine. He wants to settle the mood as soon as possible, dissipate her understandable anger with familiar banter. The three of them used to be close colleagues. A good team. The accident ended all that. He knows she still blames him, the police, for causing her to fall asleep at the wheel, for working her too hard.

'I'm getting there,' Kate says, dropping the carnations in the sink and running some water.

Silas looks around the kitchen, nodding at Strover to sit down too. They're indoors but might as well be outside. The place feels almost tropical, like an outstation of the nearby Eden Project. He took Conor there once, years ago, when he was a young boy. It wasn't a success. Conor thought it was a zoo and cried all the way round when he was told there weren't any monkeys in the rain-forest dome.

'This is Bex, by the way,' Kate says, turning to smile at a woman who has just walked into the room. Her hair is wet. 'My friend from Wiltshire.'

'Preston, actually,' Bex says.

'Nice to meet you, Bex,' Silas says, standing up to shake her hand. He wasn't expecting Kate to have company. 'You mind if we talk to your friend in private?'

'OK,' Bex says hesitantly, glancing at Kate for approval.

'Nothing personal,' he adds. He didn't mean to sound so formal or abrupt.

Bex turns to Kate. 'You alright wi'that?' she asks.

Her Lancashire accent suddenly seems to have grown stronger, more assertive. Silas likes Lancashire, used to stay at a great pub in the Forest of Bowland when he wanted to spoil Mel. Cask ales and kippers.

'It's fine,' Kate says.

'I'll take Stretch for a walk then,' Bex says, picking up a tiny dog from a cushion in the corner. Silas hadn't even noticed it. He's put bigger things in a bread roll.

They all watch in awkward silence as Bex strides through to the hall, fastens a lead on the dog and closes the front door a little too loudly behind her.

'You didn't say goodbye,' Silas says, turning back to Kate. 'Didn't let us know you were leaving the hospital – leaving Wiltshire.'

He's in danger of sounding like a jilted lover, but it upset him when she left without saying anything. They'd spent a lot of time together, working through hundreds of hours of CCTV footage, standing in cold crowds, and he'd visited her regularly in hospital, to interview her about the crash and because he was concerned for her. The whole unit was.

'It was a difficult time,' Kate says. 'New beginnings, clean break.'

'Of course.' Silas pauses, takes in the view again down to the sea. He'd like to retire to somewhere like this, maybe more traditional bricks and mortar, an old coastguard's cottage overlooking the harbour. He could keep a small boat, enjoy a spot of mackerel fishing. 'We just want your help.'

'Sounds familiar,' Kate says.

'One photo, that's all.'

'Does this have something to do with the fire last night?' Kate asks.

'You know about that?'

'Jake rang,' she says.

'I didn't think you two were in touch.'

'We're not.' She glances away, embarrassed.

Strover raises her eyebrows in disapproval at him. She's right. He hasn't come all this way to discuss Kate's love life. It's why Silas likes working with

163

Strover. She keeps him in check, brings something to the table that he never can, not even after the amount of time he's spent in nail bars.

'What's the photo?' Kate asks.

Silas turns to Strover, who pulls out a folder from her bag.

'The night of the accident,' Strover begins, 'when you were driving home—'

'I really don't remember anything about it,' Kate says, interrupting her and glancing at Silas. 'I've told you all I know.'

'It's OK,' Silas says, sensing her alarm, her reluctance to revisit the accident. For the first month in hospital she wasn't able to talk about it at all. Even when she was well enough, she couldn't tell them anything useful. 'Something new's come to light, that's all.'

'About that night?'

He turns to Strover again, keen to let her lead the conversation, allowing him to watch Kate more closely, read her responses.

'It seems you stopped off at a pub on the way home,' Strover says.

Kate flinches. 'We've been through this,' she says. 'I don't remember anything, not even leaving the office that night. It had been a pretty shit week.'

Silas had worked her to the bone. The results were coming thick and fast. And then she'd seen Jake on camera with another woman. A shit week, as she says.

'Where did I go?' she asks.

'The Bluebell in Rockbourne,' Strover says. 'It's about halfway between Gablecross and the canal.'

Kate glances up at them both, seemingly surprised. 'I went there a few times, towards the end. To clear my head.' She looks down. 'But I don't remember going that night.'

She's holding something back, Silas is sure of it.

'You ordered an Aperol spritz,' Strover continues, seeking approval from her boss.

Silas nods.

'Look, we all know I'd had a drink before the accident,' Kate says. 'And we all know why I needed one.'

Her eyes have a hint of accusation in them. Silas turns away. He pushed the team too hard, he accepts that now. He turns to face her again.

'Why did you choose the Bluebell?' he asks.

Kate looks up at him, guilt in her eyes. Christ, his suspicions are right.

'I should never have been there,' she says. 'It was a stupid idea. I was frustrated when we were pulled off the county lines job, wanted to prove a connection with the modern slavery gang we were investigating.'

Silas sighs, shaking his head. As he feared, Kate visited the pub to identify someone. She was a civilian, not a detective, with no legal powers to investigate. 'So you went there to make a spot,' he says.

'I know it wasn't my job . . .'

'Wasn't your job?' Silas can't help himself, despite Strover throwing another look of disapproval at him. 'You were acting completely illegally. Putting yourself in grave danger.'

'I didn't think it would do any harm,' Kate says. 'I just sat at the bar, watched who came in and out, that's all. I'd overheard you talking about the place, that it might be a drugs pub.'

'How often did you visit?' he asks, more calmly now. Kate was always impulsive, never a great respecter of rules.

'Twice, maybe three times, I can't remember.'

'You should have told us.'

He'd suspected that she'd stopped to have a drink somewhere, given the alcohol found in her blood, but they'd never established where. There are a lot of pubs between Swindon and the canal. He can't be too hard on her. She nearly died, spent months in recovery.

'I didn't recognise anyone,' she adds.

But someone recognised her. Silas watches as Strover produces an A4 photo from the folder and slides it onto the table.

'You didn't recognise this man, then?' Strover says. 'The barman who served you a drink that night?'

Kate picks up the photo, the blood draining from her face. Silas leans forward, watching her intently.

'You OK?' Strover asks, resting a hand on Kate's forearm.

'What is it?' Silas asks. Something's very wrong. 'Do you recognise him?'

Kate puts the photo down on the table.

'I do now.'

'You do?' Silas glances at Strover, who looks equally surprised. Neither of them was expecting this. Does Kate remember him from the modern slavery investigation?

'How do you know him?' he asks as Strover pulls out her notepad.

'Because he's in the village,' she says, her eyes moistening. 'And I think he spiked my coffee yesterday.'

CHAPTER 31

JAKE

Jake looks for the key under the flowerpot at the back of Bex's house. It's a small thatched estate cottage, on the edge of the village. He's been there many times with Kate, particularly in the early days, before the book deals dried up and Bex started to give him a hard time for not earning more money.

A black cat comes up to him, rubbing against his legs. He doesn't remember Bex having one. He leans down to stroke it, more shaken than he realises by the events of the past twelve hours.

He didn't try to catch up with the man in the forest or ask him if he knew anything about his boat or the fire. He didn't trust himself not to do something stupid. It was the sound of the striking match that set him off, bringing back memories of the flames dancing down the towpath. Of course it wasn't him – it would be too risky to hang around the next day, given the number of police in the area – but Jake is haunted by what he was told once, how arsonists like to return to the scene of their crime.

After finding the key and letting himself into the house, he gives Bex a call.

'Does the mog need feeding?' he asks. He stopped it coming in through the back door.

'Not mine,' Bex says. 'Give it milk if you're feeling soft.'

'Just wanted to say thanks,' Jake says, looking around the small kitchen. It's not much bigger than the galley on his boat. And the oven clock is wrong. He'll have to fix that. So many friends have oven clocks flashing the incorrect time. It's almost a fulltime job resetting them.

'No worries,' she says. 'You OK?'

'Is Kate with you?' he asks, ignoring her question. Her sudden kindness is unsettling. With one hand, he opens the fridge, pulls out a plastic bottle of milk and looks around the kitchen. He takes a bowl from the drying rack and pours some milk into it.

Bex pauses before she answers. 'Not right now.'

'But you're with her in Cornwall,' he says, putting the bowl on the floor. He opens the back door and lets the cat in.

'I was going to tell you yesterday, at the station . . .'

He remembers their frosty encounter on the platform. 'So that's why you didn't want to talk to me.'

'I was in a rush.'

'I'm not checking up on you. Or Kate. None of my business. It's just that I spoke to her last night.

We haven't talked for months. And then you texted me this morning.'

'Kate was worried,' Bex says. 'We both were.'

'But Rob isn't down there now?'

'He comes and goes,' she says. 'Busy man. Works hard, does Rob.'

Jake ignores the barbed comment, the implication that he's a slacker. 'Where are you?' he asks as the line crackles with wind.

'Walking Kate's daft dog on the coast path.'

'I didn't know she had one.' A sudden sadness wells up in him. Kate always wanted a dog, but he was never keen. Too many friends' cars smelling of wet fur. There's so much about her new life that he doesn't know.

'It's easy to miss him,' Bex says.

'Where's Kate, then?'

'She's with the police. Her old boss DI Hart and a female colleague. Did you know they were coming down?'

'No idea,' Jake says, surprised. Odd that they didn't mention it when they took his statement. 'I was with them both last night. On the canal. They came out to investigate the fire.'

'Maybe that's why they're down here. I didn't have time to find out before they asked me to leave.'

'They don't think it was Kate?'

'Of course they bloody don't. Kate? She loved that boat.'

'Did she? I think she hated it by the end.'

170

They must be going to talk to her about the CCTV footage, see if she remembers anything about that night. She won't like a visit from the police. Doesn't want anything to do with her past life. With him.

'Is everything OK? With Kate?' he asks. 'You sound—'

'Everything's fine.'

She pauses. He knows something's wrong. It might explain why she's being so nice to him all of a sudden. And he's happy to wait, resist filling the silence until she tells him.

'Did she ever talk to you about doubles?' Bex asks eventually.

'Doubles? Not that I remember. Except when I was ordering too many at the bar.'

Jake has a weakness for Talisker, an expensive habit that didn't help their finances.

'I'm serious, Jake. She's become fixated with the whole idea down here. Thinks that Rob might be . . .'

'Might be what?' Jake has no idea where Bex is going with this.

'She thinks Rob might have been replaced by a doppelgänger,' Bex continues. 'Apparently he spoke to her about it once, said he has this fear of meeting his double, that the double would take over his life. And what's really freaking her out, she says, is that he did actually meet someone who looked just like him, when he was younger, on a beach in Thailand. It's meant to be bad luck if

171

you meet your doppelgänger once. Meet them twice and you're toast. She's been unable to get the idea out of her head ever since.'

'That doesn't sound like Kate,' Jake says.

'I know. And last night she saw this footage on French TV, an interview with Rob about his new tech office in Brittany or something. She woke me at one thirty in the morning to watch it, convinced that it wasn't Rob. It was all very weird. Apparently Rob doesn't speak a word of French – Kate's been trying to teach him – but this guy was talking fluently. And then we found a French book in Rob's office. I told her he's just a quick learner but she's really worried by it, thinks she's going mad.'

Jake pauses for a moment, trying to take in what Bex has just said about Kate. 'Ever see *Invasion of the Body Snatchers*?' he asks. 'Nineteen fifties sci-fi horror movie about alien clones?'

He and Kate used to watch a lot of movies on the boat together, particularly in the early days, on long winter nights. But he watched that one on his own. She wasn't into horror.

'God, years ago, I think,' Bex says. 'Donald Sutherland screaming at the end?'

'That's the seventies remake. It's the original one I was thinking about. Kevin McCarthy as the doctor who sees a number of patients apparently suffering from Capgras syndrome. In fact it turns out they're "pod people" – extraterrestrial doubles with no emotion.'

'What's Capgras syndrome?'

'That's what made me think of the film. It's a very real delusion, apparently. Nothing sci-fi about it at all. I read about it after watching the film. You're convinced that the person closest to you – your partner, say, or family member – has been replaced by a double.'

Silence. And then Bex speaks, her voice quiet. 'Do you think that's what's going on with Kate?'

'Could be – I'm no expert. But it sounds a lot more likely than Rob being replaced by a French-speaking doppelgänger.'

CHAPTER 32

KATE

ate scans the beach with the pair of binoculars borrowed from the National Coastwatch lookout hut behind her, aware that her hands are trembling. The hut sits on the end of a rocky promontory, with good views of the beaches back towards the village and the other way towards Nare Head. She often drops by for a chat here on her walks. A Union Jack flutters above it whenever someone's on duty.

'This is exactly what I came down to Cornwall to leave behind,' she says, moving her focus systematically from one person to the next: sunbathers, dads playing French cricket with their children, friends throwing a Frisbee in the surf. Above them, by the footpath, a long lunch queue snakes its way towards the Secret Shack, her favourite café. Best seafood chowder in Cornwall.

She still hasn't got over the shock of the photo of the barman that Silas and Strover showed her. Afterwards, they told her they thought he'd spiked her drink at the pub too. She's sure it's the same man that she saw at the café before she went for a

174

swim. When there's a match, it's just obvious. A spot. He's also in the background of her photo of Rob, which means that he's been watching her for a while – and that it wasn't cramp that nearly caused her to drown.

'I can't promise I'll recognise him,' she adds.

Hart is aware that the accident left her without her old powers of recognition. What he doesn't know is that Dr Varma now thinks her ability to remember faces is returning. She just wishes her ability to paint them would come back too.

'Take your time,' Strover says behind her.

She's obviously still feeling guilty about the flowers. So she should. It's a while since they've seen her and they used deception to enter her house. Why did she open the door when all she could see on the security camera was a bunch of carnations? She should have known. Rob only ever sends lilies. A part of her wanted to slam the door in their faces, but there's an undeniable bond between them, forged over months of working too hard together, that Kate suspects will never be broken. They lived in each other's pockets when the unit was running, learnt to rely on each other.

'I can't see him,' she says, lowering the binoculars. 'You need to tell me if I'm right to be feeling this scared.'

She's told them what happened after she drank her coffee in the harbour café yesterday. And neither of them believes it was cramp either.

'There's no conclusive proof that your drink was spiked at the pub, or your coffee yesterday at the café,' Hart says, taking the binoculars from her and focusing on birds diving far out at sea. 'But it's looking that way. You must be careful. Don't do anything impulsive.'

He gives her a look. She knows he's referring to her unauthorised trips to the Bluebell. She should have told him earlier, but she'd crossed a line by going there. It was symptomatic of her state of mind at the time. She was tired to the core from work and devastated that night after seeing Jake with another woman. She also didn't think she'd be recognised by anyone, but it seems the barman knew exactly who she was – and tried to kill her.

And now he's down here.

'Gannets,' Hart says, binoculars still raised.

Strover rolls her eyes at Kate. Kate got to know her too, admired her technical knowhow, the way she stood up for herself in what was a very male environment. Hart also stood up for Strover, often fighting her corner, which is why Kate likes him. He just got carried away with the work, their successes. They all did.

And then she spots someone on his own at the far end of the beach. He's too far away to see his face, but his gait, his profile, is sickeningly familiar.

'Binoculars?' she says, trying to sound professional.

Hart is still distracted by gannets. Strover nudges him. 'Boss?'

He passes them over. Her hands are trembling again as she focuses on the man who wants her dead.

'That's him,' she says, lingering on his face, the features that he attempted to hide from her yesterday. Large forehead. Herman, as in Munster. Does a part of her remember him from the Bluebell, that night of the accident? Or does she just recognise him from the café and the photo?

She hands the binoculars back to Hart. 'To the right of the steps,' she says. 'Far end of the beach.'

Hart adjusts the focus. 'Ugly bastard, isn't he?'

'It's definitely him,' she says, watching as Strover pulls out the CCTV photo and passes it to her. Seeing the image again just makes her more sure. She misses this, the satisfaction of a match. It masks the fear. The professor who tested her said that super recognisers tend to peak in their mid-thirties. She should be in the zone.

'Let's have a little chat with him,' Hart says to Strover. 'Ask if he's ever worked at the Bluebell.'

They return the binoculars to the Coastwatch volunteer in the lookout and set off along the path at the top of the cliffs, heading back towards the beach. Herman is still there, but he's not settled and their pace quickens, Hart walking out ahead. It will take them a good ten minutes to reach him.

'Can I ask you something?' Kate says to Strover, who is beside her, one eye on the beach. 'About facial-recognition software?'

'Not exactly my favourite subject at the moment,' Strover says.

'Really?' Kate's surprised. Strover used to live and breathe technology when they worked together.

'It keeps getting it wrong,' she says.

'I thought you were the tech expert?'

'It's all relative,' Strover says, nodding at Hart ahead.

'I heard that,' Hart says.

'I just want to know how easy it would be to find your double – you know, your lookalike.'

'Aren't there apps that can do that?' Hart asks, chipping in. '"Find My Doppelgänger".'

Hart's not helping here. Kate's trying to have a serious conversation with Strover, distract herself from Herman up ahead.

'In theory, it should be easy,' Strover says. 'As you know, the software relies on metrics – the distance between eyes, ears – and data. The more of it, the better. Apps only have access to a limited number of photos. But law-enforcement agencies can draw on millions of images – the UK custody database is getting bigger every day.'

'And in reality . . .?' Kate asks.

'You might get a rough match, but finding your long-lost twin is by no means a given. Someone who *looks* identical might not share the exact same facial geometry.'

'It's why we turned to people like you,' Hart says. 'Faces are uniquely human. They need to

178

be interpreted emotionally, intuitively, not just measured. At least that's what I told the boss.'

'Can I ask you a favour?' Kate says. 'In return for helping you guys out with the photo.'

'Depends what it is,' Hart says.

'I want you to look for a match for Rob. My partner.'

'Isn't that a bit weird?' Hart says.

Strover gives him a look.

'He used to have this fear, a phobia, of meeting his double,' she says. 'I need to put his mind at rest, tell him there isn't anyone out there who has the same distance between his blue eyes.'

If Strover and Hart know she's not being honest, they don't show it.

'What if there is?' Strover says. 'We're all meant to have a doppelgänger, aren't we?'

Kate's about to reply when Hart interrupts them. 'Hold up,' he says. 'Our man's on the move.'

They all focus on the far end of the beach, a steep flight of steps that runs up to the coast path. Herman is taking them two at a time. Has he seen them? At the top, he turns and looks back across the bay. And then he starts to sprint.

CHAPTER 33

JAKE

Jake stares at the French TV footage on Bex's desktop computer in a small room adjoining the kitchen. It's on a sliding desk, built into a bookcase. Bex said he could use it, which is helpful as he doesn't have any data left on his phone. As far as he can tell, the geek being interviewed is Rob. And it makes for painful viewing. Rob not only comes across as intelligent and successful but charming too. And he's speaking fluent French. Jake leans in closer. The man looks like the Rob that Jake met briefly at the hospital, but it's not a face that he cares to remember.

He pulls up his notes on Capgras syndrome. Ever since Bex rang earlier, he's been researching the delusion and thinks he's found something important.

He calls Bex again on his mobile. Crazy. She's been avoiding him in the village for the past six months, but now they're like besties, bonding over the possibility that Kate might have Capgras.

'Give me a sec,' Bex says.

He hears her talking to Stretch, Kate's dachshund. 'Are you with Kate?' he asks. It's important he talks to Bex when she's on her own.

'She's still with the police.'

'She's not going back to the old job, is she?'

Her police work was a far cry from portrait painting, but it gave her some independence – and money too. And it was Jake who originally introduced her to DI Hart.

'No chance,' Bex says. 'Have you seen her house down here? The life she has now?'

Jake falls silent. He's often thought about visiting, trying to talk to Kate, but he has so far stayed away.

'Sorry,' Bex says. 'That wasn't kind. Tell me what you've found?'

'Listen to this,' he says. '"Capgras is a full-blown psychiatric disorder caused by anything from dementia to paranoid schizophrenia."'

'So why would Kate have it?'

'Bear with me,' he says, glancing at his notes again on the screen before switching to an academic paper he's just found on the Internet. 'From what I can gather, a super recogniser like Kate has a more developed fusiform gyrus.'

'What's that when it's at home?'

'The area of the brain that processes faces – the same area that was affected by her accident.'

'And how does that relate to Capgras?' Bex asks. Jake's in danger of losing her.

'Because Capgras can also be caused by traumatic brain injury – specifically, lesions in the fusiform gyrus.'

'Bloody hell, that must be what she's got then. It would explain everything.'

Jake can hear the relief in Bex's voice. 'Except that it's an extremely rare and unusual disorder,' he says, reading from the article again.

'Someone's got to have it.'

He's still not convinced. 'And it doesn't seem to affect the auditory cortex, just the visual.'

'Say that bit again,' Bex says, a sudden curiosity in her voice.

'Someone with Capgras only thinks their loved one is a double if they can see their face,' he explains. 'If they can only hear their voice, it doesn't seem to affect them.'

'When they're talking on the phone, you mean?'

'I guess so. Why?'

'Because Kate says she's fine when she's chatting to Rob on her mobile. It's when he facetimes her and she can actually see his face that she freaks out.'

Jake sits up in his chair, trying to get his head around what Bex has just said. 'You really need to speak to her about this,' he says. Up until now, the Capgras theory has seemed interesting but a little fanciful. He now thinks they might be onto something, given her past as a super recogniser. It would be a cruel irony if a high-performing fusiform gyrus, once responsible for

182

Kate's exceptional powers of recognition, was now tricking her into seeing doubles.

'She's seeing a neuropsychiatrist regularly,' Bex says. 'Paid for by Rob. I'll get her to ask him about it. I don't think she's mentioned seeing doubles to him yet.'

Jake hangs up and starts to search for more information about Capgras: case studies, related delusions like Fregoli (different people are in fact a single person who changes his or her appearance), but something's still nagging him about Rob. He's just not sure what. He begins to google him, repeating a search he's done many times in recent months. Brought up by two doctors in Douglas, Cork, entered the *Sunday Times* Irish Rich List when he was twenty-three. Always considered a bit of a loner. After a few minutes, Jake is on the Companies House website, looking at a list of all Rob's directorships: technology start-ups, mostly medical, an online art gallery. He's been here before and found nothing suspicious. The only controversy was when he briefly invested in a company that made electric-shock collars for training dogs. The product was banned before it even hit the shelves.

This time, though, a new company is listed, the one mentioned in the news report. He pastes its name into a separate Google tab, calls up the website and clicks on 'About'. The company appears to specialise in something called 'direct neural interface technology'. It's currently raising capital for electrodes implanted in the brain that can help to operate artificial limbs or control epilepsy.

A window asks him to accept cookies. He clicks on it and is about to drill down further into the site when he notices a green LED light on Bex's computer, just to the right of the camera. He's sure it wasn't on a moment ago. His first thought is that maybe Bex does a lot of facetiming and someone's calling her. But FaceTime isn't open. He closes the company website, quits Chrome and backs away from the computer. The light is still on, the camera watching him.

CHAPTER 34

KATE

'You go on ahead,' Hart says, calling out to them. 'See where he goes.'

Kate's walking fast beside Strover. They glance at each other and both slip into a run. Hart's heavy breathing fades behind them.

'This really isn't part of my Cornwall retirement plan,' Kate says as they stride out together on the coast path.

'You do the identifying, let us do the rest,' Strover says. 'Just like the old days.'

Kate's glad she's been getting fit. As well as the swimming, she's tried to run two or three times a week, on the same stretch of coast path as they're on now. Strover seems fit too, though she's not exactly in running gear. Light trousers and those telltale sensible black shoes that only plainclothes cops seem to wear.

'I've lost him,' Strover says, coming to a halt. 'Can you still see him?'

The coast path ahead broadens out into a wide grassy track, ridged with trails left by sheep. There are one or two walkers, but most people are enjoying the sea and the sand below. It's what

Kate should be doing on a beautiful day like today, not running beside a detective in pursuit of a man who keeps trying to kill her. Beyond the grassy expanse, where the steps come up from the beach, the path weaves its way through gorse bushes. For a moment, she can't see Herman either and then he appears again from behind a bush, close to where the path enters the village.

'He's up by the first houses,' she says, getting her breath back.

'If he's got a car, we're stuffed,' Strover says.

Five minutes later, they're walking quickly through the village, scanning every side road and alley for the man. Strover's already called Hart, given him an update. They try not to draw attention to themselves as they pass holidaymakers coming up from the beach laden with chairs and spades and buckets.

'He could be anywhere,' Kate says.

'Problem is, we're not officially here,' Strover says. 'Otherwise I'd call for back up.'

'How do you mean?' Kate glances at Strover.

'We're off duty.'

She gives Strover a puzzled look. She'd assumed they were down on official business.

'Sad, I know,' Strover says. 'Daytrip to the seaside with my boss at the weekend. Such is the miserable state of my social life.'

'Why are you really here, then?'

Strover looks out to sea, her neat, petite face

186

glowing from the exercise, and then turns to Kate. 'He was devastated when you were injured. We all were. When we saw the CCTV footage yesterday of you at the pub that night, he felt he had to investigate. In his own time.'

'Because his boss wouldn't have sanctioned it?'

Strover nods. Kate remembers his boss, the one who never believed in the super-recogniser unit, despite their results, and closed it down soon after her accident.

'Why now, though?' she asks. 'How did you suddenly get the CCTV footage?'

She doesn't expect Strover to answer. She learnt quickly that as a civilian she was not allowed to know the operational details of the cases she worked on.

'Jake didn't mention it, then?' Strover says.

'Jake?'

'It was him who was sent the video.'

Why would Jake be sent CCTV footage of her at the pub that night? 'Who by?' she asks, her head spinning.

'We don't know.'

'When?'

'Yesterday.'

'And someone sets fire to his boat last night?' There must be a connection. Kate lets her words hang in the air, hoping Strover will join the dots.

'I can't tell you any more. I'm sorry,' Strover says. 'Trust me, we're working on it.'

They jog down into the village, stepping out

into the middle of the road to avoid a crowd of children coming up the other way. They're all eating ice creams, peering into a small beach bucket. That's why Kate loves it here, a reminder of her childhood, of innocent days spent rock-pooling, building sandcastles. She just wishes that her past hadn't caught up with her. The spiked coffee, Jake's fire, the CCTV image of her at the pub. And a crazy, nagging sense that Rob's been replaced by a double. Overnight her idyllic life's become a nightmare.

'Caught a shark?' she says as they pass the children, glancing at their catch.

'Crabs,' one of them says, holding the bucket out for her to see.

Strover looks too, smiling at the young children. At the bottom of the bucket is a modest crab, its shell barely three inches across.

'Massive, isn't it,' another child says. 'Tried to bite me with its *huge* claws.'

Kate hears the car first. They are both still in the road, the children on the pavement. And then she's aware of Strover screaming at her, so loud it's as if her voice is in her own head.

'Watch out!'

She spins around to see a car coming up the hill, out of the village, driving too fast. Instead of slowing down, or moving across to the other side of the road, it accelerates, the driver steering directly at her and Strover. Strover moves first, pulling Kate out of the way just in time, but not

188

before Kate gets a look at the driver, who turns to glare at her. It's the same man, same forehead. Herman.

The car speeds past, its wheels inches from the pavement.

'Emmet!' someone shouts from across the street.

'Get the number plate,' Strover says as she picks up one of the kids she accidentally knocked over when they jumped onto the pavement.

Kate memorises the plate and the make of the vehicle, a BMW. She's hopeless with cars and only happens to know it because Jake used to want one when they were at their poorest. In his dreams.

'Who was that?' one of the children asks.

'Just an angry fisherman,' Kate improvises, her chest tight with adrenaline. She can hardly breathe.

'Why's he so angry?' another child asks.

She tries to calm herself. Her legs have turned to jelly.

'Because he didn't catch what he wanted,' she manages to say, peering again into their bucket to distract herself. As she holds its rim, one of the children looks up at her, aware that her shaking hand is creating ripples in the bucket's water. She manages a smile, struggling to stop herself being sick. The car tried to run her down, could have killed the children.

'Must have been jealous of your massive crab,' she says.

CHAPTER 35

SILAS

'Sure the kids are OK?' Silas asks Strover as he sips on an espresso. The harbour café is full of families in dripping swimwear and sunglasses, the air thick with the smell of sun lotion and salt water.

'All fine. Apart from the one I squashed,' Strover says. 'He'll live.'

After a long talk with Strover, Kate has gone back to her house, shaken up by the near miss. They'll call on her on their way out of the village, check again that she's alright.

Silas was hurrying down the hill when the car sped past. He managed to get its number plate, which tallies with the one that Kate memorised. A minute later, he was with Kate and Strover on the pavement, relieved that no one had been injured.

'If he knows we're police, he'll ditch the car – or lose the number plates,' he says.

Strover has already called a colleague back at Gablecross, who confirmed that the car had been reported stolen. He then rang through to the Devon and Cornwall Police Control Room, giving them details of the incident.

'Tasty?' Strover asks, nodding at a half-eaten tart beside his espresso.

'Exceptional.'

The Portuguese tart is his reward after the earlier exertions on the coast path. It's not as if he's unfit – he's been going to the gym recently. Strover and Kate are simply fitter.

'He was driving straight at us,' Strover says, more sombre now.

'Trying to scare you? Or kill you?'

'Her, not me, I hope.' She pauses. 'I'm not sure. I think he lost his nerve when he saw all the kids.'

Silas sits back on the metal stool, watching a dad on the beach below dig a speedboat in the sand with his son. He used to do that with Conor, who always squealed with excitement as the incoming tide washed all around him. Will he ever see Conor again? Every force in the country has his details, along with the UK Missing Persons Bureau.

'That's three times he's gone for her,' Silas says. 'If we believe Kate's swimming story.'

'You don't believe her?' Strover asks.

He thinks he does. When he was working alongside Kate, he trusted her with his life. It's annoying that she didn't tell him sooner about her visits to the Bluebell, but something else is bothering him. Kate said that the man had spiked her coffee in the harbour café. It was a very specific allegation, quite a leap for her to have made. Particularly as it was before they'd explained that her drink in the pub six months ago might have been spiked too.

Maybe it's nothing.

'I believe her now,' he says.

More than anything, his heart feels heavy, guilt about Kate mixed with anger. He realises he's been in denial, not quite ready to take Jake's pub footage seriously. He pushes away his empty plate and stands up. They need to find the driver.

'And we've got a problem,' he adds.

'With the boss?' Strover asks, standing up too.

Silas nods.

'He won't like it, us being down here off duty,' he says. 'He didn't like the super-recogniser unit and won't want to hear anything about Kate. Facial-recognition software is king.'

He starts to walk up the slipway towards the car park.

'But if we can prove a connection with last week's trial?' Strover says, catching up with him.

'That's over, as far as he's concerned. Gang sentenced, job done. Thirty-three years is a result – even made the national press.'

'So what do we do?'

Silas stops in the middle of the village square to face Strover, glancing around to check that no one is within earshot.

'We prove a connection with the Proactive Team's ongoing investigation into county lines.

192

The boss is right behind that one. Can't get enough of it.'

The targeting of Kate a day after the sentencing makes Silas almost certain that there's a link between the modern slavery gang that was sent to prison and the new county lines network that's infiltrating villages around Swindon. He despises drugs, even more so since he's seen the effects first hand on Conor. And the county lines gangleaders, the ones who groom the kids, some as young as ten, are no better than child molesters.

'But we still don't know who sent Jake the footage,' Strover says as Silas walks on again, faster now, more purposeful. She has to trot to keep up with him.

'Maybe someone who wants us to know there's a connection,' Silas suggests, opening the car doors with the remote.

'Another gang?' Strover asks, walking around to the passenger side.

Before Silas can answer, his phone rings. He holds up his hand towards Strover as he takes the call.

'Thanks,' he says, after listening for a few moments.

'That was the insurers,' he says to Strover. 'Our friend Jake . . . seems like he took out a new policy on his boat four days ago.'

CHAPTER 36

KATE

'I need a drink,' Kate says, frantically opening one kitchen cupboard after another.

'What's going on?' Bex asks, standing behind her.

'Why don't we have any bloody alcohol in this house?' she says, opening another cupboard. It's full of identical tins of Illy Italian coffee. At least twenty of them. All Rob's. She pushes them away to see if there's a bottle of something lurking at the back. She knows it's a forlorn hope.

'Because you've been disappointingly sensible since the accident?' Bex offers.

Bex and Kate used to despair of people whose voice went up at the end of every sentence. Now Bex is doing it.

'Not any more.' Kate slams the last cupboard door shut and rests her hands on the sideboard, head bowed.

'I've got some gin in my room,' Bex says quietly.

'I thought you drank it all last night?' Kate says, turning as Bex walks out of the kitchen and down the corridor to her room.

'Emergency rations,' Bex calls over her shoulder.

Two minutes later, they're sitting at the kitchen table, drinking strong gin and tonics at three in the afternoon. Kate used to drink at lunchtimes, when things were getting really bad with Jake. Kid herself that mints would mask the smell of alcohol. Stretch is on his bed, shattered after his long walk with Bex while Kate was out with Hart and Strover.

'I never like to travel without reserve supplies,' Bex says, turning the small square bottle to look at its artisan label: 'Lancashire Dry Gin'. 'Particularly when I'm coming down here to Prohibition Villas.'

'Thanks,' Kate says, enjoying the glowing sensation as the alcohol starts to permeate her body.

'Hair of the dog,' Bex says, knocking back hers.

'Speak for yourself.'

She'd left Bex to it last night. Been a good girl. The doctors all said she should try to avoid anything that might impair her brain's recovery, including alcohol. Rob often reminds her of their words. It was the same when she was working. Hangovers weren't compatible with intensive recognition work. It didn't stop her drinking, though. She was beyond caring.

'So what's happened now?' Bex asks.

Kate starts to fill her in about nearly being run over in the street by the man who sat next to her in the café. As she gets to the bit about Jake and the pub CCTV footage he was sent that shows the same man, there's a ring on the doorbell.

195

'I'll go,' she says.

'Call if you need me,' Bex says as she walks off down to her room.

She hesitates by the door for a moment, suddenly fearful. It must be the adrenaline from earlier. She almost laughs with relief when she clicks on the security monitor screen. It's Mark, the guy who runs the gallery and looks after Stretch when she goes for a swim. He's with Trudie, his own dog. She opens the door.

'Just wondering if you wanted me to take Stretch for a walk,' he asks, his open face all smiles.

'That's kind of you,' she says, standing back in case her breath smells of gin. Mark's a good man, always looking out for others.

'Didn't know whether you'd be up to walking him yourself,' he says, 'after what happened yesterday.'

'Oh that,' she says, playing down her swimming incident. As she feared, it's become the talk of the village: the incomer who forgets how to swim and has to be rescued by the lifeboat. At least he hasn't heard about her being nearly run over by a car today. No doubt news of that incident will soon be percolating through the village. 'I'm fine now,' she adds. 'And Stretch is good. My friend Bex – she took him out earlier. Thanks, though.'

'No problem,' Mark says, turning to go. He pauses. 'Did I see Rob just now?'

Kate's heart misses a beat.

'Rob? I don't think so,' she says, managing a thin smile. 'He had to go back to London yesterday.'

'That's what I thought.'

She'd told Mark as much when she dropped Stretch off at the gallery before her ill-fated swim.

'Where did you see him?' she asks, failing to sound casual.

'I must have mistaken him for someone else. I just thought I saw him driving past, out the top of the village. Gave him a friendly wave.'

'In a Tesla? Like that one?' she asks, nodding at the car parked on the drive.

'Yeah, a Model S, just like that one.'

Mark knows his electric cars. He was one of the first in the village to get one. It wasn't a Tesla though. There aren't any other Teslas in the village, even during the holiday period. Kate's has been sitting on the drive all day – at least she thinks it has. She was out for a few hours with Hart and Strover, but the car is where she left it when she returned from Truro yesterday. What worries her is that Rob said recently that he was planning at some point to buy a second Tesla, identical in every respect, for his use in London. He's like that. When he finds something that's right for him, he sticks with it. Cars, trainers, tennis racquets, Italian coffee. If he had a wine cellar, it would be full of identical wines.

'When was this again?' she asks.

'About an hour ago,' Mark says. 'Hey, listen, I

must have got it wrong. Rob normally waves back anyway. This guy sped past, so I made a note of the number plate, in case it had been stolen. You know me.'

Kate tells herself to calm down as she takes the scrap of paper that Mark gives her and closes the door. Rob is in London. She spoke to him earlier. Mark is right. It's just a mistake. He's a member of Neighbourhood Watch, inclined to be over-cautious. But then she remembers the woman who approached Rob at Truro station.

'Everything alright?' Bex says, coming back down the corridor from her room.

'I need another drink.'

198

CHAPTER 37

JAKE

Jake leans forward and sticks a plaster over the tiny lens above the screen. He tried to ring Bex as soon as the green light appeared on her computer, but she didn't pick up and he decided against leaving a message. It's not his business how she manages her computer settings. And he can't be sure that the light came on when he started to browse Rob's new company's website.

He's about to open Google again, see what else he can discover about Rob's investments, when his phone rings.

'You tried calling me?'

Bex.

'Pocket call, sorry,' Jake says.

'Liar.'

She knows him too well.

'Your camera came on,' he says. 'On your computer.'

'The interactive porn cam, you mean?' Bex says.

Jake swallows hard. He'd momentarily thought about watching a bit of soft porn – it's been a while since he's had any data – but the cat was eyeing him with such disdain that he'd quickly ditched the idea.

'You serious?' he asks.

'I must have left it on after facetiming my mum,' she says, letting him down gently.

He closes his eyes. 'Have you talked to Kate about Capgras yet?' he asks.

'Not yet.' Bex sounds low. 'I think it might freak her out even more right now. Being told she's delusional. I need to choose my moment.'

'How is she?'

Bex pauses before she answers. 'OK . . . considering that someone just tried to run her over in the street.'

'What?'

'She's fine,' Bex adds quickly. 'A bit pissed but fine.'

She explains about Kate's close shave with the car and then drops a bigger bombshell, telling him that the driver tried to spike her coffee yesterday and that she nearly drowned in the harbour.

'Why didn't you tell me this earlier?' Jake asks, struggling to take it all in. And why didn't Kate mention it last night when he called her? Typically, she'd been more concerned about him and the boat fire than her own brush with death.

'Because you're out of her life, Jake.'

Harsh. 'So why are you telling me now?' he asks quietly. He knows she's right. He's history.

'It gets worse. The same man who spiked her

drink yesterday . . .' Bex is finding this difficult. She's usually as hard as nails. 'He also spiked her drink the night of her car crash. Kate recognised him from that footage you were sent.'

'Really? How do you know all this?'

But before Bex has a chance to reply, Jake's phone flags up another caller.

'I've got to go,' he says. 'DI Hart's calling me.'

He cuts Bex off and sits up in the chair in front of the computer, trying to process what he's just heard and wondering why Hart is ringing him. He hopes Hart has news about the arsonist who torched his boat. Maybe something about the pub footage too. That's obviously why he went down to Cornwall, to talk to Kate, who then talked to Bex about it.

'Any news?' Jake says.

'You tell me.'

Jake doesn't like Hart's tone. The bloke can be so affable one minute, intimidating the next. 'How do you mean?' he asks, shifting awkwardly in his seat.

'Taken out any insurance recently?'

Jake breathes a sigh of relief. 'Yeah, finally upgraded to some decent cover,' he says. 'Thank God.'

Until now, he's just had the basic third-party cover – damage to locks and other boats – that's required to get a licence from the Canal and River Trust.

'Four days ago,' Hart says. 'Three days before your boat was destroyed.'

He's so naive. It never occurred to him how it might appear in the light of the fire. For months he'd been meaning to get the insurance upgraded to cover contents. Just like he's been planning to set up an ISA, buy some premium bonds and do his tax return early for once. All part of his sober, self-improvement plan.

'And that's a problem?' Jake asks.

'You can see how it might look,' Hart says. 'I'll call you tomorrow.'

The line drops. A moment later, the cat jumps up onto his lap, steps with its front paws onto the keyboard and wakes up the computer screen. A picture of Rob in Brest stares back at him.

CHAPTER 38

SILAS

'We're off back up to Wiltshire,' Silas says, finding himself standing in the doorway of Kate's house in Cornwall for the second time that day. On this occasion they rang the doorbell and smiled at the security camera. No need for carnations. He'd been hoping for a quick cream tea before they went, but they need to beat the Sunday-night traffic.

'Have a safe drive,' Kate says. 'And watch out for . . .' She hesitates, swaying slightly on her feet in front of Silas.

Is she drunk? It's four o'clock in the afternoon.

'Are you sure you're OK?' Silas asks, glancing at Strover. She'd reassured him earlier that Kate was fine after the run-in with the car, but she doesn't look herself.

'All good,' Kate says, unconvincingly.

Her friend Bex appears at her shoulder, grinning at him and Strover. Dear God, they're both drunk.

'I was just going to say watch out for the speed camera on the border with Cornwall and Devon,' Kate says, pointing in the air with her finger.

'There's a sneaky police van at the bottom of the hill – Rob is always being caught there. But then I remembered you are the police and . . .'

Bex puts a hand to her mouth to suppress a giggle.

'We'll be careful,' Silas says. 'The car was stolen, by the way. The one that tried to run you over. We'll let you know if we find it – or the driver. The local police have all the details.'

'OK,' Kate says. Silas catches a whiff of alcohol on her breath.

'And we've asked a colleague to run a match for your partner,' Strover adds.

Kate seems to sober up immediately. 'And?' she asks.

'I'll call you if we hear something.'

'Me too, if you find a match,' Bex adds. 'Then we can have a toyboy each.'

Kate elbows her friend in the ribs. Silas is beginning to regret stopping by. But he knows there's another reason why he needed to see Kate.

'There's something else I wanted to ask,' he says.

'I'm not coming back,' Kate fires back.

'I know you're not.' Silas pauses. She's made that quite clear already. 'It's actually about my son, Conor. He's been missing six weeks now. I've no idea where he is.'

This is proving harder than he thought. Kate and Strover both know that Conor had a drugs problem and was homeless, but it's still not easy.

'We used to come to this part of Cornwall for our holidays, when he was a boy,' he continues. 'I don't know, it's a long shot, but he might have headed down here – somewhere familiar. Where he was happy.'

He stops before he makes a fool of himself. Then he pulls out an A4 sheet and hands it to Kate. It's a missing persons poster, with a photo of Conor taken a couple of years back, when he was still living at home and relatively stable.

'Do you want me to put it up in the village?' Kate asks. All the giggling of earlier has gone.

'No need,' Silas says. 'Just keep an eye out for him. Remember his face. In case he should ever pass through here. You're good at spotting someone in a crowd. Very good.'

'I'll do that,' she says, looking at the photo.

The last time Silas saw Conor, he was living rough in a multi-storey car park in the middle of Swindon.

The four of them stand in awkward silence for a few moments before Silas turns to walk away.

'Can you check something else for me?' Kate calls out. 'About Rob?'

Silas stops, surprised. He thought they were quits now, her looking out for Conor in return for them searching for Rob's double on the database.

'I think Rob might have another Tesla, just like that one,' she says, gesturing at the car on the drive.

Silas glances at it and then looks back at Kate.

'Lucky Rob,' he says, forcing a smile. He's tried over the years not to feel jealous of others' wealth. In his experience, money rarely brings happiness. But the sight of a £90,000 electric whip still niggles him.

'If he has bought another Tesla, it'll be in London,' Kate continues. 'With Rob. But then someone thought they saw him in the village this morning.'

'And?' Silas asks. Last time he looked, he was working for Wiltshire CID not bloody Relate.

'Can you check? You know, the number plates. See if it was his new car?'

'If it's been stolen, Rob needs to report it,' Silas says.

'I don't think it's been stolen.'

Where's Kate going with this? She seems so ill at ease, uncomfortable. 'Can't you just check with Rob?' he asks.

'Not really,' Kate says, looking down awkwardly.

'If you give us the number plate, we'll run a search,' Strover interjects, glancing at Silas, who turns away. She's out of order, but the damage is done.

'Won't be a moment,' Kate says, walking over to the corner of the kitchen, where she finds a scrap of paper. 'Someone in the village made a note of it.'

'Thanks,' Strover says, taking it.

Silas will talk to her later.

206

CHAPTER 39

KATE

'You just need to speak to Rob,' Bex says, glancing at the missing person poster that DI Hart left on the kitchen table. 'Ask him up front if he was here this morning in a new car. End of. For your own sanity.'

She's right. Kate was about to call him when Hart and Strover dropped in to say goodbye. She feels sorry for Hart. His son has caused him so much pain in recent years. She'll keep an eye out for him, for what it's worth. Scan the summer crowds on the beaches. Old habits die hard.

'Will you also talk to Rob?' Kate asks.

'Gladly,' Bex says. 'Give him a piece of my mind.'

Kate's angry with him too. Earlier, they'd worked themselves up into a gin-soaked lather as they discussed the possibility that Rob might have come back down to Cornwall without telling her. Was it to see the woman who met him at Truro station? It might explain why Rob didn't wave back at Mark. Kate's also frightened. And still a little drunk, which isn't helping her paranoia. If it wasn't Rob in the car, who was it?

'I'll start by asking him what he's been doing today – in a casual way, of course,' she says, for her own benefit as much as Bex's. 'But we also need to see where he's speaking from.'

If he's in a car, she'll challenge him, explain that Mark from the gallery saw him driving past this morning. It would mean he wasn't in his London flat when they spoke earlier. For most of that conversation, he was just a blur on her phone.

'You going to facetime him?' Bex asks.

'On my laptop – connected to the big screen next door.'

Bex gives her a quizzical look. 'Really?'

'That way we can see the background properly, work out where he's calling from.'

Ten minutes later, they're all set up in the sitting room, Kate's laptop connected to the vast TV set. Rob is going to appear much bigger than he is in real life. Huge. As big as he was last night on the French news. If they're looking at someone else, it will show. At least, that's the theory.

They both sit on the sofa and Kate opens up FaceTime, her desktop mirrored on the large screen.

'This is so weird, Kate,' Bex says.

'You focus on him, I'll look at the background.'

Kate's still not sure whether she's strong enough to do this. Her fear is that the moment Rob appears on the big screen, she'll feel like she did before and have to end the conversation. She can't deal with the disorientation, the overwhelming sense that the man she loves has been replaced by a stranger. It's like a rug being pulled from under her feet so hard that she's spun upside down. Also, she's been trained to look at a face as soon as she sees it, beginning with the nose and then taking in the whole, studying it for likenesses. Holistic facial recognition. Will she be able to look away quick enough?

She dials his number on FaceTime. Rob answers almost immediately, an image flickering into life on the vast screen. She can't cope. Keeping her eyes averted, she gets up and walks to the door, where she hovers.

Bex looks over to her anxiously and then turns back to the screen.

'Hi, Bex. What's up with Kate?' Rob says. 'Everything OK down there?'

It sounds like Rob and he appears to be talking from a room rather than his car. The voice is loud and clear, coming from all around them, thanks to an array of sunken Bose speakers. At least he's not in Cornwall. Not visiting some floosie in Truro.

'Hi, Rob,' Bex says, casting another imploring glance at Kate.

From where Kate's standing, she can listen to his voice without having to look at him.

'She was here, but . . .' Bex falters. Kate rolls her hands encouragingly, urging Bex to carry on, to bluff. She's great at charades. 'There's someone at the door,' Bex continues. 'Rang the bell just as we were calling you.'

Kate raises both hands in the thumbs-up sign to encourage her.

'People are so friendly down there,' Rob says. 'Dropping by all the time. No one ever knocks on my door here in Shoreditch.'

Kate tiptoes into the room, stepping in far enough to be able to see the screen. Rob seems to be doing something else, eyes down. She forces herself to look away from his face, aware of his movements but not his expression. All she needs to do is focus on the background. It looks exactly as it did earlier, when he said he was calling from his flat.

She steels herself and walks over to the back of the sofa where Bex is sitting.

'Hi, babe,' she says, leaning over Bex's shoulder. The laptop is on the table in front of them. She keeps her eyes firmly averted from both images of Rob's face. She's often talked to him in the past on FaceTime while she's been doing something else – cooking, yoga, painting. It's quite common for her not to be looking into the camera.

'Who was at the door?' he asks.

'Oh, Mark from the gallery,' she says breezily. 'Asking if Stretch fancied a walk.'

She is aware of Rob smiling.

'Did you lock the front door afterwards?' he asks.

'Of course,' she says.

Bex nudges her, subtly pointing at something she's just scribbled down on a piece of paper:

This is nuts! It's definitely him. And he's gorgeous.

Maybe it is nuts, but something's still niggling her.

'So are you guys just facetiming for a friendly chat or what?' he asks.

'Don't you like our company?' Bex says, leaning into the camera in her flirt mode. She's still a bit drunk too.

'You know I love it, Bex,' Rob says. 'It's just that I've got someone on the other line and the small matter of a company to float . . .'

'It's fine,' Kate interjects. He's busy with work. He always is. 'Just wanted to ask about the pool. The automatic vacuum's stopped cleaning the bottom.' It's her turn to improvise now.

'Leave it with me,' he says.

The robotic vacuum that criss-crosses the bottom of the swimming pool all day ground to a halt earlier. It could have been worse. A few weeks back, the cover started to roll over the pool while she was swimming in it, coming up behind her. She got out just in time – it was terrifying. Rob played it down afterwards, said that the cover's sensors would have detected a body in the water and stopped, but she hasn't been in the pool since.

She takes a deep breath, telling herself that Rob's in London, that she's worrying unnecessarily. It's no good.

'Rob,' she says. 'I need to ask you something else.'

'Sure,' he says. 'Fire away.'

'About Mark,' she begins, her voice shaking.

'How was he?'

'He's good.'

Rob doesn't know him as well as she does, but he's bought a number of pictures from his gallery in recent months.

'Actually, he thinks he saw you in a Tesla.'

'When?'

She detects a faint tightening of his voice, a hint of alarm. Bex tenses too, shaking her head as if this is all so unnecessary.

'A couple of hours ago,' she says.

'That would be pushing it,' he says, seemingly untroubled by the allegation. She needs to see his face so she can read his reaction better, but she daren't look into his eyes. 'Even for a Tesla. I'm three hundred miles away. And the car's with you anyway. Isn't it? I presume you've checked it hasn't been stolen?'

She's about to reply, ask him if he's bought another car, when a military jet passes over the house, so low and loud that Bex ducks involuntarily. Kate's got used to the noise. There's been a lot of RAF activity in the area recently. And then a second one flies over.

Kate can't help herself: she looks up at Rob's face on the big screen. He is staring back at them, a fear in his eyes that she's never seen before, as

212

if he knows he's about to be found out. It's not him. She lunges forward and is about to shut the laptop when she and Bex both hear it again. One jet, followed by the roar of another. Except that this time the sound is coming from the Bose speakers all around them.

Kate stares at Bex in disbelief. 'He's in Cornwall.'

CHAPTER 40

JAKE

Jake sits down in front of Bex's computer again, keen to discover more about Capgras syndrome. He's just been back over to the canal, retrieving a few more sodden items that have floated to the surface. It was a depressing scene. People were friendly, but that just made it worse.

It seems that Capgras is brought on by physical or cognitive changes in the brain. Kate definitely had a lesion in her fusiform gyrus – Jake remembers discussing it with her doctors soon after the accident – but why would Capgras only manifest itself now, six months later? A psychological trigger, perhaps, such as Rob's alarming talk of doppelgängers. It's the sort of thing that might mess with Kate's head at a time when she's still fragile and possibly suffering from feelings of disconnectedness – another common precursor to Capgras. Bex is certainly worried about her.

Jake remembers what she said about Rob meeting his doppelgänger in Thailand when he was twenty-one, how he lives in fear of their paths crossing again. What happened at that first

214

meeting? And why doesn't Rob want to talk to Kate about it? He calls up Facebook and logs in – to Kate's account. It feels wrong, but he tells himself he's doing it for her benefit. As he suspected, she hasn't changed her email or password. Nor has she posted recently. Kate always did have a love–hate relationship with Facebook. She is clearly in a hate phase. A quick scan of her friends – he was unfriended soon after she left hospital – and he finds Rob.

The articles he's read all mentioned Rob's young age – twenty-nine – and how he's achieved so much before he's even thirty. He checks Rob's date of birth. Rob turns thirty in ten days' time. A relatively big birthday. Jake will be thirty-five later this year, an anniversary he plans to ignore. Kate is bound to cook up something nice for Rob. She was always springing birthday surprises on Jake – in the early days, anyway. For his own thirtieth, she took him away to Paris, where thirty friends met him on the steps of Sacré-Coeur in Montmartre. She also tended to leave things late, planning them at the last minute.

Jake scans through Rob's profile. He doesn't seem to have many friends on Facebook and there are hardly any posts. It looks more like a token presence, a gesture. He probably prefers Instagram and some trendy messaging app of his own to communicate with his techmates.

It doesn't take Jake long to find exactly what he's looking for: an old Facebook friend, someone who has known Rob for a long time. Kirby looks the part. American born, he used to work for him in the early days – around the time when Rob visited Thailand. It's worth a try. He must know Rob well and might be able to shed some light on what happened. According to his profile, he likes to travel and even mentions South-East Asia. Jake opens up the messages tab, enters his name and creates a new message. Kate's never been in touch with him before, which makes things easier. He just hopes they haven't met in real life yet. Taking a gamble, he begins to type:

> Hey, Kate here, I'm pulling together a few ideas for a surprise birthday party for Rob. It's his big 3-0 coming up soon! Please don't say anything to him. Any good stories to tell? Funny anecdotes from his past?! Kx

Jake sits back, reading the message. Has he over-cooked Kate's enthusiasm? He knows this is bad, that Kate will hate him for it, but he hits the return key and sends.

CHAPTER 41

SILAS

'You crossed a line,' Silas says as they drive out of the village and head towards the A30.

'Sorry,' Strover says. 'I just took the number plate. We don't have to run a check on it.'

He lets her stew in silence as he nurses the car down a narrow road. He loves Cornwall's lanes, particularly when they're in full bloom like this, wildflowers tumbling over high drystone walls. They weren't so much fun when he was towing a caravan, five-year-old Conor yelling in the back, Mel beside him, stressing over an old road atlas.

'We spent a year working together,' Strover says, breaking the silence. 'I like Kate.'

'We all do. That doesn't mean we start checking her new toyboy's number plates just because he might be having an affair.'

In truth, he's less bothered than he sounds. He just needs to put a marker down, remind her who's in charge.

'That's not why she asked,' Strover says.

Silas glances across at her, surprised. Has he

missed something? Female intuition again. 'So why did she?'

'She's asked us to do two things for her,' Strover says. 'Search for a facial match with Rob. And check that he wasn't driving around Cornwall when he was meant to be in London. It's not just Rob who's worried about doppelgängers. Kate is too.'

'And?'

'I just think we should check it out, that's all. Given everything that's happened to her in the past twenty-four hours.'

Silas's phone starts to ring on the car intercom.

'Talk of the devil,' he says, glancing at the display screen. It's the Control Room at Devon and Cornwall Police.

'Any news?' he asks.

Maybe he could put in for a transfer down here, while he's still got some miles on the clock.

'Your Beamer's been found.' It's the same officer he spoke to earlier, when he rang through to the Control Room with the car's details. 'A couple of miles up the coast, in a car park behind Nare Head.'

'No sign of the driver?' Silas asks.

'Nothing.'

'Can you get forensics to have a look? Take some prints?'

There's a pause before the man speaks, clearing his throat. 'This is Cornwall, not Swindon,' he says. 'And it's a Sunday afternoon. Do you know how many forensics we have across the force?'

Silas doesn't want to get drawn into an argument over a lack of resources. It would be a quick race to the bottom. 'The car was stolen and the driver tried to run down one of our officers,' he says.

'We've taken a good look around the area. No sign of anyone.'

He's not going to win this one. At least they've found the car. 'Thanks for your help,' he says, hanging up.

'Funny place to leave a stolen car,' Strover says, looking up the location on a map on her phone. 'Remote.'

Silas is thinking the same thing. An abandoned car near coastal cliffs usually means only one thing: suicide. It doesn't make any sense. An hour earlier, this man had tried to run down Kate. The day before, he'd nearly drowned her.

'Ask that friend of yours in digital forensics to run a check on Rob,' he says. 'See if she can find a facial match.'

Strover turns to him in surprise. 'Really?'

'Why not?' he says defensively. Strover's friend is good, a digital investigator who's helped them on previous cases.

'Isn't that crossing a line too?' she asks.

Possibly, but they came barging into Kate's new life today, reminding her of a past that she clearly wants to forget. Strover's right. It's the least they can do for an old colleague.

'And check the plates she gave you,' he says, ignoring her surprise. 'See if he's been giving her the runaround.'

CHAPTER 42

JAKE

Kirby replies almost immediately to Jake's Facebook message. He works in tech too, somewhere in Silicon Valley. No doubt another one of those beanbags-for-chairs start-ups where being on social media 24/7 is all part of the job.

> Kate! I've heard so much about you. And so far only wonderful things ☺ Great idea. What sort of anecdotes are you after? So many! And when's the party-party?!

Jake sits back. He can't introduce doppelgängers too quickly into the conversation, but he also doesn't want to be on Facebook for long, given he's using Kate's account. He's already been logged in for half an hour and it's beginning to feel increasingly disloyal. He's about to start typing a reply when a new message window pings open on the screen.

He freezes. It's from Rob.

> Hey?! Thought you'd given FB up for the summer???? Ring me? Been trying to call

you back. What happened with FaceTime? Need to get comms sorted down there. Can't get through on landline either. You OK? xx

Should he just ignore it? If he replies, he could blow everything. The chances of making a mistake are too high. For whatever reason, it seems like Kate doesn't want to talk to Rob right now.

He logs out without replying to Rob. Kirby will have to wait.

CHAPTER 43

KATE

Kate's completely forgotten that there's a beach clean this evening. Not that they need one around here. They all do their bit – runners, dog walkers, even the tourists, who are pretty good at clearing up after themselves. But Kate wants to go along tonight, to take her mind off all that's happened this weekend.

'You coming?' she asks Bex, who is sitting with Stretch on the sofa.

'Sure,' Bex says, more subdued than usual. Presumably from their afternoon gin session. Kate's hungover too. And still in shock.

They've talked long and hard about the sound of the military jets. As soon as she looked at his face and heard them on the speakers, she cut off the FaceTime call, snapping shut the laptop. She also turned off her phone again and persuaded Bex to do the same. The landline was still disconnected after Rob's earlier call.

Neither of them can be certain of what it means. Either Rob is back down here without telling her. Or it wasn't Rob on the screen, it was his double, who is now in Cornwall. It didn't look like Rob, but Bex is certain that it was him. Perhaps Kate was imagining the jets, the guilty look in his eyes?

She hopes so. She will ring him later from the beach. No facetiming, just a normal call. She can't keep contacting him and hanging up. He's used to the poor communications down here, but he'll still be worrying what happened, trying to contact her.

There's a good crowd on Pendower beach tonight, about twenty of them, thanks to Rob. Kate's always urging him to do more for the environment. He's keen, just needs reminding, like buying an electric car rather than a diesel-guzzling 4x4. For the past few months, his tech company has sponsored the local beach cleans, which means it pays for their T-shirts and for fuel for the community van that brought them over here. She's trying to persuade Rob to cough up for an electric minibus. Most importantly, the sponsorship includes putting money behind the pub bar afterwards for all the volunteers.

'They've got jets in London too,' Bex says as they start to work their way down the high-tide mark. She doesn't sound convinced and Kate doesn't reply.

Stretch is sniffing about in front of them. It's a falling tide, the best time for a clean. Behind them, a few families are still enjoying the last of the sun as it sets over St Mawes in the distance. It's been one of those cloudless Cornish days that no one wants to end, the summer heat still lingering in the sand and on glowing, sunburnt cheeks.

'You saw the look on his face though,' Kate says. 'He'd been found out.' She has to believe that Rob would never come down to Cornwall without telling her, which means she must confront this man, ask him who he really is, why he's here. 'And the time delay,' she says, picking up a clump of orange fishing line that's become tangled with seaweed. 'Two seconds, at most. He wasn't that far away.'

She drops a crumpled can of Coke into her bucket, which also sports Rob's company name, and looks up, staring back towards the village and the surrounding countryside. Is his double really down here somewhere? Watching them? And what has he done with her Rob? The Rob who has taken care of her for the past five months, nurtured and loved her with such tenderness.

'There is another explanation for all this,' Bex says.

'I told you, he doesn't have a twin.'

'It's not that.' Bex pauses, looking around the beach. 'Have you heard of something called Capgras syndrome?'

'No, why?' she asks. It sounds French, like a resort on the Riviera. 'Should I have done?'

'Jake was telling me about it yesterday. It's a . . .' Bex hesitates. Unusually for her, she seems to be choosing her words carefully. 'It's a state of mind, a condition, where someone thinks that the person they love has been replaced by an impostor, a double.'

'A state of mind?' Kate says. Bex is not being straight with her. It sounds more serious than that. She's also been chatting with Jake about her, which is unsettling.

'OK, it's an illness,' Bex says. 'A delusion.'

'I'm not deluded, Bex,' she snaps, walking on ahead, but a part of her wants to know more.

'It only affects you when you see someone with your eyes,' Bex adds, calling after her. 'You don't think they're a double if you're chatting on the phone.'

Kate stops in her tracks, turning to look at Bex. What did she just say? Kate thinks back to her conversations with Rob, how familiar and reassuring he sounds when she calls him on her mobile.

'Really?' she says.

Bex nods, smiling sympathetically. 'It can be caused by lesions in the part of the brain that was damaged in your car crash.'

'OK,' Kate says, trying to take everything in. 'I'm sorry, I didn't mean—'

'It's fine,' Bex says, interrupting her. 'Maybe you should talk to Dr Varma about it. When you see him next. It might be nothing.'

It doesn't sound like nothing. A part of her feels better already. A specific syndrome, linked to her injuries, is more reassuring than thinking that she's gone mad. It would explain the funny feelings she has every time she sees Rob, the normality of their phone conversations.

It still doesn't explain the jets though. She can hear one now, far out at sea. Maybe she's imagining that one too.

Five minutes later, Kate and Bex have broken away from the main group and are searching the high-tide line in silence, scattering seabirds in front of them as they go. Jake would know their names. *Ruddy turnstones*, he whispers in her head.

'Where's Stretch gone?' Bex asks, looking up.

'He'll be around somewhere,' Kate says.

She never worries about him straying or getting lost. The beach is dog friendly and people look out for each other's animals. And then she sees him, fifty yards away, where the sand meets a cluster of rocks at the end of the beach. They don't usually go that far. It's always damp and empty and often in shade from the cliffs above. A flock of turnstones is pecking nervously at the sand. Behind them Stretch is sniffing at something on the high-tide line, a large bundle of seaweed, partially hidden. He starts to bark.

'There he is,' Bex says. 'What's he found?'

Kate doesn't reply. Instead, she starts to walk over to Stretch, a heavy feeling in her stomach as she quickens her pace. Stretch doesn't normally bark like this.

'What is it, Kate?' Bex calls behind her, fear growing in her voice. 'What's he barking at?'

She keeps walking, transfixed by the sight of what Stretch has found.

'Come away from there, weenie toes,' she says quietly, slowing to a standstill when she's ten feet away. 'There's a good boy.'

She thinks she's going to be sick.

'Oh my God,' Bex says, now beside her, hand over her mouth.

'We'd better call the police,' Kate manages to say.

CHAPTER 44

JAKE

Jake is back at Bex's computer screen again. He's left it long enough, can't afford to miss the chance to message Kirby. Kirby will be wondering where Kate's got to.

He logs into Kate's account, moving fast. A quick check of the chat window reveals that Rob is offline. He opens up the message thread with Kirby, reminding himself that he's posting as Kate.

> Sorry, had to pop out. Anything really. Maybe a story from way back, when you were at school together? Travelling? Thailand?

Has he gone too quickly with the reference to Thailand? Maybe he should have started with something more general, but there's no saying how long he's got on here before Rob appears. Or even Bex. He glances at the list of Kate's friends on the right of the screen, scrolling up and down and up again, watching for a green 'online' icon to appear next to Rob's name.

Don't go near what happened to Rob in Thailand.

He stares at the screen, blood draining from his face. There's no going back now. He needs to remember exactly what Bex told him, how reticent Rob had been.

> Why not? He briefly mentioned it to me once. How he met his double on a beach. He seemed upset. I want to help him – get him to talk more about it.

Kirby replies immediately.

> Can I call you?

Jake starts to panic. Does Kirby have Kate's mobile number?

> Reception terrible here in Cornwall. Messaging best.

Again Jake wonders if he's blown it. Kirby takes a long time – too long – to reply.

> Not sure I should tell you . . .

Jake replies instantly, Kate's words flowing out of him.

I love Rob. In just a few months, he's turned my life around.

And you've made him so happy too. He loves you.

Jake can't stomach much more of this. Another long pause.

Give me some time. There's a lot to tell.

It's ten minutes before Kirby returns. Ten minutes in which Jake's eyes remain glued to the chat window. He scrolls up and down the list again, watching for the green 'online' icon to appear next to Rob's name. For a moment he's tempted to read some of the previous exchanges between Kate and Rob, but it would be too painful and that's not what this is about. And then Kirby's long reply drops in one go. It's worth the wait.

We were in Thailand, having a beach party for Robert's twenty-first birthday. He hasn't touched drugs for years, as you know. Let's just say we were young back then. It was late. The stars were shining. And everyone was beautiful – and intoxicated.

We all wanted a piece of Robert that night and were toasting his birthday and his incredible successes. His first two apps were already sure-fire winners – number ones in the App Store – and he was disrupting markets around the world and making his first million. Ludicrous for someone so young. He was drinking heavily and then popped something strange, we still don't know what. Next thing I knew, he'd wandered off down the beach into the darkness.

When he returned, he looked troubled, like death to be honest. He said in a rather rambling speech that he felt he would have to change if he was ever going to make it properly. He joked that all the biggest names in tech, the people he really admired, had not played by the rules to achieve their successes. Failed to pay enough tax, 'borrowed' others' ideas, misused personal data, treated staff badly. The usual stuff. All bullshit, of course, but that's what he thought, and it bothered him. He was having a moment. Like we all did at that age. Quite an important one in his case. As you know, he's a major force for good these days, doing all sorts of amazing medical stuff and charity work. So he was kind of conflicted about his achievements to date and how far he could really go in his future career, wrestling with this whole idea of whether you can succeed big time in business and still be a good person.

Afterwards, I asked him why he'd walked off like that. He fell quiet and said that he thought he'd seen an uninvited guest show up at the party earlier. This guy apparently looked familiar in some weird way and Robert wanted to find him. After searching everywhere he suddenly spotted him at the far end of the beach.

Jake sits up in his chair.

And when he caught up with him, Robert got the shock of his life. The man wasn't just familiar, he looked identical to him. And I mean identical.

CHAPTER 45

SILAS

Silas glances across at Stonehenge, glowing in the last rays of the evening sun. There could be worse places on the A303 to queue. He was going to take the M5 and M4 to Swindon, but he wants to drop in on Jake, ask him a bit more about his narrowboat insurance. The fire might be an unfortunate coincidence, but the timing still troubles him.

Strover, sitting beside him, has just taken a call about the number plate that Kate gave them. It still annoys him that Strover offered to run a check on the car in Cornwall without consulting him first, but she's right, they need Kate onside. According to Strover, the registered keeper of the Tesla is not Rob. It belongs to someone called Gilmour Martin at a 'care of' address in London N1. 'Care of' addresses are used by the DVLA when the owner of a car is abroad or of no fixed abode. It can be a friend's house or family member's. At least, that's the theory. Criminals try to abuse them too.

'Who's Gilmour Martin?' Strover asks.

'He's not Rob, that's all we need to know,' Silas snaps. 'All Kate needs to know. She can rest easy

234

– her man's not giving her the runaround. Marriage guidance over. We move on.'

He's being irritable, unreasonable. Scratchy, as his Mel used to call it. Has been ever since Conor disappeared. They inch forward in stony silence, two queues of traffic slowly merging into one. And then Strover takes another call. Her digital investigator friend has found a total of seven people whose details match Rob's facial metrics. No names yet, just images. More details to follow shortly. He's not sure if Kate will be reassured or horrified.

'Strange thought, isn't it?' Silas says, tapping the steering wheel.

'What is?'

'All these other versions of ourselves out there somewhere.'

Seven people who look like his ex. There's a thought.

'A bit like Earth,' Silas continues, warming to his whimsical theme. 'Must be other planets in the universe just like ours.'

'There's something you need to know,' Strover says, in a tone he's come to recognise. A sure sign that she's about to fess up to something.

'Go on,' he says, staring straight ahead. Is she going to tell him that her digital investigator is more than just a friend? It wouldn't bother him. Each to their own. It might explain why Strover's romance last year with Sean, the pub conspiracy theorist, didn't last long.

'Our own custody database, Europol and Interpol resources, they're all useful, but there are some much bigger databases out there,' she says tentatively. 'Legal and illegal ones, on the Dark Web.'

'And your friend accessed them?'

Strover nods. Silas drives on in silence. Technology has changed policing so much in the past few years, marginalising old-school detectives like him. He might not be much good with computers, but he still needs to understand what they can do.

'Faces scraped from every social media site you've ever heard of,' Strover continues. 'And from a lot you haven't. Weibo and Youku in China, VK and Odnoklassniki in Russia. Age-filter apps like FaceApp are also generating huge numbers of faces as everyone shares images of what they'll look like when they're ninety.'

'I'd rather not know, thanks,' Silas says.

'The same's happening with Zao, the Chinese deepfake app that lets you swap your face for a film star's. Combine all these uploaded faces with databases used by the world's law-enforcement and intelligence agencies, and you've got a big dataset,' Strover continues. 'A lot of mugshots. More than a billion of them.'

The revenge of the selfie. He's never understood the urge to ruin a good photo with a gurning face in the foreground.

'How do you search that many faces?' he asks.

'Clever algorithms, fuzzy logic, probability theory. Russian programmers are leading the way. There's a search site called SearchFace.ru that can sift through half a billion faces on VK and find a match in seconds. But there's still a long way to go.'

Silas thinks back to the last time Strover's digital investigator friend helped them. And he thought Strover was computer savvy. This woman was extraordinary, blinding him with talk of symmetric-key block ciphers and triple data encryption algorithms. He'd had to look it all up afterwards.

'I'm amazed your friend's only found seven doubles for Rob.'

'We don't know exactly who or where they are yet,' Strover says, reading from her phone. 'One was last seen in Ireland eight years ago. Two could be in Australia, another possibly in Thailand – the best likeness. The other three were last seen on MySpace and Bebo in North America more than ten years ago.'

The traffic is beginning to move when another call comes in on the intercom for Silas. It's the Devon and Cornwall Police Control Room again.

'We've located the driver of your car,' the man says.

Silas knows at once that it's bad news. 'Located' is never a good word.

'A bunch of beach cleaners discovered his body

tonight – about half an hour ago. Pendower, not far from where the car was parked.'

'Suicide?' Silas asks, wondering if Kate knows.

'We're launching a murder inquiry. Looks like he's been shot in the head.'

CHAPTER 46

JAKE

Jake is desperate to know more about the man at the beach party who looked like Rob, but for some reason Kirby has gone quiet on Facebook. He's still online but is not responding. Jake prompts him with another message.

Tell me more?

And then, after a long wait, Kirby posts another chunk of text online, taking up the story again.

I never personally saw this guy. Gil, I think his name was. There were hundreds of people on the beach that night – surfers, techies, wannabes who were after a job with Robert. He just told me about him afterwards, said he could have been his twin. Except that Robert doesn't have a twin and Gil sounded nothing like Robert as a person. Apparently, he was a total loser, a drugs bum.

Later that evening, he revealed a bit more about what had happened on the beach with Gil, wanted to show me a video on his phone. For a second I thought it was Robert, but then I saw that this guy Gil had a pistol. He was waving it at the camera, gesticulating, making threats – so much anger. Not like Robert at all. He was saying that Robert didn't have what it took to be really successful. That he was too decent – too damn nice! – and needed to channel his darker impulses. And all the time he's waving this frickin' gun around. It was terrifying.

Rob's always worried about how we're all two steps away from being homeless – just like this guy. I think he really got under Rob's skin, reminded him of how life could be if it all went wrong. Gil was clearly jealous of Rob's success and his last words were the most chilling. He said he was going to wait until Rob had become a global hotshot. Had a life worth taking. Then he'd come looking for him, wherever he was in the world. Hunt him down. And when he'd found him, he'd . . . steal his soul.

Jake stares at the screen, shaking his head in disbelief. He needs to talk to Bex, to Kate.

Thanks for sharing. This is going to help me, help Rob, us. You're a good friend to him.

I try. But you might need something a bit lighter for his birthday party! The guy's doing OK though, isn't he? Playing by the rules. Got himself a wonderful partner. Doing right by the world. And no sign of Gil – not as far as I know . . .

He's doing great things.

Jake forces himself to keep writing.

And I love him for it.

And then Rob's name appears in the chat window. He's back online. Jake types a quick final message to Kirby, his big fingers trembling.

Thank you so much – please don't tell Rob we've talked. Surprise! Must go. xx

Before Kirby can reply, Jake deletes the message thread and logs out.

CHAPTER 47

KATE

'I want to come to London,' Kate says, standing outside the pub in the centre of the village, just up from the harbour café. Bex and the other beach cleaners are all inside, trying to drown their horror at what happened tonight. News of the body found on Pendower has spread fast and the pub is even busier than usual for a hot summer night. Locals and holidaymakers are sitting at the tables outside, milling around, chatting animatedly, each with their own theory. The community is in shock.

'I understand,' Rob says.

She's told Rob about today's unexpected visit from Hart and Strover, the CCTV footage from the pub, the near miss with the car and finally the body found by Stretch. She's also explained that she recognised the dead man as the Bluebell barman, the same person who sat beside her in the harbour café and spiked her coffee. She omitted to mention how the police came into possession of the CCTV footage. There doesn't seem any point in involving Jake in all this. And she hasn't told him about Capgras, the syndrome that Bex

242

mentioned, which also seems to have come from Jake.

'I need to see Dr Varma,' she says.

It's the second time they've spoken in five minutes. She rang Rob from inside the pub, but it was too noisy. It's Bex's idea to be seen by Dr Varma. Bex is starting to think Kate's losing it. More so than usual.

'He's gone back to London,' Rob says. 'But he'll be down again at the end—'

'I can't wait that long,' Kate interrupts, her voice shaking.

'OK,' he says quietly, in that caring, unflappable way he spoke to her in the early days, when she really wasn't very well. 'I'll give him a call, see if he can see you sooner.'

'If I come up tomorrow . . .'

'Leave it with me.' Rob pauses. 'It must be tough for all of you down there, after what you found.'

He's right. The police arrived quickly, sealing off the far end of the beach, but not before all of them had seen the body, the contorted expression of surprise on the man's gaping, broken face. She and Bex stayed to give statements, explaining how they found the body. Kate didn't say that she recognised the man. She just told them to contact DI Hart of Wiltshire Police. Hart rang her shortly afterwards, said he would be in touch. He also said that it wasn't Rob's car in Cornwall earlier that morning.

'How is everyone?' Rob asks. 'In the pub?'

'I'm outside.'

'I should be with you. Honestly, I can come back down tonight.'

'Back down' after returning to London yesterday? Or 'back down' after a secret flying visit to the village this morning? She leaves it for now, closes her eyes and leans against the outside wall of the pub, trying not to think about the dead man on the beach. The wall is still warm, retaining the heat of the day. She knew at once that he was Herman, the same person who'd been trying to kill her. What looked like a bullet wound – she was exposed to some graphic crime-scene photos when she was working for the force – had left the lower forehead barely recognisable, but she could still make out the prominent brow.

She knows that she must ask Rob if he was in Cornwall when they spoke earlier. For her own sanity as much as Bex's. Settle the matter once and for all. It might not have been his car that Mark saw, but the jets are still troubling her.

'Today, when we were talking on FaceTime, some military jets flew low over the house,' she begins, determined to hold it together.

'Is Bex with you?' Rob asks. She's not sure if he's even listening to her. 'In the pub?'

'And then, two seconds later, we heard them flying over you,' she continues, ignoring him. Her lip's bleeding she's biting on it so hard. 'The same sound came through the speakers. Which means

244

you were talking to us from somewhere nearby, Rob. In Cornwall.'

'I don't know what you're talking about,' Rob says.

'Please – just tell me if you were down here this morning,' she says, as firmly as she can without raising her voice. Tears are coming now. She looks around, in case anyone is nearby. A man on the far side of the square glances over at her.

'We've been through this, Kate. I was up here. In the flat and then over at the office. I've been in meetings all day. The IPO is next week. Things are a little crazy right now.'

She knows the feeling. She wipes away a tear and closes her eyes. As his words wash over her, she decides that Rob isn't lying. Her relief is immediate, the tension melting away. It's so much easier – for her, for Bex, for Rob – to believe that he's telling the truth. And that maybe she is delusional, suffering from this thing called Capgras.

'So why did we hear the jets twice?' she asks, all conviction gone now. She knows he'll have some technical explanation, a plausible theory that will allow her to sleep tonight.

'There was a lot of delay on the line today,' he says. 'You know what reception's been like down there. Nightmare.'

Rob continues to be uncharacteristically flummoxed by the slow broadband at the house. It's good in the village, but for some reason the speed drops off up on the cliffs. Mobile reception is sketchy at best too. And so far no amount of his money or ideas has been able to sort the problem.

'Maybe you heard the sound again through the speakers,' he continues. 'Did you hear your own voices too?'

Did they? She often hears herself a few seconds after she's spoken. Has she just been imagining everything?

'You coming in?'

It's Bex, standing at the pub door, pint glass in hand. She always drinks pints, has done ever since Kate's known her. Kate nods, mouthing, 'One sec.' Bex notices she's been crying and hesitates. Kate musters a smile and Bex returns inside.

'I still want to come up,' she says to Rob. 'Tomorrow. I feel scared down here. A man tried to kill me and now he's been shot dead. It's not exactly reassuring.'

'I know,' he says. 'I understand.'

She could take the train tonight, the sleeper service, or drive up, but she's happy to wait until the morning. Bex is here, after all. Tomorrow she'll be in London, where she can see Ajay, ask him about Capgras. And she can sort things out with Rob, enjoy being looked after. Pampered. Cherished. It's what she needs right now.

'Let me know when your train arrives at Paddington and I'll meet you,' he says.

She breathes in the warm summer air, feeling so much better already.

'I'm sorry,' she says, grateful for his under-standing, 'for going all funny on you.'

'It's OK. You can go funny on me any time. Sure you don't want me to drive down tonight?'

'It's fine. Bex is here. I love you.'

'I love you too. And, hey, bring your passport.'

'My passport? Why?'

'No promises, but maybe we can finally go to Brittany together.'

She's about to reply when Mark comes out.

'Better get in there quick,' he says. 'Your nice man Rob is buying another round.'

Her head starts to spin. For a moment, she thinks he means that Rob is actually in the pub, but then she remembers. After a beach clean, he usually puts enough money behind the bar for one round, but because of the distressing scene tonight, he's been even more generous than usual.

'That's good of you,' she says to Rob, who is still on the phone. 'Buying everyone more drinks.'

'The least I can do,' he says. 'The whole thing's awful.'

'I better go,' she says. 'Brittany sounds wonderful.'

She hasn't been to France for years, not since she took Jake to Paris for his thirtieth birthday. And Rob is always talking about Brittany, how she must go there.

'Saw you on Facebook this afternoon, by the way,' Rob says. 'Thought you'd—'

'I wasn't on Facebook,' she interrupts. He must have made a mistake.

'You were definitely online.'

'When?' she asks, feeling the tension of earlier returning.

'About an hour ago?'

'It wasn't me.'

She goes in phases with social media. Right now, she's in an Instagram phase. Facebook is too bound up with her old life. She hasn't been on it for months.

'Maybe change your passwords again,' he says. 'You did change them, didn't you?'

Rob had despaired when she told him her passwords were simple, easy-to-remember names and urged her to include lots of symbols and numbers. How was she supposed to remember that?

'Of course,' she lies. 'You think I might have been hacked?'

'Maybe,' he says.

The one other person who knows her password is Jake.

CHAPTER 48

SILAS

There are only a handful of people in the Parade Room at Gablecross police station when Silas walks in. A couple of uniforms, one or two plainclothes colleagues in the far corner where CID sits. He still hasn't got used to the new open-plan hot-desking way of working.

After dropping Strover off at her flat in town, he headed straight here, aware that he now has a homicide case on his hands. He is also aware that he should be at home on a Sunday night, but life has lost its balance in recent months. If he's not working, he's looking for Conor, pacing the less salubrious streets of Swindon, checking in with the UK Missing Persons Bureau, trying in vain to find some common ground with Conor's mother, Mel.

He's already spoken to Kate but couldn't tell her much. The death of the barman who tried to spike her drink and run her over is most likely linked to drug gang rivalry, but Silas has no idea who killed him. At least there is no longer any imminent threat to Kate.

He plugs in his laptop and waits for it to fire

up. His boss won't be happy that he went down to Cornwall in his own time to investigate a suspect. Even less happy that the suspect is now a murder victim. Silas will liaise closely with Devon and Cornwall, but out-of-area cases are always messy, the sharing of resources never straightforward. Even the much-trumpeted Tri-Force Alliance between Somerset and Avon, Gloucestershire and Wiltshire has crashed and burnt.

He's about to check his emails when his phone rings.

'DI Hart,' he says, sitting back.

The call is from a detective in Nottingham. Silas has spoken to him once before, a few months back, when the detective was setting up a pilot super-recogniser scheme similar to the Swindon unit. He'd wanted some advice on recruitment and protocols.

'How's it all going?' Hart asks, expecting a routine inquiry. A number of other regional forces have established super-recogniser units, disillusioned with the failure rate of facial-recognition software, and most have sought Silas's advice.

'I wish you'd asked me that three days ago,' the officer says. 'Our super-recogniser results have been incredible, on a par with DNA and fingerprints.'

'So what's happened?' Silas asks.

He expects the detective to say that his unit's been closed down, run out of town by some new facial-recognition software contract, but the answer stuns him.

'Our main recogniser, an extraordinary bloke, has just gone AWOL, dropped off the grid completely.'

'Civilian?' Silas asks, reaching for a pen and paper.

'Community support officer. Been with us for years, always been a good spotter.'

'Family?'

'They're distraught. Wife says it's totally out of character. He's a man of routine. We're all worried sick.'

Silas stands up, walks over to the window and looks out onto the deserted car park. Not many people in tonight. They're all off on holiday, enjoying the summer, as he should be.

'Has he been involved in any serious-crime cases recently?' he asks.

'Nothing major. Indecent exposure, a few assaults, shoplifting. Why?'

Silas thinks back to Kate's track record. Should he have limited her work to identifying petty criminals? There was a lot of pressure at the time to focus on modern-slavery and organised-crime gangs. 'It's just that we've had an issue with one of our old super recognisers,' he says.

'What sort of issue?'

It's well known amongst regional police forces that Swindon's super-recogniser unit was unceremoniously wound up. Just like the Met's unit was closed, even though the force still uses super recognisers. But no one knows about Kate and the attempts on her life.

'Our best recogniser, a civilian, was injured in a car accident,' Silas says. 'The unit was shut down shortly afterwards, as you know. It now seems that it might not have been an accident. She might have been deliberately targeted – by one of the gangs she helped to convict.'

'Is that recent?' the officer asks, surprised.

'We've only found out today. Nothing confirmed, but it looks that way. Did your PCSO do much publicity? Media interviews?'

'We've kept him out of the limelight – our secret weapon.'

Silas wishes he'd done the same with Kate, not exposed her to so much media attention. It was a way of taunting his boss as much as anything. Petty.

'We'll double-check the list of recent convictions,' the detective says. 'Ones that he can claim responsibility for. I can't see anyone taking it out on him though.'

That's what Silas thought about Kate. And look what happened to her. 'Let me know if he turns up,' he says. 'How good is he?'

'How good? He's a freak. More than a hundred IDs in the past year. Don't know about you, but I've been twenty years in the force and can count the number of people I've identified on one hand.'

Silas's own record is not much better. Maybe two hands. 'And he's never disappeared before?' he asks.

'Never. Loves his job, his family. Not like him at all.'

CHAPTER 49

JAKE

It's been an hour since Jake ended his online chat with Kirby and he is still struggling to process what Rob's old colleague told him. He's been down to check on the boat again, harvesting some wild garlic from the towpath on the way back, and he is now in Bex's kitchen, rustling up something to eat. Cooking has always been his way of relieving stress.

He finds a wooden chopping board and starts to slice some shallots he found in a cupboard, thinking again about what Kirby said. He had to delete the message thread, which means he's got nothing to read through again, no evidence that any of their chat actually happened. It all seems too unreal, the beach party in Thailand far away in time and place.

Should he ring Kate? Confess that he logged into her Facebook account and conducted a conversation with an old friend of her new man? He can't. She'd murder him. On the other hand, she might welcome the information, given her current obsession with doubles.

His phone rings before he can decide whether

to call her. It's Kate. *Fuck.* She must know already about Facebook. Rob saw Kate online and presumably mentioned it to her. He lets it ring out. And then she rings again. She always used to do that, knew when he was ignoring her calls. If he doesn't answer it now, he knows she'll keep ringing until he does.

'Kate?' he says tentatively.

'Have you been logging into my Facebook account?' She's angry, fuming, like she was the night of her accident.

'No,' Jake says, protesting. He should have switched off his phone. 'What's happened? Is everything OK?'

'You're lying.'

How come Kate and Bex always know?

'OK, so I logged into your account by accident. I thought I was logging into mine.'

'You're still lying.'

And she's still angry.

There's silence as she waits for him to come clean.

'Jake?' she asks, her voice marginally less hostile.

'I'm here.'

He closes his eyes, knowing there's worse to come before the storm blows itself out. He picks up a handful of mushrooms and begins to slice them.

'Why did you log into my account?' she asks.

There's no way out. 'I didn't read any of your private messages,' he says.

'Oh, that's OK, then.' She's furious again. 'What do you expect me to say, Jake? I know you hacked into my Facebook account, but that's alright because you didn't read any of my messages? Jesus, and you wonder why I wanted out.'

Neither of them speaks for a while, all the years of their relationship stewing in the exhausted silence. Maybe it really was best that they split up. He feels empty. There's nothing left to say or give. He starts to chop the wild garlic.

'What are you doing?' she asks quietly.

'Cooking.' He pauses. 'Wild garlic carbonara.' It was one of her favourite dishes.

'Something awful happened down on the beach tonight,' she says in a low voice, breaking the silence. He can sense she's close to tears.

'Tell me. What was it?'

She explains about the dead barman.

'And he'd been shot in the head?'

He feels so sorry for Kate. She moved to Cornwall to get away from that world, her police work. It must have been awful for her. It might also explain her anger. She's clearly still in shock.

'Looked like it,' she says. 'DI Hart thinks it's drug-related.'

That would make sense if it was the Bluebell barman. 'I'm sorry it was you who found him,' he says.

'Actually it was Stretch, my dog. Poor little sausage. At least Bex was with me.'

Jake has yet to meet Stretch.

'I spoke to Bex earlier today,' he says, changing the subject. 'She said you're worried about Rob. That he has a bit of a thing about the double he met in Thailand.'

'Bex was talking out of turn,' she says. 'She also thinks I'm delusional.'

'She's concerned for you. We all are.'

Bex must have mentioned Capgras to her. Jake scrapes the ingredients together on the wooden board with a knife.

'That's why I logged into your Facebook account,' he continues.

'How do you mean?'

'I wanted to see if anyone in Rob's past knew what actually happened in Thailand, that's all.' He braces himself for her reaction. 'So I contacted one of his friends.'

'Contacted? How?'

He tosses the shallots and garlic and mushrooms into the pan, standing back as they fry in the spitting oil.

'By pretending to be you.'

He screws his eyes tight shut as he waits for the eruption.

'Me? Fuck you, Jake. Seriously, fuck you. Who? Who did you contact? I can't believe you did that.'

Jake shakes the pan around until her anger subsides. And then he relates everything that Kirby told him, as much as he can remember about the double called Gil at the party in Thailand. Perhaps he shouldn't have deleted the chat, then she could have read it for herself.

'I thought it might help,' he adds. 'I'm sorry. It was totally out of order, completely wrong of me, I know.'

It's a while before Kate speaks, and when she does, she's calmer, more composed. 'I knew it was more serious than Rob was letting on. But he doesn't . . .' She pauses, falls quiet.

Jake breathes a sigh of relief. She's no longer shouting. He finds some pasta in a cupboard, puts it on to boil. They always talked, eventually, if there was a problem, sorting things through in their own muddled way. Except for the time that she saw him on the CCTV cameras with another woman. They've never talked about that.

'Rob doesn't what?' he prompts, not sure if he wants to know the answer.

'He doesn't burden me with stuff,' Kate says in a small voice. 'Makes it hard to understand what's going on with him.'

She hesitates again. Jake focuses on the pan.

'Jake?' Kate asks quietly.

'I'm still here.'

'Do you think Rob might . . . might have been replaced by him? Gil? The man in Thailand?'

'No, Kate, I don't.' Her voice frightens him. She doesn't sound herself. He pauses, takes a deep breath. 'Did Bex mention anything about this condition called Capgras? It's a—'

'She told me,' Kate says, interrupting him.

Silence. No one likes to be told they might be delusional.

'So what do you think?' he asks.

'I'm talking to Dr Varma about it.'

'Who?'

'He's a neuropsychiatrist, one of the best in the country. Rob pays.'

Of course he does. Jake doesn't want to be reminded of Rob's wealth, or how he, Jake, was singularly unable to provide for Kate.

'That's good of him.' The words sound more sarcastic than he meant. He remembers Bex mentioning something about a shrink.

'I wish I could explain to you what it's like,' Kate says. 'One moment he looks familiar, the Rob I know and love, the next he's a total stranger.' It's her turn to pause now. 'I'd be so bloody relieved if it is Capgras, Jake. At least I could stop thinking I'm going nuts.'

Her voice cracks. Jake wishes he were with her now, there to comfort her. In truth, she always was a little bit nuts. Impulsive. Like the day gay marriage was legalised and she painted the outside of the boat in rainbow colours. Her hair has been most colours of the rainbow too, since he's known her, although she settled on a conservative chestnut when she worked for the police. He wonders what colour it is now.

'Talk to this guy Dr Varma,' he says. 'When are you seeing him?'

'Tomorrow. I'm coming up to London. On the train.'

He's not aware of her having come up-country since her move to Cornwall, but what does he know? They live separate lives now.

'Don't forget to wave,' he says. The Penzance to Paddington line runs through the village, parallel with the canal.

'Sure.'

They are both silent, neither of them hanging up.

'Did you really not read any of my messages?' she eventually asks. 'To Rob?'

'No.'

'Thank you.'

MONDAY

CHAPTER 50

KATE

Kate is sitting on the train from Cornwall to London, watching the Wiltshire countryside slide by. Bex and Stretch dropped her off at Truro station this morning, later than she planned. She and Bex both overslept, having stayed up late to talk about what they'd seen on the beach. Bex is going to hang out at the house for a few days, drive around in the Tesla with Stretch.

The train will soon be passing through Kate's old village, where she shared so much of her life with Jake, and she should be able to see their boat – what's left of the burnt-out hulk. She's not sure if she wants to.

She's still cross with Jake for logging into her Facebook account, but it was good to talk to him last night about Capgras. And to hear about the story that Kirby told him online – told *her*; she must remember that. Rob's encounter with Gil in Thailand fits with what Rob told her – his fear of being found by his double. But Jake's right, it doesn't explain her own suspicions whenever she sees Rob face to face, that he's been replaced by

263

Gil. That just doesn't make any sense, on so many levels. Take the piece of beach glass she and Rob found. How would Gil, a man Rob met nine years ago, be aware of that? He certainly wouldn't know to give it to her as a necklace. It's ridiculous. She must be suffering from Capgras syndrome. Dr Varma will know. Rob has arranged for her to see him later today.

Her phone rings.

'You alright?'

It's Bex, calling her for the third time since they said goodbye at Truro.

'Just coming up to the village,' Kate says, her face pressed against the carriage glass.

'Give it a wave from me,' Bex says, echoing what Jake said yesterday. 'I think I've been caught speeding – sorry.'

'Seriously?'

Rob won't be happy. When Kate spoke to him earlier, he agreed to put Bex on the Tesla insurance as long as she watched her speed.

'Stretch was on my lap so he can take the points,' Bex continues.

She's joking. Of course she is. Kate worries that she lost her sense of humour too after the crash.

'Goes like a rocket though, doesn't it?' Bex says. 'And it can drive itself, does the parking for you, even blow-dries me hair.'

They chat some more, Bex's usual joshing cut through with a new note of concern. The sight of a dead man has left them both frightened. Kate knows Bex is worried about her going up to London on her own. She fell very quiet after Kate told her about Kirby and Thailand – Kate had expected her to be outraged by Jake's behaviour – and she gave Kate an extra-long hug on the platform.

Kate's train starts to slow as it approaches the village. The service from Cornwall to London rarely calls here, but she'd had to take a stopping service after oversleeping. As they draw near to the platform, she catches a brief glimpse through a row of poplar trees of the wreck of their old boat, semi-submerged in the canal, the adjoining towpath blackened by the fire and ringed off with cones and police tape. The sight of it takes her breath away. The boat looks so forlorn, utterly broken. And then she sees a figure walking towards her. It's Jake, hunched shoulders, defeated gait.

She grabs her bag from the overhead luggage rail and finds herself standing at the door, waiting impatiently for it to open. One other passenger at the far end of her carriage is preparing to get off and she doesn't recognise the few people gathered on the platform. There's a delay with the door and she begins to wonder if she misheard the announcement. Before she knows it, she's slapping at the glass and the door slides open, fresh air is on her face and she's running down the platform towards the canal.

And then she stops. This is crazy. What is she doing? Jake, the narrowboat, this village – it's the old her, the life that she left behind. She needs to keep moving forward, to London. To Rob. The only other person to get off the train walks past. The woman in her carriage. Big eyebrows, like Cara Delevingne's. She must think Kate's a madwoman. The doors are still open. Kate glances up and down the platform, spots the guard at the far end, and starts to move back towards the train.

The guard shouts at her. 'Stand away!'

The doors close. And she's still on the platform.

She stands there in a daze, watching distorted reflections of herself as the shiny train pulls out without her and continues on its journey. She knows she hesitated, could have jumped back on board. When the train has gone, she's alone at the station, the sun beating down on her. Even the birds are too hot to sing. It feels like yesterday she was here, and yet it could also be an eternity ago.

She's about to turn when a movement in the doorway of the shelter on the opposite platform catches her eye. There are no windows. It's just a basic wooden hut, popular with teenagers who gather there at night to drink cans of cider. She remembers the graffiti and stale smell of urine.

She looks across the tracks again, into the hut's dark interior, and sees someone sitting on a metal bench in the shadows. It's hard to make out his face in the poor light, and he's wearing a beanie, pulled down hard. But she can glimpse enough to know that she has seen him before – staring out from a missing person poster.

CHAPTER 51

SILAS

The boss is furious with Silas, much as he expected, demanding to know why he should authorise him to spend time on a murder investigation two hundred miles away in Cornwall.

'Even when you told him about a possible link to our modern slavery investigation?' Strover asks.

Silas shakes his head. They're sitting in the canteen at Gablecross, where he is debriefing Strover about a twenty-minute roasting from his boss. He called Silas in after his email request late last night to assist Devon and Cornwall with a murder inquiry.

'Told me to leave it to Major Crime,' Silas says, nursing a plastic cup of cold coffee. 'Reckons the man was in Cornwall trying to sell drugs to the locals. Extend the Swindon county lines network.'

'So who does he think killed him?' Strover asks.

'Looks like a rival north London network supplying drugs into Truro from Tottenham. Apparently the bloke had been under surveillance in Swindon for several weeks – until he gave the Proactive Team the slip and headed west.'

268

'What about Kate?' Strover asks. 'Her accident? Nearly drowning?'

'The boss is not buying any of it. Too circumstantial.'

'The man tried to bloody run us over,' Strover protests. 'Did you show him the footage from the pub?' she asks, glancing around the canteen.

'Not interested.' Silas takes another sip of coffee. 'It's back to the nail bars for us.'

He doesn't even bother to smile. It's not funny. For six wonderful months after Silas cracked his last case, he basked in his boss's praise. Couldn't put a foot wrong. But then normal service resumed. Silas was a good detective, but he must learn to be more of a team player. Play the corporate game. Which means not meddling in another force's business. Liaise, by all means, but don't try to run the show.

In half an hour, Silas will be interviewing some poor woman from Latvia who thought she was coming to the UK for a new life and now finds herself doing acrylic overlays for eighteen hours a day. He glances around the canteen. A group of uniforms has lined up and are joking with the woman behind the food counter. He misses his own days in Response in the Met.

'Last night I looked back at some of the interviews Kate gave to the media,' Strover says. 'Just to see what she actually said.'

'And?'

There's no need for Strover to feel guilty too. It was his idea to push Kate into the spotlight. Silas waits for her to speak, but she's not confident enough to openly criticise her boss.

'It was a mistake,' he reminds her. 'My mistake.'

'The OCG would have found Kate eventually, if they were committed to harming her,' Strover says. 'With or without publicity.'

'You think so?'

Neither of them seems convinced.

'I came across something else, too, when I was searching to see if any other super recognisers had given interviews,' Strover continues.

'The Met unit did – told anyone who would listen about their success at the London riots,' Silas says.

One poxy criminal was identified by recognition software in the aftermath of the 2011 disturbances, even though the Met had gathered 200,000 hours of CCTV footage. When the footage was passed over to the spotters, a single super recogniser made 190 IDs. Interestingly, the Met gave no interviews when the unit identified the two Russian GRU officers who had travelled to Salisbury to poison Sergei Skripal with the nerve agent novichok.

'And the Australians,' says Strover. 'And the Germans. They've all been talking about their successes.'

'You were busy last night.'

'Couldn't sleep.'

Strover retrieves a sheet of paper from her jacket pocket. A printout of an article.

'Not sure it's relevant now, but I thought you might want to see this,' she says.

Silas takes it and starts to read. The article is about an Irish super-recogniser unit that was set up in Dublin at the same time as Wiltshire's. But it's the photo staring back at him that has his attention.

'She's still missing,' Strover says, but Silas is not listening. 'Their star recogniser, two years younger than Kate. Disappeared a month ago.'

Silas tears through the words. The female officer vanished late one night on her drive back from work. As with Kate, she possessed exceptional powers of facial recognition and was responsible for the arrest of a number of petty criminals. Nothing major, apart from one suspect who was caught after she'd spotted him at a football match at the Aviva Stadium in Dublin. He was subsequently charged with murder.

'You need to widen your search,' Silas says, a new urgency in his voice. 'See if any other super recognisers have disappeared. Dublin's not alone.'

He tells her about the call last night from the detective in Nottingham. She's shocked, but her eyes light up. Two small dots have been joined. It's the bit of his job that Silas likes the most, watching the bigger picture emerge.

'Search the UK first, then Europe,' he continues.

'Check with Europol too – see if they're aware of any missing recognisers.'

As far as Silas can tell, most forces in Europe either have their own units already up and running or are in the process of establishing them. No surprise, given the continuing fallibility of facial-recognition software. In the past two weeks alone, colleagues from two cities in Germany have been in touch, asking Silas for advice.

He knows that there might not be any connection between the Dublin and Nottingham mispers and Kate. Each one might have been targeted independently by aggrieved local criminals. But the fact that all three are super recognisers – and the best performers in their unit – is hard to ignore. And Silas can't shake off the feeling that the disappearances could be more coordinated, part of a pattern. A bigger picture.

'Are you going to tell the boss?' Strover asks.

'Not yet. Ask your friend to search the Dark Web too. There might be some chatter around. And get onto forensics about that pub CCTV footage. We still don't know who got hold of it or how. Or why they sent it to Jake.'

CHAPTER 52

KATE

'No, I can't be certain,' Kate says, walking down from the station towards the canal. 'But it looked like him. Same eyes.'

It's odd talking to DI Hart again about a 'spot' in the field. It used to part of her daily work. Only this time it's personal, a possible sighting of Conor, Hart's missing son. And if she's right, it's further evidence that her powers of recognition are returning. Technically it was also a 'dirty spot' – partial view, bad light. The hardest type.

'And he was on the westbound platform, you say?' Hart says.

'In the waiting room on the opposite side from me – I was going to London.'

She's already told him that she's stopped off at the village because she needs to talk to Jake. He struggled to hide his surprise, didn't buy into her casual tone, her acting as if the whole thing was planned. She's surprised too.

'Did he look depressed?' Hart asks. 'Suicidal?'

Oh God, it never crossed her mind. She hadn't

realised Conor was in such a bad way. 'I couldn't see,' she says. 'I'm sorry. He wasn't near the edge or anything like that.'

'I'll take a look at the station cameras.'

'Any news on the body?' she asks.

'Not yet. I'll keep you posted.'

He pauses. She thought he might have more answers by now, an official explanation for the death of the man in Cornwall.

'I'm sorry it was you who found him,' he adds.

Her too. She hangs up, pushing away an image of the dead man's brutalised face, and walks on down the towpath, worried that she's wasting Hart's time. Should she go back, check that the man at the station is OK? If it was his son, he might have moved on already, although she remembers teenagers used to hang around the shelter all day, not going anywhere.

She spots the boat before she sees Jake, listing to one side and partially submerged. It was their home for twelve years and now it's officially a wreck. Spent. All she saw from the train window was a glimpse through the trees. Up close the sight is even more shocking. Confirmation, as if it were needed, that what Jake and she had together is over.

And then she sees Jake, behind the towpath, sitting on the grass on his own, leaning back on his arms, tree-trunk legs stretched out before him.

A fallen giant. He is staring at the boat and is yet to see her. For a moment she stands still, thinks about walking quietly away, catching the next train to London, but she's come this far now and they should talk.

CHAPTER 53

SILAS

Silas looks around the empty platform. It took him a lot less time than it should have done to get here, his single blue light allowing him to skip plenty of red ones as he imagined Conor leaping in front of a high-speed train. He dropped everything after failing to access the security cameras on the station platform. All of them were down.

He lights up a cigarette, the first he's had in a while, and walks back to double-check on the shelter. If Conor has been here, there's no sign of him. It's deserted apart from some old cans in the corner. Silas used to know when Conor had returned in the night to sleep in their shed at the bottom of the garden. He could smell the weed in the woodwork. Perhaps he has taken a train west or retreated into the countryside. Silas looks up at the woods on the hill, wondering if he's out there somewhere.

He's about to call Kate on his mobile, ask her if she's still in the village, when Strover rings.

'Any luck?' she says.

It's good of her to check, but he knows she hasn't called about his missing son.

276

'What have you found?' he asks.

'You might need to talk to the boss again.'

Strover gives him the details, far worse than he feared. Three more super-recogniser units whose main players have disappeared. One in Madrid four months ago, another last month in Amsterdam. And a third in Hamburg two weeks ago. No publicity, all three forces keen to keep their units out of the limelight. No one yet to make the link.

'Civilians or cops?' he asks.

'Civilians.'

Strover explains how their families have been appealing for information, but so far there's been no specific mention of their police work or the units – no suggestion that their disappearance has anything to do with their job. One reason why they haven't come onto anyone's radar before.

He thanks Strover for the call and heads back to his car. More dots. The disappearance of so many key super recognisers is sounding more coordinated by the minute. There's no time to drop in on Kate now.

CHAPTER 54

KATE

Jake doesn't get up. He just smiles and watches as Kate approaches and sits down beside him on the grass in silence, both of them staring at the sunken boat. The sight of it is suddenly overwhelming. This was their home. She turns from Jake, wiping away a tear. The towpath is empty and no boats are moored nearby. People are keeping their distance, out of respect or maybe something else. The fear of fire is contagious.

'I saw it from the train,' she says eventually. 'And then we stopped and I—'

'It's good of you to drop by,' Jake says, interrupting her.

'I'm so sorry, Jake.'

'I've managed to save some of your stuff—'

'I was on my way up to London, to see Rob,' she says. 'I need to call him.'

There's no reason to introduce Rob so abruptly, but she's suddenly racked with guilt. She hasn't told Rob she's not on the train. He was going to meet her at Paddington.

'Are you OK?' Jake asks, still looking ahead at the boat. 'About seeing him?'

'Why wouldn't I be?' she says, turning to Jake for the first time.

Jake doesn't answer. No need. He knows her too well, her too-quick reply. She is nervous about the encounter with Rob. Meeting him face to face, on a crowded platform at Paddington station. Maybe that's why she jumped off the train. A part of her believes – hopes – that he will seem his old self and take her in his arms. That everything that's happened in the past two days can be forgotten as if it were a bad dream. But she can't help worrying. What if her head tells her he's his double? She's not sure she can cope with that. Not yet. She will remind herself that she probably has Capgras, and that it's likely to be temporary. But it won't be easy.

'Want some tea?' Jake asks.

She manages a smile. Jake used to believe everything between them could be sorted with a mug of tea. And for many years it could be, until things deteriorated too much.

'Back at Bex's?' he adds.

Ten minutes later, she's sitting in Bex's kitchen, a stray cat at her feet, waiting for Jake to come through from the other room. It's strange seeing him in Bex's home. She used to spend hours here, with Bex, complaining about him and their failing relationship.

On the walk up from the canal she told him that she'd seen someone who might be DI Hart's missing son, but she didn't go into details. They also talked about the dead man in Cornwall and who might have killed him. He seems to agree with DI Hart that it's drug-related, internecine rivalry. She'd forgotten that gang crime used to be his journalism beat, before he chucked it all in to write books.

'I rinsed it as best I could, but it'll need a proper wash,' Jake says, coming back into the kitchen with an old orange dress of hers. He used to like her wearing it; one reason she left it behind.

'It stinks of diesel.' She sniffs the material. The smell takes her back. All her clothes used to smell. 'Thank you – for rescuing it.'

'You need to ring Rob,' Jake says, trying to sound casual as he pours the tea. 'Tell him you're running late.'

'I will.' She casts an eye over Jake as he fetches the milk from the fridge. He's lost weight and his hair is neat at the sides, like it was when they first met. Even his clothes are smarter than she remembers. Making an effort but not for her. He didn't know she was coming. She hopes there's someone new in his life.

'You liked him, when you met at the hospital,' she says. 'The real Rob.'

'"Like" might be putting it a bit strongly.' He sits down opposite her.

His beard's trim too. She's pleased for him. Only his eyes look tired. Maybe some good will come out of the boat fire, force him into new things, a better life. She's not sure he's ever fully accepted that their relationship is over.

'Rob's a decent man,' she says, for her own benefit as much as his. 'Kind and generous.'

Jake bends down to stroke the cat. He's kind and generous too, but it wasn't enough in the end.

'I just don't know what's happened to that person,' she adds. 'Where he's gone.'

She's determined not to cry, particularly in front of Jake.

'It's pretty hard to impersonate someone, you know,' he says, straightening up and resting his hands on hers on the table between them. 'You can't just take over another person's life, assume their identity and carry on as if nothing's happened. It's not that easy. Almost impossible, unless perhaps you're an identical twin. And he hasn't got one of those, has he.'

She shakes her head and withdraws her hands, wondering why she didn't flinch when he first took them.

'Dr Varma will know more,' Jake says. 'I'm no expert, but what you're experiencing sounds remarkably like Capgras. This whole thing with the doubles – it must all be in your head. Must be.'

She turns away. It's the first echo she's heard of their old relationship. Jake used to think she imagined a lot of things, their lack of money, the leaks in the boat windows, her unhappiness. Maybe he thought she'd imagined his affair too, the one she saw with her own eyes on the cameras.

'And this lookalike who met Rob on a beach in Thailand nine years ago – is he in my head too? You tell me – you're the one Kirby poured his heart out to.'

She's suddenly angry, struggling to keep her voice down. One false step and they seem to slip so easily into their bad old ways.

'I'm just saying there's likely to be a simple explanation for all this, that's all.'

Jake was never one to raise his voice in return, always preferring to avoid conflict. It was Kate who did all the shouting.

'I shouldn't have come here,' she says. Too many memories are flooding back and not all of them are great.

'Why did you get off the train?' he asks, glancing up at her.

They look at each other in silence. And then his eye is caught by something in the other room.

'What is it?' she asks, watching him walk through to check on Bex's computer.

'It's probably nothing,' he says, coming back into the kitchen and closing the door behind him. 'The computer screen just came on, that's all.'

But she can tell he's worried.

'Will you walk me back to the station?' she asks.

It's time she went to see Rob.

CHAPTER 55

SILAS

I t's as Silas is driving away from the station that he sees Kate and Jake strolling through the village, past the vegan café, now closed and boarded up. He slows beside them, opening his window. They made a good couple. Silas is sad that their relationship ended how it did. Guilty too.

'I was going to call you, but I've got to head back to Swindon,' he says to Kate. Jake looks a little sheepish standing beside her. The last time Silas spoke to him, it was about his hastily arranged boat insurance.

'Did you see him?' Kate asks.

'No luck.' Silas pauses. 'Thanks for calling it in though. Like old times, eh?'

Kate turns away. Silas regrets the comment at once, wishes Strover were there to keep him in check. She's going to ring Kate later, tell her about the matches for Rob that they've found around the world.

'Want us to put some of those up in the village?' Kate asks, nodding at a pile of laminated missing person posters on the passenger seat. Silas has already tied one onto the metal railings down at the station.

'Would you?' he says. 'I'm out of time.'

'Sure.' Kate takes a couple and passes one to Jake.

'Maybe in the pub? Post office?' Silas suggests, but Jake is still staring at the image of Conor.

'I've seen him,' Jake says. 'In the village yesterday. Down by the water meadow.'

'Really?' Silas glances at Kate. Her own sighting suddenly seems more credible.

Jake looks at Silas, as if he's contemplating whether to tell him something. 'By the crossing,' he says. 'Waiting for a train.'

'And what happened?' Silas can hardly bear to hear the answer.

'The train came and I pulled him out the way.' Jake says the words quietly, no suggestion of heroics on his part.

'You didn't tell me any of this,' Kate says, turning to Jake.

Jake shrugs. 'We went for a walk afterwards, up in the woods. I left him there.' He pauses, studying the photo again. 'Is this really your son?'

Silas nods.

'We need to talk.'

CHAPTER 56

KATE

'I'm so sorry about the boat,' Kate says to Jake as the train draws up at the platform. They haven't discussed where he might live. They haven't talked about a lot of things.

'Thanks for coming,' he says, avoiding eye contact.

'Thanks for the dress,' she says.

She's folded it up in a separate plastic bag, to stop the smell of diesel from infecting her other clothes.

'You'll feel better once you've seen Dr Varma,' he says, looking at her.

'Rob first,' she says, trying to sound upbeat.

She rang Rob after they met DI Hart in the high street, told him that she'd changed onto the wrong train at Exeter and would now be arriving an hour later. That suited Rob better, he said, as, predictably, he was running behind with work.

'It'll be fine,' Jake says. 'And that beach-bum Gil in Thailand? I bet he looks nothing like Rob these days.'

Jake is always full of optimism. It's what did for

285

them in the end, blinded him to the reality of their circumstances.

'Wait, there's something else I saved from the boat,' he says as she boards the train. In his big hand is a tiny paintbrush, a kolinsky. It was a present from him when she was struggling with a difficult portrait. At the time she knew they couldn't afford it and she'd been cross with him.

'I hope you're painting again,' he says.

'I am.' She takes the brush as the door closes and mouths the words, 'Thank you.'

But Jake is distracted, looking down the platform. She presses the button and the doors open again.

'What is it?' she asks, peering out of the door.

'Ah, just some late-runner cutting it fine,' he says.

'You'd know all about that.'

Jake always used to leave it until the last minute when he was a commuter, jogging down the towpath, waving at the train driver to wait for him.

They smile at each other and the doors close.

CHAPTER 57

SILAS

'He was standing over there, by the kissing gate,' Jake says, pointing across the water meadow towards the railway track.

Silas takes in the scene, trying to imagine what was in Conor's head as he waited for the train to come. Was he full of anger towards Silas? Maybe even guilt? Silas is flattering himself. If Conor's drug-soaked brain was thinking of anyone other than himself, it would have been his mum. They were always close. He will have to tell her that their only son nearly took his own life. And he will be blamed.

'Thanks,' Silas says. 'You know, for saving him.'

'I don't think he was that committed, to be honest,' Jake says. 'We chatted about it afterwards. I'm no expert, but I'm guessing it was a cry for help.'

And Jake answered it. Silas was planning to head back to Gablecross to talk with Strover about the missing super recognisers she's discovered, but he's decided to stay in the village. He waited around while Jake saw Kate off on her train and the two of them then headed out here.

'What else did you talk about?' Silas says as they cross the water meadow towards the railway. Jake suggested earlier that there was something Silas needed to know.

'It's not my business, but Conor, he . . . He didn't look too well.'

'He's had some issues,' Silas says. 'Drug-related.'

It started with skunk at university, which led to psychosis, dropping out, homelessness and heroin.

'As I say, this really isn't my business, but I think he might be dealing in drugs too,' Jake continues. 'Might have got himself involved in county lines.'

The sun is warm on their backs as they reach the railway line, but Jake's words chill Silas to the bone. The suggestion is sickeningly plausible. 'What makes you think that?' he asks.

'I took a punt, asked him about the Bluebell, which you'd told me was a drugs pub.'

'Did he know it?' Silas asks.

'He said he didn't, but I think he was lying.'

'How come?' Silas asks, but he isn't surprised. Lying has become second nature to Conor.

'Because I also asked him if he'd "gone cunch". He didn't deny it, just told me he had no choice and that he operated out of Swindon. I'm guessing the Bluebell is part of the same set-up. It would make sense.'

They have reached the kissing gate where Conor contemplated killing himself twenty-four hours earlier. Silas rests his hands on the curved metal bar and closes his eyes. This is about as bad as it could be. If Conor has got involved in a county lines network, he'll soon be arrested, and Silas's own shame will be complete. His career could be over too.

'Why here?' Silas asks, looking across the water meadow back towards the village. 'In this village?'

'That's the other thing I wanted to talk to you about.'

Silas turns to face Jake. He doesn't want to look at the track any more, imagine what could have happened here. He's seen the results before.

'I can't be certain,' Jake says, hesitating, 'but I think he might have been the one who torched my boat.'

The two men stare at each other. Silas doesn't know whether to laugh or cry. He senses at once that it's true. Jake asks some awkward questions at the Bluebell and that night his boat is set on fire. The county lines ringleaders would use someone else to do their dirty work, someone expendable like Conor.

'Oh Christ,' Silas says. 'I'm so sorry.'

'Not your fault,' Jake says, trying to make light of it.

But Silas knows he is to blame, in more ways than Jake will ever understand. He was close to his son when Conor was a young boy, a toddler on the beach, playing in the park. It was all so easy back then. Build a sandcastle. Fly a kite.

Kick a ball. *Look at that new man, what a great dad he is. So in touch!* The teenage years were the problem: as Silas's working day got longer, Conor became more withdrawn. They seemed to lose touch with each other, drift apart. No common ground or shared interests.

'It's just a hunch,' Jake says. 'And maybe I'm wrong. But I've never seen him around here before. And then he's hanging about the next day, lighting his cigarette with a match. Most people have lighters now, and, well, I heard a match being struck just before the boat caught fire.'

'The investigation's ongoing,' Silas says. 'If Conor's involved, he'll be brought in, of course.'

He doesn't know why he's saying all this. It's for his own benefit as much as Jake's. The reality is that the investigation is going nowhere. No fingerprints on the abandoned jerrycan. No witnesses. More serious crimes to deal with. And Jake's hunch is hardly compelling evidence. As flimsy as matchwood.

Silas is about to turn and walk back towards the canal when his phone rings. The mobile number is not familiar. For a moment he considers letting it go to voicemail, but something makes him answer it.

'DI Hart,' he says.

Silence, but Silas knows someone's there, with something to tell him. He's had calls like this before, can hear the breathing. Informants, witnesses, whistleblowers. You just have to wait until they're ready. He gestures at Jake, who has stopped up ahead.

'Can I help?' Silas asks, turning away.

More breathing, this time familiar. Silas's stomach tightens. He looks up at the hills beyond the canal. And then he hears his voice.

'Dad?'

CHAPTER 58

KATE

Rob isn't there when Kate arrives at Paddington. He rang, full of apologies, shortly after her train left the village. More meetings, not enough time. If she'd been on the earlier train, he could have met her, but now that she's more than an hour late, it's knocked things back and . . . She told him not to worry. She didn't say how relieved she was.

He's sent a car with a driver though and wants her to make herself at home in his flat in Shoreditch until he gets back. She's intrigued finally to see the place for herself. They've often talked about her coming to stay in London, but she's never felt strong enough for city life. Not until today.

She heads across the concourse at Paddington and finds the car waiting for her on Praed Street. London seems full of people with not enough time, the press of urban life etched on sunless faces. The stress in the air is almost palpable, like a taste at the back of the mouth. Or perhaps it's just the pollution. She also feels alive here, the heady mix of cultures far removed from her safe little routine in Cornwall. At least it used to be safe, until someone tried to kill her and a dead body washed up on the beach below their house. That all seems so surreal now, a different world.

Her driver – stocky, faint eastern European accent, gimlet eyes – instantly makes her think of the Russian president, Vladimir Putin. Except that Putin doesn't have a scar on the side of his shaven head. He takes her bag and opens the car's rear door. She doesn't feel comfortable being looked after like this, but his eyes glint as she moves to get in. And then she remembers the orange dress. She looks around and spots a bin across the street.

'One sec,' she says to Putin.

She walks over to the bin with the bag. She knows she should ditch the dress, but she can't bring herself to do it. Damn Jake. Damn his sentimentality. Her brief stop in the village has affected her more than she expected. It was good to be back. Good to see Jake. For months after the accident, every memory of the place – of the narrowboat, of Jake – was tainted by the image of him kissing another woman on the CCTV. But today has changed things. They talked without sniping at each other. Maybe they can be friends after all.

As she walks back across the street with the bag, she sees someone familiar. Cara. The woman who got off the train with her in the village. She struggles not to stare. What's she doing here? It's definitely her. Big eyebrows. She's waiting for a bus on Praed Street, glancing briefly in Kate's direction, but there's something odd about her manner.

Kate turns away, trying not to panic, and looks back at her again. Is she a tail? Kate saw it in her old job, when colleagues were pursuing suspects in crowds. The telltale glance. Why would Cara be following her? She must have got back on the same train as her in the village. The late runner. Kate was distracted, chatting with Jake.

Half an hour later, Putin pulls up outside a converted factory on Nile Street, between Hoxton and Shoreditch. Rob told her about its history once, when he was facetiming from his bedroom. He was shy about showing her the rest of the flat, embarrassed by its size. A former printworks, it was given the Manhattan loft treatment in the late 1990s and transformed into fashionable warehouse apartments. His is the penthouse, of course.

She takes her bags and reassures Putin that she's fine as she stands outside the main entrance. She tries the door but it doesn't open. Putin points to the camera above the patchwork of buzzers.

'Smile and it will recognise your face,' he says.

She presses the number for the penthouse and waits. A moment later, the door swings open and she's in the foyer, waving goodbye to Putin. How does the camera recognise her if she's never been here before? She takes the lift to the third floor, presses the buzzer and pouts like a movie star in front of another camera. Childish. She does that when she's nervous. Why was Cara watching her at Paddington? And then she's standing in an open-plan living area that makes the home in Cornwall seem like a garden shed.

The space is huge! At least twenty yards long and almost ten yards wide, with a kitchen bar in one corner, dining table in another, all reclaimed-wood floors, industrial-brick walls and loading-bay doors. There's a pool table, a cinema zone and a bedroom at the far end. She wonders for a moment if she's come to Rob's office by mistake and everyone's out. It's even bigger than she expected. How does one person live here?

She wanders around, taking in all the art. Vast canvasses and installations, including one that she recognises, a grotesque 'data-mask'. It's a 3D-printed sculpture of a face and was in the house in Cornwall for a while, but she found it too disturbing. Rob explained it to her once: the artist, Sterling Crispin, reverse-engineered facial-recognition algorithms to show how human faces are seen by machines. And then her heart misses a beat as she come across three of her own works. They are the same paintings that Rob exhibited in the hospital show, the sight of which had so lifted her spirits.

She stands in front of them and stares. Of course she immediately starts to see things that are wrong with them, but they aren't so bad. Her goal was to paint unflinching, raw portraits, to create a sense of confrontation between artist and sitter, the latter usually wide eyed, as if they'd been caught doing something untoward. She leans in closer to a portrait of an old man who used to sell gas bottles and sacks of coal on the canal; his lined, world-weary face. She remembers layering on the oil paint with a scalpel, impasto style, mixing the lumpy colours to create coarse, textured flesh, chatting quietly with him.

The sight of these pictures makes her want to cry with happiness – and to paint again. She had a very similar reaction in the hospital. She walks on down the wall and sees another portrait, by the late Sarah Raphael, one of her heroes. It's jewel-like and intense, an early work and full of empathy. She feels honoured to share a wall with her, but it's a salutary reminder of her own limits as an artist.

Upstairs she finds a second bedroom, a wet room, and a spacious roof terrace complete with real grass and a scattering of wicker chairs around an outdoor bar. The views of London, bathed in early evening sunlight, are breathtaking. Can she see Rob's office from here? They're close to Old Street roundabout, where he works. She's suddenly desperate to see him, to pick up where they left off before things started to go wrong in Cornwall. She's just been imagining things, as Jake says, suffering from Capgras syndrome. Dr Varma will be here shortly. He'll confirm the diagnosis, she feels certain of that now. The more she thinks about Capgras, the more it sounds like her.

She looks out across the London skyline again. Is Rob watching her from his desk? She waves, trying to dissipate some of her impish joy. And then she cartwheels across the grass, remembering her pictures on the wall downstairs, and peers over the wall to the street below.

The car that brought her is parked across from the entrance to the apartment block, partially obscured. She leans further over the wall and can just see Putin on the pavement, talking to someone she recognises. Her mouth dries, all joy gone. It's Cara, the woman on the train, the same person she saw at Paddington.

CHAPTER 59

SILAS

Silas follows the track through the woods until it opens out into a grassy area, hazy in the evening light and buzzing with the low drone of summer insects. If it were mown, it would make an idyllic cricket pitch, hidden away amongst the trees. On the far side, there's a gamekeeper's hut that could easily double up as a rustic pavilion.

It's here that Conor has asked to meet him, which somehow seems fitting. Conor used to play cricket when he was younger. He was good, but bat and ball were alien to Silas and he didn't show any interest. His own dad brought him up on a strict diet of football. Given the chance again, Silas would watch every one of Conor's cricket matches, offer to do the scoring, make the teas. Be a father.

No one else is around as he approaches the hut. There's an open barn area, for large machinery, presumably, and a shed to one side. Conor didn't say much on the phone, just that he wanted to meet here. He could see Silas down by the train track, had been watching him for a few minutes from the woods above.

298

'Conor?' he calls out. 'You there?'

Silence. A red kite enters the far end of the clearing and sweeps over the grass, twisting and turning in search of carrion. Silas moves forward, pushing open the hut door. Inside, some logs, a row of pheasant feeders, neatly stacked, a collection of white plastic scarecrows piled up in the corner. The familiar smell of weed.

It takes a few seconds for Silas's eyes to adjust to the darkness. And then he sees Conor on the floor, propped up against the far wall. The relief knocks him sideways. For the past six weeks, Silas has had to consider the possibility that Conor might be dead. And here he is, arms wrapped around his knees, rocking gently like a child.

Silas has seen him in better shape, but at least he's alive.

CHAPTER 60

KATE

Somewhere below her a phone starts to ring, so Kate returns downstairs from the apartment's rooftop terrace. She can't find the receiver at first and then she works out that the ringtone, more of a futuristic pulse, is coming from the bedroom. She pushes open the door and sees the handset by the bed. She hesitates before she answers it.

'You've found the bedroom then,' Rob says.

'I heard the phone and thought I should answer,' she explains, feeling like an intruder as she glances around Rob's private world. They've never shared this space before – the bed, its white cotton sheets. On one wall there's a large canvas photo of them together on Porthbean beach, smiling at the camera. She looks tired but happy. In her mind, Rob's life in London has always felt so separate, but the connections to Cornwall, their life down there, are here, plain to see. Another surge of happiness runs through her.

'It's OK, I meant you to pick up,' he says. 'Make yourself at home. I hope you like it.'

'It's beautiful,' she says, lying down on the double

300

bed. 'And so big. Amazing. I can't believe you've been keeping it from me all this time.'

'I wanted you to be ready, well enough to enjoy it.'

She can smell his scent on the pillows, clean and fresh as heather. It feels so good to be here – secure, cossetted, safe. Her worries of earlier are falling away with every passing second.

'When are you coming back?' she asks.

'Late, I'm afraid,' he says.

'No worries,' she replies, but she feels a pang of disappointment.

She turns to look at a photo on his bedside table. It's of her, walking out of the surf in her bikini, a little chubbier than she'd like. Should she ask him about Cara? Tell him that she thinks she's being followed? It sounds so paranoid, on a par with thinking that he's been replaced by a double. Maybe it's just another symptom of Capgras.

'Dr Varma should be with you shortly,' he says.

'That's good.' She pauses, feeling awkward at the prospect of Ajay's visit. She hasn't told Rob the real reason why she wants to see Ajay and she wonders if she's wasting his time. Once again, Rob sounds like himself on the phone. 'Will I be asleep when you get back?' she asks.

'I hope not. We've some catching up to do.'

'Shall I get some supper for us?' she asks, smiling at the thought of what they might do together later.

'I've put a few things in the fridge,' he says. 'You go ahead. I'm sorry.'

'It's OK. Really.'

This time she fails to hide her disappointment. She's genuinely looking forward to seeing him, to being in this bed with him. The two of them here together, in his flat, is exactly what she needs right now. It's a new stage in their relationship, the first time she's been in London with him, and she can't wait to celebrate that. She's moved on from her old life, the village, Jake, and she's going to put her fears behind her – no more stressing about the dead man on the beach, about Cara, about Rob's double.

'What are your plans after seeing Dr Varma?' he asks.

'I thought I might pop out to visit a gallery,' she says. 'It's been a while.'

'Nice.'

'Then come back, run a deep bath, light a few candles. Get myself ready.' She pauses. 'I can't wait to see you.'

'Me too.' He hesitates before continuing, his voice less confident. 'I bought you a few clothes. They're in the wardrobe. See you later – I've got to go.'

He hangs up.

She lies there for a few seconds, smiling to herself, and then slips off the bed, pulling open the cupboard door like an excited child on Christmas Day. It's full of new clothes, all her size and just her look. Bohemian summer dresses from Ghost, Rubina slides from Paul Smith, linen kaftan-neck tops from Toast. There's some night-wear too – thin cotton pyjamas from the White Company. Rob knows her so well. She should ring him back to thank him, but he sounded busy.

After going through all the clothes and setting out each item on the bed, she lies down beside them, holding the photo frame, and starts to cry. Happy tears but also sad ones. Jake bought her White Company pyjamas in their last days together, but she gave them back, told him to get a refund and spend the money on fixing the boat's leaking windows. They were broke, but it was still unkind of her. He knew she loved the pyjamas, couldn't understand her reaction. She gets the orange dress out of her bag and hangs it in the wardrobe.

Something catches her eye as she places the frame back on the bedside table. Another photo is hidden behind the first, one corner just visible. Rob with a different woman? Does he change the photos depending on who's staying in his flat? She tells herself to relax as she slides the photo up. It's of Rob when he was much younger, on an exotic-looking beach. Could it be Thailand? There are palm trees, small islands on the horizon. He isn't smiling at the camera.

She examines it more closely, scrutinising the photo for clues. Is it him? It looks exactly like Rob. He's wearing a floral shirt, shorts and espadrilles and seems drunk, almost leering at the camera. Then she notices a watch on the left wrist. Rob is left-handed. Maybe the picture was printed incorrectly, as a mirror image. He wears his watch on the right, doesn't he?

CHAPTER 61

JAKE

Jake pushes back his chair, staring at the screen as he calls Bex on his mobile. Her computer is behaving strangely. First, the camera came on unprompted yesterday, and then it woke up without any reason when Kate was here today. He's checked the settings and it hasn't been programmed to sleep or wake at certain times. And now the screen cursor seems to move occasionally by itself. It might just be a hardware fault, but it's making him jumpy.

'Technical support here,' he says. 'Have you been experiencing any problems with your computer recently?'

'How was Kate?' Bex says, ignoring his attempt at humour.

Kate's obviously told Bex about her flying visit to the village and Bex obviously doesn't approve.

'Fine,' he says. 'I put her back on the train.'

'How did you find her?' Bex is sounding like she always used to when she talked to him – dismissive, short. It's as if their recent conversations about Kate never happened.

305

'It was good to catch up,' he says, not sure where the conversation is heading. 'We talked some more about Capgras.'

'And?'

'I think she found it reassuring – she's going to talk to Dr Varma about it.'

Bex doesn't reply.

'She also told me about the body on the beach,' Jake continues. 'I'm sorry.'

'Nothing personal, but I can't believe she jumped off the train like that,' Bex says, choosing not to pick up on his mention of the dead body. 'She was so focused on getting to London. Being with Rob.'

'She wanted to see the boat,' Jake says defensively. 'How are things down there now?'

'The dog's doing my head in, but otherwise fine, thanks.' She pauses. 'Actually, not great. I can't get the image of the dead man out of my mind. And because I was one of the first to see the body, everyone wants to talk to me about it.'

'Better out than in,' Jake says, struggling to find the right words. 'Talking about it, I mean.'

'I've been thinking,' Bex says. 'I might come back up to the village – I need to get away from here, the beach.'

'Tonight?'

Jake glances back into Bex's kitchen. He will need to tidy up, find somewhere else to stay.

'In Rob's car,' she continues. 'He said I can use it. I'll bring the dog too.'

'Do you want me to move out?' he asks.

He's become quite settled in Bex's house.

'Don't be daft.' She pauses. 'I'd rather not be on my own right now.'

Bex doesn't sound like herself at all. She's usually so ballsy. Jake pushes open the sitting room door. The sofa isn't the biggest.

'Kate told me about Facebook,' she continues, changing tack again. 'The double on the beach in Thailand called Gil.'

Jake braces himself for another tirade, but Bex isn't angry with him for hacking into Kate's account. Far from it.

'I really don't know what she's got herself into,' she continues.

'With Rob?' he asks, surprised. 'I thought you approved.'

'I did. Still do. But . . . It sounded right weird, that man threatening to come back and take over Rob's life. What sort of a knob would say a thing like that? Makes me wonder if Kate might be onto something.' She pauses. 'If she hasn't got Capgras.'

'If it's not Capgras, it's something else in her head,' Jake says, for his own benefit as much as hers. 'Rob hasn't been replaced by a double. That sort of thing just doesn't happen. You and I know that.'

He leans forward and glances at the Google results for Kirby, Rob's Facebook friend. He's been searching all evening, ever since he left DI Hart in the water meadow. Was it wrong to accuse the detective's son of arson? There's no proof. He looks at the screen again. He hasn't been able to find anyone who fits Kirby's Facebook profile. Odd. No one even close to a match.

'You're right,' Bex says. 'I saw Rob on Paddington station and I've talked to him on FaceTime down here. It's ridiculous, the whole idea.'

She still doesn't sound sure. 'So what's the problem?' Jake asks.

She hesitates before speaking.

'The Thailand story's changed things, that's all. Got me thinking. What if there really are two of them? The one I saw in London and the one Kate met down in Cornwall? Rob and this bloke Gil?'

'It's easy to get carried away,' Jake says, trying not to sound patronising. Too many years in journalism have left him with a default cynicism that he's not proud of, but it prevents him from leaping to fanciful conclusions.

He lets Bex talk some more. She has a lot to get off her chest, including a couple of jets they heard during a FaceTime chat that apparently proved Rob was still in Cornwall. It's clear to him that things have got out of hand for Bex and Kate in their seaside bubble.

'I was going to call Kate after she's seen this Dr Varma,' he says, typing in some new search terms for the elusive Kirby. 'But maybe it's best if you do it.'

'Leave it with me,' she says. 'And sorry, you know, for being a bit off with you earlier.'

'No worries.'

Jake hangs up and then he freezes, staring at the screen. At last he's found a Kirby who matches the criteria. Worked at one of Rob's companies, looks like the photo on Facebook – and died five years ago.

Jake reads the information again, eyes widening in disbelief. Kirby's definitely dead. He reaches for the phone to call Kate, recalling the chat he had on Messenger. If he wasn't talking to Kirby, who the hell was replying to his messages?

CHAPTER 62

KATE

'Rob said you wanted to see me urgently,' Ajay says, glancing around the apartment as they make their way over to the kitchen area.

Kate wonders if he's been here before. 'Thanks for coming,' she says.

Is it urgent? Or is she wasting Ajay's time?

'Can I get you anything? Tea? Coffee? Glass of wine?' she asks as he perches awkwardly on a high kitchen stool.

'I'm fine, thanks,' he says, smiling. And then his expression becomes more serious. 'Rob mentioned what you saw on the beach in Cornwall. I'm so sorry. It must have been very distressing for you.'

Of course. Ajay thinks he's here to debrief her about the dead body. That's what Rob must have told him after she rang from the pub in a state last night. It was upsetting, but it's not what she wants to talk about.

'We were both shocked – I was with my friend Bex when we found the body,' she says, wondering how she's going to turn the conversation to

310

Capgras. Doctors must hate it when patients try to self-diagnose.

'Would you like to tell me a little more about it?' he asks. 'How you felt?'

'Actually, I wanted to ask you about something else,' she says, hesitating. Ajay smiles, encouraging her to continue. 'It sounds a little crazy.'

'Crazy?'

She realises it must be a loaded word in his world, one that he probably tries to avoid.

'Delusional,' she offers instead.

'Tell me,' he says.

She takes a deep breath. 'Every time I see Rob,' she begins, shifting her position on the kitchen stool, 'I think it's not him.'

Jesus, she does sound crazy. Unhinged. Ajay looks at her, unblinking, as if she's the only person in the world. She likes that about him, his undivided attention.

'Who do you think it is?' he asks quietly.

'An impostor, a double, I don't know,' she says. 'Just not Rob. It's as if he's been replaced by someone.'

'And this has been happening for how long?' he asks.

She's reassured that he's taking her seriously. A diagnosis would make it so much easier when she next sees Rob.

'The past four days. Since he came down to see me in Cornwall on Friday.'

She remembers the look in his eyes when he

watched her painting that day. The mug shattering into pieces on the concrete floor, the sudden certainty that she was talking to a total stranger. Stretch trotting away in fear. 'My best friend Bex, she thinks I might have something called Capgras delusion.'

Ajay looks up at her, cocking his head to one side.

'Capgras? Interesting. It's a rare condition.'

'But you have heard of it?' she asks, noting that he pronounces it with a silent 's'. It suddenly all feels a little too real, hearing the word repeated by a leading neuropsychiatrist.

'Of course,' he says. 'Technically it's classified as a delusional misidentification syndrome – an extremely unusual disorder.' He pauses, looking at her again with a certain detachment, what she's come to recognise as clinical interest. Maybe it's not such a long shot after all. 'It's more common in women than men,' he adds. 'And it can occur in association with migraines.'

She stares at him. They both know she suffered from migraines after the accident.

'And is it true you only think someone's a double when you see them?' she asks. 'Not when you talk to them on the phone.'

'That's correct – connectivity between the auditory cortex and memory appears to be unaffected. In fact, auditory cues can be used to help patients restore the association between a person and a face.' He pauses. 'But there's a lot we still don't understand about Capgras. And at present there's no known cure. In some cases, when it's caused, say, by a right hemisphere lesion, only the left visual field is affected.'

'Meaning?' she asks, her head beginning to spin. *Only the left visual field is affected.*

'You only think the person is a double if they're to your left.'

Her eyes start to well up.

'As I say, it's a rare condition,' Ajay repeats, noticing her discomfort. 'Very rare.'

She doesn't know whether to be pleased or frightened. The thought of no cure for Capgras isn't great. Nor is the prospect of seeing Rob as a double for the rest of her life. But at least it might explain what's been happening to her. Her own brain injuries from the accident were all on the right hemisphere, which controls the left part of her body, including her left eye. Does she only think Rob is a double when he's in her left field of vision? When she dropped the mug of tea on Saturday morning, he was on her left. And at Truro station, when the woman approached Rob . . . he was to Kate's left too.

CHAPTER 63

SILAS

Without speaking, Silas sits down next to his son in the hut in the forest, wincing at the pain in his knees as he pulls his legs up and wraps his arms around them. The last time he sat like this was in the cubs more than forty years ago, trying not to look up Akela's skirt.

'I just want you and Mum to be together,' Conor says after a while.

Silas closes his eyes. 'It's not that easy,' he says.

And he doubts whether it would fix anything in Conor's life if they did give it another go. His problems run far deeper. Mel blames him for not being tough enough on their son when he was younger. Silas tried to explain that it was hard to play the disciplinarian when you were feeling guilty about being an absent father, but it never washed.

'Have you even tried?' Conor asks, rocking more violently now.

Silas senses the anger beneath the surface. He doesn't want to do or say anything that might provoke it further.

314

'It needs us both to want to get back together and I don't think Mum—'

'Mum wants it,' Conor shouts, interrupting him. 'She told me.'

'OK,' Silas says, taken aback by Conor's sudden outburst. He's glad they are up here in the woods, far from anyone. 'So Mum wants it.'

Neither of them says anything. Silas closes his eyes and becomes aware of a nearby buzzing. He looks up and sees a wasp nest in the far corner, under the green corrugated-iron roof. A mass of delicate, beautiful swirls, like one of the big brown-sugar meringues that Mel used to make with Conor when he was little.

'When did she tell you she wanted us to get back together?' he asks.

'Yesterday,' Conor says. 'When I phoned her to say goodbye.'

From the train track. Silas remembers seeing the missed calls from her, the ease with which he'd ignored them. Was that after Conor had called her?

'I heard what happened,' Silas says. 'And I'm glad you didn't go through with it.'

'Are you really?'

Conor is calmer now, more reflective, his body no longer rocking.

'Of course I bloody am,' Silas says. 'What made you want to do it?'

'You?' Conor says.

Silas winces. It's painful, like a knife between the ribs, but a part of him knows that he needs to hear this if the two of them are ever to patch things up.

'My shitshow of a life,' Conor continues.

'If you're in trouble . . .'

'Trouble?' Conor laughs. 'I'm not a child any more, Dad.'

'There's always a way out, that's all I'm saying.'

'Not from this there isn't.'

'From what?'

Conor remains silent.

'I'm not interested in the boat fire,' Silas says, worried that he might be overplaying his hand. He's learnt to keep back how much he knows, at least when interviewing suspects. But this is his own son.

'You're a cop,' Conor says. 'Of course you're interested in the boat. That's why you're here – in the village.'

'I came here today because someone saw you – recognised you from the missing person posters I've been putting up everywhere.'

'You're lying. I saw you two nights ago, down by the boat. With the firemen.'

So Jake was right: his own son is an arsonist. He lets the thought sink in. Conor must have been watching the boat fire unfold from a safe distance. How did it come to this? His own flesh and blood. Thank God no one was injured.

'OK, so I was here that night because of the fire,' Silas says. 'As a cop. I happen to know the owner of the boat, Jake. The man I was talking to down at the railway just now.' Silas pauses. 'The same man who saved your life.'

Conor looks up at him, seemingly shocked by the revelation. Silas lets the implications sink in for a few moments before continuing.

'But I'm here today as a father, to find my son. Your mum and I, we're . . . we're worried sick about you. Been looking for you everywhere. Both of us.'

He's not good at this, talking so openly about his emotions. It's why he's always declined Mel's requests to attend joint counselling sessions.

'So why didn't you ring Mum back yesterday?' Conor asks quietly.

Because she only ever gives Silas grief. Bucket-loads of it. Conor must have called her again later in the day, told her he was safe, no longer feeling suicidal.

'You're right,' Silas says. There seems no point in arguing. 'I should have called Mum back.'

'Then you'd have known that your own son nearly killed himself yesterday.'

Silas closes his eyes. 'We need to get you help,' he says. 'For whatever . . . difficulties you're in.'

Conor reaches for a cigarette from his pocket.

'Here, have one of mine,' Silas says, pulling out his own packet.

Conor hesitates and then takes one, studiously avoiding any eye contact.

'We can get you out,' Silas says quietly. 'That's all I'm saying.'

'You don't know these people,' Conor says, lighting up with a match.

'Oh, I wouldn't bet against it.' Silas lights up too. 'I've met some pretty objectionable individuals over the years.'

He feels happier talking about police work, on safer ground.

'These people are from London, Dad. They don't give a fuck about anyone. One mistake and you're dead.'

Silas knows Conor is right. Rural knife crime has soared since county lines got a toehold.

'Life means nothing to them,' Conor continues.

'And these people, they asked you to torch the boat?'

Conor nods.

'And threatened to kill you if you didn't?'

Conor nods again. 'I hung around till I saw the bloke living on the boat had got off.'

That was good of him. 'It's coercion – not your fault,' Silas says. 'I see it all the time. And the courts understand.'

'The courts?' Conor looks up. 'You arresting me?'

'Of course I'm not. I'm just saying you're not automatically to blame.'

Silas gets to his feet and looks out through the door to the grassy area outside, his back to Conor.

'I'm guessing you're recruiting for them too?' he asks, trying to bury his revulsion, the shame of it all. 'Drug mules. Schoolkids.'

'Jake tell you that?'

'He put two and two together.'

'They didn't like him asking questions at the pub.'

'That's what I want to talk to you about. The Bluebell. I need your help.'

It's a long shot, but Silas can see a way of playing Conor back into the organised crime gang. If he can discover more about the night Kate's drink was spiked – who ordered it to be done – he might be able to help bring down the entire county lines network and expose any links it has with the modern slavery gang in Swindon that was recently sentenced. His boss won't like it, but this is personal now. He also wants to know who sent Jake the CCTV footage.

'Help you?' Conor says. 'Why should I?'

'Because then I can help you,' Silas says, turning to face him.

Once the drugs network has been disbanded, Silas can make an argument for Conor, cite the assistance he's given the police, the mitigating circumstances. Would that really work? Or is he deluding himself?

'I'm off,' Conor says, gathering up a small rucksack and brushing past him out of the hut door into the evening light.

'I just need to know who gave the order to target Kate, the super recogniser who worked for me,' Silas says, calling after Conor as he heads off into the sunshine. 'And find out who sent the CCTV footage of her drink being spiked at the Bluebell.'

He follows Conor out of the hut, but Conor is already ten yards away, striding across the open grass. A startled pheasant crows in the distance.

'The CCTV footage was sent to Jake, the guy whose boat you torched,' Silas calls after him. 'Someone might know that the pub cameras were hacked.'

Conor is not interested. Silas scans the forest, as if searching for something else to say, but he knows there's only one thing that will get his son's attention.

'I'll make an effort with Mum,' he shouts, his voice echoing through the trees. Are they mocking the hollowness of his words?

Conor is thirty yards away now. He stops and turns.

'We'll try to sort things out,' Silas continues, eyes locked on Conor's across the long grass. 'Maybe get some counselling. I promise.'

CHAPTER 64

KATE

Rob was being a little disingenuous when he said there were a few things in the fridge for supper. Like he'd said there were a few clothes in the bedroom wardrobe. Kate's just finished an exquisite crayfish salad, moist and meaty. He knows it's her favourite seafood. Readymade, of course. Rob is a hopeless cook, buys all his meals from a high-end delivery service. There was a bottle of Sancerre too and she treated herself to a glass. What the hell. She's not meant to drink, but tonight feels different, as if she's turned a corner.

Ajay couldn't stay long, but they talked some more about Capgras and he didn't rule out that Kate might be suffering from it. In fact, the more they chatted, the more he seemed to entertain the possibility, particularly once they'd worked out that she only ever thinks Rob's a double when he's to her left. Weird. The whole auditory cortex thing also fits with her experience of talking to Rob on the phone and feeling fine. Ajay gave her a coping strategy too: if she should find herself again thinking that Rob is a double, she should close her eyes and listen to Rob's voice. It might encourage the brain to re-establish the neural pathways that link his face to the person she knows.

After Ajay left, telling her that she could call him any time of day or night, she went up to the terrace and did some sketches, inspired by the sight of her work on the walls downstairs, and for once the pencil flowed and she's reasonably happy with the results. Big harsh skylines, void of all people. If she starts to paint portraits again, she wants the landscape to be more prominent, to interact more with her subject, hint at the insignificance of humankind. She also keeps thinking about the man she spotted in the station shelter. DI Hart sent her a text earlier, confirming it was his son and that he'd met up with him. He just wanted to say thanks – and to congratulate her on her 'dirty field spot'. The old skills are definitely back.

Her only problem is Jake. He's been trying to call her all evening and she hasn't answered. She will always love Jake, but they've both moved on. She doesn't want him to think there's any chance they might get back together again. It's not fair on him. He's been texting her too, but she hasn't read any of his messages and she's now turned her phone off. Rob called again on the landline a few minutes ago, confirming that he'll be back by 11 p.m.

So she's got a few hours to herself in town.

There's a Tate Late at Tate Modern tonight. She will head over there for a bit and then be back in time for Rob's return. She's told herself to stop worrying so much about Rob and his past, the photo by the bed. What does it matter which wrist he wore his watch on when he was younger? His taste in coffee? What side of the bloody bed he sleeps on? She's also come up with a plan for when he arrives, based on Ajay's advice. Something to stop Capgras in its tracks.

She checks herself in Rob's bedroom mirror, applying some carmine lipstick. There's a lot of male grooming stuff here and in the bathroom. She likes a man who takes care of himself – it's still quite a novelty for her. It's all in the hands, the cuticles. Rob's are manicured, as unlike Jake's oil-stained, nail-bitten fingers as you could get.

She glances around the bedroom, checking that everything is ready for later. This is where she's going to be with him tonight. And she feels good about it, confident. She deserves all this, a clean start, her new man. A lucky break. *Go for the money, girl*, as Bex said. And why not? Her ridiculously comfortable new life is just a happy consequence of their relationship, not the reason for it.

She skips and twirls across the vast living area in one of the Ghost dresses Rob bought her. It's a while since she's dressed up to go out for the evening. Scooping up her shoulder bag, she reaches for the front door handle and pulls.

It doesn't open.

She's always had a thing about these sorts of doors, the ones that require you to press a release button before you can open it. She sees a button on the wall to her right, shakes her head at Rob's obsession with security, and presses it. There's a satisfying click and she pulls on the door handle again. It still doesn't open.

She presses the release and tries the handle several more times before admitting defeat. God, she hates technology sometimes. There must be something obvious she's missing. She closes her eyes, opens them again, imagines that she's an intelligent person walking up to the door for the first time. *Look around, press release, pull on door handle.* Nothing doing.

Two minutes later, she's back in the bedroom, talking on the landline to a receptionist who is trying to connect her to Rob.

'It's me, sorry to disturb,' she says.

'You OK?' Rob asks. It sounds like him. 'Thought you were going out.'

'That's the problem. I can't open the door.'

She explains the issue she's having with the release system, playing up the silly-woman-doesn't-understand-tech thing. She's got no shame tonight. Whatever it takes. She just wants to head out into the summer evening in her new dress.

'I'm missing something obvious,' she says.

'First it's the pool cleaner, then the gas hob, and now this,' he says. 'I'm so sorry, it must be this end.'

'How do you mean?'

She wasn't too bothered that the pool cleaner in Cornwall was broken – she prefers to swim in the sea anyway – but he fixed it quickly. The gas hob too.

'Both properties are run on the same operating system,' he says. 'It's been experiencing a few problems since the most recent upgrade.'

'It's a home, Rob, not a bloody computer.'

Hear yourself, Kate, as Bex would say. She sounds like a spoilt brat.

'I know, I know,' he says.

She can hardly complain that there's a glitch in the door software of the luxury penthouse apartment in Shoreditch where she's lucky enough to be staying. Talk about a First World problem.

'So how do I get out of here?' she asks, glancing around at the windows. They're all sealed; the apartment is regulated by a smart air-con system. 'I wanted to head over to the Tate for a couple of hours. Before you get back.'

'Give me ten and it'll be sorted,' he says. 'I'm really sorry.'

Kate walks across the living space and goes upstairs to the roof terrace. It's a stunning evening: the sun's beginning to set, softening London's harsh, jagged skyline with its warm hues. If she is genuinely stuck, could she get out of the building from up here? She peers over the wall. It's a sheer drop to the street more than a hundred feet below. No chance. The phone starts to ring again downstairs.

'The door's going to take a while to fix,' a voice says. It belongs to the irritating woman in Rob's office who she spoke to earlier.

'Can I talk to Rob?' Kate says.

'He's a little busy in a meeting right now,' the woman replies. 'He'll call you right back.'

Kate slams the phone down, mimicking the woman's silly voice. *He's a little busy in a meeting right now.* The vast apartment suddenly feels airless. This is ridiculous. She's trapped, a victim of modern technology. She walks back over to the front door, looks around and notices a small security camera mounted in the corner of the room, to the right of the entrance. Rob wanted cameras inside the house in Cornwall, but she put her foot down. So he installed some around the outside of the property instead. This camera is definitely pointing into the room, straight at her. She walks over to it and peers up into the dark lens, trying to ignore a growing sense of dread.

CHAPTER 65

JAKE

'She's probably at a gallery or something, turned her mobile off,' Bex says, calling from the car. The drive up from Cornwall has been traffic-free and she reckons she'll be home within the hour.

'I've been trying her all evening,' Jake replies, putting away some cutlery. It's the last bit of tidying up he needs to do before Bex arrives. 'Texts, calls.'

He knows what Bex is thinking. It's none of his business what Kate's doing in London, why she's not replying.

'Did you have a row today?' Bex asks. 'When she stopped by the village?'

'Nothing like that.'

Quite the opposite. Jake felt they'd got on almost too well.

'Maybe she's just feeling guilty,' Bex says. 'You know, seeing her ex on her way up to be with the new man in her life.'

'Maybe.'

There's no one new in his life. He can't imagine it. An image of them in their first few months together flashes through his mind. Walking back from the pub to the boat 12 years ago, drunkenly singing 'Alarm Clock' by The Rumble Strips, the two of them wrapped in his tatty old overcoat. He blinks away the memory. He'll be crying in a minute.

'What's the urgency anyway?' Bex says.

Jake glances at the computer in the other room, thinking back to the light that came on beside Bex's 'interactive porn camera', the cursor moving by itself. And the way the screen woke up when Kate was here earlier. Was the computer's built-in microphone listening to their conversation? It can happen. Either way, he's increasingly confident that Bex's computer has been compromised in some way.

'That guy Kirby I was chatting with on Facebook Messenger, when I was signed in as Kate,' he says, stepping out of the back door into the cool air, away from the computer, 'it was a fake account. "Kirby" died five years ago.'

He wanted Kate to be the first to know, but there's no harm in telling Bex.

'Died?' Bex says, unable to conceal her shock. 'So who the bloody hell were you chatting to?'

'I don't know.'

Jake has been trying to find out all evening. Using a virtual private network in an attempt to remain anonymous on Bex's computer, he logged into Facebook as Kate and searched through the list of Rob's twenty-five other friends – not many for a leading techpreneur, but that was Rob's personal account not his public one. Jake was unable to find matches in the real world for any of them, apart from Kirby, which suggests they might all be fake accounts.

'It makes no sense,' Jake continues. 'If Kirby's dead, the whole story, what happened in Thailand, could be fake.'

There's something about the story though that Jake can't ignore. His newspaper boss used to hold up an old wine glass and flick it whenever he was presented with a story that bordered on the fanciful. 'Does it have the ring of truth?' he'd ask as the glass resonated around his office. Jake can hear the ring now.

'Maybe it was Rob you were chatting to?' Bex says, her voice quieter.

The thought has crossed Jake's mind too. 'He's not the sort to play games,' he says. 'To make things up.'

The irony of defending Rob isn't lost on him. 'Unless, of course, he wanted to deliberately frighten Kate,' he adds, unable to resist a dig.

'He'd never do anything like that,' Bex flashes back. 'He loves her, Jake. I know you don't want to hear it, but he truly loves her.'

'I'm sure he does.' *Cherishes her.* Jake has heard it all before.

He glances up at a flock of Canada geese circling late and low over the canal. Something must have disturbed them.

There's another explanation for the chat he had with 'Kirby', one that would change everything. 'Or perhaps I was chatting with Gil himself, the double on the beach,' he suggests.

'Gil?' Bex says, surprised. 'I thought you were Mr Sceptical about all that doppelgänger stuff.'

He is. Just not quite as sceptical as he was.

'All we can be sure of at the moment,' he says, 'is that someone who isn't Kirby wanted Kate to hear about Thailand.'

'But how would they have known Kate would message Kirby out of the blue? It was Kate – *you* – who contacted *them*.'

That's what's troubling Jake too. He walks out across Bex's lawn in the moonlight, peering down at the well-kept flowerbeds, feeling the wet grass beneath his bare feet. Kate used to keep an allotment in the village.

'What if, just for a moment, we buy into this whole doppelgänger narrative and assume that it was Gil who replied to me, pretending to be Kirby,' he says. 'He's back in the UK after nine years, jealous of Rob, of all that he's achieved, and with only one thing going for him in this world: he looks identical to Rob. If you were set on taking over someone else's life – becoming that person – social media would be as good a place as any to start. And maybe he's already begun. If all Rob's friends are fake accounts, monitored by Gil, it wouldn't matter which one of them Kate contacted.'

'And I thought it was just me,' Bex says. 'You really think that's what might be happening?'

Jake can't be certain about anything any more, not since he discovered Kirby was dead. 'We have to consider it,' he says.

'But why would Gil break cover and let Kate know what he's up to?' Bex asks.

'To send a warning to Rob? A blackmail sting? I don't know, Bex, but if the story about the birthday party is true, he's got form threatening others. Maybe he's in no rush, assumes that Kate will eventually tell him.'

Jake is starting to sound like the resident conspiracy theorist in the Slaughtered Lamb. He blames the internet. He's been reading a lot of stuff about doubles, and there's ample evidence online that what Rob told Kate is true: it's so much easier now to track down your lookalike. And Jake can't forget how Kate explained to him what it was like to see Rob and believe he was an impostor. She sounded utterly convinced, professional. Like she used to in work mode, when identifying a criminal.

'Whoever it was, Kate needs to know that Kirby's dead,' Bex says. 'I'll try her now. Nothing personal, but she might pick up if I ring her.'

'Good luck with that,' Jake says. 'And drive carefully.'

'This car drives itself.'

He'd forgotten that Bex is in Rob's fancy Tesla.

'I'm sure there's an innocent explanation for all this,' he adds, without much conviction. 'I just worry that something else might be going on – that Kate might be in real danger.'

CHAPTER 66

KATE

Kate lies back in the roll-top bath and turns on the hot water tap with her big toe. She's been in here almost an hour and has become quite adept at the manoeuvre. Her trip to Tate Late has been well and truly scuppered. Rob has tried his best to get the front door sorted, but there's a problem with the facial-recognition software. The contractor is not answering, but Rob thinks he'll be able to override the system with his master key when he returns.

They've also discussed couriering the key over here to let her out, but Rob is now at another office across town and by the time the key's arrived, he'll be back here in person. He's also nervous about handing the master key over to a stranger, which is fair enough. She's a woman on her own and he doesn't want anyone turning up to let themselves in.

She reaches across and takes another sip of Sancerre. She knows there might be an alternative explanation for what's happened here tonight: the front door could be fixed sooner, but Rob is being over-cautious about her personal safety.

He doesn't want her wandering the streets of London so soon after the court trial in Swindon. A part of her would be furious if that were the case. How dare he decide what she can and can't do? But in light of what happened in Cornwall – her drink being spiked, her nearly being run down in the street, the dead body on the beach – she can hardly be angry with him if he's being over-protective of her. She's lucky to have someone who cares.

And it's turned into a good night in, given the circumstances. She has watched a movie on Netflix, drunk too much wine and eaten a whole bar of Peruvian dark chocolate, which he also bought for her, and she's now feeling sick. She still hasn't turned on her mobile and talked to Jake. Their worlds feel further apart than ever as she lies here in Shoreditch, sipping Sancerre. If Jake saw her now, he could be forgiven for thinking that the only impostor is her.

A call on the landline disturbs her drunken reverie. She reaches across to pick up the receiver, careful not to get it wet. It's Rob again.

'You still in the bath?' he asks. His voice is gentle, reassuring. Familiar.

'How did you guess?' she says, wishing he were here with her. To her right, of course.

'I'm sorry, this isn't how I wanted it to be,' he says enigmatically.

'How you wanted what to be?' she asks, her smile fading.

The tone of Rob's voice is beginning to scare her. Does he mean their evening together?

'Don't wait up for me,' he says, sounding almost tearful now. 'I love you.'

'Wait,' she says, sitting up.

The line dies. At the same moment, the lights go out, plunging her into darkness. The bath suddenly feels very cold. Her thoughts try to follow a rational route, like flowing water, feeling their way along the most sensible, scientific path, obeying the laws of physics. It must be a power cut, connected in some way to the faulty front door. The house is over-engineered, too much can go wrong. Something else has come up at work and Rob won't be back until even later. He was interrupted on the phone, didn't sign off.

She sits in the darkness for a few moments, aware of her quickening pulse. There's a noise in the main room. Automated, an electrical hum of some kind. Maybe there isn't a power cut, just an issue with the lighting. She steps out of the bath, feels for the dressing gown, and shivers as she wraps herself in its soft cotton embrace.

She walks into the main room and watches with horror as the space begins to steadily darken around her. Steel security blinds are sliding down the inside of the windows and the last of the London skyline is disappearing behind them. Within seconds the blinds have shut out the remaining light of the city and she's now in total darkness. Is the apartment going into lockdown, turning into one big panic room? It's the sort of paranoid security feature Rob might have. Jesus, just how dangerous can Shoreditch be?

She remembers the roof terrace, turns and feels her way towards the door at the bottom of the stairs. Pulling it open, she's relieved to see evening light spilling in through the terrace door that she left open earlier. She scrambles upstairs as fast as she can, as if oxygen-starved, and rushes out onto the grass. She feels better already.

The night is balmy, London bathed in a lambent halo, at odds with the drama playing out below. She pauses to get her breath back, tells herself to stop worrying. Why was Rob talking like that on the phone? His voice sounded so fragile, conflicted.

She has a sudden urge to call Jake. He'll know what's going on, what's happening to the house. Where to find the fuse box or master switch or whatever. He's so practical. This was always her favourite time of day when they were living on the boat. In summer, the two them would sit out in the cockpit, chatting and laughing in the twilight glow, glasses of wine in hand, their heads full of dreams and madcap plans. In those moments, everything used to seem possible.

She looks around at the other buildings, lights shining out into the London twilight. No one else is without power. It's just Rob's apartment. And then she's aware of another light in the sky, red and flashing, heading towards her. For a second she doesn't know what it is until she hears the telltale buzz of a small drone.

She stands back, stepping towards the doorway as it approaches. Is it one of Rob's toys? Maybe it's delivering the master key? It's the sort of childish thing he'd do, now that he's invested in a drone courier company. But there's nothing playful about the hum of its four small propellers. Or the camera, suspended below the drone, its dark lens angled straight at her.

The drone is hovering a few feet away now, at eye level. It starts to move forward, as if ushering her inside. She backs away, but it continues to follow her. Christ, can drones fly indoors? Without thinking, she ducks inside and slams the door shut behind her, frightened of being hurt by its blades.

There's a sickening click as the glass door locks. She knows what will happen next. Breathless, she stares at the drone, still hovering outside, as the apartment's final steel blind begins its inexorable descent.

CHAPTER 67

SILAS

Silas heads for the CID corner of the Parade Room, where he can see Strover at a desk, deep in conversation with someone on her mobile. She's working late again, without being asked. At least she doesn't have a family.

As soon as he left Conor in the woods, he called Mel, told her that he'd seen their son. He also announced that he wanted to accompany her to a joint counselling session.

'Are you doing this for Conor or for you and me?' she asked.

'All three of us.'

She said she'd think about it, which is a start.

He sits down next to Strover, now off the phone.

'That was the Major Crime Team in Truro,' she says. 'The SIO's been trying to contact you.'

Silas turned off his phone in the forest, a belated attempt to focus on his son. He then phoned Mel in the car, ignoring calls from the office in an attempt to focus on her.

'The County Lines Coordination Centre has confirmed the dead man was involved in a

338

network operating out of Swindon,' Strover continues. 'He used to work at the Bluebell until six months ago, but they don't think he was down in Cornwall selling drugs.'

'Because he was there to target Kate,' Silas says, unable to hide his frustration. It would be so much easier if he could take the lead on this case, but his boss thinks otherwise. Devon and Cornwall are running the show and his role is to liaise with their Senior Investigating Officer.

'I told them that,' Strover says.

'Do they have any idea who might have killed him?'

'That's why they were calling.'

Silas looks up.

'Forensic ballistics has come back with some data on the bullet that was retrieved from the victim's skull.'

'Go on.'

Strover consults her notes.

'According to NABIS, the only other bullet with barrel markings like this was fired in Thailand. Nine years ago.'

Silas sits back in his chair. The National Ballistics Intelligence Service specialises in firearms-related criminal activity in the UK. It normally only holds data on a case abroad if a UK citizen is involved in some way.

'Remind me why I've heard about Thailand recently?' he asks.

Strover throws him a scornful look. Unlike him,

she never seems to forget anything. 'One of the seven people in the world who looks like Kate's new boyfriend was last seen in Thailand,' she says. 'The one who bears the closest resemblance.'

It's probably nothing, but Thailand doesn't often cross Silas's desk in Swindon twice in one day.

'Does your friend have more details yet?' he asks. 'A name would be useful. His age too.'

Strover turns to her laptop and starts typing.

'And did NABIS have any other information?' he adds, watching her.

'Very little,' she says. 'The file just says the gun was fired in a drugs-related incident. No trace of it since.'

Strover has found the mugshot of the man in Thailand and adjusts her laptop screen so that Silas can see it.

'A bit blurred,' he says as she displays an adjacent image of Rob, Kate's partner, 'but it's a striking likeness, isn't it? Uncanny.'

'Some more intel on him has just dropped,' Strover says, opening up a new window on her screen. She freezes, her fingers suspended above the keyboard.

'What's the matter?' Silas asks.

'His name.'

'And?'

She points to a line of small print on the screen. 'Gilmour Martin.'

He stares at the words. It's one of those moments

when an investigation comes alive. The name matches the registered keeper of the Tesla that was seen by Kate's gallery friend in her village. Kate asked them to check as she was worried that Rob might have been in Cornwall when he was meant to be in London. Silas is just not sure what this new lead means or where it will take them.

'Do we know where he is now?' he asks, eyes narrowing. Gilmour Martin is not a common name.

Strover shakes her head. 'Last seen in Thailand nine years ago,' she says, reading from the screen. 'Police took his picture because he was involved in some sort of disturbance at a beach party. Subsequently released without charge. Bit of a loser, by all accounts.'

'And never heard of again – until yesterday. We need to find out everything we can about him. And look into that "care of" address the car was registered to in north London.' He should have checked when Strover first mentioned it, been less scratchy.

'I'll run his name through every database I'm allowed to,' Strover says.

And some that she's not. Silas has learnt not to ask. He likes it when Strover's got the bit between her teeth.

He peers more closely at the image, comparing it with the one of Rob. 'Can you find a photo of Rob when he was younger?' he asks.

He watches, impressed by his colleague's digital

dexterity as she finds a picture of Rob from an old cover of *Wired*, taken in his early days when he was a buccaneering young techpreneur. Silas wishes he could reverse his own ageing so easily. There must be an app out there. It's the sagging jowls that upset him the most.

Strover positions the image side by side with the Thai mugshot of Gilmour Martin. The likeness now is even more striking.

'Have you told Kate yet?' he asks. 'About the matches we've found? We should let her know about Gilmour Martin.'

'I can't get through to her,' Strover says. 'Left a message on her mobile.'

He's not sure how Kate will react to the news that Rob's not only got an identikit double but one who's been driving around the lanes of Cornwall in a matching Tesla.

CHAPTER 68

KATE

Kate stumbles back down the stairs from the roof terrace in the darkness, the buzzing of the drone fading with each step. The machine was like a demented insect, menacing. She knows where she needs to go. Before her bath, she prepared a few scented candles in the bedroom, ready for Rob's return. All part of her plan to combat Capgras.

She feels her way through the door and finds them on the bedside table. A moment later, she's holding a match and trying to strike it. The match snaps. She tries another and then another, her hands trembling. Finally, she manages to strike one and the room lights up with the faint glow of the candle. It's not how she imagined it would be tonight. She thought they'd be in bed together, drinking wine, making love. Like a normal couple. But it's turning into a nightmare.

The candle's shaking so much in her hand that she spills some wax on the floor. She puts it down beside the bed and lights two others she brought with her in her luggage, calming candles from Cornwall. *Relax.* She needs to get everything in perspective. The power cut, the dead phone line, the shutters – there's a perfectly rational explanation. They're all part of the problem with the apartment's software, the same issue that prevented her from leaving earlier tonight. It's either an accident or an over-cautious Rob. The drone is more problematic. There was nothing accidental about that. Maybe its appearance was a coincidence, an envious neighbour who enjoys buzzing the rich kids in their penthouse suites.

I'm sorry, this isn't how I wanted it to be.

What did Rob mean? Will he be back tonight? And which Rob will it be? The old thoughts are returning like smoke, seeping in under the door, circling and swirling around her. She is certain it was Rob's voice on the phone earlier, but she won't be able to cope if someone else turns up here now. An impostor, his double. The man from Thailand.

She looks around for her phone to call Ajay. She needs his reassurance that her damaged brain is playing tricks, nothing more. She knows she should ring Rob first, ask him what's going on, but she's lost her nerve.

She finds her mobile on the sideboard in the kitchen. No signal. She purses her lips, trying not to cry. The steel blinds must be blocking reception. What sort of security measure is that? Protection against bloody cold-callers? She just wants to be back in Cornwall with Bex and Stretch.

And maybe even with Jake too, camping on the rainy hillside like they used to.

There's hardly any power left on her phone either. Perhaps the landline's working again. She finds the receiver in the bathroom. Dead. She looks around. There's a ticking sound high up in the corner. The blades of a wall fan are turning lazily in a faint breeze. Climbing up onto the end of the bath, she can see the evening light outside. No sign of any steel blinds. She holds the phone up by the fan and looks at the screen. One bar of reception appears. Balancing carefully, she dials Ajay's number. Engaged.

And then a distinct sound echoes through the apartment. The front door. She listens for a moment. Silence. On an impulse, she decides to try Jake's number.

'Hello?' she calls out, waiting for the phone to connect. More silence. 'Rob?'

The door again, closing behind whoever has just come in.

'Rob?' she repeats, louder now, her voice shaking. 'Is that you?'

Why hasn't he said anything? The silence is scaring her. She climbs down off the bath, knocking over the candle as the phone connects through to Jake.

'Rob?' she calls out.

He doesn't answer. It must be someone else.

CHAPTER 69

SILAS

'Boss, your phone.'

Silas turns from the window in the Parade Room and takes his mobile from Strover. She doesn't say anything, but it's clear from the display that it's Conor.

'You OK?' Silas asks, walking over to a quiet corner.

'I've just spoken to Mum,' Conor says.

Silas glances around the room. No one is within earshot, but it's still not the sort of conversation he'd like colleagues to overhear. Not even Strover.

'And?'

'Thanks – for calling her,' Conor says. He sounds in a better place, more together. 'She was chuffed about the counselling.'

She didn't seem particularly chuffed when Silas spoke to her, but he's glad if they've made progress, however slight.

'I've also been up at the Bluebell, asking around,' Conor continues. 'I overheard a conversation in the back room – went the distance for you, Dad.'

'You're not to put yourself in danger,' Silas says,

346

checking again to make sure that no one can hear him. He's being disingenuous. If Conor is to find out anything useful at the Bluebell, it's going to be dangerous. And it sounds like Conor took a big risk. For him.

'I was almost caught listening at the door, but I got away with it,' Conor says. 'Had to pay someone off to keep quiet.'

'How much?' Silas asks.

'We can talk money later. The whole place was in turmoil anyway. You heard the ex-barman's been killed? The one who used to work there a while back.'

'In Cornwall,' he says, sighing. 'Yesterday. Anyone know who shot him?'

'That's what's pranging everyone out.'

'What are they saying?'

'Turns out he had to do a runner six months ago. He'd been told to target that woman you mentioned, the one who was sick at recognising people. Apparently she was causing all kinds of carnage.'

Silas is hit by another pang of guilt about Kate. *He'd been told to target that woman . . .* He should have been more careful. The irony of what Conor's saying is not lost on him either. He always hoped his son might show a bit more interest in his old man's job and now he's giving him a blow-by-blow account of his working life.

'So anyway, after he spikes her drink that night, he drives off after her, just to be certain,' Conor continues, speaking in the mockney accent that used to so annoy Silas. He can live with it now. At least they're talking. 'And sure enough he comes around the bend and sees her car smashed into a tree. Not nice, quite peak actually, but job done. I didn't know any of this shit until tonight. He's a hard bastard and just sits there, lights out, having a toke as he watches her life ebb away. What he doesn't realise is that she managed to call 999 before she passed out.'

Silas remembers listening to the recording of her anguished voice, barely able to breathe let alone speak.

'Just as he's about to head off, he sees this other car pull up silently next to the crashed one,' Conor continues. 'A man gets out and checks on the driver. But this geezer doesn't wait around. He drives away when he hears the ambulance approaching.'

'What sort of car was it?' Silas asks. *He sees this other car pull up silently.*

'The barman is shitting himself in case this other man was following him,' Conor continues, ignoring his dad's question. 'He thinks he might have seen the same car at the pub earlier that evening – in the car park. So he drives off too, in the other direction. Stays low. Disappears. Six months later, it's show-trial time and a lot of people are banged up for fat sentences. The remaining gang members are not happy and send the barman down to Cornwall, where your

348

woman's recovering, to finish the job. And then he's shot dead.'

'This could be very helpful,' Silas says, way too formally.

He's having a conversation with his own son, not taking down a witness statement. Just how dysfunctional a dad has he become? He glances around the Parade Room, over towards Strover. Mel will kill him if she ever hears about this. He reassures himself that the only way to get their son out of the trouble he's in is by dismantling the entire gang. And to do that, he needs to understand the network, its rivalries.

'Is there any chance you could ask a bit more about this other man? What he looked like?' Silas asks. 'And maybe the make of car he was driving?'

Silence.

'You always did want more from me, Dad, that's the problem,' Conor says. 'Never fucking happy. I've risked my life for you tonight. Stood outside the boss's office with my ear to the door. I could have been killed.'

Silas rubs the stubble on his chin. 'I'm sorry,' he says.

Conor's right. His default response is invariably disappointment, like the time Conor achieved Bs and Cs in his GCSEs. It was only afterwards that they discovered Conor was dyslexic.

'It might have been a Tesla,' Conor says, and hangs up.

CHAPTER 70

JAKE

'Smells good in here,' Bex says, walking into her kitchen with a suitcase in one hand, tiny dog in the other.

'Welcome home,' Jake says awkwardly. Bex's house suddenly feels very small. 'I've made some dinner.'

He's repeated his offer to move out, but Bex is insistent that he stay.

'So this is the new man in Kate's life?' Jake adds, looking at the dog.

'Meet Stretch.' Bex lets him down onto the floor. 'Whined the whole way up here, but otherwise he's alright.'

Jake bends down and tickles the tiny dog behind his ears. He'd always imagined something big and smelly whenever Kate talked about getting one. This one's long and thin, like a narrowboat.

He serves dinner once Bex has taken her stuff upstairs.

'You're not eating?' she asks as she tucks into hogweed gnocchi. He found the hogweed stems earlier, picked them before the leaves fully opened.

'Bit late for me,' he says. 'It's almost midnight.'

'You shouldn't have stayed up. This is delicious. Like asparagus.'

'Did you manage to speak to Kate?' he asks.

Last time they chatted on the phone, Bex was going to call Kate after she'd seen Dr Varma.

'Voicemail. Rang Rob too, left a casual message asking him to get Kate to call when she has a moment. I didn't want to alarm him. You know, in case . . .' She falters.

Jake looks up. He knows what she was going to say. *In case Rob has been replaced by a double. By Gil.* Jake has other ideas. He's spent the evening digging into Rob's past again, his business interests, what he's doing in Brittany. Jake's been here before, after the split from Kate, when he spent too many hours googling Rob. This time he thinks he might have found something.

After Bex has finished her dinner, he takes her through to the sitting room to show her what he's discovered online.

'On the surface, Rob and his tech empire – his "unicorn" company in the UK – is all about something called "direct neural interface" technology,' he begins.

'In English?' Bex says as Jake juggles various open windows on the computer.

'Helping the human brain to interact better with machines,' he says. 'Devices implanted in the cerebral cortex to operate artificial limbs, that sort of thing. He's also invested in loads of other medical start-ups, including one that makes portable headsets for assessing brain injuries.'

'That's what he's been using with Kate's recovery,' Bex says.

'All good selfless stuff, improving the health of mankind.'

'Why do I think you're not convinced?' Bex asks.

'It's the recent trip to Brittany that's worrying me,' Jake says, gnawing on a thumbnail. 'Brest is a tech hotspot in France, has deep roots in military encryption and communications. An investigative website over there has been looking into Rob's R and D unit, what's he's going to be investing in tomorrow. And they think it might be facial-recognition technology. He certainly needs to do something – apparently his company is massively overvalued, and some people are worried about him investing in the French tech sector.'

'Is that such a problem?' Bex asks, yawning. 'If he's into facial recognition?' She must be knackered after her long drive, even in a Tesla.

'They're a bit more uptight about that sort of thing over in France,' he says. 'This website thinks that Rob is there to flog some secret new system on the quiet to the French government, to help them combat terrorism.'

'Can't see a problem with that either,' Bex says. 'I mean, apart from it all being a bit Big Brother.'

'Don't you think it's a strange coincidence?' Jake asks. 'Given his relationship with Kate, a former super recogniser?'

'Maybe that's what sparked his interest in the whole facial-recognition thing. After he met her and heard the amazing things she'd been doing with Wiltshire Police.'

'That's what I thought. Until I remembered something – the first time I met Rob, at the hospital.'

It wasn't an easy encounter. Jake knew as soon as he walked onto the ward and saw Rob sitting at Kate's bedside, paying her attention, that it was over between him and Kate.

'I just had this feeling it wasn't the first time I'd seen him,' Jake continues.

'How come?' Bex asks, showing more interest now.

'I'd clocked him in the car park at Gablecross police station.'

'You sure?'

'It was the day before Kate's accident. I'd been in to talk to DI Hart about some research for my latest book.'

They'd ended up chatting more about winter migrant birds than police procedure.

'Was he driving a Tesla?' she asks.

'I don't recall. Just saw him walking towards the police station entrance.'

And wearing a baseball cap. It had stuck in his mind because Jake had wondered if he could get away with one at his age. Probably not.

'So you'd seen Rob before – that doesn't mean Kate had,' Bex says. 'They met because he happened to be putting on an art show at the hospital where she was a patient.'

'I know that's what everyone says. All very romantic. I get it. But what if Rob was at the hospital specifically to meet Kate? This incredible super recogniser who had outperformed every facial-recognition software program.'

Bex sighs. 'I know it's not easy, Jake,' she says, walking through to the kitchen, 'but he's been incredibly good to her over the past five months, nurtured her back to health because he loves her. Loves her art. Wants her to paint again.'

'I hope you're right.'

Jake is about to get up from the computer when his phone rings.

It's Kate.

'Jake,' she says quietly.

The line's terrible, but Jake can hear enough to tell that Kate's frightened. He signals furiously for Bex to come back from the kitchen and listen.

'Where are you?' he asks, putting Kate on speakerphone as Bex rushes over.

'Jake, can you hear me?' Kate says, her voice now a desperate whisper.

Jake cracks his big knuckles, increasingly worried by the tone of her voice.

'Where are you, Katie, my love?' Bex says, leaning in towards the phone. 'Why are you whispering?'

They both strain to hear what Kate says next. Maybe something about Rob's flat. It's hard to tell.

The line drops.

CHAPTER 71

SILAS

It's late and Silas is driving Strover home through the deserted streets of Swindon. A light rain has rinsed the roads, leaving them black and shiny. They were the last two in the Parade Room tonight, going through automatic-number-plate-recognition records from six months ago, grateful that they're kept for one year at the National ANPR Data Centre. Conor's revelation that the car at the scene of Kate's crash was a Tesla has changed everything. Silas can't be certain that it was Rob at the wheel, but it's beginning to make sense, at least to him.

'Remember when we showed Kate a still from the CCTV footage at the pub?' he asks.

'And Kate recognised the barman,' Strover says, tired, unimpressed.

'When we asked her how,' Silas continues, 'she said that the same barman had spiked her coffee in the harbour café the day before.'

'So she never forgets a face.' Strover is still sceptical. 'At least, she never used to.'

'Exactly. But she didn't just say that she recognised him. She said that he'd spiked her coffee. That's quite a specific charge to level at someone.'

It's been bothering Silas ever since Kate told them in Cornwall. He steers the car across Swindon's infamous magic roundabout, five small ones linked in a circle.

'I still don't get how this relates to Rob,' she says, staring out of the window into the Swindon night.

'Because I think it was Rob who suggested to Kate that her coffee had been spiked.'

'Rob?' She looks across at him.

'He'd seen it happen before – six months earlier in the Bluebell.'

'How could Rob have seen it happen?' Strover asks, more engaged now. 'He wasn't at the Bluebell that night.'

'What if he was?' Silas says as they approach Strover's road, a row of mid-Victorian terraced houses close to Swindon station. 'According to the barman, a Tesla was at the scene of Kate's crash. And he thinks he spotted the same vehicle in the pub car park earlier.'

'That still doesn't put Rob in the pub,' Strover says.

'It does if he was sitting in the corner, watching her.' Silas parks up and turns off the engine. 'He sees the barman do something suspicious with her drink. When she leaves, he follows Kate home in his Tesla.'

'You make it sound like he was stalking Kate,' Strover says, struggling to hide her frustration.

'Or protecting her,' Silas says. 'Unfortunately, Kate's success as a super recogniser was all over the press.'

It's still just a hunch. Silas can't prove that Rob was in the pub – most CCTV cameras only keep footage for up to a month before they start to overwrite.

'All we know is that someone who drives a Tesla was definitely looking out for Kate that night,' he continues, checking his own enthusiasm. 'Keen to keep her alive after she crashed.'

As if on cue, an ambulance appears from a side street, lights flashing, and pulls onto the main road, heading back towards the nearby Great Western Hospital in eerie silence. No need for a siren tonight.

'Six months later, someone seems to be protecting her again,' Silas continues. 'And we have to consider that it might be Rob. Her guardian angel. A man tries to spike Kate's coffee and then attempts to run her down in the street. Now that man's dead.'

Strover sits back, blowing out her cheeks. Silas is happy to wait, let it all sink in. There's no proof that Rob has taken the law into his own hands. Not yet.

'What about Gilmour Martin?' she asks. 'It could have been him. I mean, why would Rob be keen to protect Kate before he'd even met her?'

'We know nothing about the man except that he happens to look like Rob,' he says.

'And he was seen driving around Cornwall in a Tesla when the barman was shot dead – by an unusual gun fired in Thailand, where Gilmour was last seen. Kate said Rob was worried about having a double.'

Silas glances at Strover. Her interest in Gilmour is starting to niggle like a sore tooth. They need to talk to Kate again, Rob too. Ask them about his weird fears, why he thinks he's in danger from his doppelgänger. Wouldn't he have alerted the police if he was really worried? Asked for protection?

'You saw the security at Rob's house in Cornwall,' he says. 'Cameras everywhere. I think Rob has always feared that Kate has been at risk from the people she identified. And perhaps from other people too.'

CHAPTER 72

KATE

There's a person standing in the main room of the apartment, Kate's sure of it. She slips the phone into her dressing-gown pocket. It was good to hear Jake's voice again, even if his words were barely audible.

Making her way out of the bathroom, she peers towards the front door, her body trembling beneath the thin dressing gown.

'Hello?' she calls out.

Rob would have said something by now.

A faint light from the candles in the bedroom is slowly taking the edge off the darkness in the main room. She strains to see who it is. Someone definitely came in through the front door – she heard the telltale click – but there's only silence.

'Rob?' she calls out again. 'Is that you?'

Why isn't he saying anything? She starts to retreat towards the bathroom, barely daring to breathe. Could it be a burglar? An intruder? Rob is always going on about the dangers of London. And then the person speaks. The familiar trace of Rob's southern Irish accent is reassuring, but the absence of all empathy is not.

'Who were you calling?' he asks.

'Thank God it's you,' she says, trying to ignore his question, the cold, accusatory tone. The only other time she's heard him speak like this was during a work call, when he was ordering someone to 'boil the ocean' for new customers. 'I thought it might have been . . . Where are you?' she asks. 'Why didn't you say something sooner? I can't see you.'

She takes a few steps forward, in the direction of the door, where she can now make out the faintest outline of Rob. Even though he's to her right, she has no wish to see him more clearly.

'I heard you talking to someone,' he continues.

Her fear turns to anger. She's just been through hell because of Rob's bloody apartment and all he can do is stand there asking questions.

'Rob, the landline's down, there's no power, I couldn't even get out the fucking front door tonight. Where are you? I can't see you. I've been scared stiff.'

'You should have called me,' he says, his coldness starting to thaw.

He's right. She knows she should. Instead, in her moment of crisis, she tried to ring Jake. Why didn't she call Rob back again? They'd been talking on and off all evening until the landline dropped.

'I was frightened,' she says. 'The power cut, the security blinds . . . I thought Jake might know what was going on with the apartment. The

360

electrics. He was always good at fixing things on the boat.'

The faintest sniff of derision. She's rarely heard Rob like this. He's usually so sure of himself, of them. It's what attracted her to him in the first place: his quiet self-confidence, the lack of jealousy, his never passing judgement on the modest life that she led with Jake on the boat.

'And I didn't know when you were coming back,' she continues. 'You sounded so busy. And then the phone died and the blinds came down and this bloody drone . . .' She can't hold it together any longer.

'Come here,' he says, his voice kinder now, softer. A moment later, his arms are around her and she's sobbing on his shoulder.

'I'm sorry,' she says. 'For calling Jake.'

This is so strange. They've never had a scene about their exes before. And now here they are, in the middle of a power cut, having their first row.

'I'm the one who's sorry,' he says. 'For what happened here tonight.'

She can cope like this, when she's in his arms and cannot see his face. The world is back on its axis, free from all thoughts of doubles. It's how it used to be when they first met and moved down to Cornwall, thrilled by each other's bodies.

She finds his mouth and kisses him. Darkness is her friend.

CHAPTER 73

JAKE

'Apologies for calling so late,' Jake says, sitting in the heated leather passenger seat of Rob's Tesla. Bex is driving and Stretch is asleep on his lap.

'No doubt it's still daylight in Lapland,' DI Hart replies.

'Ouch,' Bex whispers, looking ahead.

Hart never misses the chance to remind Jake that his books are only published in Finland.

'Kate just called us,' Jake continues, ignoring the barb. They're heading into London. Neither of them knows exactly where Rob lives, only that it's somewhere in Shoreditch. 'She sounded distressed.'

'Us?' Hart says.

'I'm with Bex,' Jake says. 'Her friend.'

He's not used to talking into the air like this. Kate's Morris Minor didn't exactly stretch to a built-in car audio system.

'Hello, Bex,' Hart says drily.

'You alright?' she asks.

Jake has noticed it before. Bex's Lancashire

362

accent becomes more pronounced when she's nervous. Alright becomes *alreet.*

'We met down in Cornwall,' she adds for Jake's benefit.

'Where was Kate calling from?' Hart asks.

'We think from Rob's flat in London,' Jake says.

'Shoreditch,' Bex adds.

'If she's with him, she's fine,' Hart says, almost matter-of-factly.

Jake glances at Bex, who looks equally confused by Hart's relaxed response. 'How can you be so sure?' he asks.

'Trust me,' Hart says.

'OK,' Jake says, failing to hide his irritation. Kate used to adopt a similar tone when he'd asked one too many questions about her police work. 'She didn't exactly sound happy, that's all. I know it wouldn't normally be a police matter, but given what happened in Cornwall, I just thought . . .'

'How long ago did she call?'

Jake looks across at Bex.

'Ten minutes?' she offers.

After Kate tried to ring them, Jake and Bex immediately agreed that they should drive up to London, even if they didn't know precisely where Rob lived. The call had distressed them both.

'And what exactly did she say?' Hart asks.

'The line was terrible . . .' Jake turns to Bex again for support.

'We think she mentioned Rob's flat,' Bex says, 'where she was heading tonight.'

'She hasn't been picking up all evening,' Jake adds. He knows how it must sound to Hart. Bitter ex unable to get over break-up.

'Kate's undoubtedly been a target in recent months,' Hart says. 'A result, I'm afraid to say, of the work she did for us.'

It's the first time Jake's heard Hart admit that. He wishes he'd said something earlier – like before the car crash.

'But we think that threat has now passed,' Hart continues. 'And, as I say, if she's with Rob, I'm not worried. If anything, I'm reassured.'

Why's Hart sounding so damn relaxed about Rob all of a sudden?

'I don't think Rob met Kate by chance,' Jake says. He doesn't like the way Kate has dropped off the radar, as if everything's now fine. 'In the hospital, that first time.' Again, Jake is worried how he's coming across, as if he's obsessed with Kate's new partner. But Hart's tone changes.

'Tell me,' he says, more interest in his voice.

Jake explains about seeing Rob in the car park at Gablecross when he came in to ask Hart some questions about police procedure for his latest book.

'Remind me when that was?'

'A day before Kate's accident. We ended up talking about Bewick's swans.'

'I remember,' Hart says.

'Rob's also involved with facial-recognition software,' Jake adds, now that he's got Hart's attention. 'Some new hush-hush outfit, possibly based in France, according to an investigative website over there. He's known for all his medtech stuff, but I think he engineered a meeting with Kate at the hospital because he was professionally interested in the recognition work she was doing for you.'

This is met by a silence so long that Jake wonders if Hart has hung up. Even Stretch raises his head to see what's going on. Bex glances across at Jake, who dials up the volume on the in-car audio system.

'And you think Rob was visiting Gablecross police station?' Hart asks eventually.

'I assume so.'

'Leave it with me,' Hart says. 'I'll call you tomorrow, first thing.'

'What about Kate?' Jake says, worried that Hart will hang up. 'We just want to check that she's OK. If you've got his address, we could—'

'We don't have Rob's exact London details at the moment,' Hart says, sounding embarrassed. So it's not just Jake who can't find his address. 'I'm sure she's fine.'

CHAPTER 74

KATE

It's like a switch has been flicked – in Rob and in Kate. The old Rob is back, the handsome Irish boy who has cared for her unquestioningly these last five months. The Rob she loves. Her fears of a few minutes ago are already fading, like the receding tide. She can't see him, thanks to the power cut, but the voice is definitely Rob's. She can cope like this. She must be suffering from Capgras syndrome. Why else would he appear different but sound so familiar? She just hopes it's temporary, as Ajay suggested. She can't spend the rest of her life with Rob in the dark.

'We're trying to establish what's caused the outage,' he continues, his arms still wrapped around her as they stand together in the inky blackness of his apartment, their bodies pressed together. 'The whole system went into lockdown and then there was a local power failure.'

'How did you manage to get in here?' she asks.

'The front door runs off a different power source – part of the main building.'

He's always happiest talking technology, never

366

likes it when she tries to discuss the two of them, their feelings for each other.

'Was everyone else shut in then?' she asks.

'I assume so.'

He doesn't sound very convinced and she wonders again if the lockdown was orchestrated by Rob for her safety. 'You can be honest with me, you know,' she says. 'About tonight. I understand.'

'How do you mean?'

Should she continue? She's no longer angry with him.

'If the "outage" wasn't an accident,' she adds.

Do his arms momentarily slacken around her?

'Next time, you can just tell me if you think I'm in danger,' she continues. 'I'm a big girl, worked for the police for a year, remember? Someone tried to kill me in Cornwall – scary for me, but for you too. I get that now. But they're dead, so there's no need to worry any more.'

'I'd do anything to keep you safe, you know that,' he says, his tone more relaxed. 'But what happened tonight wasn't deliberate. The only thing I'm not being honest with you about is that this system is still in beta testing mode and—'

'Ssshh,' she says, finding his lips with her fingers in the darkness. She's heard enough tech speak for one night. She doesn't know whether he's telling the truth or not. She doesn't care any more. All she knows is that she's got her man back.

'I've lit some candles in the bedroom,' she says, running a finger around his mouth.

'I'm enjoying the darkness,' he says, sliding a hand inside her dressing gown.

'Me too.'

Because she can't see his face. And she has no wish to, either. Not in this moment, not tonight.

'So what did you say to Jake?' he asks. 'We don't want anyone worrying unnecessarily.'

'I didn't get through to him,' she says, wishing they could talk about something else now. 'I think the blinds shut out the signal.'

'They're a bit excessive, I know, but it comes with the package. I'll get them fixed in the morning, when the power's back.'

'Why do you need to lock down this place anyway?'

'Can't be too careful,' he says.

They've talked about it before, his obsession with security. It's one of the few things they disagree about, and now's not the time for another argument.

Two minutes later, they are undressing each other in the bedroom, where the candles cast a faint, votive light on their naked bodies. She keeps her eyes averted in what she hopes he interprets as shyness. As she thought, it's not bright enough to see his face, but she doesn't want to take any chances. She also makes sure he's in her right field of vision.

'Close your eyes,' she says, disentangling herself from him. 'Surprise time.'

'That sounds exciting,' he whispers.

She reaches for the drawer beside the bed and removes a burnt-orange silk scarf that Rob bought her. She put it there earlier, before the power cut helped her out. All part of the coping strategy that Ajay suggested – using her brain's auditory pathways to re-establish a connection with Rob. She's not sure a scarf was quite what Ajay had in mind, but she blindfolds herself with it, tying the silk tightly, and lies down on the bed, wondering if it's still necessary given the power cut. She can't risk the lights coming back on without any warning.

'You can open them now,' she says, her heart racing.

She hears a small intake of breath. And then he's moving towards her, bending down, kissing her neck and breasts, her stomach. She knows it's Rob – his voice, his touch, his smell and taste, each sense heightened by the darkness. She can feel herself relaxing.

Their hands start to explore each other, reaching down and slipping between, searching and caressing. She could get used to wearing a blindfold. It makes her feel powerless and empowered, vulnerable and in control. Rob seems to like it too. His young body is taut and smooth, like a swimmer's, hard and firm in her blind hands. He's been dropping hints recently about being more adventurous in the bedroom, but she hasn't had the energy until now. And then she tastes salt and realises that he's crying. He's never cried in front of her before.

'What's the matter?' she says, pulling away.

'It's nothing,' he says. 'I just don't want this to end.'

'It doesn't have to,' she whispers, rolling over on top of him. The darkness is thrilling; it's like it's their first time as she feels her way around his body. She'd forgotten the intensity of physical attraction. Sex with Jake had become numbed by habit. No sparks any more. She leans down to nibble Rob's ear and lets him in with a gasp. 'As long as you can keep going.'

And he does, gently at first and then more urgently, bringing her to a climax so intense that she finds herself shouting, purging her mind of tonight's earlier dramas, all thoughts of doppelgängers. Maybe of Jake too. At least the shutters have some use, insulating their cries from the neighbours. Even creating ripples around the narrowboat used to make her self-conscious.

Afterwards, they lie on their backs in the dim candlelight, Rob to Kate's right. She's taken off the blindfold and her eyes are closed. She knows she hasn't got long before he falls asleep. She needs to ask him about what happened on the beach in Thailand nine years ago and she hopes that he will answer her questions in the afterglow of their lovemaking.

'Rob?' she asks.

'Mmm?'

She's already losing him, but she needs to make a confession.

CHAPTER 75

JAKE

'I think we should turn around and head home,' Bex says as they drive along the almost empty motorway towards London.

Jake glances across at her. The light from the car's large landscape touchscreen between them casts an eerie glow on her face.

He knows she's right. They've discussed what Hart said about Rob, how Kate's safe if she's with him. Hart didn't tell them why he's so sure, but an iMessage has also come through to Bex's phone from Rob. It's in reply to the voicemail message Bex left earlier, explaining as casually as she could that she had been trying to contact Bex.

Jake looks at her phone again and rereads the text, stroking Stretch, who has stirred on his lap.

Hi Bex, just picked up your message. All good. Kate sleeping in the flat. Think the journey wiped her out! Sure she'll call you tomorrow. R x

'When do you think it was sent?' Jake asks, putting the phone back in the dock. 'Before Kate rang?'

'Could have been any time tonight – iMessages seem to turn up when they want on my phone.'

'Before she rang us?'

'I don't know.' Bex glances at a road sign that looms up in the darkness outside. 'I'm coming off at the next junction, unless you've got any better ideas?'

Jake thinks again about Kate's voice on the phone. They don't know exactly where Rob lives, that's their problem. He's never been able to find an address for Rob other than the house in Cornwall, where every one of his business interests seems to be registered. He suddenly despairs at the thought of driving around Shoreditch all night.

'You're right,' he says.

But he doesn't feel comfortable at the thought of abandoning Kate. To distract himself, he starts to skim through the various settings on the touchscreen. He hears Kate's voice again, her worried tone. And he's haunted by the thought that Rob might not have met her by chance at the hospital.

'Does Rob know his car's not in Cornwall?' he asks, still fiddling with the screen. It's bigger than his old TV on the boat.

Bex glances across at him and then the screen. 'How could he?' she asks.

'This thing's a computer on wheels, Bex. And there's a feature here called "Tracking".' He opens up a new window on the screen. 'I'm guessing it all works off an app on Rob's phone.'

'Shit, really?' Bex throws him a nervous look.

They drive on in silence, the Berkshire country-side slipping past them in the darkness. Jake hasn't been this fast in a car for a long time. Another sign says that the next junction is in half a mile.

'Thanks for letting me stay in your house,' he says after a while.

'Glad I could help. Not every day your boat's gutted by fire.'

The arson attack seems a long time ago already.

Bex starts to tap her fingers on the steering wheel, as if she's suddenly nervous. 'Your beard's nice by the way,' she says. 'Much better trimmed.'

'Thanks.' It's the first compliment Bex has ever paid him. He hopes Kate liked it too. Noticed he's making an effort with his appearance. She always hated his hands, but he hasn't been able to do much about them. The oil stains seem to be ingrained, impervious to brushing.

'You'll blend in right well in Shoreditch,' she adds.

Jake is not sure if her compliment has just turned sour. He's never seen himself as an urban hipster. More of a washed-up hick. They drive on in silence. Bex starts to indicate to turn off at the approaching junction. And then Jake has an idea.

'Hang on,' he says, leaning forward to use the display screen again.

'What you doing?' Bex asks, glancing at him.

'This is Rob's Cornwall car, right? But I'm guessing he's kept it in London too at some stage?'

'Nothing would surprise me,' Bex says. 'Although Kate did mention once that he was thinking of buying another one for London. Never likes to do things by halves, does Rob.'

Jake googles the postcode for Shoreditch High Street and then fires up the satnav on the car's display screen.

'If I put in "Home" on the satnav,' he says, typing on the screen, 'it will take me to . . . Cornwall. OK.' He glances at Bex's phone again. 'But what if I type in the postcode for Shoreditch . . . N1 . . . Bingo.'

Predictive typing has kicked in, as he suspected, and a full postcode in Shoreditch is now displayed on the screen, which means it must have been entered at least once before.

'I bet you this is where Rob lives,' he says, activating the route. 'And where Kate called from.'

'Keep going?' Bex says, turning off the indicator.

'We owe it to Kate.'

CHAPTER 76

KATE

'I have a confession to make,' Kate says, pulling up the sheet, her eyes still shut.

'Were you faking it?' Rob mumbles, barely awake.

She prods him in the ribs. They've just had the best sex she can remember.

'You know when you said you'd seen me on Facebook and I denied it?' she says.

'Mmm . . .?'

She takes a deep breath.

'Well, I was on there.'

'Worse crimes have been committed on social media,' he says, his voice almost inaudible now.

'I was talking to one of your old friends.'

'Who?'

That's woken him up. Is she making a mistake?

'I'd rather not say,' she continues. 'It's not important. I was just trying to arrange a surprise.' She thinks back to what Jake told her, keen to stick as closely as she can to his story. 'For your thirtieth birthday.'

'You know I don't like being reminded of my age. Or surprises.'

'That's why I'm telling you now,' she lies. 'You liked my surprise tonight.'

'That was different.' His voice is fading. She hasn't got long.

'This friend of yours told me what happened in Thailand,' she says, 'on the beach.' She tries to conceal her nerves, but her voice is shaking. 'I realise you don't want to talk about it,' she continues. 'I just want you to know that . . . well, that I know. And I understand. It must've been frightening.'

It's a while before he speaks. 'That's all in the past,' he says. 'And you're right, I don't want to talk about it.'

She should leave it at that, but she can't help herself.

'Why?' she asks. 'Are you worried that he'll come back?'

Silence. And then he speaks again, his voice so quiet that she can hardly make out what he's saying.

'Every day I wake up scared, wondering if he has found me.'

She lies there, frozen. Can he hear her heart? She's suddenly conscious of how loud it's beating.

'Then we should talk about it,' she manages to say, opening her eyes, relieved that he's finally opening up. 'Share these things.'

But her relief doesn't last long.

'And do you know what frightens me the most?'

he continues. 'The thought that he might do a better job at being me.'

'How do you mean?' she whispers, her mouth drying. 'You're doing so well. Look at everything you've achieved. No one could beat that.'

More silence, broken only by the sound of his slow breathing.

She stays awake for a long time, replaying his words. How could someone else do a better job of being him? She thinks of the Rossetti painting in Cornwall, the books on his shelf, including the du Maurier, the unnerving sight of him talking in fluent French on the TV.

Just as she's drifting off, the power comes back on, flooding the room with light.

She blinks in the brightness. Rob is sound asleep beside her, his body turned away. She rolls off the bed, removing the scarf completely, and walks over to the light switch. The main bedroom light must have been on when the power went, but she hesitates as she reaches to turn it off. Trying to ignore a rising nausea, she creeps back over to Rob's side of the bed and closes her eyes, standing to his right. One. Two. Three. And then she looks down at his him and gasps, this time in pure fear.

Is it Rob? She needs to be brave, sort this once and for all. Feeling dizzy, she forces herself to kneel down beside his sleeping body. Her scalp begins to tingle as she looks at his legs first, tucked up towards his smooth, flat stomach, and then his chest, his bony shoulders, his long arms. Taking a hand in hers, she feels his fingers one by one, so clean and delicate, and rubs them gently. His breathing is steady, uninterrupted. And then she summons the courage to look at the full lips she has kissed, the curve of his resting eyelids, the hollow of his cheeks, careful to study each feature individually rather than look at the whole face, as she's been trained to do. She reaches out, touches his hair. Is this the man she loves? He stirs a little. Has he heard her thumping heart? The voice in her head? Leaning forwards, she moves her mouth close to his ear. '*Je sais qui tu es*,' she whispers. '*Et je sais pourquoi tu es venu ici.*' She knows who he is – and why he's come here.

Rob's blue eyes flash open. They stare at each other, his face a picture of pure shock. It's not Rob. She gets up and starts to back away, one hand to her mouth, telling herself it's all in her mind, that Rob's had French lessons, that it was his voice tonight, that she's suffering from Capgras syndrome. But it's no good. He was to her right, she can't deny it. She doesn't have Capgras. When she's out of the door, she runs to the bathroom and throws up just as she reaches the loo. Tears stream down her face as she retches and retches again. Every sense in her body told her it was Rob who came tonight. Every sense except her sight, her trusted eyes, and she did her best to stop them from ruining things.

She so wanted to believe it was him, to prove to herself that she hasn't been going mad. Now, though, it seems she's wrong. The man in the bedroom is a stranger. The smoke has returned, swirling and choking. Should she go back into the bedroom and challenge him again? Ask him straight out if he's his doppelgänger, Gil from Thailand, here to take over Rob's life, this apartment, her?

'Kate, are you alright?'

Rob's voice, behind her. She clutches at the loo bowl for strength. Or is it to stop her hands shaking?

'I'm OK,' she says, her back still towards him. Please don't come any closer. 'Must have been something I ate,' she adds.

'Kate, I'm sorry, I hope it wasn't the crayfish. It's usually so good.'

'I don't think it was that,' she says. 'Maybe I just drank too much wine tonight.'

'Can I get you anything?' he asks.

Is he coming nearer? Please God, keep him away. She can't cope with this any more.

'I'm OK, just need to stay in here for a bit. On my own. You go back to bed.'

'You sure?'

Rob's voice, Rob's sympathy . . . What's wrong with her? She should turn around to look at him again, but she can't.

'I might sleep in the other bedroom, so I don't disturb you,' she manages to say.

379

'Let me know if you need anything,' he says kindly.

She closes her eyes as she hears him walk back to the bedroom.

CHAPTER 77

JAKE

'Do you trust him?' Jake asks as they drive on towards London.

'Who, Rob?' Bex asks, moving to overtake a solitary lorry on the motorway.

Jake nods, shifting in his seat. It might be his imagination, but it's feeling a little warmer in the car than it was.

'He's been great for Kate,' Bex says. 'The Rob I know. The real Rob.'

'But do you trust him?' Jake repeats.

'Yes, I trust him.' Bex casts him another glance, as if wondering where he's going with this. 'So does Kate.'

Jake turns away and stares out of the window, watching a group of workmen in high-vis jackets behind a line of flickering traffic cones on the motorway's hard shoulder. He used to write from dusk until dawn in his last days with Kate, but it wasn't because he was a natural night owl. It was because she was asleep in their bed and he couldn't bear to feel lonely lying beside her.

'She trusted you too,' Bex continues.

He squirms in his seat. It was inevitable that

at some stage they'd talk about what happened between him and Kate. And now seems as good a time as any. According to the satnav, it's another hour before they reach Rob's house in Shoreditch.

'That's what made it so hard for her,' Bex says. 'We all know she can be a bit skittish, likes to flirt with everyone, but she would never have been unfaithful to you. Not in a million years.'

'I know,' he says. 'I messed up.' He thinks about opening a window. Maybe it's hot in the car because he's burning with shame.

'Who was she, by the way?' Bex asks, failing to sound casual. 'Kate never said.'

Jake tries not to think about that day if he can help it. It was not his finest hour. One of the worst in his life, in fact.

'Kate never asked,' he says. 'And I never told her.' He pauses. 'I didn't even get her name, her real one.'

'No way.' Bex throws him a mischievous smile.

'I'd been drinking in Swindon,' he says. 'Dark days. Things were pretty bad between me and Kate. For some reason I decided to download a dating app. I'd never done anything like that before – no need – but I'd just read an article about the online dating scene and thought I might include it in the next book. At least, that's what I told myself.'

'All in the name of research.'

'Exactly. So I downloaded the app and headed

for the busiest area I could think of, the Brunel Shopping Centre.'

'Romantic.'

Jake and Kate used to prefer the Designer Outlet at the old Great Western Railway works. When Jake got bored with shopping, he'd slink away to look at the steam trains.

'And all these people wanting no-strings sex come up,' he says. 'A hidden layer of promiscuity just beneath the surface. Who knew?'

'Welcome to my world.'

Bex has never made any secret of her use of dating apps. He should have asked her how they work – it would have saved him a whole lot of trouble. His relationship too.

'And one of them looks nice enough, says she's up for anything, so we meet and the next thing she's kissing me,' he continues. 'I can't say it wasn't exciting – it was the first time I'd been kissed by anyone other than Kate in twelve years.'

'Glad to hear it,' Bex says.

'We went back to her bedsit, but I couldn't go through with it. I left in a hurry. That didn't matter, of course. The damage was done. I never saw her again, but Kate did – our meeting had been filmed.'

He will regret for the rest of his life the manner in which Kate found out. It must have been such a shock. The chances of her seeing the CCTV footage that caught the moment they kissed in the shopping centre were slim, to say the least, but it happened. He has to live with that.

'Maybe it brought things to a head,' Bex says.

'I still wish it hadn't.'

One crazy, midlife moment had ruined everything. It's all behind him now, but that doesn't mean he's stopped caring for Kate, worrying about her.

'Is it roasting in here or just me?' Bex asks.

'It's hot,' Jake says, pleased that it's not only him.

He opens his window and searches the touchscreen for the climate-control settings. 'The heating's on full,' he says, turning it off.

'I didn't touch it,' Bex says.

A second later, loud music starts to play through the speakers. Heavy death metal.

'Turn that off.' Bex glances across at Jake, who's still fiddling with the touchscreen.

'That wasn't me. I promise,' he says.

He manages to shut down the music, but it comes on again, even louder this time: growling vocals and fast, incessant drumming.

'I'm going to pull over while you sort it.' Bex slows the car down on the hard shoulder. 'I can't drive with that bloody racket on.'

'I'm trying.'

She brings the car to a safe standstill, the music still playing.

'Shitters, I knew it was too good to last,' she says as Jake finally manages to turn off the sound system.

'What?'

Bex sits back, shaking her head. 'The car's been disabled.'

'Really?'

She tries again, but a message confirms that the car isn't going anywhere. They sit there in silence, staring ahead in the heat and the dark as Bex tries in vain to start the car. And then a video of a burning log-fire flickers into life on the touchscreen.

'What the hell?' Jake says.

The death metal music starts up again. Jake reaches for the door. He can't seem to open it.

'Shit, it's locked.' He's starting to panic. 'It's so hot in here.'

There's a click and the door is unlocked. Jake's not sure if it was him, Bex or someone else. The cool night air floods into the car as Bex and Jake look at each other, both of them shaken.

'I don't think Rob wants us to drive to London,' she says.

TUESDAY

CHAPTER 78

SILAS

Strover is already in the Parade Room when Silas arrives. He glances at his watch. Seven a.m. He's only been away from this place for six hours. They both need to get some balance in their lives.

'Please don't tell me you've already been for a run,' he says, sitting down next to her.

Strover's hair is wet, as if she's recently showered after an effortless dawn 10k. His own fitness regime couldn't be going worse. Fifteen sit-ups this morning, feet wedged under the bed, and he began to feel dizzy. He didn't sleep well last night either, troubled by what Jake had told him. Why was Rob visiting Gablecross – and before he met Kate for the first time at the Great Western Hospital?

Maybe Silas was too relaxed last night about Kate staying at Rob's London apartment.

'I wanted to talk to Thailand,' Strover says. 'They're six hours ahead.'

'Anything interesting?' He's asked her to look into the gun used in Cornwall, last fired in Bangkok nine years ago, and the Thai police file on Gilmour Martin, the same name as the registered keeper of a Tesla recently seen in Cornwall. It's too much of a coincidence to ignore, but his boss will no doubt dismiss it as circumstantial.

'The police over there are proving helpful about Gilmour,' Strover says.

They could do with some more information. The Royal Thai Police file was not exactly bulging with detail.

'I managed to get through to one of the detectives who interviewed him after he crashed the party,' she continues, glancing at her notes. 'An officer called Manu Jabthian. He's teaching these days, at somewhere called the Bang Kaen Detective Training School.'

Nice work if you can get it. Maybe Silas should offer his services. He fancies a trip to Thailand.

'How long have you been in?' he asks, knowing that this sort of spadework takes time.

'I couldn't sleep,' Strover says.

'You'll make yourself ill,' Silas says, particularly if she eats a single apple every morning and insists on calling it breakfast. Kate was pushed too hard. He's wary of Strover going the same way.

'Manu says he remembers the case well,' Strover continues, checking her notes again.

'What exactly was Gilmour arrested for?'

'Causing trouble at a private party on Ko Samui – Chaweng beach, in the northeast of the island.'

'Is that all?' he asks.

'Off his head on drugs, apparently. But get this – someone saw Gilmour on the beach waving around a handgun. That's why the police were called.'

Silas looks up.

'Do we know what sort of gun?'

'According to Manu, Gilmour was unarmed by the time the police arrested him. They let him go in the end – nobody at the party was willing to give statements. He had no ID or passport on him and wasn't making a lot of sense, but they assumed he was British.'

'What happened to him afterwards?' Silas asks, looking at the police mugshot again, his mind racing.

'That's why Manu remembers the case,' she says. 'Two days later, a body washes up on the same beach, gunshot wound to the head. The police try to call in Gilmour for questioning again, but they can't find him. He's vanished.'

'And the bullet?'

He already knows the answer.

'Same markings as the one fired in Cornwall.'

His boss is going to love this.

'Who was the victim?' Silas asks.

'Small-time drug dealer from Bangkok. Police weren't too concerned.'

He knows the feeling. But the Royal Thai Police would have filed a report linking the Ko Samui case to Gilmour Martin, suspected of being a UK citizen. No real evidence, but enough for the National Ballistics Intelligence Service to flag up a possible British connection.

'Do we have any idea where Gilmour is now?' Silas asks.

'The Home Office doesn't have a record of anyone of that name matching his age,' she says, turning to her laptop. 'I've looked everywhere else too. Mispers, Europol, Interpol.'

He knows Strover would have been thorough, doesn't want to think how long she's already been working on this.

What about the DVLA?' he asks. 'Anything on the "care of" address in London?'

'I'm still trying to establish exactly who lives there,' she says. 'No other vehicles registered at the property. Seems like it's owned by a shell company in the Cayman Islands. Wouldn't mind taking a look in person.'

'And maybe get your friend in digital forensics to help with information on Gilmour,' he says.

'She's already had a trawl. No social-media footprint, nothing. But she did find one thing.'

Silas looks up. He's come to recognise Strover's tone when she's onto something.

'A person calling himself Gilmour Martin appears to have flown into Stansted from Cork on a British passport six months ago,' she says. 'And given the Home Office has no record of a Gilmour Martin matching his age, it must have been a fake.'

Silas is aware that passports aren't always checked as closely as they should be on flights from Ireland to the UK, but there's also been a recent rise in convincing counterfeits. And many of the best are coming out of Bangkok.

'I'm trying to get a photo and flight manifests, but it's going to take time,' Strover says.

'Just don't tell the boss what you're doing,' Silas says.

'We should tell Kate, though – she asked us to look for a match for Rob and she still doesn't know about Gilmour Martin.'

The discovery is hardly going to put her mind at rest.

CHAPTER 79

KATE

Kate knows she's woken late. Not because of the daylight outside – the steel blinds are still down and it's dark in the apartment, a faint light seeping in from the bedroom. It's just a feeling. She sits up on the sofa, the memories of last night flooding back. She's here in the main room with a blanket because she was sick – after thinking again that Rob had been replaced by a double. *Knowing*, not thinking. There's no way her Rob would have known what she was saying in French, given her that look of understanding. He could barely speak a word when she tried teaching him. She hasn't got Capgras.

At least the power is still on. She gets up from the sofa and walks towards the bedroom. Rob's not here, she can sense it. The flat feels empty. Sure enough, the sheets have been stripped back, the bedside light left on, a note beside it. She reads the message without picking it up:

Sorry you had such a rough night. Hope you're feeling better. Power working but blinds still not responding. I'll call mid-morning. Had to leave early for Brittany – looking forward to you joining me . . . R xxx

Her passport, which he'd asked her to bring to London, is beneath the note. She doesn't want to go to Brittany. She wants to get out of here, back to Wiltshire, to Bex's house, where she feels safe. The events of last night have left her shaken, disorientated. She reads Rob's note again, the breezy tone, written as if nothing happened. But then she thinks of the strange man lying on the bed, the shock and the nausea. She tried so hard, wanted to believe in Rob, in the two of them, but she was being naive, wishful, by avoiding the sight of his face all evening. Denying her eyes, her most reliable sense.

She spots the phone and picks it up. At least there's a dial tone. She calls Jake's number, but the line doesn't connect. She tries Bex's, but it's the same. No outgoing calls. She searches for her mobile phone, but she can't find it anywhere. Has Rob taken it?

Ten minutes later, she's showered and changed, filled with a deepening unease. She's still trapped in this apartment and she's not convinced it's for her own safety. She's about to brush her hair when she hears the front door open. Her whole body stiffens. It's like a repeat of last night.

She creeps out of the bathroom into the main room, turns on the lights and sees . . . Ajay. He is standing inside the front door, wearing his usual dark-blue suit and holding an attaché case, bigger than the one he normally brings to their meetings.

'Thank God it's you, Ajay,' she says, with a loud sigh of relief.

'I'm sorry, I was told to let myself in,' he says apologetically, glancing at the hairbrush still in her hand.

'By Rob?' she asks.

Ajay nods, walking over to the kitchen table. Rob would have been worried by her behaviour, would have told him to visit her again.

'I tried ringing you last night,' she says, watching Ajay as he puts his case down beside the kitchen stool. His manner is subdued today; there's no sign of his usual bonhomie. Something's not right. 'You were engaged.'

'I'm sorry. Was there a problem?' he asks.

'Yes, there was,' she says, trying not to revisit the events of last night. 'I don't think I have Capgras.'

'As I think I said yesterday, it's a very rare condition and I'd be surprised if you—'

'I saw him on the other side,' she interrupts. 'In my right field of vision, not my left. And it wasn't Rob.' She moves her head from side to side, trying to reinforce her words. 'If I had Capgras, I would only see a double on my left, isn't that what you said?'

Ajay looks at her. Is it pity in his eyes? For a second she thinks it might be fear.

'How did he sound?' he asks, ignoring her

396

question as he opens up his attaché case. 'Did you try closing your eyes and just listening?' He pulls out his laptop and a reporter's notebook and puts them on the table.

'He sounded like Rob,' she says quietly, thinking of the scarf. Her plan seems so naive now. 'But it wasn't him. It's scaring the shit out of me, Ajay. This isn't him either,' she adds, nodding at the blinds. 'Shutting me in like a bloody prisoner.'

'I can understand,' he says in his best bedside voice. The one he used when he first came to visit her at the hospital.

'What's going on, Ajay?' she asks, walking over to the sink. Her hair's still a mess after her shower – there isn't a hairdryer in Rob's bachelor pad – and she starts to brush it as they talk, tilting her head to one side.

'How do you mean?' he says.

'You have a key. So does Rob. But oddly I don't seem to have one. That's not right, is it? Not bloody normal at all.' She sounds deranged as she vents her frustration on the tangles in her hair.

'Rob's nervous about you being in London,' Ajay offers.

She's brushing too vigorously now. 'Is that so?' she asks, unable to disguise her anger. She walks over to the bathroom and checks her hair in the mirror. 'I'm thirty-bloody-three, Ajay,' she calls out through the open door, still looking at herself. God, she's a wreck. 'I'm not a child.'

She doesn't mean to be angry with Ajay. They

normally speak so freely at their meetings. He's helped her through a difficult recovery, become a friend.

'What's that for?' she asks, coming back over and nodding at the laptop.

'Rob wants me to run some final recognition tests.' Ajay manages a pinched smile. 'The results from the weekend were so encouraging.'

She shakes her head in despair. She's too tired. She was hoping that Ajay might have come to get her out of this place.

'I'm not doing any more tests,' she says, glancing at his laptop as she sits down on a stool opposite him.

'I understand,' Ajay says, writing something down in his notebook. 'Rob thinks you're still at risk from the criminals you helped to identify,' he continues. 'Hence all this.'

He gestures towards the blinds, the front door. She follows his gaze and spots the camera. It's been angled further into the room. Is Ajay reassuring her or trying to warn her? Let her know that they're being filmed? He adjusts his laptop with one hand, positioning it so that the screen is facing towards her. His other hand is on the notebook. She watches as he makes sure it's turned towards her too. And then she glances down at what Ajay's written on the page.

Please do the tests – for my sake and yours.
He can see and hear everything.

CHAPTER 80

SILAS

'I know this is difficult, Silas. Kate was a good friend of yours as well as a colleague. We were all upset by her accident. And the decision to close the super-recogniser unit was not one that I took lightly, as you know.'

Silas looks out of his boss's window. He's never heard such tosh.

'I still think we should call Rob in for questioning,' Silas says. 'At least ask him what he was doing on the night of Kate's crash.'

His boss, Detective Superintendent Ward, is ten years younger than Silas, and the talk in the force is when, not if, he'll become Detective Chief Superintendent. Silas has always tried to like him, but he's not making it easy today.

'You say a Tesla was spotted at the scene of the accident, but we have to look at where this information's come from,' he continues. 'An anonymous local drug dealer who was told by the barman of the Bluebell, now deceased. It's not exactly gospel, is it?'

Put like that, Silas can see Ward's point. Except that he hasn't come clean, told him that the

399

anonymous local drug dealer is Conor, his own son. How could he?

'And Rob's not the only person in Britain who drives a Tesla,' Ward adds.

He's trying not to make Silas sound stupid. Silas's lack of a university degree never used to be a problem, but he is finding it increasingly hard these days, and not just because his boss happens to have a first from Oxford. Every new officer who joins the force seems to be a graduate, challenging his own education at the 'university of life', as his dad used to call it.

'But Rob did visit Kate in hospital and is now her partner,' Silas continues. 'Don't you think it's a coincidence worth investigating if he was there that night?'

'We don't know who was there.'

Silas is not going to win this one. He hasn't even tried to explain a possible connection between the gun used in Cornwall and Gilmour Martin, Rob's double in Thailand, who has also been seen driving a Tesla. There's only one thing left to try.

'I think Rob might have visited here before the accident,' Silas says.

'Here, as in Gablecross?' Ward asks calmly, but Silas detects the subtlest shift in his boss's tone.

'He was seen in the car park,' he says. 'The day before the crash.'

Silas has now established an exact date:

400

13 February. Jake said he saw Rob when he was coming in for a chat about his book, a meeting that Silas had written in his diary.

'Do we know who he was visiting?' Ward asks.

'No.'

Ward lets the word hang in the air. No need to say any more, point out the further lack of evidence. There was no record of Gilmour or Rob having signed in to visit the station. Silas checked earlier. He's had enough.

'The Major Crime Team in Truro is struggling, sir,' he says. 'Doesn't think the death in Cornwall was drugs-related. I'd like to take the lead on the case.'

'I know you would,' Ward says. 'Leave it with me. I'll talk to the SIO down there, see what he wants. And I'd rather you don't go troubling Rob unnecessarily. He's proving a very good friend to Swindon.'

A very good friend to Swindon. What the hell does that mean? All Rob's done is put on an art show in the local hospital. Silas is about to ask when Ward knocks the wind out of him with a parting question.

'How's Conor by the way?' he asks, standing up to signal that the meeting is now at an end. 'Heard he's fallen in with the wrong crowd.'

'He's fine, thanks,' Silas says, doubling up inside. 'We're getting him help.'

'Glad to hear it. Wasn't sure if it was just more

hearsay. You know how gossip can spread around here – like wildfire.'

The bastard. How much more does he know about Conor? Silas walks out of his boss's office, keen to put some distance between them.

CHAPTER 81

KATE

'The weekend results were truly exceptional, you know,' Ajay says, glancing up at Kate from across the kitchen table. His manner is forced, as if he's playing up for the cameras. 'You're almost back to how you were before the crash.'

Kate tries not to think too hard about the words he's just written in his notebook. Ajay is attempting to act normally and she must do the same.

He can see and hear everything.

The whole apartment must be wired up with hidden microphones and cameras. Is it the same with the house in Cornwall? Has Rob been monitoring her every move? This isn't about her security. Something else is going on.

'I missed one,' she says, recalling the rapid series of faces she was shown down in Cornwall. She spotted Jeff but Brucie got away.

'It was a hard test,' Ajay says. 'No one's ever spotted both.'

She would have done in the past. And she wants

403

to again. Ajay explains that she'll be shown a mugshot of one person for ten seconds. She must then watch up to sixty minutes of real CCTV crowd footage and try to spot the person. Analysing CCTV is particularly draining, but she will do this final test – for Ajay. And also for her. She's determined to recover – identifying Conor at the station in the village gave her a surprising thrill – but she never wants to revisit the police life she's left behind. She just wants to paint people again, see them for who they really are.

'Would it be useful if you also looked at some of my latest drawings?' she asks.

'Sure,' Ajay says, 'I'd like that.' But she knows he's humouring her.

'And afterwards?' she asks. 'I must go to Brittany?'

He nods, but his manner's become forced again, not like Ajay at all. He turns to his attaché case, open beside the laptop, and pulls out a circular device of some sort.

'Rob wants you to wear this for the next test,' he says, holding up what looks like a grey rubberised necklace punctuated with flat metal contact points. He places it on the table next to the laptop.

'What is it?' she asks, suspecting that it's another fitness gadget that Rob's company has invested in.

'The latest wearable technology,' he says, but he's not looking at her. He's busy on the laptop.

'It measures various biometric data while you're studying the CCTV footage. Blood flow through the carotid artery, that sort of thing.'

He stands up and comes over to her side of the kitchen table.

'We'll need to take this off,' he says, nodding at her beach-glass necklace. 'It might interfere with the readings.'

She lifts her chin up and unfastens it, then lets him slip on the rubber device in its place. His hands are warm, sweaty.

'Comfortable?' he asks.

She's not listening. She's looking at the image on Ajay's laptop, her target mugshot. It's a photo of Rob, staring directly at the camera. At least she thinks it's Rob.

'Are you ready?' Ajay says, following her gaze and then glancing at his watch. 'Ten seconds.'

She leans in to examine the photo more closely, searching the eyes for a clue. She's no longer sure.

'Is that Rob?' she asks quietly, slipping a finger inside the neckband to loosen it. It's too tight.

'It doesn't matter who it is,' Ajay says. 'You've just got to spot his face in the crowd.'

CHAPTER 82

SILAS

After Silas has finished with his boss, he picks up his laptop from the Parade Room and heads straight for the station's main entrance. He knows the reception staff well. These people are on the frontline, dealing with the drunk and the drugged, the violent and the damaged, anyone that Response brings in off the streets.

'Still coping with the fame?' he asks 'Bodie', one of the two female receptionists who were recently featured in a fly-on-the-wall TV documentary about Gablecross. It's not her real name but everyone at the station calls her Bodie.

'Graham Norton this week, Hollywood the next,' she says drily. 'You know how it is.'

He waits as a pair of uniforms walk past, escorting a young homeless man out of the main door. It could so easily be Conor.

'I need to look at the car park cameras out front,' he says, once they've gone. 'From February this year.'

'You're in luck,' she says. 'We've both been watching Marie Kondo.'

Silas cocks his head quizzically. What are they on about?

'Netflix?' she says, turning to open a cupboard behind her. 'Japanese decluttering expert?'

'She tells you how to vertically fold your socks,' 'Doyle', the other woman, says. No one can remember who first started calling them Bodie and Doyle. Some of the younger officers must wonder why too. *The Professionals* was a long time ago. 'You should try it sometime.'

Silas has enough trouble finding a matching pair of socks let alone folding them.

After searching in the cupboard, Bodie hands a small box over to Silas. 'Here we go,' she says. 'Neatly sorted by date. If you'd come last week, it would have taken me all morning to find it. You can't take it away though, not unless you want me fired.'

Silas was expecting as much. It's why he brought down his laptop.

'Thanks,' he says, nodding at one of the small interview rooms that adjoin the reception area. 'I'll be in there.'

'Keep only those things that give you the spark of joy,' Doyle says as Silas walks away with the box.

'Have gratitude for what you're discarding,' Bodie calls out.

Silas shakes his head in disbelief as he closes the door of the airless interview room behind him. Sitting down at the small desk, he starts to work his way through the USB sticks, each one with a month and year written on it. It takes a few moments to find the February file and insert the stick into his laptop but a lot longer to scroll through to 9.30 a.m. on 13 February, when Jake came in to see him. Jake said that he saw Rob after their one-hour meeting, on his way out. He moves forward to 10.25 a.m. and starts to watch the footage in real time. The screen is split into four camera feeds, the top two from the public car park, the bottom left from the adjoining staff car park and the final one from the main entrance.

At 10.32, Silas recognises the bulky figure of Jake walking out of the station entrance, his back to the camera. He leans in closer to the two feeds from the public car park. Jake appears in the bottom left frame, approaching a blue Morris Minor Traveller. He remembers Kate's car, the mangled wreckage that was taken away on a low-loader. As Jake opens the door, he looks across the car park at something. Silas switches to the other feed and watches. And then he sees it. A Tesla in the far corner, barely visible. It must be the only parking space that's not covered completely by the cameras. Silas swallows as the driver walks away from the car. He's wearing a baseball cap, but Silas can just see his face. It's Rob.

CHAPTER 83

KATE

It's almost forty-five minutes into the CCTV footage when Kate spots him. Rob is wearing a baseball cap pulled over his eyes and has his head down, as if he's trying to avoid being seen. He's approaching a ticket barrier at what looks like a London Underground station.

'There, that's him,' she says.

Ajay stops the footage and rewinds a few seconds. His hand is shaking.

Kate watches again as Rob approaches the barrier. 'Stop,' she says, pointing at the figure on the screen.

Ajay bows his own head for a moment and then looks up at her, his normally bright brown eyes dulled by a sudden sadness.

'Am I wrong?' she asks, disappointed.

He is close to tears. 'No, you're not wrong. You're ready. Rob will be thrilled.'

'So what's with the long face?' she asks, her whole body relaxing after the intensity of the last forty-five minutes. What does Ajay mean by 'ready'?

The phone starts to ring in the bedroom.

'Because that's incredible,' he says, glancing into the other room. 'Barely 10 per cent of his face is visible, maybe less. The resolution's low, the light's poor, it's a bad angle. Recognition software would never have identified him.'

Another dirty spot. She must be better.

'You ought to get that,' Ajay says, writing something in his notebook. 'I'll pack up.'

She walks over to the bedroom, concerned by Ajay's downbeat demeanour, and answers the phone.

'How are you feeling? Any better?'

It's Rob, but her heart doesn't soar. Not like it used to when he would ring her in Cornwall and she'd lie back on the bed, listening to his plans for her art, a possible solo exhibition in London, his love for her. She can't trust him any more, can't be sure that it's him.

'OK,' she says, her voice determinedly neutral. She'd forgotten about the device around her neck, but it starts to feel tight again.

'How did you get on?' he asks. 'With the final test?'

Is it even Rob's voice? She doesn't trust herself any more.

'I've just finished,' she says, suspecting that he already knows the result. She runs her fingers over the neckband, hoping to find a clip so that she can release it. The data from it will already have been downloaded onto Ajay's laptop.

'Did you spot him?' he asks.

410

Him? Wasn't it Rob in the footage?

'What's going on, Rob? The blinds are still down here.'

'I'm sorry.' He pauses. 'There were problems with the system last night, but it's all sorted now and you're right, the blinds should be up.'

'But they're not,' she says, trying again to find a way to release the neckband.

It's a while before he speaks.

'I think someone's still trying to harm you,' he says, his voice heavy with concern.

She doesn't believe him. Not after the scribbled note from Ajay. There are too many unanswered questions. Why can't she make outgoing calls on the landline? And where's her mobile phone?

'Who's trying to harm me?' she asks.

'The same as before. People you identified.'

She still doesn't believe him.

'I can look after myself, Rob,' she says, glancing through the door at Ajay, who has finished packing up and is waiting for her. 'And he's dead now, the man in Cornwall who tried to kill me.'

'There are others,' he says.

She hesitates. Maybe she's being naive and there are still people out there who want to harm her. She should be grateful that Rob, if it's him, is being so protective.

'Am I allowed out of here now?' she asks. 'I've passed the test.' *You're ready.*

'You must be patient.'

'How about the roof terrace?' She just wants

some fresh air. And perhaps the possibility of escape, however high the walls.

'My car's waiting for you downstairs,' Rob says. 'Same driver as yesterday – you'll recognise him.' Putin. 'You've found your passport, I hope? The driver will accompany you.'

'Rob, this is crazy, I don't need accompanying—'

'He'll bring you to the house in Brittany,' Rob interrupts. 'I think you'll like it. Home from home. I can explain more then.'

'Do I have a choice?' she asks. 'If I don't want to go with him?'

She's always wanted to visit Brittany, see if it's really like Cornwall, but not in these circumstances.

'I'm so pleased you're better, Kate,' he says, ignoring her question as if she's a truculent teenager. 'Now I need your help.'

'My help?' What does he mean? It's a while before he speaks.

'I think he's here,' he says, quietly.

'Who?' But she knows already.

'Gil – the man from Thailand.'

She should be pleased that he's talking about his double again, sharing his anxieties. It's how she always wanted it to be between them – no secrets. But she's not. She's scared. She can't even be sure who she's talking to.

'How do you know?' she asks.

'His face was picked up on the Underground earlier this morning. I need to know where he turns up next, where he's heading.' He pauses.

'He's here to destroy me, Kate. All that I've achieved. My work, my new life with you. We both might be in danger.'

'And I'm the one to help?' she asks, thinking back to the assessment she's just completed, her ability or otherwise to identify someone. Was it Gil that she just spotted on the Underground? She's sure it was Rob.

'There's no one better,' he says. 'I can't wait for you to be with me in Brittany.'

He hangs up. She stands there holding the receiver for a few seconds before replacing it. She tries to focus on Rob, the man who came to her hospital bedside and talked about art, helped her to get better, helped her to become the person she has always dreamt of being.

She walks back to join Ajay, who is still by the desk. The room's spinning and she wonders if she's going to throw up again.

'Are you OK?' he asks, looking at her with concern.

'I need a glass of water.' She goes over to the sink to steady herself. 'Are you coming to Brittany too?' she asks, still trying to process what Rob's just told her.

'I've got more appointments this morning,' he says. 'And I must lock up here. Your driver's waiting downstairs.'

'Can you take this off?' she asks, touching the neckband.

Ajay casts his eyes downwards, as if in shame.

'Rob will remove it when you reach the house,' he says.

'Why not now?' she asks, increasingly alarmed.

'He wants to download the data himself,' he says. 'It's early days, still in beta testing.'

He looks up at her, knowing that she doesn't believe him.

She shakes her head slowly. The device suddenly feels even tighter. Is it a tag of some sort? Like offenders wear under curfew? A tracking device?

'How was Rob?' Ajay asks, determinedly changing the subject.

'OK,' she says, one hand still on the neckband.

'He sounded himself, though?' Ajay looks up at her, waiting for her answer.

'I think so.'

In truth, she no longer knows.

'I've got some exercises for you to do in France,' he adds, passing her a piece of paper. His back is towards the door and the camera. She looks at him for a second and then she glances at what he's written. One word, underlined.

Run.

CHAPTER 84

JAKE

Jake stands at the train doors, waiting for them to open. Bex is behind him, surrounded by commuters. It's a long time since he's been on an early train to London. And he remembers now why he gave up commuting. The train was delayed and overcrowded. They were lucky to get a seat.

'I need a coffee,' Bex says as they step onto the platform at Paddington.

'Me too,' Jake says.

They eventually got back to Bex's house at 3 a.m., sitting in the cab of an RAC recovery vehicle. After snatching a couple of hours' sleep, they dropped Stretch off with a neighbour and caught the first train of the day. Jake wanted to leave the Tesla on the motorway hard shoulder and walk home – it would have only taken a couple of hours – but Bex felt more responsibility for the vehicle, despite it refusing to move another inch. There was also Stretch to think about.

Jake is sure Rob remotely disabled the car, which worries him, makes it even more important that

415

they get to London as soon as possible, check that Kate's OK.

They grab a coffee on the station concourse and take the Underground to Old Street. Jake hasn't been in London for a while – he hasn't been able to afford it – and the sheer volume of commuters on the Tube makes him yearn for the wide-open spaces of Wiltshire. The only wildlife on offer is a rat that he sees scuttling beneath the blackened Tube tracks at King's Cross.

It's a five-minute walk from Old Street to Nile Street, which seems to be one big building site. Almost every property is being restored, shrouded in scaffolding and plastic sheeting. Workmen in hard hats and high-vis jackets are everywhere, stopping pedestrians as diggers reverse and lorries arrive. The postcode Jake took down from the Tesla's satnav is for the whole of the street, but Bex thinks she knows where Rob lives.

'Kate mentioned once it was in a renovated factory of some sort,' she says as they walk down the narrow road, looking up at the tall anonymous buildings on either side. Jake can hear the anxiety in her voice. They are both nervous, worried for Kate.

'Has she been here before?' he asks, trying not to pry.

'No.' Bex raises her eyebrows. 'I told her to be careful not to live separate lives, but she loves Cornwall and he has to be in London and France for his work.'

They walk back up the street, Bex trying to figure out which building might have once been a factory. Jake is tempted to shout out Kate's name, see if someone opens a window. Anything to relieve the stress. He barely slept on Bex's sofa, counting the minutes until they could take the first train.

'I think this might be it,' she says, standing in front of a solid corner building with old brickwork and metal period windows.

Jake walks up to the entrance and looks at the panel of buttons. None of them have anything so helpful as a name.

'Penthouse?' he says, standing back to gaze up at the high building. A row of small palm trees is visible on the roof. Properties here must be worth millions.

'How did you guess?' Bex says.

'Do you think it makes him happy?' Jake asks. 'Having so much money?'

'You'd always want more,' Bex says.

'Let's walk around the back first,' Jake says. 'Maybe there's a tradesman's entrance.'

They set off down Shepherdess Walk, a narrow street that runs down one side of the building. Jake glances up at the roof again. Kate would want a garden if she lived in London, just like she kept an allotment when they were on the boat. Is she up there now? He's convinced she wouldn't have rung him last night if there hadn't been a serious problem.

'Can't get much sunlight if you're in a ground-floor flat,' Bex says as they approach the back of the building on Underwood Row, also narrow. 'What's the time?'

But before Jake can answer, his phone rings. It's DI Hart.

'Are you with Kate?' he asks, sounding concerned. He seemed so relaxed last night.

'We're outside Rob's apartment in London,' Jake says, scanning the street. 'At least we think we are. Why?'

He puts his mobile on speaker and calls Bex over to listen.

'It's just that she asked us to see if Rob has any doubles out there,' Hart says. 'You know, doppel-gängers. Apparently, Rob is worried about it. She is too.'

'And?' Jake asks, peach-stoning his unshaven chin as he listens intently. A lorry starts to reverse at the end of the street, alarm beeping.

'We've found some lookalikes,' Hart continues. 'And one of them is very convincing – based in Thailand.'

Jake glances at Bex. 'Don't suppose he's called Gil, by any chance?' he says, turning his back to shield him from the noise of the reversing lorry.

It's a while before Hart answers. 'Gilmour Martin – he entered the UK six months ago. How did you know his name?'

'Long story.' There's no time to explain how he impersonated Kate on Facebook and chatted to

Rob's dead friend Kirby. It seems increasingly likely that he was actually talking to Gil, who presumably wanted to send a message to Rob that he was coming for him. And now he's here in the UK, ready to fulfil his threat.

'A Tesla registered to him was seen driving around Cornwall at the weekend,' Hart says. 'I thought Kate should know. She's not answering her phone. Maybe you could pass it on when you see her?'

'We would if we knew where she was,' Jake says. 'We don't have Rob's exact address.'

'We're still struggling to find one for him too,' Hart says. 'Seems like he uses his Cornwall address for everything. Businesses, car, tax returns, the lot. What was Rob so worried about anyway?'

'Doppelgängers are meant to be a sign of your imminent death,' Jake says, not sure how much to elaborate. 'It's all a bit Brothers Grimm, but Rob thinks he met his doppelgänger – a man called Gil – at his twenty-first birthday party in Thailand. This bloke Gil apparently threatened to hunt Rob down one day and destroy him, ruin his career.'

'I'll call you,' Hart says, hanging up.

Jake and Bex start to walk back down towards Shepherdess Walk, but they both stop in their tracks as they reach the corner. A Tesla is slowing down by the building's entrance. They watch as it parks across the street, two wheels up on the pavement. The rear windows are dark. Nobody gets out. It appears identical to the one that ground to a halt on the hard shoulder last night.

Jake doesn't have a good feeling about this. 'Let's wait here,' he says, holding out a hand to stop Bex from walking any further.

CHAPTER 85

SILAS

Silas looks on in the Parade Room as Strover runs the number plates through the DVLA database, confident that the Tesla caught on CCTV in the Gablecross car park will turn out to be Rob's. Kate mentioned that Rob was considering buying another Tesla and Silas has no desire to believe in doppelgängers. What was it that Jake said? *A bit Brothers Grimm.*

'Any luck?' he asks, leaning in to look at Strover's screen.

'I thought it was familiar,' she says, scrolling down through the data. 'Same number plate as the one Kate was given in Cornwall by her gallery friend. Registered keeper: Gilmour Martin, at the "care of" address in N1.'

'Oh Christ,' Silas says, running a hand through his hair. It's not what he was expecting at all.

'And the timing fits,' Strover says. 'Gilmour flew into Stansted six months ago, a week before the 14th of February, the date of the CCTV footage.'

'We need to visit this "care of" address,' Silas says. 'Where is it again?'

'Nile Street. Shoreditch.'

'Shoreditch?' Silas looks up. He pulls out his mobile and calls Jake, remembering that he was looking for Rob's flat somewhere in Shoreditch.

'You found where Rob lives yet?' he asks, glancing around the Parade Room.

'We know the road,' Jake says. 'Nile Street.'

Silas has a terrible sinking feeling, similar to when he found Conor on the floor of his bedroom, unconscious from a heroin overdose. Rob wouldn't have registered his own car at his own apartment using a 'care of' address. Gilmour, whoever he may be, is one step ahead. He's also mocking Silas. Rob too. Why else would he use Rob's address? If he didn't want to be traced, he could have covered his tracks, given the DVLA a false address or a mailbox. It's almost as if it's deliberate, a taunting message.

After giving Jake the exact address in Nile Street, Silas gets up from his desk and stares out of the window at the station car park. It's still raining. Silas likes rain. It's less distracting than sunshine, helps him to focus. See things. Join the dots. Gilmour Martin, Rob's lookalike, flew into the UK on an illegal passport and acquired a matching Tesla, which he promptly registered at Rob's London address. He was then seen at Gablecross a day before Kate's accident. Does that mean it was him at the scene of the crash too and not Rob?

'Jake mentioned that Rob is worried about

seeing his his doppelgänger again, the one he met in Thailand,' Silas says, turning to face Strover, trying to make sense of it all. 'Apparently Rob fears that his double will come back to ruin his life. Rob even mentioned his name – Gil. You know doppelgängers are meant to be a sign of your death? Harbingers of doom.'

Strover gives him a circumspect look. 'You believe all that stuff, boss?'

'I didn't say that.' He pauses. 'But let's just suppose this Gilmour has come to the UK to destroy Rob, for whatever reason. How would he set about taking down Rob, a successful tech entrepreneur?'

'Attack his business?' Strover offers. 'I don't know, do something that triggers a share price crash?'

'Or he might try to frame him.'

'How?'

'Rob's company is under pressure, way over-valued, according to Jake,' Silas says, warming to his theme. 'He also said that Rob could be getting into facial-recognition software. A boom industry right now, as we know. Soon to be worth twenty billion dollars, so they say. Everyone's trying to crack it. Law enforcement agencies everywhere are begging for a system that actually works. Rob probably sees it as a lifeline. But what's its biggest threat?'

'Apart from the fact that it's intrinsically shit, you mean?' Strover asks.

'Apart from that.' Silas allows himself a smile. Strover's in danger of becoming a fellow Luddite.

'Privacy legislation?' she offers. 'Too much faith in faulty algorithms?'

'And?' Silas says. 'What do you and I know works better than facial-recognition software?'

Strover pauses before answering. 'Humans,' she says. 'Super recognisers.'

Silas nods. 'Experts reckon it will be a good ten years before the software can match the super recognisers.'

'And a number of them have gone missing in the past six months,' Strover says.

'Ever since Gilmour Martin arrived in the UK.'

Strover looks up at Silas. 'You think he's responsible?'

'We have to consider it.'

He thinks back to what happened to his own super-recogniser unit. Kate, its best operator, was nearly killed in a car accident, denting the unit's performance as well as its morale. One month later, his boss closed the unit down and signed a contract for Centaur, a new facial-recognition software system that's yet to go live.

'Why a Tesla, though?' Strover asks. 'Quite a top-end car to abduct someone in.'

'Not if Gilmour's trying to frame Rob, a well-known techpreneur who's already got one himself.'

'It's also electric,' she says. 'Silent. And Teslas have a chill mode – it softens out the throttle response.' Strover really should consider a job on *Top Gear*. 'A person wouldn't even be aware that there was a car behind them,' she continues.

'Get on to the super-recogniser unit in Nottingham,' Silas says, a new urgency in his voice. Gilmour might be trying to destroy Rob's career, but Silas isn't going to allow him to ruin his. 'Ask them to go through ANPR records for the night that their star performer disappeared and look for a Tesla registered to Gilmour Martin. Then check in with Dublin, Madrid and Hamburg.'

CHAPTER 86

JAKE

Jake stands with Bex at the corner of Shepherdess Walk, looking down towards the Tesla, still up on the kerb.

'Something's happening,' Bex says.

The driver of the Tesla gets out and walks over to the entrance to the block of flats where they now know Rob lives. He disappears inside and reappears a minute later with a woman. Kate. He takes her by the arm and walks her over to the car. Is she going willingly? Maybe she's unwell? The driver now has one hand on Kate's elbow, either to steady her or to restrain her.

'It's her,' Bex says.

'Kate!' Jake calls out from down the street and starts to run towards her.

Kate turns to look at them. Jake knows at once that she's under duress. There is nothing but fear in her face. A moment later, the driver bundles her into the back of the car, helped by another woman standing nearby, who gets in after Kate.

'Wait!' Jake calls again, still running. Bex is close behind him.

But the car is already accelerating silently away from them.

'Get the number plate,' he says, making a note of it himself. 'You got it?'

'I think so,' Bex says, out of breath.

They confirm what they've both remembered. Bex writes the number down on the back of her hand with a biro as Jake calls DI Hart on his mobile to tell him what's just happened.

'She was definitely not going willingly,' Jake says.

'Number plate?' Hart asks.

Bex holds up her hand. He reads it out to Hart, glancing around him. Someone else is coming out of the apartment door. A tall, dignified Asian man with an attaché case in one hand.

'Dr Varma?' Bex asks the man tentatively. He clearly recognises Bex but tries to ignore her as he walks off down the street.

'I've got to go,' Jake says to Hart, hanging up.

'Dr Varma?' Bex says again, following the man like a reporter in pursuit of a politician. 'What's wrong with Kate? We saw her get into a car just now and she didn't look too happy.'

'I'm late for another appointment,' the man says, almost breaking into a run.

Bex is undeterred and grabs the man by his arm. He stops, visibly shocked by the physical contact. He looks down at his arm and then at Jake, who's caught up with them. Bex has mentioned the neuropsychiatrist that Kate's been seeing, how

427

good he is. This must be him. Jake moves around to stand in his way, in case he tries to make a run for it.

'What's going on?' Bex asks. 'With Kate? Where was she going?'

Dr Varma scans the street, shifts his feet. He couldn't look more guilty if he tried.

'Is Rob in the flat?' Jake asks, gesturing up at the building behind them.

Dr Varma shakes his head.

'Where is he?' Jake says.

'I can't say anything,' Dr Varma says, still staring at the pavement. He then looks up at Bex. 'You have no idea who you're dealing with here. If he knew I was even talking to you now, he'd—'

'Who?' Jake says, interrupting him. 'Who are we dealing with?'

Dr Varma bites his lip. 'I can't tell you anything, I'm sorry. I have two children. A wife.'

Jake is unable to control himself any longer. He checks the deserted street, then grabs Dr Varma by the lapels of his suit jacket and rams him up against the wall.

'Jake!' Bex protests, but he's beyond listening.

'You need to tell us now where Kate's been taken,' he says, his face close to Dr Varma's. Jake is not a violent man, but the last six months seem to have suddenly caught up with him, all the anger for being so stupid that day with a stranger in Swindon, the hatred he feels for Rob, the boat fire.

'Jake,' Bex says insistently, a hand on his arm. Jake ignores her. Dr Varma looks from her to Jake and back to Bex again, his frightened eyes darting between them.

'Tell me where she's gone,' Jake repeats, tightening his grip on Dr Varma's lapels.

'I can't,' he says breathlessly.

'Tell me,' Jake says, lifting the doctor off his toes. 'We need to know.'

'Jake,' Bex pleads again.

Jake lets him go, pushing him away like a repulsed lover. Dr Varma is still breathing hard as he adjusts his dishevelled tie. There's a rip down one side of his jacket.

'I'm sorry,' Jake says, shocked by his own violence. He looks up and down the street, as if searching for an explanation for his own behaviour. 'Kate's in real trouble,' he says. 'We need to help her.'

'I know,' Dr Varma says, his voice barely audible.

'You know, but you can't tell me where she's been taken?'

'If I do, they will kill me.'

The two men stare at each other, both still breathing hard. Jake searches his face, pleading now in silence. 'I get it,' he says, raising a hand to Dr Varma's shoulder, tidying up the ripped suit material before patting him. 'It's OK.' Time to go. Jake's done all he can here. The man has a wife and children to think about. It was wrong to ask.

He's a loyal family man. And then Jake remembers the man's profession.

'First, do no harm,' he says, his eyes fixed on Dr Varma's. *'Primum non nocere.* Isn't that the Hippocratic principle you're all supposed to follow as doctors?' Jake's father was a GP. 'If you don't tell me where Kate's been taken, she's going to come to a lot of harm, believe me. You're the only person who can stop that happening.'

A siren wails in the distance. It's a long time before Dr Varma speaks.

'Brittany,' he says, his voice almost a whisper. 'Rob's got a house in Brittany, beyond Brest.'

Jake looks at him in disbelief and then turns to Bex.

'North of Le Conquet, west of Illien,' Dr Varma continues. 'It's on its own – on a headland.'

He pauses for a moment before hurrying away.

'He was terrified,' Bex says as they watch him disappear around the corner of the street.

'So was Kate,' Jake says, trying not to dwell on what fate might await Dr Varma. 'How the hell do we get to Brittany?'

CHAPTER 87

SILAS

'I've double-checked and Rob definitely only owns one Tesla,' Strover says, looking at her phone. 'And that's registered at his Cornwall address.'

'Get Jake on the phone,' Silas says. He is driving into London as quickly as a blue light and endless roadworks will allow. Whose idea was it to make the M4 a 'smart' motorway? Ten minutes ago, Jake rang from London in a state, saying that Kate had just been bundled into a Tesla outside Rob's flat in Shoreditch. He had the presence of mind to take down the number plate, which Silas recognised immediately as the car registered to Gilmour Martin.

'Any luck?' Jake asks as soon as the call connects.

'Not yet,' Silas says. 'You sure you didn't see Rob in the car?'

'No. Just a driver and a woman,' Jake says. 'I also had a little chat with the shrink who's been overseeing Kate's recovery. Someone called Dr Ajay Varma. He came out of Rob's flat shortly after Kate.'

Silas turns to Strover, who writes down Dr Varma's name.

'Varma says Kate's heading for Brittany,' Jake continues. 'Rob's been doing a lot of business over there, in Brest. Has a house on the coast.'

Jake gives more specific details of the location, which Strover also notes.

'And you're certain Kate didn't look like she was going on holiday?' Silas says.

'Absolutely not.' Jake pauses. 'I thought you said that she would be safe with Rob last night.'

'I did.' Silas wonders how to phrase what he's going to say next. 'I'm just not sure that it was Rob she was with.'

It's a long time before Jake speaks. 'Who's the car registered to? The one that took her away?'

Silas suspects Jake knows already. 'Gilmour Martin. We've put an ANPR marker on the vehicle index and we'll get checks on all ferries leaving Portsmouth, Poole and Plymouth, as well as Eurostar and all major London airports. There's only one direct flight a day to Brest Bretagne and that left Southend at seven o'clock this morning – but she might be going via Paris.'

Silas and Strover drive on in silence. He only uses the siren when he has to. If Kate's being taken through the centre of London, they'll soon get a hit on the Tesla, he's sure of it. There's ANPR everywhere, ever since Transport for London gave the Met access to its cameras for the low emission zone, congestion charge and traffic monitoring.

Their priority is to secure Kate's safety. And then find Rob. He could be in danger too, if Gilmour is serious about destroying him, taking over his life.

Twenty minutes later, the phone rings. Silas recognises the Nottingham number at once. It's the detective who runs the local super-recogniser unit, the one he spoke to before.

'You need to tell me who Gilmour Martin is,' the detective says.

Silas adjusts his grip on the steering wheel. ANPR must have spotted his car in Nottingham. He was right. It's all about identifying patterns. And the one that's emerging now is far worse than he ever imagined.

'When did ANPR pick him up?' Silas asks.

'A day before our PCSO went AWOL,' the detective says.

The PCSO was the Nottingham super-recogniser unit's best performer, like Kate.

'Is he still missing?' Silas asks.

'Not a word. Family are keen to go public – we're putting out a national misper appeal tomorrow.'

'Where was the hit on Gilmour Martin's vehicle?' Silas asks.

'New ANPR camera on the corner of Fletcher Gate and Victoria Street in the city centre. You need to tell us what's going on.'

The detective is owed an explanation. Silas is just not sure he can provide one.

'We're investigating a possible connection

between Gilmour and our own super recogniser who was badly injured in a car crash,' he says.

'And you think he's linked to our PCSO's disappearance?'

'Possibly,' Silas says. 'I'll be in touch as soon as we know any more.'

'It's just that we're struggling to find anything on Gilmour other than the "care of" address he's given the DVLA,' the detective says.

Silas glances at Strover. She did well to establish his arrival in the UK six months ago on a forged passport.

'And up here, "care of" addresses tend to have a funny smell,' the detective continues. 'Have you visited this place in London? Nile Street?'

'We're on our way now.'

'You really can't tell us anything else?' the officer says. 'The PCSO was a good man.'

'Not yet, I'm sorry.'

Silas hangs up. He can't tell anyone, not even his boss. Not until he's got more evidence. A moment later, another call comes in. Dublin number this time. Gilmour Martin's been a busy man.

CHAPTER 88

KATE

Kate's legs are shaking as the car accelerates away through the London traffic in silence. It's a Tesla, identical to the one in Cornwall. Putin stares at her in the rearview mirror. How did he get the scar on his head? She turns away, her heart still racing, head in turmoil. She can hardly breathe. What's happening? Where's Rob? The woman next to her on the back seat has said nothing since they left his flat. She knows it's Cara. The same woman who boarded the train with her in the village, watched from across the street when she got into the car at Paddington. This isn't opportune. It's a well-thought-out plan. She presses her lips together, tries to be brave. The neckband feels tighter than ever.

They're driving south, over Blackfriars Bridge. She should have stayed in Cornwall. Should have stayed with Jake. She wanted to call out when she saw him in the street with Bex, but she didn't dare. Not after what happened a few minutes before. When she left Ajay in Rob's apartment, she walked out to the lift, where Putin met her. But he wasn't all smiles as he had been yesterday at Paddington. He just stood in silence to one side of the open lift doors, waiting for her to enter. And then she glanced back into the flat and made a run for the stairs. Wrong move.

She didn't get further than a few paces before she dropped to the floor as if she'd been shot, clutching at her throat. She'd never felt pain like it in her life. Strangled and electrocuted at the same time. She's not sure if she cried out – she doesn't think she could, her throat was so constricted. The pain stopped after a few seconds. She lay stunned on the shiny tiles, aware of Putin walking over to her, Ajay rushing out of the flat door, protesting.

'Too high,' Ajay cried. She'd never heard him like that before. Hysterical with anger. 'Way too high.'

'Do exactly as I say and it won't happen again,' Putin said, ignoring Ajay as he squatted down beside her. She stared ahead in shock, curled up in a ball, frozen with fear. 'Try to run away, talk to anyone, make any kind of fuss and the pain will be worse, much worse.'

The palm of his hand came into focus. He was holding out a small remote control with a dial on it for her to see. It was set at three – on a scale of one to ten.

Putin wasn't smiling then and he's not smiling now as they head down towards Southwark. Kate read about them once: electric-shock collars used to train dogs. And now she's wearing one for humans, disguised as wearable technology. She can't believe Ajay put it on her, knowing what it was, the pain it could inflict. She's being treated like an animal. Ajay must have been acting under duress. Why else would he also tell her to run? Protest so loudly?

'Where are we going?' she asks Putin, not expecting an answer. He doesn't give one. She tries to loosen the neckband. He flicks a glance at her and then at the empty passenger seat, where the remote is lying.

She closes her eyes, tries to calm her frayed nerves. If only Jake was here. His presence in the street means he must have heard something when she tried to ring him from the bathroom last night, enough to come looking for her. Bex will be worried sick too. She will have written down the number plate when Kate was driven away. She's good like that. But what can they do for her if the Tesla doesn't get stopped? The large touchscreen to the left of the steering wheel is showing a map with London's static ANPR cameras clearly marked, and Putin is navigating a long, circuitous route to avoid them. Her only chance is if they're spotted by a police patrol car equipped with ANPR.

Jake and Bex won't know that she's being taken to Brittany. Or who she'll meet there. She's not sure either. She touches the neckband, thinks of the beach-glass necklace Rob had made for her.

The one that Ajay removed. And then she hears a siren behind them. The sound has never felt so sweet. She turns around to see an unmarked police car indicating for them to pull over.

'Listen very carefully,' Putin says, picking up the remote and handing it back to Cara beside her. 'You're on your way to see your partner in France. No names. I am his driver, and she is here for your security.' He nods at Cara, who is now in charge of the remote. 'And she's not as nice as me.'

He pulls the car over and stops. Kate knows this is her moment and she must be brave. *Run*. But the pain was unbearable last time; it felt as if she was about to die. And the dial was only set at three. She glances at the door, her hand muscles flexing.

Cara turns, fixing her dispassionate eyes on Kate. It's as if she's read her thoughts. Without blinking, she begins to turn the dial.

Kate grabs her throat, doubling up with the sudden shock of pain.

'OK, OK,' she begs, sliding into the footwell, barely conscious. 'Please.'

Cara smiles down at her and looks away.

CHAPTER 89

SILAS

Silas glances at the satnav. They're still eighty minutes from Nile Street. Jake is on the phone again, asking if they've had any luck tracking the car that Kate was taken away in.

'I'm sorry, nothing,' he says. Silas is equally disappointed, having expected an ANPR hit by now. 'And no word from Border Force.'

It's almost an hour since Kate was taken away. Jake is now at St Pancras, about to board a Eurostar train to Paris, from where he's hoping to catch a flight later today to Brest Bretagne. Silas admires his doggedness, wonders if Kate will ever love him again, whether Mel will take him back. She rang earlier, but Silas let the call go to voicemail. He didn't want to talk about counselling in front of Strover. Or Conor. Their son drove them apart, the stress of his mental illness proving too much in the end. It would be fitting if Conor were responsible for getting them back together again.

'You think we can trust him?' Strover asks, after Silas has ended his conversation.

'Jake? I've known him a long time.' And Jake's

439

never lied to Silas before, apart from about how well his books have sold.

'It's just that he was living with Kate on a crappy canal boat and now she's with this new man in his million-pound apartment in Shoreditch, second homes in Cornwall and Brittany. Maybe it was sour grapes on Jake's part – that she looked unhappy when she was leaving the flat.'

'Maybe.'

Strover hasn't stopped since they took calls from the missing persons units in Nottingham and Dublin, looking at the facts from every angle. They're both fired up. Gilmour Martin's Tesla was spotted in each location a day before what they're now treating as abductions. The European super-recogniser units that have lost someone will contact him too with similar news, he's sure of it.

His phone rings again. It's an officer with the Met's SCO15, the Traffic Operational Command Unit, calling him about the marker he put on the ANPR vehicle index. Silas's specific instructions were to contact him first.

'We've got an intercept for you,' the traffic officer says. 'I'm about to talk to the driver now. Tax, insurance and MOT all check out. What exactly am I looking for here?'

Silas doesn't like his tone. In his experience, traffic officers are only ever interested in traffic offences, ignoring the bespoke crime markers that detectives put on vehicles. There's no hard evidence to suggest that Kate doesn't want to go Brittany, just Jake's word that she didn't look too keen. And as Strover says, he's also Kate's aggrieved ex, which has to be taken into account. The doppelgängers and disappearing super recognisers, the matching Teslas and the gun in Thailand – they count for nothing at this stage. At least in terms of Kate's immediate movements.

'There's a suspicion the car might have been stolen,' Silas says, thinking on his feet. He has no evidence yet, but it wouldn't surprise him. And he doesn't want to lose the traffic officer's interest. 'We just need to know who's on board and where they're heading.'

CHAPTER 90

KATE

P utin steps out of the car with a folder of documents and starts to talk to the police officer on the pavement in Southwark, beside Kate's window. The noise of the passing traffic makes it hard for her to hear what they're saying, but Putin looks relaxed as they skim through the paperwork together. Cara is beside her, remote in hand. Kate's neck still aches from the shock she gave her a few seconds ago. Is this her moment? If she smacks the glass and shouts as loud as she can, makes a scene before Cara has time to trigger another shock, tells the officer she's being abducted . . .

'Don't even think about it,' Cara says, nodding at the traffic officer. 'He's one of ours.'

Kate sits back, too embarrassed to look at Cara. For the second time the woman has read her thoughts. Is she also lying about the officer? 'Where's Rob?' Kate asks.

A moment later, a knuckle rap on the window and the officer gestures for Kate to get out. She glances at Cara, who seems momentarily thrown. And then she nods.

'We're just making a few checks,' the officer says as Kate steps out of the car. 'A Tesla like this one was recently reported as stolen.'

It feels good to be out in the fresh air, the bright sunshine. Has someone slipped up? Without thinking, she raises one hand to the neckband and touches it; she's barely able to breathe. All she needs to do is speak, tell the officer what's happened. Is he really one of theirs? She glances back at Cara, who's staring at her through the window, and remembers the pain.

'May I ask your destination today?' the officer continues.

She glances at Putin and then back at the officer. 'To France, to see my boyfriend,' she manages, recalling Putin's instructions. *No names.*

'Would you like to speak to him?' Putin interrupts, holding out his phone to the traffic officer. Putin's suddenly full of charm, like he was yesterday when he greeted her at Paddington. 'My boss – he is calling me now.'

The traffic officer hesitates for a moment, as if weighing up his options, and then takes the phone out of what looks like a bored sense of duty. Is this a charade for Kate's benefit?

'Am I speaking to Gilmour Martin, registered keeper of a Tesla Model S?' he says formally, leaning over to look at the number plate, which he proceeds to read out.

Who's Gilmour Martin? Gil from Thailand? Kate closes her eyes, hoping in vain that she may

443

have misheard. Rob's right. Gil is here – to destroy Rob, her, their life together. She thought it sounded like Rob on the phone this morning, but perhaps it wasn't. It was definitely somebody else on the bed when the lights came on last night, Capgras or no Capgras. Was it Gil? Did she sleep with a total stranger? She should have been brave and confronted him, asked him outright. She feels sick, their intimacy sullied all over again.

She tries to keep it together as the officer asks for a date of birth and address, checking it on his own phone, and then listens for a while. A part of her wants to grab the phone, hear Gil's voice, ask him what he's done with Rob. Does he sound the same as him too?

'Three people.' The officer sighs and looks briefly at Kate. 'Your partner, your driver, named on the insurance, and another female passenger, also a named driver.' A longer pause this time. 'Thank you.'

She watches, transfixed, as the officer passes the phone back. She is about to say something, protest that her partner's called Rob not Gilmour, when Putin catches her eye. She glances at the car, where Cara is still glaring at her through the window, the remote visible in her hand. *No names.*

'We're going through the Tunnel today,' Putin says to the officer cheerily. 'The boss needs his car in France.'

'Have a safe journey,' the officer replies, walking back to his own vehicle.

Kate watches him get in and sit there for a moment, talking to someone on the car radio. All around her busy Londoners are going about their day, chatting on phones, carrying coffees back to the office. She wants to stop one of them, explain about the neckband, but she knows she can't. *Run.* Not yet. She must bide her time.

CHAPTER 91

JAKE

'What do you mean you can't stop them?' Jake says, glancing around him. He's about to board the Eurostar at St Pancras International and is talking on speakerphone to DI Hart. Bex is standing next to him on the platform.

'According to the traffic officer, Kate showed no visible signs of distress,' Hart says. 'They're driving to Dover, taking the Eurotunnel and then heading out to Brest. You've about ten hours to get there.'

'Aren't you coming?' Jake asks, despairing. Why didn't Kate say something, make a scene when the police officer stopped the car?

'We'll liaise closely with our colleagues in France,' Hart says, 'but there's not much we can do until we get more evidence.'

Jake looks at Bex, who shakes her head with resignation. Behind her, at the far end of the station, an LED installation by Tracey Emin lights up one wall with its message to Europe: 'I want my time with you.' Kate's a big fan of Emin. Of Europe too. He closes his eyes, fighting back the tears. They both know the police should be doing more for Kate. Jake is doing all he can, helped by Bex. She's paid for his train ticket, put some data on his phone and withdrawn some cash for him, but she isn't coming herself. Her passport is back in her house in Wiltshire. Jake has been carrying his around for the past three days, ever since he rescued it from the boat.

'Talk to Dr Varma if you want evidence,' Jake says. 'He was terrified when we spoke to him. I had to . . . persuade him to tell us where Kate was going.' He is not proud of having lost it with him in the street.

'And you need to tell us everything you know about Gilmour Martin,' Hart continues. 'How you knew Rob's doppelgänger in Thailand was called Gil.'

'Have you found him then?' Jake asks. According to Hart, Gilmour arrived in the UK on a false passport six months ago.

'Not yet, but the traffic officer who stopped Kate appears to have spoken to him on the phone. That's where Kate's heading – to see Gilmour in Brittany.'

'Jesus, you need to stop her.' Jake is panicking now. 'Gilmour told Rob in Thailand that he was going to destroy him, his life. That's what Rob's been so worried about, why he confided in Kate about his fear of doppelgängers. Seems like he's coming for her too.'

'We'll do everything we can,' Hart says. 'An

447

all-ports marker is already in place with UK Border Force. We'll try to delay her departure until we've questioned her. And we'll ask the French authorities in Brest to visit Rob's house. But if Kate's happy to be there, our hands are tied. Until we can prove what's going on.'

'She's not happy, believe me,' Jake says. 'You need to talk to Dr Varma.'

CHAPTER 92

KATE

It doesn't take long for Kate to realise they're not going to France via the Tunnel. Continuing to use the map to avoid static ANPR cameras, Putin heads west along the south bank of the Thames. After a circuitous route through Vauxhall, they drive on past the new American Embassy and cut down to the river in Battersea, where they pull up at the London Heliport.

Putin gets out of the car, followed by Cara, who hands him the remote then gets back in, behind the steering wheel. Putin opens Kate's door. She thinks again about making a break for it. Her only chance of escape is if she can put enough distance between herself and the remote. It must have a limited range. She just doesn't know how limited. And the pain . . .

Run.

'Do exactly as I say,' Putin says, gesturing for her to get out as he looks around. Why have they chosen to fly her out of the country from here? Presumably there will be checks like any other airport and her name will trigger an alert of some sort.

'Do you need my passport?' she asks.

'It's not necessary.'

'Why not?'

He doesn't answer.

Twenty minutes later, she's watching London below her turn into a diminishing patchwork of houses and roads, laced through with the glistening thread of the Thames. Her chances of escape are diminishing too. She prays that Jake and Bex are down there somewhere, looking for her. Will Jake have contacted DI Hart? There were no Border Force officers at the heliport, no last-minute intervention by the police. It will be too late if anyone notices after she's left the country.

She's terrified of what will happen when they arrive in Brest, who will be there. The airport represents her last chance of escape. Crowds, people, police. She suspects she'll be on her own once she gets to Rob's house. Just her and . . .

'Who's Gilmour Martin?' she asks Putin, recalling what he said to the policeman who stopped their car.

'No questions,' he says. 'No names.'

She hopes Rob's safe.

CHAPTER 93

SILAS

Silas parks up in Queen's Square, north of Holborn, and waits. He needs to calm down. They are here to see Dr Varma, who works out of a private practice in the square.

'You want a coffee, boss?' Strover asks.

'I need something stronger than that.'

A moment ago, he hung up on a liaison officer with Border Force, the law enforcement command within the Home Office that's meant to patrol all gateways into the UK via air, sea and rail. The officer rang Silas in response to his earlier request for an all-ports marker on Kate. According to the officer, Kate left the UK via London Heliport in Battersea ninety minutes ago – information that's only just been relayed to Border Force in a general aviation report that was filed by the pilot once he'd touched down in Brest.

'And there were no Border Force officers at the heliport?' Silas asked incredulously.

'We keep no permanent presence there,' the officer said. 'Only at times of heightened security.'

'Glad to hear it.'

It wasn't much consolation and it still rankles with Silas now as he gets out of the car and walks across Queen's Square with Strover.

'Let's see what this Dr Varma's got to say for himself,' he says.

Two minutes later, Silas is sitting with Strover in a bleached-out waiting room, staring at an illustration on the opposite wall of the human brain. Strover is flicking through a copy of *Auto Express*. Silas started to get more interested in neurology when he set up the super-recogniser unit, learning about the fusiform gyrus, the part of the brain where human faces seem to be recognised and processed. As he begins to trace the temporal lobe, a man comes out of Dr Varma's consulting room. Silas and Strover haven't made an appointment to see Dr Varma, but his secretary said he would see them between patients. Silas gets up and passes by the man, who keeps his face averted.

'Did you clock that?' he says to Strover, knocking on Dr Varma's door.

'Didn't want anyone to see him,' Strover says.

They wait for a few more seconds, but there's no answer from behind the door. A flicker of concern. Silas knocks again and waits, glancing around the empty waiting room. Dr Varma's next patient has clearly not shown up yet.

'Dr Varma?' Silas calls out, head close to the door. His stomach starts to tighten. He looks at Strover, takes a deep breath and opens the door.

452

'Oh Christ,' he says, taking in the scene. 'Quick, out the front,' he adds. Strover spins around and runs.

Silas walks forward into the spacious room. An Asian man, presumably Dr Varma, is slumped behind a large desk at the far end. The wall behind his head is sprayed with filigree red patterns. For a split second, Silas thinks it's one of those strange images that psychiatrists show to their patients. And then he realises it's blood, from a gunshot to Dr Varma's forehead. His eyes are open, staring up at the ceiling, as if permanently in awe of the sky.

Silas checks outside the large sash window. A car drives off at speed, chased by Strover, who runs after it for a few yards before stopping. Silas turns away, walks over to Dr Varma and feels in vain for a pulse, scanning the mass of papers on his untidy desk.

'Too late. Sorry, boss,' Strover says, coming back into the room.

'Check his diary with reception,' Silas says, still beside Dr Varma. He needs a few moments on his own. 'Find out if his killer made a booking.'

Once Strover has left the room, he pulls out his phone and takes photos of various sheets of paper on the desk, careful not to touch or dislodge anything. Dr Varma's laptop is to one side, angled towards where he's sitting. Silas pulls out a hanky and carefully presses the space bar, waking up the screen. Leaning closer, he starts to read, glancing up at the closed door.

When he's finished, he peers at the entry wound in Dr Varma's forehead, wondering if it was made by the same type of bullet that killed the man in Cornwall. An even bigger, nineteenth-century illustration of the brain looms above Dr Varma on the wall behind him. Silas straightens up to look at it, wondering which parts of the brain the bullet passed through. And then he notices the white lumpy flecking on the picture, sprayed across the right temporal lobe, and reaches for his hanky. For the first time in years at a crime scene, he throws up.

CHAPTER 94

JAKE

Jake glances up and down the Eurostar carriage, scanning the passengers for anyone who might be following him. DI Hart's on the phone, explaining about Dr Varma and warning him to be careful. Jake wishes Kate were here. She'd be able to spot a tail, give them a silly nickname. For some reason, old ladies were always Ethel, bald guys were Bill, gingerheads Rich. She saw lots of 'serial killers' too – at least that's what she used to call anyone who looked dodgy.

'Maybe Dr Varma was trying to warn Kate about something,' he says to Hart.

'According to the doctor's diary, he had a 9 a.m. appointment with her,' Hart says.

'We met him coming out of the apartment.'

'And that's when he told you the address in France?' Hart asks.

'He wasn't exactly forthcoming with the information.' Jake closes his eyes. An image of Dr Varma slammed up against the wall comes and goes. The doctor must have known what he was doing when he decided to put his Hippocratic oath before his life and tell Jake where Kate had been taken.

Jake looks around the carriage again. The man who has just returned from the buffet car throws him a suspicious scowl. The woman across the aisle is still talking in whispers on her phone.

'He said he couldn't tell us anything,' he continues. 'He had a wife and children, said that we didn't know who we were dealing with.'

'But you managed to persuade him,' Hart says. There's no accusation in the detective's voice, only procedural interest. Hart must have persuaded a number of people in his time to tell him things that they didn't want to reveal.

'I reminded him of his Hippocratic oath,' Jake says.

'I guess words are your business,' Hart says.

'His family will need protection.'

'We're on it already.'

Jake's relieved. He didn't know Dr Varma, but he's still shocked by the news of his death, feels guilty about their encounter in the street. Bex will be even more upset. She liked Dr Varma. So did Kate. Bex has gone back to Wiltshire to relieve her neighbour of Stretch and sleep for a few hours before being on hand to help. It was an early start. He's knackered too, knows he must keep going.

'There's more bad news, I'm afraid,' Hart says. 'Kate's already in Brittany.'

'You're joking.'

'I wish I was.'

Hart explains how the Eurotunnel plan was a deliberate misdirection and that she flew out on a private helicopter from Battersea. Right under everyone's noses.

'No one was there to stop her?' Jake asks incredulously.

He has already had his passport checked once in London and will have it checked again at Gard du Nord. His face too, ironically. According to the investigative website he was trawling earlier for information on Rob, the Paris Eurostar terminal is one of only three places in France where the government allows facial-recognition cameras. The other two are Orly and Charles de Gaulle airports.

'Stay safe,' Hart says. 'And keep in touch. We've flagged up Varma's death with Europol – they're putting out an arrest warrant for Gilmour Martin.'

After signing off with Hart, Jake calls up the investigative website again. He will tell Bex about Dr Varma in a while. It's not the sort of news anyone wants to be woken up to hear. Dr Varma's murder will soon be on the news and he needs to alert the website to the connection between Dr Varma and Rob. But then he sees a small story about a super recogniser who has gone missing in France. According to the report, she was part of a secret surveillance unit in Paris that had been set up to target the gilets jaunes, the yellow-vest protestors who'd been bringing Paris to a standstill in their calls for economic justice.

The story is full of indignation that such a unit even existed – further proof that France, champion of civil liberties, is becoming a Big Brother state – but Jake is more interested in the missing woman. She doesn't look like Kate, but she's of similar age and was the unit's star super recogniser. And someone thinks they might have seen her after she disappeared – in Brittany.

CHAPTER 95

KATE

Kate touches the neckband again as Putin follows the coastal road around the bay. If she were there in different circumstances, she could appreciate the scenery more. Rob was right. Brittany and Cornwall are uncannily similar, like twins: the hidden sandy coves and rocky headlands, high hedgerows and Monterey pines, windfarms and gorse. It's enough to make her cry. Rob has often raved about Brittany – Cornwall without the crowds – but she knows Jake would love it here too. And she has a terrible feeling that she's never going to see him again.

There were no checks when they arrived at Brest Bretagne airport. No opportunities to put some distance between her and the neckband's remote. They were waved through the VIP channel and Putin picked up a car from the car park. Rob must have passed through the airport many times. He never talked about it though, not until recently, when he suggested they visit Brittany together. And now she's here, wondering if he is too.

As far as she can tell from the car's satnav, they've since headed west from the airport, skirting around the north of Brest and through Saint-Renan and Ploumoguer to the coast. They're now somewhere northwest of Illien, driving down an increasingly narrow lane to a headland.

'Is this the house?' she asks.

'No questions,' Putin says. 'He will explain everything.'

Who will? Kate holds her breath as the car rounds what she assumes is the final bend. The countryside feels so familiar – glimpses of the sea through five-bar gates, the fresh salty air, the promise of holidays – but there's nothing reassuring about it. And then the lane opens up and she struggles to take in what's before her. They could be at Rob's house in Cornwall. The property looks identical: the same modernist mix of glass and oak and concrete, cut into the hillside and overlooking the sea.

They pass through high open gates that close behind them and head down the gravel driveway. A man and a woman are waiting for them in front of the house. One looks like Rob. And the other . . . looks like her.

CHAPTER 96

SILAS

'First it was Cornwall and now it's central London,' Detective Superintendent Ward says on the phone. Silas rolls his eyes at Strover. They are both standing on the pavement outside Dr Varma's practice in Queen's Square. 'You seem to be making a habit of investigating murders committed outside Wiltshire.'

'I think they're related, sir,' Silas says, watching as more scene of crime officers in white oversuits enter Dr Varma's practice. The square has been sealed off to traffic and there are a number of police vehicles parked up, including a Major Incident mobile command van. He misses his time in the Met, envies their resources.

'I don't need to remind you that you are employed by Wiltshire Police, with a publicly funded remit to prevent crime in the county,' Ward continues. 'I've just had the Met's SIO on the phone, wanting to know why the first person on the scene was a Keystone Cop from Stonehenge.'

'Sir, Dr Varma worked for Rob,' Silas says, mindful of what Ward said last time about Rob

461

being a 'very good friend' to Swindon. 'He was assessing the mental recovery of Kate, the former super recogniser, who is currently in a relationship with Rob. I think someone's trying to frame Rob with this murder and possibly the murder in Cornwall, as well as the abduction of a number of super recognisers in the UK and Europe, including France.'

Jake has just rung him about an item on a French website, suggesting that a super recogniser has disappeared from a covert unit in Paris. Silas wasn't even aware of the unit's existence; he'd assumed that the use of super recognisers in France was not permitted under the country's tougher regulatory framework.

'All news to me, Silas,' Ward says. 'You really need to keep others in the loop, particularly your immediate boss. That's how these things are meant to work. I thought we'd talked about you being more of a team player.'

'A lot of the evidence has been circumstantial until now. And I know you don't like—'

'Do we have any idea who might be trying to frame Rob?' Ward asks, interrupting him.

'Our prime suspect is a man called Gilmour Martin, who happens to bear an uncanny physical likeness to Rob.'

'His "doppelgänger", you mean,' Ward says.

'He arrived in the UK on a fake passport six months ago,' Silas continues, ignoring his boss's cynical tone. 'And we have reason to believe he's

462

been impersonating Rob as part of a long-held grudge to destroy him – and possibly Kate too. Kate left the country earlier today, we think under duress.'

'Anyone see her go?'

Silas glances at Strover again. 'Her ex-partner.' He doesn't want Ward to linger on the unreliability of his source. 'Her best friend also saw her leave. Kate could be in real danger.'

'Where is she now?' Ward asks.

'Brittany, where Rob has a number of business interests and another home. I've alerted Europol – they've issued a European arrest warrant alert for Gilmour Martin.'

'So I gather.' Ward pauses. 'What do you want from me, Silas?'

'Twenty-four hours. Strover and me.'

'Twenty-four hours when modern slavery is allowed to tighten its pernicious grip on Swindon. You're a pain in the arse, you know that.'

And the last time his boss's arse hurt, Silas caught a serial killer, but he stays quiet.

'Twenty-four hours,' Ward confirms. 'And that's it. I don't want Rob being unfairly framed for anything.'

'Thank you, sir,' Silas says, smiling at Strover.

CHAPTER 97

KATE

Kate sits in the back of the stationary car, staring ahead. She can't bring herself to look at him. Or at the woman. Is it Rob? She needs to hear his voice before she sees him.

He steps forward and opens the rear door on her side. She closes her eyes.

'How was your journey?' he asks.

It sounds like Rob.

'Shocking,' she says and turns to look at him.

It's not Rob. Rob was always awkward, restless, buzzing with a warm, infectious energy. This man is focused and withdrawn, dead-eyed.

She manages to step out of the air-conditioned car into the warmth of a French summer's day, hoping her legs don't buckle beneath her. Waves break somewhere below the house, seagulls cry above. For four months in Cornwall, this was the soundtrack to her happiness. Now these noises fill her with dread. Is the house the same inside too?

She forces herself to look at him. It's easier than before. He's no longer an unknown impostor, no more not-Rob. He's Gil from Thailand – Gilmour

464

Martin, Rob's doppelgänger. She can't believe she slept with this man. She wheels away in disgust at the thought. The tarnished memory. Rob was right to be worried. They both were. His past has finally caught up with him, just as he feared. She prays that Rob, her Rob, is still alive, wherever he is, whatever this man has done with him. If only she had pushed Rob harder when he first mentioned his fear of doppelgängers, persuaded him to tell her more. She might have been able to do something, help him, save them both.

And then she turns to the woman. It's like standing in front of a mirror. Kate glances at the ground. It's early afternoon, a high sun. No shadow. Her stomach lurches. And this must be her own doppelgänger. She thinks again of the Rossetti painting in Rob's office in Cornwall, the couple confronting their doppelgängers. *How They Met Themselves*.

'Meet Catrine,' he says.

The woman seems subdued, broken, dark rings below her eyes. Kate hopes she doesn't look that unwell. Catrine is wearing a summer dress from Ghost, identical to the one that Rob left for her in the wardrobe, and her hair is up, like Kate's, exposing a similar neckband. It looks so innocent on someone else. Innocuous. Sporty. Kate shudders again at the pain it inflicted.

'Catrine's learnt that life here is more comfortable if you smile,' he continues. His Irish accent is cold, indifferent. Fake. If it were Rob, he would already have kissed her by now, held her close, checked his phone.

Catrine forces a watery smile. The two women stare at each other, each still trying to take in the other's appearance.

'I found her in Finland,' he says. 'Amazing how easy it is to track down a double in the digital age.'

Poor woman. Kate can't bear to think what she's already endured, the pain that lies ahead for both of them.

'What have you done with him?' she asks quietly.

'Who?' he asks, taking the car key and remote from Putin.

'Rob.'

He shakes his head and turns to Catrine. 'Kate appears to be suffering from a rare delusion called Capgras,' he says to her. 'At least that's what the esteemed Dr Varma believed.'

Believed? She doesn't like the past tense. Ajay also had his doubts, said how rare Capgras was. It was hardly a formal diagnosis. She thinks back to their conversation in the London apartment. Either the place was bugged, as she thought, or Ajay briefed him afterwards.

'Sufferers are convinced that the one they love most in life has been replaced by an impostor,' he continues, holding up his hands in innocent protest.

'Why are we wearing these collars?' Kate asks,

466

touching her neck. 'Rob would never have done this. It's barbaric. Demeaning.'

She looks at him again, searching his blue eyes for a trace of the man she loved, in case she's got this all wrong.

'I'm sorry,' he says. 'Not everyone understands what I'm trying to do here . . .'

Everyone? She glances around. The place feels empty, isolated. Up behind the main house, further along the headland, another building, long and low, is cut into the side of the cliffs and linked by a gravel pathway. It looks more industrial, like a warehouse. She tries to picture the replica property in Cornwall. The warehouse here has replaced the tennis court. Behind it, the blades of a solitary turbine turn idly in the sea breeze.

'. . . but it soon becomes clear why they've been chosen,' he adds, blinking.

Catrine throws her a look, her eyes dark with meaning.

'And, really, there's no point in trying to *run*,' he says.

Jesus. He saw the note, knows that Ajay tried to warn her. She prays that Ajay is OK.

'I need your passport,' he says.

She doesn't hear his words at first, or at least she doesn't understand their meaning, and he has to ask her again. She finds the passport in her bag and hands it to him.

'The driver will show you around,' he says, giving her passport to Catrine. 'We have to go.'

He steps forward to kiss her. She jerks her head away as he holds her firmly by the wrist. The neckband remote is in his other hand. She wants to spit in his face, but he doesn't try to kiss her.

'Ajay said that you've made a full recovery,' he whispers in her ear. He's sounding so like Rob again. Tender, kind. And then he speaks again, this time in fluent French. *'Je n'ai jamais voulu tomber amoureux de toi.'*

Kate's whole body starts to shake as he chucks the remote to Putin and gets into the car with Catrine. He never meant to fall in love with her.

CHAPTER 98

SILAS

'Have a read of this,' Silas says, passing Strover back her iPad. 'It's the article that was on Dr Varma's desk.'

They are sitting in a café around the corner from Queen's Square. Silas has already given one statement to the Met and the senior investigating officer wants to talk to him again shortly, find out why a prominent neuropsychiatrist was shot dead in cold blood in his central London consulting room. Silas has a good idea. Varma knew too much and had already started to talk, telling Jake where Kate was being taken. It's what else Dr Varma knew that's worrying Silas.

He watches Strover as she reads from the iPad. There were a number of interesting documents on Dr Varma's desk, but two in particular caught his eye. One was a sheet of results for a recognition test he'd conducted at the weekend on Kate – something to do with a P3 brainwave. Another was a printout of a story headlined 'The Frozen Addicts'. He took pictures of them both on his iPhone and called up the article on Strover's iPad while she was fetching the coffees.

'Seems like the drug that the addicts took induced an advanced state of Parkinson's,' Silas says.

'This is awful,' Strover says, scrolling through the article.

Awful doesn't come close to describing what happened. In 1982, six drug users in the San Francisco Bay area consumed an impure form of synthetic heroin that turned them into living statues, rendering their bodies rigid and twisted. The neurotoxic contaminant, later identified as MPTP, had targeted dopamine-producing neurons in a part of the brain, the substantia nigra, that coordinates movement. The results were devastating, much like the debilitating last phase of Parkinson's. Although the addicts' bodies were catatonic, their minds were normal, alert and fully aware of the world around them.

'Dr Varma had highlighted the line about the local neurologist who found the addicts in various jails and psychiatric wards,' Silas says. 'Apparently he reversed their condition with a drug called levodopa.'

'And kickstarted research into Parkinson's in the process,' Strover says, finishing the article. She looks up, waiting for an explanation, a connection with what they're investigating.

'We can't assume there's a link,' Silas says, 'but Dr Varma had also highlighted the line about the addicts' minds remaining normal. And there was another article open on his laptop.' Strover looks up. Silas knows she's wondering if he left any fingerprints on Dr Varma's screen, but she's too polite to ask. He didn't. 'It was about locked-in syndrome,' he continues. 'Those patients who appear to be in a persistent vegetative state but are in fact fully conscious. They're also frozen, in a sense, unable to move their bodies – except for one part. Their eyes.'

Strover glances down again at the frozen addicts story on her iPad.

'As I say, there might not be a connection.' He pauses. For once in his life he's not sure if he wants to join the dots, but he knows he must, however shocking the final picture might prove to be. 'If Dr Varma's notes are anything to go by, Kate's P3 results were extraordinary, suggesting an almost complete recovery. Apparently, this P3 wave is an involuntary response in the brain when you recognise someone – and it's much more pronounced in a super recogniser. Kate was shown hundreds of images in rapid succession – at least ten a second – and her brain made a spot. "Jeff." She's clearly got her old recognition skills back. Her eyes are working again.'

He can see Strover's still not sure where he's heading with this, how it relates to the bigger picture: Rob being framed by Gilmour. She looks tired. They both are.

'What's Rob's latest project?' he asks, keen for Strover to see the pattern emerge for herself, know what it feels like.

'Facial-recognition software,' she says.

'What else is he into?'

'Medtech, fitness gadgets, drone deliveries, charity art shows.'

'And?'

Strover's done a lot of digging into Rob's business empire. She closes a window on her iPad and opens another file. 'Direct neural interface technology,' she reads. 'Man and machine.'

She looks up at him, eyes widening, the horror dawning on her face.

'In this case a P3 spike in the human brain, and recognition software,' Silas says. 'And if that brain belongs to a super recogniser, so much the better. The more the merrier, wherever you can find them, but only the best. Nottingham, Dublin, Hamburg, Paris, Swindon . . .'

CHAPTER 99

JAKE

'I'll call you again when I get near the coast,' Jake says, checking the rearview mirror of the rental car he's just picked up at Brest Bretagne airport.

'Be careful,' Bex says, still tearful. He's rung her several times since breaking the news to her about Dr Varma, first from his Eurostar train and then while he was waiting for his flight from Paris to Brest. She's taken Dr Varma's death badly and is worried what that means for Kate. For him too.

'DI Hart's alerted Europol about Gilmour Martin,' Jake says.

'And no one knows where Rob is?' Bex asks.

'I'm hoping I'll find one of them at the house,' he says. 'And Kate.'

'Jake, I really think you should leave this to the French police.'

He wonders whether he should too. Dr Varma's death has escalated things, made the authorities sit up, but he still wants to be here in France, wants to do something. Kate called him last night clearly in distress and he failed to stop her being taken away from the flat this morning.

'Gilmour must have friends in high places,' he says. 'How else did he get Kate into France?' He's still haunted by Dr Varma's words. *You have no idea who you're dealing with here.*

Twenty minutes later, as he's queuing through roadworks in Saint-Renan, Jake idly glances across at a Carrefour supermarket. Beside it is a petrol station. The traffic lights in front of him turn green and he's about to pull away when someone catches his eye on the station forecourt. It looks like Rob, standing beside a car as he refuels. There's someone in the passenger seat too: a woman.

He turns around at the next junction and pulls off at the petrol station, drawing up behind the car. Rob, if it's him, has gone inside to pay, leaving the woman on her own. Scanning the tills, Jake gets out, careful to keep his face turned away, and walks up to the car. The passenger window is down and the woman is wearing sunglasses, staring impassively ahead. Jake's mouth goes dry. Could it be her?

'Kate,' he whispers, checking the tills again. Rob is out of sight, must be buying something.

The woman turns, but not with the speed of someone responding to their own name. Is it Kate? She's tired and sallow. Possibly drugged.

Jake hangs his head. It looks like her.

'Jesus, Kate, what's going on?' He puts a hand

474

through the open window, touching her shoulder. 'Are you alright?'

The woman recoils from his touch as if he's a pariah.

'Please, you mustn't talk to me,' she says. 'Move away from the car, I beg you.'

Jake stares at her in disbelief. She looks like Kate, but she doesn't sound like her. There's a trace of another accent in her voice, but he can't place it. Scandinavian?

'Oh God, where is she?' he asks, looking up at the tills. The man has just paid and is turning to leave the shop. He's no longer sure it's Rob. 'What's he done with Kate?'

'You must go – please.' The woman has tears in her eyes now, and she's nervously fingering a rubber necklace.

'Just tell me where she is and I'll go.' Jake takes a step back. Has the man seen him? He's striding across the forecourt with what looks like a key fob in his outstretched hand.

Jake turns his back and bends down to fiddle with his rear tyre, out of sight, pretending to unscrew the valve cap.

'She's at the house,' the woman says.

A moment later, Jake hears the car drive off. He stands up, barely able to breathe, and pulls out his phone.

'I thought it was her, Bex,' he says as an angry pump attendant comes towards him. 'But it wasn't.'

'*Que faites-vous?*' the attendant demands, gesticulating wildly for him either to buy fuel or to bugger off.

'Was she with Rob?' Bex asks.

'I don't know any more,' he says, trying to pacify the attendant with an upheld hand. 'It looked like him. But I think it must have been Gilmour. I'm driving on to the house.'

'What's going on, Jake?'

'I wish I knew,' he says, getting into the car. The attendant is still cross with him. 'She looked really unwell, whoever she was,' he says, driving off. 'And I think she might have just taken Kate's place in the world.'

CHAPTER 100

KATE

'We haven't got long,' Putin says, opening the front door of the house. 'I don't know why you need to see inside, but he insisted.'

'Who?' Kate says, following him into the hall, eyes widening. 'Who insisted?'

'He likes us to call him "Gil" when he's here.'

She shakes her head, looking around in disbelief. The interior is identical to the house in Cornwall, down to a copy of the *Financial Times* neatly folded on the chair in the hall. The same Persian rug on the concrete floor, white lilies in an identical glass vase. And then she hears the unmistakeable sound of little feet. A dachshund comes trotting out of the kitchen to greet them, sniffing at Putin's leg.

'He's a rat,' he says, kicking the dog away.

Kate winces, desperate to scoop him up in her arms. He looks just like Stretch.

'What's his name?' she asks, leaning down to beckon the whimpering animal, but he's already retreated to the kitchen. She doesn't blame him. She'd run away if she could.

'What does it matter?' Putin says. He picks up a plastic supermarket bag of what looks like clothing and throws it to her. 'You need to change into this,' he says. 'In there.' He nods at the bedroom, waving the remote at her. She looks inside the bag and then at him. It's a hospital patient gown. A pair of flip-flops too.

She walks into the bedroom, expecting it to be the same as the one in Cornwall. And it is, including the canvas photos on the wall. Except that the couple are on what must be a local beach in Brittany and it's Catrine, not her, emerging from the waves. She can't tell if it's Rob or not behind her. She assumes it's Gilmour.

She closes the door and leans against it, breathing heavily. It's such a relief to be on her own, even for only a couple of minutes. Every inch of her is slick with sweat. She tries to calm herself, to trawl through her super-recogniser training, find some-thing – anything – that might help her. Nothing. She takes off her clothes and puts on the gown with a terrible sinking feeling. It's a bad fit. They always were. She hated her time in hospital, the sterile smell, the nylon sheets, the machines winking at her bedside through the night. Only the staff were nice – and Rob, who came to visit her that day. Why is she wearing a gown again? It's as if the past six months haven't happened and she's back in hospital.

Something awful is about to happen to her, that's all she knows. She sits on the end of the bed, staring out at the terrace and the sea beyond. Brittany might look like Cornwall, but it feels very different now.

She gets up and tries the outside door. Locked. No surprise. She's been brought to this place for a reason. She thought it was by Rob, who wanted her to help him spot his doppelgänger, but it's too late for that. Gilmour is already here.

A knock on the door. Putin enters the room before she has time to answer.

'We need to go,' he says, looking Kate up and down.

She slips on the flip-flops and follows him through the atrium, past an easel with one of her unfinished paintings of Stretch. She guesses it was too much to find a doppelgänger who could paint too. The kitchen area is tidier than in Cornwall, but apart from that it's the same.

'If he likes something, he sticks with it,' Putin says, waiting for her to catch up with him. She doesn't want to walk in front, conscious that her gown barely ties up at the back. 'Houses, cars, women.'

'Is there more than one of you?' she asks.

'He's looking,' Putin says, touching a hand to the scar on his head. 'These things take time. I also like to think I'm unique.' For the first time since he picked her up at Paddington, he smiles, creasing his tiny eyes.

She doesn't smile back. 'What happened?' she asks, nodding at the scar.

'Gil made me well again. I was fitting twenty, thirty times a day. Then he put a neural probe in my brain.'

'No more fits?'

He shakes his head, grinning again. 'But I seem to enjoy the pain of others more than I did before. An added bonus.'

She shudders and looks away. Rob once told her he'd invested in a medtech company that implanted electrodes in the brains of epileptics.

'Please, drink some water,' he says, gesturing at a jug and a glass on the sideboard. He must assume he has quicker reactions than Kate. For a moment, she thinks about hurling the jug at his face, reaching for a kitchen knife. She knows where everything is, after all. He seems to read her thoughts and unnecessarily checks the remote in his hand.

'Where am I going?' she asks as they walk past the sitting room. She peers in, sees a big TV screen on one wall.

'Not in there.' He smiles. 'That's his porn room.'

She thinks back to the couple she saw on the TV late at night in Cornwall. A porn habit still doesn't fit with the Rob she knows.

Putin accompanies her through the back door of the kitchen and out onto the gravel path that leads up to the warehouse. This time he waits for her to walk in front.

'Where are we going?' she repeats.

'To work,' he says as they near the warehouse.

Is this her last chance to escape? It's up to her now. Jake, Bex, Rob, DI Hart – no one else can save her. She glances around at the grounds of the house. A high security fence dotted with cameras encloses rolling lawns, an overgrown vegetable patch, a small apple orchard. Her heart sinks. Nowhere to run to.

On the seaward side, there are only sheer cliffs. She hadn't realised how remote the house is. No other properties are in sight in either direction. She looks out across the English Channel, wondering if Cornwall is visible through the sea haze, and inhales a large lungful of air. And then, as she turns around, she notices a delivery van drawing up at the gates. The driver gets out to talk into an intercom. Her heart starts to race. A path runs down from the warehouse, around the main property and out to the drive. This is her moment. It's more important that the driver hears her than that she reaches him. She won't get five yards before she's electrocuted.

She takes a deep breath and runs.

'Hey!' she shouts at the top of the voice, sprinting down the path, away from Putin, dreading the imminent agony. 'Hey! Help!'

She gets further than she expected – almost five yards – before she's cut down by the shock and thrown to the ground. The pain is so much worse than before. Far worse. She's in too much agony to scream or shout. This time she might actually die.

'That was so stupid,' Putin says, walking over to her. 'So fucking stupid.' He's mad with anger, the veins bulging at his temples.

'I'm sorry,' she gasps. The pain has stopped, but she's terrified by what he might do next.

Putin looks around, checking to see if anyone has heard her shouts. Then he kicks her in the stomach. And again, harder this time. And again.

'Stop it! Are you crazy?' a woman shouts as Kate begins to pass out. 'Stop it!'

CHAPTER 101

SILAS

Silas gazes up at the palm trees spilling over the top of the roof. He doesn't expect to be able to enter the penthouse suite, he just wants to see the area for himself, get a feel for Rob's wealth, the Shoreditch side of his life.

'Average price paid for properties in this street?' Strover says. '£1.9 million.'

'The penthouses must go for way more,' Silas says. '£4 million? £5 million?'

He's given a second briefing to the SIO in charge of the Dr Varma homicide and told him that he'll be staying in London for a few hours. The potential link to the Cornish murder was relatively easy to explain – NABIS has all the ballistics and Silas expects a match with the markings on the bullet that passed through Dr Varma's skull. That there might also be a connection with the disappearance of several super recognisers from across the UK and Europe left the SIO scratching his head. One thing did become clear: the Met need to interview Rob and Gilmour as a matter of urgency. Silas refrained from muddying the waters further by suggesting that one was being framed by the other.

At the moment, no one knows where either of the men are.

Silas's phone rings. It's his boss, Detective Superintendent Ward.

'I owe you an apology,' Ward begins, wrong-footing Silas. His boss never apologises. 'You're right. Someone is trying to take down Rob. And it sounds like it's this "doppelgänger", just as you suspected. I was wrong to respond so cynically to your earlier suggestion.'

What's got into Ward? Silas has never heard him like this before. 'That's OK, sir,' he says. 'It's a complex case. May I ask what's made it clearer?'

'Rob did. He's just been in to see me. Brought Kate along with him too – a pleasant surprise. Seems to have made a full recovery from her accident.'

Silas can hardly believe what he's hearing. 'Sorry, sir, did you say Rob and Kate have just been in to see you at Gablecross?'

Strover looks up from her own phone. Silas shakes his head in disbelief.

'And I know what you're going to say,' Ward continues. 'Rob brought his passport and driving licence along. Kate had her passport too. I made a point of asking.'

Silas's head spins as he tries to process his boss's words. Kate definitely flew to France earlier today. The general aviation report submitted to Border Force confirmed it.

'How did Rob get there?' Silas asks.

'I didn't inquire,' Ward says. 'Apparently, he's

484

been meaning to talk to us about his fears for some time. And then yesterday he was sent a speeding fine for a car he doesn't own, which focused his mind. It's registered in the name of Gilmour Martin, this lookalike who made threats against him in Thailand nine years ago. And now one of his employees, Dr Varma, has been murdered. He's quite frightened, actually. I explained that the Met wants to interview him and he's on his way up to London to talk to the SIO now. They also offered to hand in their passports until the matter's resolved, and I agreed.'

Silas is speechless, doesn't know where to begin. 'Did you ask him about the missing super recognisers?' he asks.

'I would have done if you'd told me more about them, Silas. In due course, he'll need to account for his movements when these super recognisers apparently disappeared. He's not going anywhere, said he's staying at his London apartment tonight.'

Silas still can't get his head around the timings. Kate must have turned around as soon as she touched down in France, flying back to the UK with Rob in his private helicopter and landing somewhere near Swindon. Beats crawling along the M4.

'It's not all bad news, though,' Ward continues. 'Rob confirmed that Centaur's finally coming on-stream tonight. Our all-new facial-recognition software. Man and machine working in perfect harmony.'

CHAPTER 102

KATE

'He shouldn't have done that,' a woman is saying. 'You were not to be harmed. Strict orders. He will be in trouble.'

Kate's at the kitchen table in the house, barely conscious, sipping from a mug of mint tea. The woman is young and pretty and wearing what looks like a nurse's uniform. Kate can't place her foreign accent, but it's similar to Putin's. Slavic. Kate's neck is still sore, but it's her ribs that are throbbing. They feel badly bruised, possibly broken. Her lower back's agony too.

'Thank you,' she says to the woman, feeling a little stronger. 'For the tea.'

It's so weird to be sitting in this familiar kitchen, the light flooding in from all directions, a painting of Stretch on the easel to her left.

'If he laid a finger on your head, he would have been killed,' the woman says, glancing up at the rear kitchen door that leads out to the warehouse.

'My head?' Kate says, thinking back to Putin, how he aimed all his blows at her torso.

'Your brain.' The woman nods at Kate's tea. 'Drink it quickly.'

486

Kate closes her eyes. 'What's outside?' she asks. 'In the warehouse.'

The woman casts her eyes downwards, pressing her lips together. 'It's better you don't know,' she says.

'Tell me,' Kate says, almost shouting, eyes alert with an animal fear.

'I wish there was a way I could help you,' the woman says, turning away. 'You're lucky he didn't throw you into the swimming pool. He did that to me once, knew that I can't swim. Can you?'

'I prefer the sea,' Kate says, remembering how she was nearly suffocated by the pool cover in Cornwall.

The woman stares at Kate for a moment. 'You're a strong swimmer?'

'When I don't get cramp. Why?'

'Nothing.' But Kate knows she's holding something back. The woman checks the kitchen door again. Kate does the same.

'Why are you here?' Kate asks, her voice quiet now. She glances up at the woman's head, searching for scars.

'I'm not like the others who work here,' the woman says. 'I'm desperate to leave.'

'So, why don't you?'

'I can't. I've tried. Like you. Several times.'

'But you're not wearing a neckband.'

'I used to.' She touches her throat, as if remembering the pain. 'Now I have an implant.' She pulls down the top of her blouse to reveal a scar across her chest, above her heart. 'If I leave here, go beyond the perimeter fence, pick up a mobile phone, do anything to try to escape, my heart will . . .'

The back door swings open. Putin breezes in and Kate recoils, tensing her legs and stomach. More pain.

'Time to go,' he barks, avoiding eye contact with her.

Putin says something to the woman that Kate doesn't understand, then marches Kate out of the kitchen and up towards the warehouse. It's agony to move, but he ignores her pleas to slow down, dragging her by her wrist when she tries to stop. In his other hand he's holding the remote for the neckband.

'Try anything and I will use this again,' he says, waving the remote in her face as they approach the warehouse.

When they reach the door, Putin looks around and pulls out his phone, which is buzzing.

'One minute,' he says, holding a finger up at her. He seems distracted and starts to chat quietly but urgently on the phone.

Kate stares at the warehouse door, wondering what lies behind it. A chill runs through her. The sky is pewter grey now, the sea dark and choppy. The woman's right. There's no escape from here. Her one attempt failed. The van driver was too far away to have heard her. It's hopeless.

Putin is becoming more animated on the phone,

defensive. Is he being reprimanded for beating her up? She turns away and her heart misses a beat. On the far hillside, across the bay, a familiar figure, a distinctive lumbering gait. She stays very still, aware that she mustn't alert Putin. Despite the distance, she knows at once that she's made a spot. It's Jake. His ursine profile.

Putin hasn't seen him. He's still talking on his phone.

'Can I wave goodbye to Cornwall?' she manages to say, loudly, to Putin. 'To England.' The urge to scream, call out to Jake, is almost unbearable, but she knows that the pain from the neckband will be far worse. 'It's somewhere out there.'

He puts a hand over his phone, glances at her and then at the sea, before returning to his conversation. She's not sure if he's understood her question. The wind ruffles her hair as she starts to wave out to sea. She checks on Putin and looks towards Jake in the far distance again. She can hear the waves thumping against the rocks, somewhere out of sight far below her. The drop must be vertical. She scans the bay again. High tide, the sea right up against the cliffs where Jake is still visible. She became obsessed with tides in Cornwall, living in tune with their ebb and flow.

And then Putin is off the phone and grabbing her by her wrist again.

'Come,' he says, dragging her to the door.

'You're hurting me,' she protests as he pulls

out a card with his other hand and holds it against the lock of the warehouse door. She turns to look back one last time. Is that a wave from Jake? Has he seen her? She feels stronger just knowing that he's nearby. Braver too as she is dragged inside, the door locking behind her.

CHAPTER 103

SILAS

Silas is still on the phone to his boss, Detective Inspector Ward, stunned by the news that Centaur is about to go live. News that was apparently confirmed by Rob in person.

'Sir, what exactly has Rob got to do with Centaur?' he asks, standing outside Rob's apartment in Shoreditch with Strover.

For a while now Strover has been trying without success to find out who is behind the force's imminent new facial-recognition software. The details surrounding the Centaur contract are opaque, to put it mildly.

'It's one of his start-ups,' Ward says. 'He invested in it a while back.'

'Why didn't you tell me this?' Silas asks incredulously.

'Believe me, I would have done if I could, Silas, but these things are very commercially sensitive. There were also some teething problems. Delays.'

'And you don't think his involvement in a facial-recognition firm has any bearing on Kate's accident or his subsequent relationship with her, a super recogniser?' Silas knows he's out of order now, adopting the wrong tone for speaking with his boss.

'Not as far as I can see,' Ward says. 'Except perhaps in the context of Gilmour Martin trying to frame him. From what Rob's told me today, it seems certain now that it was Gilmour at the scene of Kate's accident that night.'

'How many other forces are using Centaur?' Silas asks.

'Just us at the moment, but then Swindon has got more surveillance cameras than most. We're in a position to make the best use of it. If the software lives up to its promises, Centaur's going to drive crime off the streets of this town.'

Rob is proving a very good friend to Swindon.

'The Irish are also looking at it,' Ward continues. 'So are the Germans. And I had a call from my opposite number in Nottingham last night. I'm not surprised. It's a potential game changer. Promises closer interaction between humans and computers. No more embarrassingly high error rates.' He pauses. 'Are you liaising with the Met over Dr Varma? I don't want any reports of non-cooperation.'

'I've told them everything I know,' Silas says. Almost everything.

Silas signs off and briefs Strover about Centaur. She'd already got the gist of it and is equally shocked.

'I can't believe he didn't tell us,' Silas says.

'It's the name that's bothering me,' Strover says, searching for something on her phone. 'Know what a centaur looks like?'

Silas nods. He'd read about them when he visited the Pelion peninsula in Greece a few years back, when Conor still came with them on family holidays.

'Half man, half horse,' Strover continues, holding out her phone to show him a picture. 'The combination of a computer's artificial intelligence and the human brain is also known as the centaur model. After Garry Kasparov lost against IBM's computer Deep Blue in 1997, he invented "advanced chess", or "centaur chess", in which grandmasters play against each other with computers.'

Silas made the mistake once of challenging Strover to a game. And he considers himself a half-decent player. He thinks about the documents on Dr Varma's desk. The P3 brainwave, the articles on frozen addicts and locked-in syndrome. Centaur's coming on-stream tonight – the day Dr Varma was killed, the day Kate was taken to France after having finally recovered her recognition skills.

His phone starts to ring. It's Jake.

'Where are you?' Silas asks.

'On a hillside in Brittany overlooking Rob's house.'

The man is a like a dog with a bone. If he'd shown the same dedication to writing crime thrillers, he'd be a bestselling author by now.

'Have the French police been alerted?' Jake continues. 'I can't see anyone around.'

Silas takes a deep breath and surveys the street. 'I'm sorry, it's not as straightforward as that.'

'How do you mean?' Jake says. 'I thought there was an arrest warrant out for Gilmour? Kate's in real trouble. I think I've just seen her. Behind the house, up on the cliffs.'

There's no easy way to tell him. 'Kate's back in the UK, Jake,' Silas begins. 'With Rob. He's just visited Gablecross police station. Claims he's being framed by Gilmour.'

'What?' Jake's sense of disbelief is even greater than Silas's. 'That's not possible. It can't be Kate. It must be someone else. You've got to believe me.'

Jake describes his encounter at the petrol station in Saint-Renan.

'And you're sure it was Rob the woman was with?' Silas asks.

'I'm not sure, no. It definitely wasn't Kate, though. She had a different accent, different . . . I don't know, presence. Physically, sure, she looked just like Kate, but . . . I lived with Kate for twelve years. I'd recognise her anywhere. And this woman looked terrible. Pained. Terrified. Kept begging me to leave. She also told me that Kate was back in the house. You've got to help me. I'm on my own here.'

CHAPTER 104

KATE

The low lighting in the warehouse is a sickly blue, like a morgue at dawn. The temperature is low too. Putin is beside Kate, letting her take in the hideous scene.

'Your new home,' he says, but she's not listening. She's staring ahead, trying to comprehend the nightmare laid out before her, the saline tubes and TV screens, the smell of disinfectant. She's back at the hospital again, bruised and battered in the dark early days after the accident, listening to the anguished cries of other patients as they call out through the night. The flickering screens remind her too of the very worst days in the super-recogniser unit, the endless scrutiny of human faces in a cramped, late-night office.

Her hands start to shake. She clutches her arms, pulling the thin gown tighter around her sore ribs. She's got to get away from here.

She forces herself to count a total of eleven people, six men and five women. They appear insensate, lying in separate cubicles, torpid faces staring up at large display screens suspended from the low ceiling above them. Their eyes are pegged open in some strange way, giving the impression of gross, misshapen eyelashes. They are all wearing gowns and what look like EEG headsets, identical to the one she was made to use, and they're breathing through ventilators. Drips are attached to their arms.

'Gil wanted you to see this first,' Putin says. 'He's very proud of what he's achieved. But this is not normal, you being here like this. We usually induce catatonic stasis before they are brought in.'

He nods towards a door off to their right. Kate tries to speak, ask what he means by catatonic stasis, but she's too choked up for any words to come out. Her whole body is shaking now. One bed, at the far end, is empty. Her bed. She knows what's on the screens. Human faces, at least ten a second, just like Ajay showed her. And then she notices that several of the screens are showing moving images. It's hard to see clearly because of the angle, but the footage – it looks like CCTV – seems much faster than normal, as if it's been sped up.

She wonders if she's imagining all this and starts to pinch the skin on her forearm, squeezing it harder and harder, twisting the fold of flesh until it hurts too much, hoping that she'll wake up from this bad dream.

The woman who gave her mint tea enters the warehouse from the far end with a clipboard and starts to check on the people, moving from one bed to the next. Kate tries to catch her eye, but the woman doesn't look in her direction. Daren't risk her heart.

'We have to put moisturiser in their eyes,' Putin says, almost proudly, observing the woman as she leans over one of the captives. 'Otherwise they dry out. They hardly ever sleep – the drug we give also induces hyposomnia. But we can tell when they do from the EEC monitors. And then we close their eyes. But it's never for very long.'

'Are they conscious?' she manages to ask. Her voice is barely a whisper.

'Fully.'

She closes her own eyes, trying to imagine what these people are suffering. She assumes they are all super recognisers, like her. She had a repeat nightmare in her last months in the police unit. Told to identify a decapitated head, she had to watch a stream of thousands of contorted, disfigured faces until she could bear it no more and woke up in a cold sweat. For a second she wonders if Rob's lying here too, whether they'll be incarcerated together, side by side, but she doesn't recognise any of the faces.

'Sometimes we let them see a movie,' Putin says, glancing at his watch. 'It's a little in-joke of ours – we call it the Ludovico hour.'

CHAPTER 105

SILAS

Silas moves fast after ending the call with Jake. Ward isn't happy about forensics coming into his own office to check for fingerprints, but he agrees when Silas tells him on the phone about Jake's encounter at the Carrefour petrol station with Kate's double – and possibly Rob's too.

What worries Silas is that Ward must know Rob well, certainly better than he knows Kate, whom he only met once, when the super-recogniser unit was set up. They would have been talking about Centaur for months. Did he meet Rob enough times to realise that it wasn't him walking into his office?

'The boss isn't stupid,' he says to Strover as they grab a coffee in a Pret opposite Moorfields Eye Hospital. 'Even if he did go to university.'

'You think it's Gilmour?' Strover asks.

'Let's see.'

All Silas knows is that Rob's fears about Gilmour one day taking over his life don't seem so incredible any more.

It doesn't take long for the results to come back

498

on Kate's passport, which was still on his boss's desk. Her fingerprints are on file – it was part of the vetting procedure when she was recruited to the super-recogniser unit – and they have been duly found all over the passport. But so have more recent fingerprints, which forensics have checked against IABS, a new Home Office database that contains the prints of all foreign nationals entering the UK. And they belong to a woman from Finland who went missing six months ago, shortly after arriving in the UK.

'Her name's Catrine,' Silas says, passing his phone across the table to Strover. Jake was right.

'Uncanny,' Strover says, studying the picture. Unsettling too. Silas thought he knew Kate well, but the likeness is striking. Enough to convince Ward.

It's another ten minutes before the initial results on Rob's passport come through. Only one person's fingerprints are found on it, apart from Ward's, but it's not clear whose they are. Rob's prints aren't on file and IDENT1, the police database of prints for everyone taken into custody, has failed to find a match.

They are now waiting for the Royal Thai Police to call back. Strover's new best friend, Manu Jabthian at the Bang Kaen Detective Training School, unearthed another old file overnight on Gilmour Martin that includes his prints.

Strover's phone rings.

'It's Manu,' she says, glancing at the international number.

'Answer it,' Silas says, trying to remain calm.

He watches her as she listens and then hangs up.

'The prints on Rob's passport match Gilmour Martin's from Thailand.'

500

CHAPTER 106

JAKE

Jake scrabbles down through the dunes and onto the beach. The tide is in, but there's a thin strip of sand that runs halfway around the bay to a tiny inlet, where a couple of small boats are moored. Beyond it the dunes give way to rocks and then sheer cliffs. There must be a drop of at least fifty feet from the house where he saw Kate, and there's no beach directly beneath it. No obvious way up.

He still can't be sure it was Kate, but her hand movements were familiar. In the early days, when they'd drunk too much on the narrowboat, she would stand on the bow and wave energetically at passing boats, putting her whole body into it, determined to get at least a smile in return, even from the grumpiest passers-by. It was a private joke of theirs.

He has no idea how he can reach the house. It's also much further away than he thought. There was no way in through the main gate, which he observed from a distance, and the perimeter fence is too high and monitored by CCTV. Approaching from the sea is his only hope.

He loves Kate more than ever, will never take her for granted again. 'We could go somewhere if you like,' the woman in the Swindon shopping centre said. He flushes at the memory of it. One stupid moment. Her mouth tasted bitter, like yarrow.

He looks across the bay, then bends down to pluck some moist samphire shoots pushing through the sand. He's starving, but there's no time to forage properly. It's up to him now. DI Hart said there was nothing more they can do, at least for the moment. If a couple who look like Rob and Kate have walked into a police station in the UK, Jake has only one option left. He glances at the boats again and starts to run towards them, wishing he were fitter, praying that he's not already too late.

502

CHAPTER 107

KATE

Kate watches as the woman in the nurse's outfit comes towards her and Putin, studiously avoiding eye contact. Does Putin control her too? As if on cue, he pulls out the remote. But for who? He stares at the woman's firm figure, making no effort to be subtle, before checking his phone again. The woman immediately looks up at Kate, giving the faintest nod in the direction of the main door.

Did Kate imagine it? Her stomach starts to churn. What does the woman mean? Kate heard the door lock behind them when they arrived; it clicked with a sickening finality.

The woman turns to smile at Putin, who appears surprised, flattered. It must be the first time she's paid him any attention. The woman smiles again, coquettishly this time, and starts to walk towards him, hips swaying shamelessly as she passes close by Kate, one hand holding the clipboard across her chest, the other down by her side. Kate feels the plastic card before she sees it, brushing her hand. A card like the one Putin used to let them in.

Kate grasps it and watches as the woman continues to flirt with Putin, leaning in to whisper something to him. Men can be so weak. He momentarily turns away, as if he doesn't want Kate to hear their exchange. And then the woman looks over his shoulder at her and mouths one word.

Jump.

CHAPTER 108

JAKE

Jake's heart sinks as he reaches the end of the deserted beach. Both boats moored in the inlet are old and unloved. Earlier he'd seen some buoys marking lobster pots, strung along the coast like beads on a giant necklace, and he'd thought the boats might be in decent condition. He'd also expected to find a tender pulled up on the sand somewhere, hidden at the back of the beach, but he can't see one. He'll have to wade out.

Five minutes later, he hauls himself onto the nearest of the two dilapidated boats, checking again that there's no one around. He's hidden his phone and wallet behind some rocks on the beach. The water was cold and his wet trousers are heavy as he gets his bearings on board. He's always loved boats and has long dreamt of owning one like this, maybe a Plymouth Pilot with an enclosed cuddy and dual helm positions. He'd keep it down in Cornwall.

He scans the cliffs again, where he thought he saw Kate. It's at least a mile away, but if he can get the engine going, he can cut straight across the bay and search for a way up. He lifts the

505

inspection hatch and peers down at a rusty, single-cylinder, ten-horsepower diesel engine. The last time he had to hotwire anything was when he lost both sets of ignition keys for the narrowboat's ancient engine. All he needs is a piece of cable. The owner of the boat seems re-assuringly untidy, like him, and Jake soon finds a rusty length in the depths of the engine bay, semi-submerged in the bilge's oily seawater. After turning on the fuel, Jake touches one end of the cable to the starter motor, the other to the posi-tive terminal of the twelve-volt battery, bypassing the ignition switch. A few sparks – enough contact to crank the engine. Bingo. Removing the cable, now hot, he grabs the tiller and sets a course for the cliffs.

Kate used to hate how much time he spent with his head in the engine. Maybe now she'll think it was worth it.

CHAPTER 109

KATE

Kate grips the card in her hand and slides off the flip-flops, trying to control her breathing. She can't stay here a second longer. The ventilator masks, the IV tubes, the screens – she's never going to subject herself to all that again. She'd rather die than get trapped here, in this grey torture zone between life and death. Her body might be weak, boot-marked and sore, but her mind is strong.

Jump.

The lock clicks and the door is open before she hears the first shout behind her from Putin. The woman will do her best to stop him; Kate prays that her selflessness won't be the death of her. Kate doesn't care about the pain that's about to rip through her own body. The urge to escape is overwhelming, visceral.

Fresh air, blue sky. The sea stretching out before her. Kate runs as she's never run before, ignoring the pain in her swollen ribs, forcing her legs to go faster, focusing on the sea. The sea that extends all the way to Cornwall, to where she and Jake used to camp in the drizzle, water dripping through the flysheet, their Morris Minor failing to start, just enough money for a pint in the pub across the soggy cornfield, Jake stopping to pick her stitchwort and bluebells, her cursing him, loving him.

Her chest is heaving with the effort now, and she feels nauseous, faint, but she's got nothing to lose. It was Jake out there on the cliffs, she's sure of it. His profile is hard to mistake. It's why she recognised him in the CCTV footage. He looked surprised when the woman kissed him, she'll give him that. Shocked, even, by what he was doing. It had to happen, though. She and Jake were going nowhere, not communicating, too poor and too tired and too stuck in a rut, clinging to the wreckage of their waterborne life together, taking each other down to the cold lonely depths of a world where they'd forgotten how to love. Then along came Rob. And now Jake's come looking for her.

She keeps running, forcing her bruised body forward until there's nothing solid beneath her feet any more. She doesn't stop. The sea is waiting for her far below, waiting to engulf her in its salty embrace, and she is a child again, jumping from the harbour wall. For a split second she thinks about arcing her body into a swallow dive, but she's never jumped from this height before. She's going to die. The cliffs are too tall. Better a quick death now than a slow, wide-eyed one back there. She tries to force her hands down to her sides, keep her feet pointed as she plummets. A pencil jump, like the one that impressed the Cornish boys in Mousehole. But then the shock hits, hot fiery pain like she's never felt before, twisting and folding her screaming body until it's snuffed out by the smack of watery darkness.

CHAPTER 110

JAKE

Jake hears the scream before he sees the body tumbling through the air. He knows at once it's Kate and all he can do is watch from the boat, praying that she will survive the fall. Or did she leap? She always loved to jump and these cliffs are sheer and there is water below, but she must have been desperate to risk it. A second later she hits the surface, leaning too far back but feet first.

He's still five hundred yards away. The engine's cooling system isn't working and he's worried it's about to overheat, but he tries to squeeze more power from it even so. A man appears on the clifftop, peers over the edge and disappears. Did he see him? Jake is now two hundred yards from where Kate hit the water. He can see her body, floating in the sea, listless, head down.

'Kate!' he shouts about the noise of the motor. Thick black smoke has started to billow out of the engine bay. 'Kate!'

Her body is not moving. A gown of some sort is floating on the surface beside her. He's still a hundred yards away.

'I'm here,' he calls out, breathless. He reaches forward to turn off the fuel, one hand still on the tiller. The engine cuts as he pulls up alongside her. She's still not moving. The sea is deep and dark, even though they're close to the shore. Cursing the choppy water, he braces himself against the gunwale and reaches over the side. He grasps repeatedly at Kate as he leans out – grasps and misses, tries again – and then finally he manages to grip a hank of her hair, a shoulder. Big heart thumping, he leans out even further, dangerously far, gets both hands under her torso and turns her. He lifts up her head, trying to keep it above the waves. Her eyes are shut and her limbs are limp. Floppy. Tears are streaming down his face now. He can't bear the sight of her like this. With one last effort, he scoops her up, heaves her out of the water and lays her in the bottom of the boat. She's not breathing.

He checks in vain for a pulse at her wrist. Leaning forward, he breathes into her mouth. Her lips are cold. Deathly. He throws back his head in a howl, a wounded roar at the sea. Who did this to her? His Kate? The love of his life. He looks down at her broken body again. It's OK. He can do this. No one else can save her. He starts to compress her chest, desperately trying to remember the first-aid course he attended in the village hall, something about the rhythm of 'Staying Alive'. Kate loves the Bee Gees, used to dance around the boat to it when he was trying to write. She dived off the bow once when he'd had enough and had started to chase her. He glances up at the clifftop. Something awful must have happened up there to make her jump. After thirty compressions, he breathes into her mouth again: one, two, three.

Kate starts to cough, throwing up chestfuls of seawater.

'Oh, thank God,' Jake says, shaking with relief as his heart soars. The tears return. He rolls Kate onto her side and thumps her back as she's sick again.

'Ow,' she moans. And then they're both crying and he's cradling her in his arms as he scans the wide empty sea.

Five minutes later, Jake has got the engine going again and he's heading back across the bay, getting them as far away as possible from the house. No one has appeared again on the cliffs, but he's not taking any chances. Kate is sitting in the bottom of the boat, out of the wind, wearing his jacket. And he is standing at the stern, steering a steady course for the shore as a coastguard rescue helicopter hoves into view.

CHAPTER 111

SILAS

Silas and Strover watch from a doorway across the street as the black cab slows outside Rob's apartment in Nile Street. Silas has arranged for backup and Armed Response officers are in position at either end of the street, ready to assist in the arrest if he needs help, but he's still nervous. NABIS has just confirmed that the bullet that killed Dr Varma matches those fired in Cornwall and Thailand. And the man who pulled the trigger is still on the loose.

Silas has a weird feeling when he sees the couple step out of the cab. He knows it's not Kate, but he still does a double-take. And he now knows who the man is. The fingerprint match from Thailand with Gilmour Martin was the final piece of the puzzle. In consultation with the Met's SIO, Silas requested Air Traffic Control to monitor the man's earlier helicopter flight from Swindon to London, and two unmarked cars from the Met's Specialist Crime and Operations Branch tracked the taxi journey from Battersea Heliport to Nile Street, considered the safest place to make an arrest.

'Here we go,' he says. They cross the street, approaching the couple as they're about to enter the apartment. The adrenaline rush is almost overwhelming. He never thought he'd be back on the streets of London again, making arrests with armed support. Conor would be impressed, maybe Mel would be too. That's the problem. They never get to see these moments, can't share in the professional satisfaction that makes him get out of bed every morning.

Strover moves towards the woman, flashing her ID as she takes her to one side, while Silas confronts the man, who visibly tenses.

'I'm arresting you on suspicion of ordering the murder of Dr Ajay Varma,' Silas says. 'For the abduction of twelve super recognisers, the murder in Cornwall of a barman at the Bluebell pub in Wiltshire, the false registration of a car with the DVLA, and entering the UK on a false passport. You do not have to say anything. But it may harm your defence if you do not mention when questioned something which you can later rely on in court. Anything you do say may be given in evidence.'

'Very good,' the man says, glancing up and down the street, where armed officers have now broken cover and taken up closer positions. He looks so young, barely older than Conor. 'But aren't you supposed to give a name?' he asks. 'My name?'

Silas takes a deep breath, watching as Strover hands the woman over to another female police officer. To his right, he clocks an Armed Response officer shifting his feet, gun trained on the man in front of him, elbows high. This is it. What Silas lives for. Strover is back at his side again. She's done well. He stares at the man, tries to imagine what it must have been like for Kate when she looked into these hollow blue eyes, blinking now in the bright London sunshine. Whose soul did she really see?

'Your name?' Silas repeats.

Strover looks across at him, waiting for him to confirm that it's Gilmour Martin.

He pauses, savouring the moment, the evening light of east London.

'Your name's Rob,' he says. Strover flinches beside him. 'Robert Colwan.'

The man looks at Silas, blood draining from his face, and checks up and down the street. Has Silas got it wrong? This is Rob before him, no question. It always was Rob, wasn't it? But the man doesn't speak. He just stares at Silas as he slips a hand inside his jacket pocket. A moment later, shots ring out as the man slumps to the ground, armed officers running towards them from either end of the street, the air full of urgent cries.

ONE WEEK LATER

CHAPTER 112

SILAS

Silas pushes back his chair in the Parade Room, resisting the urge for a smoke. He and Strover are in their usual corner, but he's only been at Gablecross for an hour. It's been another long day in London and he has to be up there again tomorrow to assist the Met with its ongoing investigation into Rob's double life and sudden death. Armed Response were right to think that Rob was pulling out a gun. A pistol that matched the one in Thailand was found in his jacket. But Silas is in no doubt that Rob would have turned the gun on himself and taken his own life if they hadn't dropped him first. They've yet to find the person who shot Dr Varma. All they know is that the assassin must have returned the gun to Rob sometime between him landing his helicopter in Swindon and arriving in Nile Street.

Strover has returned to local duties, patrolling the nail bars and pop-up brothels of Swindon. Ward's orders. She's not happy, wanted to stay on the case. The boss is still embarrassed by his closeness to Rob and he's been throwing his weight around, lashing out at junior officers. Silas will have a quiet word, tell him to back off Strover, not that she can't look after herself.

He checks his watch. The first counselling session with Mel is at nine tomorrow morning. Should he cancel? He was hoping for an early night, but that plan is already out the window. He's short-tempered when he's tired, uncompromising. Scratchy. Maybe he should delay the session for a week, wait until he's on top of his work, less exhausted, more willing to listen. He feels better already and reaches for the phone, but it's started to ring. Conor.

'Hi, Dad, just checking you're still on for tomorrow?' Silas has never heard his son sound so upbeat, optimistic. 'Mum's well happy you're coming.'

'Of course,' he says, spinning in his chair away from Strover. He doesn't want her to see him wiping a tear from his eye. 'I'll be there.'

It's early days, but Conor's rehab is going well and the information he's supplied has led to the arrests of the remaining members of the modern slavery OCG, who were also running the county lines network in Swindon, just as Silas suspected. The Bluebell pub too has been shut down. It also looks like Conor will be spared from prosecution in return for his cooperation. As for the boat fire, no one has considered Conor's possible involvement and Jake has no wish to press charges.

'Can I ask you something?' Strover says five minutes later as they walk out of Gablecross

520

station to the car park. It's dusk and feels more like winter than summer, dark clouds brooding over the Swindon skyline.

'Sure,' he says. He's got a grip now.

'When did you first realise that it was Rob and not Gilmour?' she asks.

Silas looks across at her as they reach his car. She's been uncharacteristically quiet since Rob's death. It happens a lot in police work, when you back the wrong horse. She was convinced Gilmour Martin existed. He was too, for a while.

'There never was a Gilmour Martin,' he says as they both get into the car. Rain has started to drift across the deserted car park. 'Gilmour didn't frame Rob. Rob framed Gilmour, created him – a French-speaking figment of his imagination. His darker side made flesh.'

'What about the matching fingerprints from Thailand?' she asks.

He reaches for the ignition and then pauses as the rain intensifies, hammering down on the car roof. She's owed an explanation.

'That's the moment when I knew Gilmour and Rob were one and the same,' he says, sitting back. 'Rob changed in Thailand, came up with his big plan. Whenever he needed to break the law, he decided he would adopt Gilmour's persona. He would always blame his double, claim he was being framed. The brain farm in Brittany? Gilmour Martin's idea. When Rob shot the man in Cornwall, he was driving around in a Tesla registered to

Gilmour. The backstory he created online? The fake Facebook friends like Kirby? They all added to the myth that Gilmour wanted to bring him down. And of course he fed Kate with the same tosh too – just enough disinformation to make her question her own sanity.' Silas shakes his head. How's Kate ever going to recover from this? Jake's support will be crucial, if she'll accept it.

'But how did Rob expect to get away with it, that's what I don't understand,' Strover says.

'The arrogance of the psychopath,' he says. It never ceases to amaze him.

'And the night of Kate's crash? The video sent to Jake?' Strover asks. 'Was that all Rob too?'

Silas nods, glancing out at the car park. It seems a long time ago now. 'Back then, Rob was beginning to assemble his team of super recognisers. He just hadn't bothered to consult any of them. He came here the day before the accident, to check out Kate's work movements. The following night, he's sitting in the corner of the Bluebell pub, watching, waiting to abduct her, but then someone else gets to Kate first.'

'The barman.'

'He spikes her drink, on the orders of the OCG, whose members she had identified.'

'And who'd recently been arrested,' Strover adds.

Silas starts up the car, watching the rain dancing in the headlights. 'Rob's noticed the barman's sleight of hand and follows Kate home, worried about her. Imagine his shock when he rounds the corner and finds her Morris Minor smashed up against a tree. It's his worst nightmare. His best super recogniser is suddenly fighting for her life, possibly brain damaged. He does everything he can but leaves moments before the ambulance arrives – he'd been about to bundle her into the back of his car, remember.'

'And the pub CCTV?' Strover asks as they drive out of the car park.

'After the crash, Rob goes back to the Bluebell and hacks into its cameras, studies the footage.'

'Man-in-the-middle attack,' Strover says. 'Unencrypted password.'

'Piece of cake for a techie like him. After confirming that her drink was spiked, he searches everywhere for the barman. Rob now knows he must protect Kate at any cost, allow her time to recover. The last thing he needs is for her to be targeted again by the OCG. But the barman has already gone to ground, spooked by this mysterious man in a silent Tesla.

'Six months later, the gang members are sentenced and Rob fears for Kate's life all over again, even though he's installed heavy security down at the house in Cornwall. But he hasn't been able to find the barman. So he sends the pub footage to Jake, knowing that he will pass it on to us, hoping we'll realise the danger Kate's in. It also keeps Jake busy – as Kate's ex, he's been doing some unhelpful digging into Rob's business affairs.

And then the barman tracks Kate down to Cornwall, spikes her coffee at the harbour café, and she nearly drowns.'

'He also tries to run her over in the street,' Strover says. 'And me.'

Strover is still indignant about the incident in Cornwall, has taken it surprisingly personally.

'This time Rob's onto him,' Silas says, picking up the story again. 'He drives down to Cornwall – in a car registered to Gilmour Martin – and shoots the barman, making sure he uses a gun that can be linked back to Gilmour in Thailand.'

'So you were right,' Strover says, sitting back. 'Rob was her guardian angel.'

'More of a fallen one. He was keeping her safe – for his own hell on earth.'

CHAPTER 113

KATE

'Eyes closed!' Bex says, taking Kate's hand. Kate is back in the village for the first time, standing on the doorstep of Bex's house on crutches. She does as Bex instructs, but Bex has no idea how hard she's finding it. How hard she's finding all of this. It's not her leg, which is in plaster. Or her ribs, which are still bruised and sore. It's her eyes. She never wants to close them again.

'OK!' Bex says.

Kate opens them like a surprised child. Bex's kitchen has been decked out with balloons and banners, a large 'Welcome Home' strung across the dresser. Bex has always loved throwing parties – 'Jacob's joins', as she calls them, where everyone brings along a dish. All Kate's old friends from the village are here. Jake too, standing at the back, stooped a little because of the low ceiling. Kate wants to cry, but she knows she must hold it together. This is her past, but it's also her future.

And then she spots Stretch, who trots over to see her, and she is unable to hold back the tears any longer.

'Weenie toes,' she says, scooping him up.

'And he's got a bestie,' Bex says, looking across at Jake. The crowds part and Kate sees another dachshund, tiny in Jake's big arms. It must be the one from the house in Brittany. She hobbles over and takes it from him.

'Hey, he's mine,' Jake says, pretending to hang on to him. 'He's called Banger,' he adds, as she holds the two dogs up to her face. 'DI Hart's choice.'

She kisses both dogs. And then she kisses Jake too. Nothing lingering – it's early days – but a cheer still goes up around them.

'Like the dress,' Jake whispers.

'Thanks,' she says.

It's the orange one he retrieved from the canal – and still reeks of diesel.

They've talked a lot in the past week, starting with her rescue, how he managed to resuscitate her – 'just like jump-starting an engine,' he'd quipped. And then they talked more seriously. She's even let him try to explain what happened at the shopping centre. She can't forgive him. Not yet. He was by her hospital bedside all the time in France and then he took her to her mum's, where she stayed for a few days. It was healing to stand back from everything, try to get some perspective on all that's happened. She still can't believe what Rob was planning to do to her – to her brain.

'You alright?' Bex says, finding her on her own in the kitchen a few minutes later.

She's lucky to have Bex as her best friend. 'Fine,'

she says, looking out of the window into the garden, where Jake is talking to a couple of friends she remembers from the canal. Single men in their forties, both fleeing broken marriages, trying to start again. Stretch and Banger are chasing each other around the flowerbeds.

'He's alright, is Jake,' Bex says, clocking the direction of her gaze. 'Pulled his finger out when it really mattered. Managing to suss what Rob was about. Going looking for you like that. Not such a lazy git after all.'

It's good to hear Bex say nice things about him. For so long she disapproved of Jake.

'I'd be dead now if it wasn't for him,' Kate says quietly. She's not sure she'll ever be able to make sense of everything that's happened, to process the nightmare of the Brittany house, her suicidal leap off the cliff. 'I was unconscious when I hit the water. Passed out with pain. And fear.' She gives a rueful smile. 'The cliffs were a little higher than I realised.'

Bex turns to Kate and hugs her, long and hard. 'Bit of a hero, isn't he, our Jake?' she says. 'You know he saved DI Hart's son too?'

'So I hear.'

Jake mentioned something but only in passing. It was DI Hart who filled her in with the details, during one of the interviews he conducted at the hospital in France.

'And he's really sorry,' Bex says. 'You know, about what happened.'

'I know he is,' she says.

'He's still daft about you,' Bex adds.

Kate smiles and catches Jake's eye in the garden.

CHAPTER 114

SILAS

Silas approaches the village, shuddering at the memory of what he and Strover saw in France: the dimly lit warehouse, like a hospital ward. The French police discovered eleven other super recognisers, all in a catatonic state. By the time he and Strover reached Brittany, they had been taken to hospital, where they remain. Doctors are confident that they'll eventually regain full mobility, thanks to the notes that Silas found on Dr Varma's desk about the cure given to the frozen addicts in California in the 1980s. A nurse's life was saved too. Her heart had stopped, but the paramedics managed to resuscitate her. Another body was found – a man who had died of a seizure.

'What about the other super recognisers?' Strover asks as they pull up outside Bex's house. Silas will leave Kate's homecoming party to Strover, get an early night before tomorrow's counselling session. 'Were they all taken by Rob too?'

'Their abductions went much more smoothly,' Silas says. 'He kidnapped each of them in the Tesla registered to Gilmour. In England, Rob tried to avoid ANPR, but if any cameras did pick him up, the car was registered to Gilmour. Kate was the prize though, the brain he coveted the most, the fusiform gyrus that lit up like no other, and he was prepared to wait for her to recover. Centaur would have to wait too. Only when she was well again could he begin to roll out the system, using the super recognisers' exceptional P3 brainwaves to recognise faces from hundreds of thousands of images. And all this time, if he ever was discovered, he could claim he was being framed by Gilmour Martin, the double from his past who had apparently promised to destroy him.'

'So there was never a Gilmour Martin in Thailand either?' Strover asks quietly.

Silas shakes his head. Rob's properties in Cornwall, London and Brittany have been painstakingly searched by forensics in the past week. Silas would like to have questioned Rob, but the evidence against him is still overwhelming.

'Thailand was Rob too,' he says. 'An old phone was found hidden in his Shoreditch apartment. There's a video on there of Rob talking to himself on a beach on Ko Samui. The date it was recorded fits – nine years ago, just before his twenty-first birthday. Forensics showed it to me tonight. It was a long drunken dialogue with himself but set up to look as if another person was addressing him.'

'And we're sure he wasn't talking to Gilmour?' she asks.

Strover won't let it go. Getting it wrong about Gilmour will make her a better detective in the long run.

'Rob was looking straight at the camera, telling himself that if he was to really succeed in business, he must be prepared to do bad things, questioning whether he had it in him. "You'll need to do this, you might even need to do that." And they were pretty bad things, including taking another's life.' Shortly afterwards, he was arrested, after being seen waving a gun around at someone else's party.'

'It wasn't his twenty-first party then?' Strover asks.

Two people come out of Bex's front door. It sounds like a good evening, full of laughter. Silas will catch up with Kate properly when things have settled down.

'We think he was travelling alone,' he says. 'Two days later, Rob found a drug dealer on the beach and shot him dead. At least, that's what the Thai police now think happened, based on the video. Cheap life, no big deal. And that's when Gilmour Martin, the name Rob had given to police two days earlier, came of age.'

CHAPTER 115

KATE

'The boss sends his apologies,' DI Strover says to Kate as they stand in the corner of Bex's sitting room. The party's been going a while, but Strover has only just arrived.

'He's a busy man,' Kate says. She wants to see DI Hart, thank him for his help, but now's not the time.

'How you feeling?' Strover asks, glancing at Bex's computer in the bookcase beside Kate.

Kate follows her gaze. The screen's just lit up. Someone must have knocked it. 'My body's still sore,' she says.

'And . . . psychologically?' Strover asks quietly.

'The good news is that I don't seem to have Capgras,' Kate says.

'I'm so pleased,' Strover says.

The psychiatrist Kate saw in France was adamant that she was never suffering from the rare delusion. And who was she to argue with a Frenchman about Capgras, given it was named after a psychiatrist from Toulouse? Rob's talk of doppelgängers undoubtedly messed with her head at a time when she was suggestible and

532

suffering from feelings of disconnectedness, but the psychiatrist also had another explanation.

'One day I just woke up and saw Rob for who he really was,' she says.

'I like that,' Strover says.

'Me too.'

When she was well enough, when her powers of recognition returned, she was able to see right through him, beyond Rob's public face and into his dark heart. It means that, in a way, she was right when she thought she saw an impostor in his tennis gear in Cornwall, heading off from Truro station, asleep in his London apartment. He was an impostor, always was, whether he was in her left field of vision or her right. And she was too, for a while, living a life that wasn't hers.

'Does that computer normally come on like that?' Strover says, clearly troubled by the screen. A green light has lit up next to the small camera.

'Better ask Bex,' Kate says.

After finding Bex and introducing her to Strover, Kate slips out to the garden. Her plan is to live here for the foreseeable future – Bex says she can stay as long as she likes. Jake is camping up in the woods – the boat is too much of a wreck to be salvaged – but he's just had some good news from a publisher. There's some interest in a new novel idea he shared with his agent while she was with her mum. A high-tech spin on an old gothic trope, apparently. He's already talking of getting another boat, wants her to help him choose it. As she says, early days.

If Rob hadn't died, Hart says he would have been charged with two murders and twelve abductions, including her own. At first she pleaded with DI Hart in the French hospital that he keep looking for Rob. She was still convinced that Rob had been replaced, that he couldn't have been responsible for such depravity. That the last five months had been one elaborate play-act at her expense was too much to comprehend. It took her a long while to absorb Hart's lengthy and patient explanations that there never was a double called Gilmour. He also gave her a book: *The Private Memoirs and Confessions of a Justified Sinner* by James Hogg. It's the copy she picked up in Rob's office but never got around to reading. One of the Devon and Cornwall police officers who searched the house fancies himself as a bit of a bookworm and told Hart there's a possible connection. She'll read it one day, when she's feeling stronger.

Je n'ai jamais voulu tomber amoureux de toi. Kate has replayed over and over her time with Rob and she doesn't believe he did fall in love with her – it's obvious now that he was incapable of loving her, or anyone. But that doesn't make it any easier to come to terms with his deception. The cold calculation of it all. His cruel patience. He nurtured her back to health because he coveted her ability to recognise a human face. Nothing more. It wasn't out of love. Or a shared passion for art. Bex tried to joke that she should be flattered – he desired her for her brain, unusual in a man – but they both know there's nothing funny about what happened to her and to the others.

Everyone has their darker side, Kate's aware of that. The face that they hide from the world. Sometimes they might even glimpse it in another, in one of their shadowless doubles that roam this earth, but most people learn not to act on their worst impulses. With Rob it was different. All that talk of doppelgängers, the Rossetti picture, the books – she suspects his fears were genuine, deep-seated, but he used them to blame someone else, to avoid taking responsibility for the evil that lived within him.

Her super-recogniser brain made the spot in the end, once it had healed. That's the real irony. He nurtured her back to good health, only for her to identify him for who he really was.

'Want to go for a walk?' Jake asks, finding her at the end of the garden. 'I think I saw an otter on the canal this morning. Beautiful place, down towards Crofton. Not far. We could take Stretch and Banger?'

She looks up at him and smiles. Jake is a good man.

'I'd like that.'

ONE MONTH LATER

CHAPTER 116

SILAS

Strover's phone rings. It's her digital forensics friend.

'I better take this,' she says to Silas.

They're in their usual corner of the Parade Room, just back from raiding a nail bar in Swindon Old Town.

'Sure,' Silas says, returning to his laptop. He wonders again if there's anything between Strover and her friend. None of his business. Just like his own personal life is none of hers, although he wouldn't mind talking about it. Not now that things are looking up. He's got another counselling session this afternoon with Mel. And Conor's going round to her place for dinner tonight. She asked if he'd like to join them. He might just do that.

'Anything interesting?' he asks casually. Strover has finished her call, but she's sitting in silence, staring ahead.

'What if Rob was right?' she says quietly.

'About what?' Silas starts to compose an email to Ward on his laptop.

'About Gilmour Martin.'

'We've been through this. Many times.' He glances up at Strover. She never raises something without a reason, doesn't like to waste his time. 'He doesn't exist.'

'But what if he does? A living, breathing person. And what if, nine years ago, he really did threaten Rob in Thailand, told him he would one day destroy him? I haven't been able to stop thinking about it.'

The first turn of a knot begins to tighten in Silas's stomach. He's never heard Strover like this before, so animated.

'Maybe Rob was terrified, took the threat seriously, wanted to do all he could to nullify it,' she continues. 'Wanted to be ready when Gilmour came looking for him. And to do that, to understand him better, he had to become more like Gilmour. Live like him in France. Break the rules. It's then that he devised his ungodly plan, abducted the best super recognisers he could find in Europe, wired them up to live CCTV footage from airports and railways and shopping centres, and Centaur was born. But he didn't develop Centaur for commercial reasons. It was for his own personal safety – an early warning system.'

'What's your friend in forensics found?' Silas asks quietly, not sure if he wants to hear the answer.

'I asked her to run a check on the desktop computer in Bex's house,' Strover says. 'It was

540

playing up at that party they threw for Kate. Jake said he'd been worried about it too.'

'And?'

'She found some malware on the hard drive,' Strover says. 'A remote access Trojan that hijacks the computer's camera and microphone.'

'Sounds like Rob,' Silas says, relieved that Strover's friend hasn't unearthed anything else.

'It was activated several times when Jake was staying there, when he was researching Rob. And at the party – a week after Rob died. It's impossible to trace exactly where it was accessed from, it was routed through too many proxies, but she thinks the last time, at the party, the hacker might have been somewhere in South-East Asia.'

Thailand. Silas has a sudden urge for a cigarette.

'There's something else,' Strover says.

'Go on,' Silas says, dreading what Strover might say next, how he's going to break all this to his boss. Dinner with Mel is already looking unlikely.

'Seems like Centaur came on-stream for a few hours on the day Rob was arrested, before the house in France was raided,' Strover says.

'Are you serious?' Silas asks. The thought that any real data might have come via the brains of comatose people on a cliffside in Brittany is too sickening to contemplate.

'No one was monitoring it,' Strover continues. 'My friend took a look this morning, out of curiosity. Decided to input Gilmour's biometrics,

541

based on the old Thai files. Just to see if anything came up.'

'And?'

Strover pauses before she speaks. 'It picked up a match.'

Silas turns to look at her, closing his laptop. He definitely needs a cigarette. 'Where?' he asks.

'Heathrow. Terminal 2. Waiting to board a flight to Thailand. She's checked the airport data. No matching names on the manifest, no passport photo matches. Just a dirty spot made by Centaur – she's sending over the smudge now.'

Silas leans across as Strover opens an email on her own laptop and clicks on the frame grab from the CCTV footage. He doesn't see the figure at first, but then he notices him in a queue, wearing a baseball cap – and glancing up at the camera.

'That's him,' she says, pointing at the screen.

Could it be? Silas leans in closer. There's a taunting look of triumph in the man's eyes that Silas doesn't like. Doesn't like at all. An air of mission accomplished. Of a job well done.

'Maybe Gilmour didn't need to frame Rob to destroy him,' Strover offers, sitting back. 'Just the threat of his arrival was enough to lead Rob astray. It became self-fulfilling, made him bend the rules, abduct super recognisers, kill barmen. He was desperate by the end, would have done anything to stop Gilmour coming for him. And he finally knew the game was up, that Gilmour had won, when we confronted him outside his flat in

542

Shoreditch. There was only one way out. Give Gilmour what he wanted, what his doppelgänger had come for. His life. His soul.'

Silas stares at the image in stunned silence. It must be one of Rob's other doubles. There were seven in total, weren't there? And his features are barely visible. The likeness is only passing. It's a software error. A case of mistaken identity.

Just another face in the crowd.